Th

A Stryker Legacy Novel

Ann Markim

Blue Heron Books

This is a work of fiction. Names, characters, places, and incidents are a product of the author's imagination. Locales, events, public names, and public figures are sometimes used for atmospheric purposes and historical accuracy. Any other resemblance to actual people, living or dead, or to businesses, companies, events, institutions, or locales is completely coincidental.

The Cause/Ann Markim
ISBN: 978-1-7346150-4-3

Dedication

To the brave and persistent suffragists
who fought for women's right to vote,
and
to my mother, who instilled in me
the importance
of exercising that hard-won right.
Thank you.

Chapter One

December 15, 1896
Cedar Falls, Iowa

Dear Rachel,

As I had hoped, McKinley won the election. My stepfather voted for the Republican ticket, and he is pleased with the outcome.

I am still submitting occasional articles to the Dannevirke. *The editor has asked me to cover the National American Woman Suffrage Association Convention in Des Moines in January. When I asked President Seerley for time off to attend, he grudgingly approved my request to be excused from teaching my classes that week so I can go. The newspaper is paying for my train ticket. My mother wants me to stay with her friend's daughter who lives close to the Christian church where the convention will be held. Marie is six years older than I am, and I haven't seen her since I was a child, so I am uncertain if this will be a satisfactory arrangement.*

I have been eager to see Susan B. Anthony again, since we went to hear her speak while we were at Oberlin.

The lack of interest in woman suffrage here at the Normal School is somewhat surprising, given the large number of female students. They don't actively oppose it. There just seems to be a general indifference in Cedar Falls, not just at the college.

Did you get the journalist position at The Conservator? *I've been hoping that since the editor's wife is also an Oberlin College graduate that she'll put in a good word for you.*

Are you coming to the convention in Des Moines? I hope so. Graduation seems like a long time ago, and I'd like to have a chance to catch up on what you are doing.

I wish you and your family a merry Christmas.

Lovingly in friendship,
Inga

Tuesday, January 26, 1897

Standing at the entrance to the auditorium in Des Moines, Inga Stryker perused the sea of gray hair, looking for a dark head that might belong to someone she knew. Someone closer to her own age. The smell of warm, damp wool permeated the air. How many of these women had been working on the cause since 1848? After nearly fifty years of effort, they would need to succeed soon, or they would never have the opportunity to vote.

She stepped closer to one of the heavy walnut doors to allow new arrivals to pass through. Never before had she seen such large conference space in a church. And this wasn't even the sanctuary.

Again, she scanned the room for a familiar face. If more young women didn't become involved, the movement was in danger of dying out. Perhaps that could be the perspective from which to approach her article. Or perhaps not. The idea could give aid and comfort to the anti-suffragists.

She shifted her weight from foot to foot and fidgeted with the handle of her handbag. Her stories about this conference had to be just right.

Behind her, the front door screeched open, admitting a blast of cold air. Inga shivered. She turned to see who had come in.

A burst of joy waved through her. "Sarah!"

"Inga! It's good to see you again." Sarah Jefferson lowered her hood and shook out her thick, brown curls. Snowflakes on her shoulders melted into her black cloak. "I wasn't sure if we would make it. The snow is blowing so hard we could barely see beyond the horse's ears. Luckily, Mr. Eberhart knew the route."

"I'm glad you're here." Inga hugged her friend.

"The thermometer at the guest home read twenty-four degrees below zero. Can you believe it?" Sarah removed her mittens and rubbed her hands together. "I wish they could have held this meeting somewhere warmer."

"I feel the same way," Inga whispered.

"But I'll try not to complain anymore since all these old ladies are here, and they probably arrived on time, which I did not."

"Really, Sarah." Inga narrowed her eyes. "Many of these women have dedicated their lives to the cause."

Sarah chuckled. Her eyes sparkled with amusement. "Is Rachel here?"

"She said she was coming, but I haven't seen her yet." Inga stood on tiptoe to search the room. "Maybe she was held up by the weather."

"Has Governor Drake said anything of note?" Sarah lifted her gaze to the well-dressed man at the podium.

"No. Mostly he's been trying to congratulate the association without committing to support giving women the vote." Inga gestured to the right. "There are two seats over there. Let's take them."

They picked their way down the row without stepping on any feet, excusing themselves as they worked their way to the vacant chairs.

Inga pulled her handkerchief from her pocket and covered her nose. She pinched her nostrils together to prevent a threatening sneeze.

Trying to ignore the overpowering scent of floral and spice perfume the woman sitting next to her wore, Inga took out her paper and pencil. She jotted notes as the various dignitaries welcomed the suffragists to Des Moines. Finally, Reverend Breeden stood to address the assembly.

Sarah leaned closer.

"Have you ever seen a church as big as this one?" she whispered.

Inga shook her head and focused on the pastor's words.

"...I have a robust faith that you are right, and also that churches are with you in sympathy and heart. I belong to one which welcomes women to its pulpit and to all its offices. I should distrust the Christianity of any that would deny to my mother and my wife the rights it accords to my father and myself."

Inga nodded as she scribbled his words.

His talk was followed by welcoming greetings from state and local organizations, even by reading lengthy greetings from those not present. Her eyelids drifted closed.

She caught herself and jerked her attention back to the speaker.

Shifting on her chair, she met Sarah's glance. Her friend crossed her eyes, as she had done in many of the classes they shared at Oberlin when professors droned on and on. Inga suppressed a giggle.

Finally, Miss Anthony took the podium. Inga sat up straighter. This was the speech she had most anticipated.

Miss Anthony mentioned the hostility suffrage meetings encountered in the olden days. "...I do rejoice with you over the immense revolution and evolution of the past twenty-five years, and I thank you for this cordial greeting."

Applause met her words.

Inga tried to envision meetings that had occurred before she was even born. How could these women have persisted for so many years in the face of so much hostility and obstruction?

This huge room held plenty of sources who could provide information and quotes about past conventions. She had already scheduled an interview with Miss Anthony near the end of the week.

Progress in 1896 was reviewed. Inga scribbled the highlights to include in her article.

January 6 - Utah became state w/ constitution guaranteeing equal rights to women, including full suffrage.

November - Idaho Supreme Court declared amendment granting woman suffrage carried constitutionally.

Inga shifted in her seat, trying to angle her face away from the offending perfume.

California - defeat of suffrage amendment. Susan B.'s analysis: passed in properly organized counties, defeated by "liquor men" in unorganized counties. Lesson for future endeavors.

Also mention: Colorado - first state to enact woman suffrage by popular referendum in 1893.

Wyoming, 1890 - first state admitted w/ constitution guaranteeing equal rights to women, including full suffrage.

The audience applauded and Susan B. Anthony stepped away from the podium. Inga was pleased to have noted a brief history of states granting woman suffrage as background for her articles.

When the session closed, Sarah turned to Inga. "Would you like to join me at the guest home for dinner?"

"Thank you, but I need to go to Marie's and write my article while the details are still fresh in my mind."

Sarah frowned. "This is the piece you're writing in Danish?"

"Yes." Inga sighed. "It's my first important assignment. Like all the others, it is about a 'woman's subject,' but this topic is not about the Woman's Club's gossip session or some domestic issue like Mrs. Smith's daughter's visit from down the block."

"Didn't you write some articles for them when we were in college?"

Inga nodded. "But if I do a good job on the ones I write about this meeting, the editor might give me more significant assignments."

"Are you still sending stories to *Vogue*?"

"No. I only had so many dog and cat stories in me that pleased Josephine Redding." Inga pulled her cloak around her shoulders. "And I couldn't care less about New York society."

"Too bad." Sarah tucked her curls into her hood. "Those animal tales were always fun to read."

"But I want to be a serious journalist. To write

stories that matter."

Sarah patted her arm and sighed. "Good luck."

Inga wasn't counting on luck. In addition to her newspaper articles, she was going to write a serious story she hoped would be published in a national magazine. It would have to be her best piece ever.

When Inga and Rachel Jones found each other in the crowded auditorium Wednesday evening, they hugged.

"I'm so glad you made it." Inga studied her friend. "Were you delayed by the weather?"

"That, and a conductor who didn't want Negroes on his train." Rachel narrowed her eyes. "Ida protested, but we had to exchange our tickets. The stationmaster said he couldn't guarantee our safety if we didn't."

Inga frowned. "Oh, Rachel, I worry so much for you and Mrs. Wells-Barnett when you travel in the south. Especially when she speaks against lynchings."

"It isn't just the south," Rachel said through clenched teeth. She stood nearly a head taller than Inga. "There are so many people here tonight. Ida said the church's auditorium was supposed to hold fifteen hundred, but I don't think everyone will fit inside."

"Rachel!" Sarah's excited squeal reached Inga's ears before she came into view. "It's a good thing you stand out in this huge crowd. I would hate it if I missed seeing you tonight."

Rachel smiled. "I'm glad to see you, too."

Inga perused the crowd, looking for three empty seats together.

A woman Inga had spoken with earlier rushed up to them. "They're going to hold an overflow meeting," she confided breathlessly. "They think the big crowd is here because Carrie's going to speak. She's originally from Iowa, you know."

The woman moved on, spreading the word.

Rachel narrowed her eyes. "Carrie Chapman Catt?"

"Yes." Sarah knitted her brows together. "Do you

know her?"

"No, but Ida thinks she might be allied with Mrs. Stanton in wanting to keep Negroes out of suffrage associations."

"I've never heard of her saying anything like that. I hope Ida's wrong." Inga stared at her.

Rachel shrugged. "Time will tell."

"Let's find seats while there are still some left." Sarah led them into the massive auditorium with row after row of seats. The large windows were dark with the night beyond.

"There are three together." Sarah hurried to a row with vacant chairs on the aisle. Rachel and Inga followed.

Once they had settled into their places, Inga pulled her paper and pencil from her handbag.

"Another article today?" Sarah asked.

"Yes. Marie, the woman I'm staying with, took the first one to send via train this morning." Inga wrote Carrie's name at the top of a blank sheet. "And she'll send tonight's article. She's so helpful."

"Why didn't she come tonight?" Rachel asked.

"I invited her, but she said she had too many papers to grade. I'm not sure if it was true or a convenient excuse."

The meeting was called to order, and they turned their attention to the podium.

"I'm proud to introduce one of Iowa's own daughters, Mrs. Carrie Chapman Catt."

Mrs. Catt - Wyoming, Utah, Colorado, and Idaho had moved ahead of Iowa in her heart because they have recognized the equality of men and women.

Quote: "If today we could prove to Republicans or Democrats that every woman would vote for their party, we should be enfranchised."

Q: "When the first woman desired to study medicine, not one school would admit her. Since that time, only half a century ago, 25,000 women have been admitted to the practice of medicine. If a popular vote had been necessary, not one of them would yet have her diploma. We have gained these advantages because we did not have to ask society for them."

Inga glanced at Sarah and Rachel. If Oberlin had required approval from society, it was unlikely that any of them would have been allowed to earn their degrees, especially Rachel.

How many young women were being denied higher education because of their gender? If women were enfranchised, they would have the power to change that situation. Inga was determined to do all she could to win the right to vote.

Late that evening, Inga returned to Marie's boarding house.

"Three of the state Senators came in person to invite the convention to visit the Senate tomorrow morning. Come with us." Inga pleaded with her friend across the small table in Marie's sizable room. Even with the bed, two dressers, sofa, two chairs and three tables, the room was more spacious than Inga's. "Just this once."

Marie combed her fingers through her light brown hair and pursed her lips. "Tomorrow is Friday. It's a school day. I have classes to teach."

"But they've invited Miss Anthony and some of the other leaders to speak at the state capitol."

"I can't." She stood. "Do you have your article ready to send?"

Inga handed her the envelope. "It's the last day. Are you sure you don't want to go with me?"

"I'll arrange for a hack to take you to the train station Saturday morning."

"Thank you." Inga cocked her head to one side, wondering why Marie so adamantly refused. "Don't you support woman suffrage?"

Marie reeled around, her hazel eyes flashing. "I don't know what to think." She placed her right hand on her hip, still holding the envelope in her left. "My mother wants the vote. Jess and my father think it would ruin the sanctity of a woman's place in the home. Their disagreement is a source of bitter friction within my family."

Inga winced. "That has to be hard."

"At least I'm not living with them, so I don't have to deal with it every day." She dropped Inga's article on top of the pile of graded student papers. "My mother said Erik moved to the Alaska territory to look for gold. Have you heard from him since he got there?"

Inga frowned, but accepted the change of subject. "*Moder* got a letter that said he staked a claim somewhere in Canada." She missed her brother and wished she heard from him more often. "I don't know much more than that."

"I can't believe he'd just go off into the unknown."

"This must be his way to ensure he doesn't get pressured to operate the farm when Moder and Halvor get too old."

Marie shook her head. "Isn't moving to Alaska a bit extreme?"

"Maybe." Inga sighed. "He's supposed to be sending articles about his adventure back to the *Dannevirke*, so you can keep track of him that way if you want."

"I'll ask my parents to send me their newspapers when they finish with them." Marie picked up a washcloth and towel. "I'm going down the hall to the lavatory, and then I'm going to bed. It's late."

"I'll get ready, too." Inga's glance slid to the sofa, where her hostess had stacked the pillow and blankets.

When Marie was finished, Inga took her turn at the lavatory, extinguished the lamp, and snuggled under the covers.

"I'm sorry I snapped at you about suffrage." Marie's contrite voice drifted through the darkness.

Inga wished she would have known about the conflict within the Holden family. "I shouldn't have nagged you. I'm sorry. I really appreciate your hospitality."

"I've enjoyed your visit." Her voice mellowed. "Good night."

Inga stared into the blackness. How lucky she was that her mother and Halvor both supported suffrage.

But then, Inga's stepfather had supported her mother for as long as Inga could remember. Since Marie's mother had partnered with Moder in the produce business, Inga had presumed that Marie's father was more progressive-minded. She knew better than to make assumptions.

When Inga awakened the next morning, Marie had already left for the high school where she worked. Inga hurriedly dressed and ran to the church to meet Rachel and Sarah in time to ride with them to the state capitol.

They followed the other suffragists across the marble floor of the rotunda. When they reached the Senate chamber, they squeezed in among the other women crowding into every inch of available space. Caught near the back of the gallery, Inga was unable to see the speakers. There was no room to take notes. If she hadn't overslept, they might have gotten a better spot.

After Lieutenant-Governor Parrott's welcoming remarks, Miss Anthony pointed out that Iowa women had been requesting suffrage for nearly thirty years, to no avail. Representatives from each of the four states with full woman suffrage spoke briefly. Three of the other leaders presented short speeches.

As soon as Inga and her friends escaped the throng back into Mr. Eberhart's waiting carriage, Inga scrawled all that she could remember. She asked Sarah and Rachel for whatever they could recall and noted their observations.

When they arrived back at the Christian church, Mr. Eberhart handed Sarah a basket. "The wife sent lunch for you girls." He grinned, exposing the absence of his left canine tooth. "You can return the empty basket when I pick you up tonight."

"Thank you," Rachel and Sarah chorused.

"This is so nice of you and your wife," Inga said. "Please give her my appreciation."

"I will, miss."

They hurried out of the cold and into the

auditorium.

Crystals of frost had settled around the edges of Inga's ham sandwich, but she was so hungry she barely noticed.

Afternoon: debate - should association's literature remain non-partisan? It will, for now.

Final session: one last celebration of victory in Idaho and other three states with woman enfranchisement.

"Did you hear that Susan B. accused the General Assembly of playing cat-and-mouse with the suffragists?" Rachel asked.

"She said that when I interviewed her, too, and she's right. In one session, the House passes the suffrage amendment, but the Senate fails to consider it or votes it down. In the next session, the Senate passes it, but the House doesn't. Moder says they've kept this up for many sessions." Inga sighed. "One house gives us hope, the other dashes it."

Sarah raised a brow. "Are you going to put that in your article?"

Inga considered the idea for several moments. "Probably not in the one for the *Dannevirke*, but I may write one on the entire convention and submit it to other newspapers."

"You should." Rachel gave a firm nod. "Maybe you should try that new magazine, *The Chronicle*."

"Maybe. I've been impressed with the issues I've read."

"How does the Normal School feel about woman suffrage?" Sarah asked.

Inga swallowed. "Surprisingly indifferent. Especially since so many of the faculty and students are women. People hardly ever talk about it."

"Write your article." Rachel grinned. "Maybe you can stir up some conversation."

When the meetings concluded for the day, Inga tramped over the snow-crusted route back to Marie's boarding house. To take her mind off the cold, she mentally reviewed the highlights of the convention for her overarching article. Her thoughts wandered to potential markets.

Cosmopolitan, The Chronicle, and *McClures* were read by general audiences, and wasn't that who she was trying to reach? Could she dare submit to *Scribner's, Harper's,* or the *Atlantic Monthly?* Such reputable periodicals most likely would dismiss her sizable collection of *Vogue* and *Dannevirke* articles as inconsequential. Except maybe not those she had written about this convention.

She smiled to herself as she knocked on Marie's door.

"Come in." Marie's voice reached her through the wood panel.

Inga stepped into the room. "I'm going to write—"

Marie's brother, Jess, sat on the sofa that had been serving as Inga's bed. He was wearing his Sunday suit, and his brown hair was neatly combed.

The last thing she had expected was to see him in Des Moines. Her body tensed. "What are you doing here?"

He stood and faced her, smiling broadly. "I came to fetch you back to Cedar Falls."

His hazel eyes twinkled.

Inga bristled. The man was nothing if not persistent.

"I'm taking tomorrow's train. I already have my ticket." She shifted her gaze to Marie.

Her friend shrugged. "I had no idea he was coming."

"I'll escort you home." His smile faded. "I've got a ticket on the same train."

Inga squared her shoulders. "I'm a grown woman with a master's degree. As a college student, I traveled between Oberlin and home by myself. I don't need an escort."

Marie chuckled. "Looks like you'll be on the same train, whether you sit together or not."

Jess's grin returned. "So we might as well sit together."

Inga released an exasperated sigh. "Only if you don't talk. I have articles to write."

"You'd better sit at opposite ends of the car," Marie teased. "It's a long ride."

Inga clenched her teeth. She removed her cloak, began gathering the belongings she had strewn around the room, and packed them into her small trunk. "Where are you going to sleep tonight, Jess?"

"I've got a room in a nice hotel downtown. How 'bout I take you girls to its restaurant for supper tonight?" His expectant gaze drifted from Inga to Marie.

Marie frowned. "I really don't want to go out in the cold again."

Inga nodded her agreement. "Me either."

"If you like, I'll ask the cook if she can accommodate you for dinner," Marie said. "But they usually require a two-day notice for guests, especially men."

Please, no. Inga massaged her throbbing temples.

Jess's mouth had become a thin line. "That would do."

"I'll be back in a few minutes." Marie left.

Jess strode to Inga and planted himself directly in front of her. "Why won't you let me court you?"

She met his gaze. "For the hundredth time, because I want to concentrate on my career."

"But we're twenty-one years old." He lifted a hand to her shoulder. "By the time our mothers were our age, they were both married and had children of their own."

She took a step backward. "I'm still twenty, and I worked very hard for my master's degree. I want to use it."

He raised his eyebrows. "I know. You skipped three grades in school, so you're smart enough for raising a family and to help our mothers in their produce business. My father told me I can live on the old Ringe place when I marry. We could build a house just the way you want it."

Inga propped her hands on her hips. "I'm not

interested in running a produce business. I want to teach. I want to write. My adult life is just beginning, and I don't want to be tied down by a husband and babies, especially a husband who does not support woman suffrage."

He narrowed his eyes. "You'll never find a husband worth his salt who does."

She took a step backward.

"I don't need to find a husband because I'm not looking for one." She fought to keep her voice quiet. "I plan on having a fulfilling life without a man."

Inga's office at the Normal School was cluttered with work that had piled up during her absence. She considered the stack of assignments her students had turned in. If she worked on them every spare minute, day and evening, she might be able to get through them by the end of the week. She sat down at her desk to sort them by course.

A knock sounded at her door. She set down the papers. "Come in."

"Excuse me, Miss Stryker." A dark-haired young woman, bundled in a bulky cloak, stepped over the threshold. "Dr. Bender would like to see you in his office."

"Dr. Bender?" She wasn't even in his department. What could he want?

"Yes, ma'am."

"Now?" Inga's glance slid back to the piles of papers on her desk.

"Yes, ma'am."

Inga frowned and reached for the coat that she had removed only a few minutes ago. "I'll be right there."

She shrugged into her heavy wrap, placed her hat on her head, and wrapped her scarf around her neck. After picking up her gloves and pad of writing paper, she followed the young woman back into the frigid air, over the icy sidewalks, to the office of the Advanced Department of the Training School.

The floorboards creaked as she entered the room.

"Good morning, Miss Stryker." Dr. Wilbur Bender sat behind a wooden desk that dominated the space. "Please sit down." He gestured toward an oak armchair directly across from him.

She removed her gloves, loosened her scarf, and unbuttoned her coat, before sitting.

"Miss Mitchell has taken ill and is not able to perform her evaluations of the student teachers in their language classes."

Inga tilted her head, her brow furrowed. She bit her lip.

"President Seerley has assigned you to fill in." He picked up an envelope from his desk and handed it to her. "He had to go out of town for a meeting, so he left you this letter."

"Me?" She gulped. "I don't understand. I'm not in your department. I don't know anything about training teachers."

"President Seerley believes that you can perform these tasks credibly. He told me that you are an intelligent woman and a promising associate professor."

Dr. Bender's benevolent smile only irritated her. Were his words true or merely flattery to make her feel better about the assignment?

"And you are the only available person on the faculty who is fluent in Latin, besides teaching classes in English. You know the subject matter that the student teachers will be presenting."

Inga swallowed. "Am I being transferred to your department?"

"No." He stood. "You'll still be teaching your classes. We'll fit your student teacher evaluations in around your regular classes."

Stifling a gasp, Inga stood, too. "How long is this arrangement going to last?"

"It's all in your letter." He pointed to the envelope in her hand. "At least through the rest of winter term. We'll re-evaluate it at the end of February." He walked across the squeaky floor and opened the door. "We'll meet tomorrow morning and go over the expectations. Thank you, Miss Stryker."

"Thank you, Dr. Bender." Inga straightened to her full height and strode out the door.

She tamped down the anger rising within her. With all this additional work, how was she ever going to find time to write and polish her overarching article in support of woman suffrage?

Chapter Two

Cedar Falls, Iowa
February 18, 1897

Dear Sarah,

I don't know if you saw the article in the Iowa State Register *about the convention, but it had some encouraging passages. In case you didn't, I'll share the highlights.*

"The convention in this city this week will, no doubt, exert a large influence on this community and state. There is something infectious in a cause which has so many capable women pleading for it constantly. Other women are influenced by it and every time we lose a woman (we speak now from the anti-suffrage side) we are in danger of losing from one to half a dozen men..."

I have to wonder if this last statement is true. I certainly hope all those men will support our cause.

The article went on to say "The women who believe in suffrage are entitled to a full hearing..." which surprised me because this is an anti-suffrage paper, but the reporter later qualified it.

"The very chivalry which is the stronghold, or at least the boast, of the anti-suffrage side, compels us all to yield them that. In the meantime, we hope that the good women will not desert us and go over to the side of "Our Susan" for we would be lonesome and powerless without them. For the success of the anti-suffrage cause reliance must be placed in women, not in men."

I haven't found the anti-suffragists to be particularly chivalrous, so their boast may actually be delusional. But I hope the statement that the cause is in the hands of capable women is correct. I believe that if we persist, we can prevail.

I wrote the article we discussed and submitted it to The Chronicle. *Fingers crossed.*

Please write soon and advise me of your summer plans. Perhaps we and Rachel can get together before the sweltering heat sets in.

I won't have time before mid-June. President Seerley has dumped extra work on me, because, as he said in the assignment letter, "I don't believe these extra tasks will be too great a burden since you were able to take a whole week off, even though we are in the thick of the winter term."

I won't know until the end of the month whether or not he will expect me to continue the extra duties into the spring term.

Lovingly in friendship,
Inga

Inga gazed at the wallpaper in the large dining room. The slender willow branches flush with sage green leaves lent a calm, soothing note to the otherwise chaotic atmosphere that always ensued whenever the family gathered. Even though the farm was only about five miles outside of Cedar Falls, it seemed a world away from the Normal School.

All three of her half-sisters and three of her four brothers gathered around the table. Only Erik was absent. She missed her oldest brother, who was away in the Yukon.

Mrs. Jensen appeared in the kitchen doorway. The housekeeper carried the cut-glass cake stand holding a frosted cake-topped with flaming candles-which she set on the table in front of Inga.

The group erupted in shouts of "Happy Birthday."

Grinning, Inga swept her gaze across her assembled family.

"Blow out the candles before they burn up the cake," Greg, her youngest brother, called.

"Don't forget to make a wish," her half-sister, Karoline, said in her angelic voice.

Inga made a show of inhaling a deep breath then expelled it, moving her head from side to side. By the time she ran out of air, the flames had been extinguished. Waxy-smelling smoke lingered in the air.

"Did you wish that Jess would propose?" Although twelve-year-old Ella's teasing tone amused Inga, she shot her half-sister a narrow-eyed glare.

"Hardly."

Her mother handed her the special-occasion cake knife, and Mrs. Jensen set a stack of dessert plates on the table. Inga picked the candles out of the white frosting and set them in an empty bowl.

"I'll bet she wished that William Jennings Bryan was the one who was going to be inaugurated next month instead of McKinley." Her stepfather, Halvor, grinned.

Inga turned to him. "I don't wish that, even though he might have been for suffrage. I'm hoping McKinley can be convinced to support the cause. Maybe you could write and ask him for his support since you voted for him."

She picked up the knife and began slicing and dishing up the cake.

"I'll bet she wished she could have voted," her younger brother, Poul, said. "Am I right?"

"I don't think I'm supposed to make a retroactive birthday wish." Inga turned her attention back to her task. "Besides, I can't tell you what I wished for or it won't come true."

When everyone had a piece of cake, her brother stood and tapped his spoon on his glass. "I have an announcement to make." He waited until the room was quiet. "I'm going to change my name."

"What?" Their mother stared at him with wide eyes.

Poul smiled at her. "Well, not exactly 'change.'" He paused. "I'm going to spell my first name the American way, P-a-u-l. So be sure you spell it this way."

"Thank goodness, that's all," Halvor said. "I don't think I could get used to calling you Henry or Ralph."

Inga raised a brow. "Why now?"

"I'm going to start looking for a job that isn't on the

farm." He glanced at Halvor. "I've promised to stay long enough to help with this spring's planting, but I want to leave in the summer."

"Where will you go?" their youngest brother, Greg asked.

Poul shrugged. "I haven't decided yet."

Inga smiled. "I wish you the best of luck whatever you decide."

Later, when Inga and her mother were finally alone, her mother asked, "Are you well? You look so pale and thin."

"I'm just tired." Inga dropped onto the velvet and satin quilt that covered her mother's bed. "It's that extra assignment I told you about. I had plenty to do before, with the classes I'm supposed to teach."

Moder sat down beside her. "What, exactly, does it involve?"

Inga sighed. "I have to sit in a high school English class or Latin class, and watch a student teacher give her lesson. I then make notes on what she does well, what she does poorly, and sometimes when she makes mistakes. If the pupils get out of control, I have to take over and restore order."

"That must take time." Her mother gave her a quick hug. "Not to mention the mental energy."

"It does. So, I have to grade my students' assignments and make my lesson plans in the evenings since I spend my little bits of free time during the day meeting with students or faculty."

"How much longer will you have to keep this up?"

"I don't know. Maybe until President Seerley thinks I've been punished enough for taking time off to attend the suffrage convention." Inga shrugged. "I have a meeting with him on Tuesday to determine if the assignment will continue into the next term. As far as I know, Sadie Mitchell is still too sick to work. She has pleurisy."

Her mother's brows furrowed. "Does your contract allow him to do this?"

"I don't know." Inga shrugged again. "But if I don't

do what he asks, he might not renew my contract for next year."

"Well, you should make yourself familiar with the legal stipulations." Moder stood and walked to the large, mirrored dresser.

Inga smiled. When she was a small child, she had loved to stand on a chair, make silly faces, and watch her reflection in that mirror. Although tempted to make one now, she resisted.

"I have a birthday gift for you." Moder handed Inga a silver bar. "Keep it as security, in case you need it in the future."

The bar was heavier than Inga expected, and she nearly dropped it. "Oh, Moder. You're too generous."

Her mother returned to the open drawer and pulled out several bills.

"I want you to speak with my attorney about your contract." She handed the bills to Inga.

"But, I already told you. That doesn't really matter."

"Yes it does."

Inga jerked at the sharpness of her mother's tone.

"Whether you hold the Normal School to the terms or not." Her voice was gentler but still firm. "You should understand their obligations and yours."

Inga sighed. She couldn't imagine when she would find time to meet with the attorney. Besides, it probably wouldn't make much difference anyway.

On Tuesday, Inga sat in the straight chair across the desk from President Seerley. An oak chair with arms stood against the wall behind her. He sat in one padded in the back and seat. To her left, a fire crackled in the heating stove that had been inserted in fireplace. Bright sunlight steamed through two big windows.

Inga worried her lower lip as she waited for him to speak.

Finally, he looked up.

"Miss Stryker." With his thumb and forefinger, he

stroked his neatly-trimmed beard, brown with strands of gray. "Dr. Bender has noted that you did an excellent job in supervising student teachers. He also states that you were accommodating and quickly learned the expectations for student teacher performance."

Pride swelled within her chest. "Thank you, sir. It was an interesting temporary assignment."

"And a very demanding one." He laced his fingers together and rested his hands on the desk. "Consequently, I am hiring a temporary instructor to take over the duties of evaluating the students teaching Latin, so you will only be responsible for evaluating those teaching English."

Which was the largest portion of the student teaching. She swallowed. "For the entire Spring term?"

"That's right." He shifted the papers on his desk. "While you are here, there is one more item I want to address."

She nailed her gaze to his face. "Yes?"

"I have received translations of the articles you wrote for the *Dannevirke*." He lifted the top sheet. "The Normal School is a state institution. I must ask you not to write any more articles about woman suffrage. And you must not promote it with the students and faculty."

She lost her breath. "What about my right to free speech?"

"You may write articles about education or laudatory ones about the Normal School." He frowned. "Woman suffrage is like a lightning rod, especially so soon after the convention you attended. We need to keep a unified front here on campus."

She lay her hand on her chest. A unified front? What if she didn't agree with him?

"Then there's something you should know." She lifted her chin. "I have submitted an article to *The Chronicle*, but I haven't yet heard whether it will be published."

He closed his eyes. "If they decide to use it, I expect you to give me a copy of your piece before it is issued."

Inga already knew he wouldn't approve of her story. She swallowed. "Yes, sir."

At the close of the winter term, Inga gave her room in the boarding house a thorough cleaning. Having everything tidy gave her a sense of control she hadn't felt for a while.

On Tuesday, her mother stopped by, carrying a basket in each hand. A faint aroma of almond rose through the wicker. Inga's mouth watered.

"Come in." She opened the door wide.

Her petite mother bustled into the space. "I brought you a kringle, a puff, and some canned bing cherries, apples, peaches and pears." Moder set her parcels on the floor next to the table Inga used as a desk. "I fear they aren't feeding you right here."

"The food here is fine." Inga shut the door and joined her. "I didn't have time to eat noon meals because I was too busy last term. But, thank you. I'll enjoy these treats."

"Speaking of that, what have you learned about the next term?"

"That I'll still have to do about two-thirds of the extra work." Inga held out her hand for her mother's cloak and gestured to the upholstered chair.

"Did you contact my attorney?"

Inga hung the cloak on a peg. "I haven't had time."

"I'll take you this afternoon when Halvor picks me up." She settled on the chair.

Inga seated herself on her bed. "That isn't necessary. President Seerley told me not to write more suffrage articles. I told him I had sent one to *The Chronicle*. This came yesterday." She picked up the letter she had received and handed it to her mother.

Moder unfolded the page and read. Moments later, she lifted her head. A broad smile lit her face. "They've accepted it."

"President Seerley said if it was accepted, I should

give him a copy before it comes out." Inga sighed. "I transcribed it last night."

"It doesn't seem right that he would demand to see the article."

Inga shrugged. "But I don't want to risk my job, which is why I'm going to take this copy to his office today."

Four weeks later, a month into the spring term, Inga again found herself in President Seerley's office.

"I've written an article on how teacher education at the Normal School benefits the education of children in Iowa." Inga placed a copy she had transcribed into English on his desk.

"Sit down, Miss Stryker." He picked up the papers and skimmed the words. "This is very good."

"Thank you. I'm turning it in today."

"Your suffrage article has created a lot of conversation." President Seerley raked his fingers through his dark brown hair.

Inga smiled. "I hope it has created support across the country."

"That's not the conversation I've been hearing." He opened a desk drawer and pulled out a stack of magazines. "These have all come to me from legislators—and the mayor."

Her smile faded. She clasped her hands together in her lap.

He pulled a sheet of paper from under the cover of the top one. "Since when is the Normal School taking positions on political policy issues?"

She worried her lower lip. "But I didn't mention the school in the article or my byline."

He shifted another magazine to the top and read, "'If the Normal School is publicly supporting woman suffrage, I will support building new normal schools in other parts of the state instead of consolidating teacher training in Cedar Falls, the next time that issue comes to a vote'"

"What?" She frowned. "More normal schools?"

"In 1894, when I was trying to get money to build this building for more classrooms and a bigger library, many representatives proposed having small normal schools around the state – in their districts – instead of increasing the size of the college here in Cedar Falls."

"I was in college in Ohio then." Her voice was soft. "I didn't know—"

"It was a hard fight, but in the end I was able to secure $35,000." The line of his mouth was grim.

"And this is a fine building."

"But the fight against multiple small normal schools is not over, as our state representative and many other legislators have reminded me." He tapped the stack of magazines.

"The majority of the legislature does not support woman suffrage, and I have to work with these men on behalf of this school. Our enrollment is growing. As you know, we have over 1400 students this year. So we will need an increase in our annual funding now, and more buildings in the future. That won't happen if they establish additional schools."

Inga cast her eyes downward. "I didn't mean to jeopardize the future of the school or to make your job more difficult." She raised her gaze to meet his. "I'm sorry."

"I know you are, but I can't risk alienating the lawmakers' support of this Normal School." He frowned. "You are a good writer, Miss Stryker. You are an excellent instructor. The students and faculty like and respect you. So, I regret to inform you that I will not be able to renew your contract for the next school year."

Inga blinked back her tears. She refused to let him see her cry.

On Saturday afternoon, Moder stopped by Inga's boarding house on her way home from delivering her farm produce to her customers in town.

Moder listened silently while Inga poured out the story of what had happened in her meeting with President Seerley. When Inga finished, she dabbed her cheeks with her already damp handkerchief, then walked to her dresser and picked out a clean, dry replacement.

"So he didn't terminate your contract." Her mother sat on the upholstered chair, her hands clasped tightly together in her lap. She locked her blue gaze on Inga. "And you're going to finish teaching until the end of the term."

She nodded.

"But you won't be working there next school year."

Inga swallowed. "That's right."

"Have you thought about what you want to do after the term ends?" Moder's voice was soft, tender.

"I've come up with several options." Inga paused. She pulled the straight chair from her table and moved it across from her mother. "I could write full time. But my wages from the *Dannevirke* aren't enough to support myself, and I have no way of knowing whether *The Chronicle* or any other periodicals will buy enough to pay my rent."

"You have the silver."

"Yes, but I don't think this is the kind of emergency you meant it for."

"Good girl." Moder brightened. "You could move home. I'd love to have you stay with us."

Inga managed a small smile. "That's very nice of you. And I may have to while I look for something permanent." She sighed. "I could look for an editorial position at a publishing company."

"And move far away?" Her mother's shoulders slumped.

"Probably. I was far away when I was at Oberlin." Inga fiddled with a curl. "But I would miss teaching, and I don't want to waste my degree. I worked too hard for it."

"Are you going to apply for positions in area high schools?"

"No. At colleges."

Moder's eyes widened.

"Dr. Seerley said that if I turn in a letter of

resignation he could give me a good recommendation without having to sully it by explaining why he is not renewing my contract."

"What did you tell him?"

Inga inhaled a breath to stave off the tears that memories of the conversation triggered. "That I'd think about it."

"What are you going to do?"

Inga shrugged. "I'm thinking about it."

Chapter Three

Cedar Falls, Iowa
May 4, 1897

Dear Rachel,

I read that the American Negro Academy was formed in March. Were you assigned to cover it for your newspaper, or are you still traveling with Mrs. Wells-Barnett?

Although I'm still furious about President Seerley's ultimatum, I decided to tender my resignation to the Normal School. It made me aware that I really will be leaving at the end of the term. I didn't realize how sad I would feel, but I do.

Now I am submitting applications for teaching positions to other colleges. I have identified half a dozen, all in states where there is full woman suffrage. Susan B. and Carrie C. seem to both be partial to Wyoming, which is my first choice. My theory is that since woman suffrage has been in place there for the longest time, there should be far less resistance to it than in states where it was only recently implemented.

Hopefully, I will receive an offer before the next letter I write.

Unfortunately, I may have to move home for a while before I find an acceptable position. I love my family, but I can't help feeling like a little girl when I'm with my parents for any length of time. I think they shift to seeing me as a child, as well.

I will keep you posted.
Lovingly in friendship,
Inga

"Inga?" A second knock sounded at the door of her room. "Inga, Mr. Holden is down in the parlor. Can you come down and talk with him?"

Inga groaned. "Can you please speak with him for

me?"

Winnie, one of the other boarders, chuckled. "No."

"I'll be down in a few minutes." Inga set down the pen she had been using to grade papers and stood. Glancing in the mirror, she noted that her curls were messy and her skirt was wrinkled. She shrugged.

Steeling herself, she trudged down the stairs. She'd only seen him once since Des Moines, when he stopped by to apologize for starting their argument.

Jess stood as she entered the parlor. He held out a bright red tin. "My mother sent you some molasses cookies."

Inga grinned as she accepted the gift. "Please give her my thanks." Gesturing to the gold velveteen couch with her free hand, she set the tin on the marble-topped table. "Please sit down."

"It's a beautiful day." He remained standing. "I thought we could go for a walk."

Inga glanced out the window and then picked up the tin. "I'll take this upstairs and get my jacket."

After changing into a freshly-pressed brown skirt, she combed her hair and tied it back with a matching ribbon. She selected her dark-green jacket from the wardrobe and donned it and a matching hat. Resisting the temptation to eat a cookie, she returned to the parlor.

Jess held the door for her. Gently grasping her elbow, he escorted her down the sidewalk. The sweet scent of blooming lilacs engulfed them.

"Mother told me that your mother said you lost your job," he said quietly.

Heat crept up her neck and into her cheeks. "I wasn't fired. I will be finishing the school year."

"But you're not going to be teaching at the Normal School next fall, right?"

She nodded. "That is correct."

"Then it's a good time for us to marry." Jess stopped walking and looked her directly in the eye. "I can take care of you."

The man never listened to her, or at least he didn't take her words seriously. Inga crossed her arms in front of her chest.

"Oh, Jess." She managed a weak smile. "We've been good friends ever since we started the first grade together. I like you. I want to continue to be your friend, but I don't want to be your wife."

"But I'm offering you a home, security."

"And that's what many women want." She swallowed. "But I'm not one of them. You would be a good catch for someone looking for a home and security."

His shoulders slumped. "But we always talked about getting married someday."

"Back when we were both in country school." She dropped her hands to her sides. "We were children then. Things have changed since we've grown up."

"For you, maybe." Frowning, he took her elbow again and turned back toward the boarding house. "But not for me."

"I'm sorry, Jess."

They returned to the porch in silence.

He turned to leave.

"Goodbye," she said quietly.

He walked toward the street.

She watched until he was out of sight.

Birds sang. The first tender green blades of grass dotted the brown lawns. A gentle breeze blew. The sun's rays warmed Inga as she strode across the campus.

"Miss Stryker?"

Inga turned to see a tall, plain-faced student from the rhetoric class she was teaching this term. She was one of the brightest, most contemplative scholars Inga had encountered at the Normal School. "Miss Lund."

"May I talk with you?"

"If you can talk and keep walking at the same time." Inga smiled. "I'm on my way to teach a class next period."

The student chuckled. "I can do that."

She walked alongside Inga, matching strides.

"What can I do for you?"

"I've written a draft of my final term oration." She pulled out a few sheets of paper from the textbook she carried. "I was hoping you could look at it and tell me how to improve it."

"I'm impressed." Inga said. "You still have four weeks before you have to present it."

"Will you look it over, please?" She held out the draft.

Inga stopped, accepted the papers, and slipped them into one of the folders she was carrying. "I'll look it over tonight and meet with you after last period tomorrow."

"Thank you."

"You're welcome." Inga started walking again. She turned left onto the walkway leading to her destination.

Miss Lund fell into step beside her once again. "Miss Stryker, are you really leaving the Normal School at the end of the term?"

Inga was growing tired of answering that question. "Yes, I am."

"I just wanted to tell you that I was sorry to hear it. You're the best teacher of all the professors I've had since I've been here."

"Thank you, Miss Lund." Inga sighed.

"It won't affect me because I'll be graduating. But I feel sorry for the other students who won't get to have you for an instructor."

"That's nice to hear." Pressure built in Inga's temples. She picked up her pace.

"Are you going to another college?"

Inga's grip tightened on the books and folders she was carrying. She paused before climbing the steps. "Are you on the staff of *The Normal Eyte*?"

Miss Lund smiled shyly. "No. I was just curious." She cast her eyes downward. "I apologize. I didn't mean to pry."

Inga gently touched the girl's arm. "It's okay. And yes, I hope to find a position at another college, but now I have to teach my class here." She climbed the first few steps then paused and turned back. "I'll see you tomorrow afternoon."

Near the end of the term, faculty members, students, and the public filed into the rows of pews in the Assembly Hall. Footsteps and conversations bounced off the wooden floors and high ceilings.

Etta Suplee, the supervisor of the Training School, led Inga into the fourth row, her lavender scent trailing after her. Myra Call, Associate Professor of Latin, followed. They settled onto the hard wooden seats.

"Have you heard anything about the positions you interviewed for?" Etta asked.

Myra leaned into the conversation.

Inga smiled. "I've received offers from both the University of Idaho and the University of Wyoming. I haven't heard from the others yet."

Etta grabbed her arm and shook it back and forth. "But you said Wyoming was your first choice, didn't you?" She grinned broadly. "So the rest don't matter, do they?"

Inga suppressed the giddiness she felt about her new position. "I'm accepting the Wyoming offer."

"I'm so happy for you," Etta said.

Myra's brows knit together. "Why did you choose Wyoming?"

"For one thing, it's a lot easier to get there from here than to Idaho, and I want to be able to visit my family and have them visit me." Inga looked from Myra to Etta, "But the biggest reason is that women have full voting rights in Wyoming, and they were the first state in the country to grant those rights to women. They did so even when they were still a territory."

Myra's eyes widened. "Do you really believe women have the expertise to offer useful opinions about political issues? That we know enough about issues to vote on them?"

Inga straightened in her seat. "Yes I do. I know

more about the candidates and the issues than most of the men I know, but here in Iowa, the men get to vote and I don't."

"Yes, but you're a journalist. Most women aren't."

"Most women, probably more than men, can read the newspapers and magazines, so they have the same access to information as the men do." Inga pushed away the frustration this situation always engendered.

"Ladies," Etta intervened. "They're getting ready to start."

Inga directed her attention to the podium at the front of the Assembly Hall.

"We are here today to hear the scheduled orations by our students who are expected to graduate at the end of the term," President Seerley began. "As you know, in order to meet the graduation requirements, candidates must not only satisfactorily complete their coursework, they must also submit a thesis on an assigned topic, and they must prepare and present an oration under the direction of a faculty member. Today, these students are completing their final oration requirement."

Inga studied the multi-paned windows at the front and around the sides of the room. Her gaze wandered to the high ceiling, divided into decorative sections of squares and rectangles. The wallpaper and borders were light and bright, giving the room a feeling of cheerful formality. This hall had always been one of her favorite places on campus.

One by one, the students gave their presentations. Because she was the Professor of Rhetoric, Inga dutifully jotted evaluations for each.

Miss Lund's name and the title of her talk, *The Importance of Teaching Languages Other Than English to High School Students*, were announced. Inga sat up straighter in her seat. She hoped the student's oratory skills would do justice to her excellent thesis.

Miss Lund's voice wavered slightly as she began speaking, but soon smoothed into her well-practiced style.

When she finished, Myra gently elbowed Inga. "That was a well-argued position," she whispered. "I especially liked what she said about learning Latin to understand the basis of many languages, as well as English."

"She's very bright." Inga purposely kept her tone even and her words to a minimum. "She'll make a good teacher."

After the final speaker finished and the president made his closing remarks, Inga stood with the rest of the audience. She gently ran her fingers over the back of the pew in front of her and scanned the room again.

This would be one of the last times she would see the inside of this lovely Assembly Hall.

A heavy sigh escaped her. She hoped she would love teaching at the University of Wyoming as much as she had loved her work here at the Normal School.

"You can visit whenever you want to," Inga folded the quilt that had covered her bed ever since she'd moved into the boarding house. "All you have to do is to take a train to Omaha, then one to Laramie."

"I still don't think it's fair that your contract wasn't renewed because of one magazine article," her mother groused. "Did you tell the people in Wyoming about it when you interviewed?"

Inga packed the quilt into the trunk her mother had brought. "Yes. I gave them a copy, because I wanted to make sure I would be allowed to write similar articles if they hired me."

"And they didn't object?" Moder pulled the sheets from the bed and stuffed them into a crate. "We'll take these home for washing before you pack them."

"They didn't object because women have full voting rights in Wyoming." Inga swiped her forehead with the back of her hand. "Their only concern is that many of the students will probably be my age or older, but I assured them that was the case here, and it hasn't been a problem."

They packed the clean clothes from the dresser and wardrobe into the trunk and put those that needed to be washed in the crate.

Inga picked up the small blue vase her brother had given her for Christmas.

"Is Poul going to legally change the spelling of his name?" She asked as she scanned the room.

"No. Your Uncle Peder said he wouldn't need to, so he's just going to use the American spelling." Moder's lips tightened into a thin line. "He's changed his spelling, you changed your spelling. I wonder if your brothers and sisters will all want to change theirs, too."

Inga tucked the vase into the trunk, and gave her mother a quick hug. "At least neither of us adopted something entirely new."

"I suppose that's some consolation." The corners of Moder's mouth tipped slightly upward. "You both still have your legal birth names."

"Is Poul planning to keep living and working at Uncle Peder's brewery?"

"At least through the summer."

Inga relaxed. She smiled.

"Are we ready to start taking these downstairs?" She gestured to the trunk, the crate, and the rocker that Halvor had made.

Her mother smiled. "Good thing you sent your winter clothes and things home with me earlier this spring. It makes a lot less work for us today."

They each grasped a leather handle on either end of the trunk and carried it down the steps, then out the back door.

As they loaded it into the wagon box, her mother patted the case. "My grandfather made this and three more like it for me when I crossed to America." She gazed into the distance, a wistful expression on her face. "There is a secret compartment in the bottom. I'll show you how it works when we get to the farm."

Inga's jaw dropped. "A secret compartment?"

Her mother's focus shifted to Inga's face. "Yes. *Bedstefa* filled it with gold bars so I would have them if I needed money. I used one of the bars to pay your tuition at Oberlin."

"He was very generous." Inga blinked several times. "I loved when he visited us. I always hoped he would come back."

"Me, too." Her mother turned and headed back toward the house. "Let's get the rest of your things."

When everything was loaded and farewells were said, Inga and her mother climbed onto the wagon seat. Inga lifted the reins and signaled the horses to move.

"We'll be coming back with a fuller wagon in only two weeks," Inga observed as they rolled down the street at a slow pace.

Her mother frowned. "I still don't understand why you have to leave so long before the school term starts."

"I need time to find a place to live, get settled in." She paused. "And hopefully, I'll be able to find a newspaper that will hire me to write a weekly column."

The passenger train stood next to the platform of the Cedar Falls depot. The summer afternoon sun beat down on the passengers and loved ones seeing them off.

Pressure built behind Inga's eyes as she hugged her brothers and sisters. Even Poul had come to see her off.

"You be careful out there in the wild west." He grinned.

She pulled him into a quick embrace. "I will."

He stepped back.

Tears streamed down her mother's face. Halvor draped his arm around her shoulders.

"Just think of this as you did when I went off to college." Inga swallowed back a sob. "In a way, I *am* going off to college, only not as a student."

"I know." Her mother sobbed. "But this feels more permanent."

"And Erik left just a little over a year ago." Halvor's tone was sympathetic. "It's hard to watch you children grow up and go out on your own."

"I won't be that far away. You can come and visit me, and I'll be back from time to time."

Moder threw her arms around Inga and pulled her close. "I know, but I've gotten used to having you close by. I love you." She sniffed. "And I'll miss you."

"I love you." Inga inhaled a sharp breath. "And I'll miss you, too."

Halvor patted her shoulder. "Write and tell us when you get settled."

She turned to meet his blue gaze. "I will."

He smiled. "And I will take good care of your mother."

Inga smiled back. "I know. Thank you. I love you, too."

Her mother hugged her one more time before releasing her.

"I'd better go so I can find a seat." Inga drew her ticket out of her handbag and pasted a smile on her face. "Good-bye, everyone." She lifted her hand in a wave.

"Good-bye, Inga," her siblings chorused.

She let her gaze linger on her parents.

Her mother's lips were pinched tightly together, her eyes blinking.

Halvor handed Inga her satchel. "Take care of yourself."

"I will," Inga mouthed as her voice failed her. She turned and strode to the train.

After finding a window seat in the nearly-empty car, she stowed her satchel and handbag on the seat beside her.

More passengers boarded. A hefty man smoking a pungent cigar sat two seats ahead of her. She wrinkled her nose.

A shrill discharge of the train's whistle blasted through the car. She jerked.

The conductor passed by, checking tickets. When he finished, he called, "All aboard!"

Resting her forehead against the glass pane, she stared at her family still waving on the platform. Fighting sobs, she waved back.

The whistle blew again.

The car lurched, shifting Inga forward and then throwing her back against her seat.

With much chuffing and clickety-clacking, the locomotive pulled away from the station. The coach swayed rhythmically as they rolled along.

Inga twisted around and watched until her family and the depot disappeared from view.

The train rounded a gentle curve.

She dropped her hand into her lap and turned her gaze to the upcoming countryside. Her heartbeat quickened as the train rushed toward her uncertain future.

Chapter Four

Rolling through the West
July 2, 1897

Dear Sarah,

I am en route to Wyoming so if my handwriting looks shaky, it's because of the swaying and jerking of the train. The trip has been uneventful thus far.

When I finish this letter, I will also write to Rachel. If we are going to get together this summer, it will probably have to be in Wyoming. As soon as I arrive in Laramie, I will have to look for a boarding house. I'll also approach newspapers to see if they'll hire me to write a weekly column. The college has no objection to my working for a paper, as long as it doesn't interfere with my contractual responsibilities. I must run potentially controversial articles through the president's office for approval before I submit them. No more last minute submissions for me.

Please let me know if you think you can visit. I will arrange for a post office box as soon as I get to town, and ask that any mail to me be forwarded to my box. I always wondered if others at the boarding house in Cedar Falls went through, or even read, my mail. I also think a post office box address will look more professional to magazine editors when I submit.

I'll admit to you that I'm a little nervous about starting a new job in an unfamiliar place. At least I've had experience teaching. Hopefully, all will go well.
Lovingly in friendship,
Inga

Laramie, Wyoming, July 1897

Holding onto her hat to keep the wind from sailing it away, Inga scrutinized the fragments of peeling paint, the slightly-askew sign, and the weathered porch floor of 'the best boarding house in town.' She checked the address the clerk had scribbled on the back of the hotel's card when he'd recommended this place. *Ma Campbell's. Seventh and Thornburg.* The name and street signs matched.

Inga frowned and returned her gaze to her possible future home, then glanced up and down the streets that intersected at Ma Campbell's corner. The surrounding homes were large with big yards, and most were in good repair. Only two blocks from the college, the location would be convenient when she began her teaching position in September. She could see the main building from here. The town's center was five blocks in the opposite direction. She'd be close to the newspaper office, as well.

A cheerful patch of bright pink cleome bloomed in front of the wide porch. She sighed. This might not be such a bad place to live.

Standing here staring only postponed the inevitable. She marched across the brick walk and up the main steps. The scent of bacon and cinnamon wafted through the open window. Her stomach growled.

A small cardboard sign was stuck between the door and the jam. Shaky letters had been scrawled in black ink. *Vacancy. To enquire bout room come to side*

Inga rounded the corner of the L-shaped porch and rapped at the screened door.

"C'mon in," a raspy female voice called. "I'm back here in the kitchen."

Letting herself in, Inga walked past a servants' back staircase and into a bright yellow kitchen with a large flour-covered table in the center. A pan of cinnamon rolls was cooling on the counter. Two loaves of bread were rising near the heat of the stove. A short, stocky woman, with mostly gray hair tied back from her face, kneaded a blob of dough in the middle of the flour.

"I'm Inga Stryker." She breathed in the warm, comforting aromas. "It smells good in here."

"I'm Mary Campbell." The woman smiled, but kept working. "You here 'bout the room?"

"Yes." Inga's mouth watered. She glanced at the cinnamon rolls.

Mrs. Campbell slapped the dough into a loaf pan and brushed her hands together over the table. "I'll wash up and be right with you."

The woman dipped her hands in a basin of water, soaped, then rinsed them.

Inga turned her back to the rolls.

Mrs. Campbell crossed the kitchen, drying her hands on her apron, as her mother's housekeeper, Mrs. Jensen, often did. "Well, little lady, let's see the house."

Inga smiled.

"You saw the back steps when you came in." The landlady gestured in the general direction of the door Inga had entered. "They're closest to your room."

"Yes, I noticed them."

"You can use them or the front stairs. And boarders are welcome in the kitchen." She pointed to a closed door. "That leads to my quarters. You're not allowed in there. Breakfast and supper are served in the dining room." She led Inga through a butler's pantry with floor to ceiling cupboards.

A swinging door panel opened into a room with a large table surrounded by chairs. A massive oak built-in breakfront made up a wall opposite a marble fireplace. Slightly faded green wallpaper and oak wainscoting rounded out the decor.

"Meals are served on the sevens. We go by the grandfather clock in the hallway."

Through an open door, Inga spotted a corner of the clock. "Are boarders allowed to invite guests for dinner?"

"If you let me know a day ahead and pay five cents." Mrs. Campbell strode through the large squared archway.

As Inga passed into the parlor, she noticed pocket doors. A sofa and two chairs faced each other on either side of the fireplace. Another pair of chairs, separated by a lamp table, stood in the corner by the window. An electric chandelier graced the center of the ceiling. The upright piano caught her eye. "Are boarders allowed to play the piano?"

"As long as no one else in the room objects." Mrs. Campbell cocked her head. "Do you play?"

"Yes. Do you?"

She shook her head. "No. But my husband insisted that our children learn."

"Do your children live here in town?"

"Three died of cholera when they were young 'uns, but I have a daughter that married a farmer. They live upstate."

She spoke so matter-of-factly of losing three children. Inga's heart clenched. When her baby brother died many years ago, her mother's grief had been inconsolable.

"My son runs a bank in Chicago. Stayed there after college." The pride in her voice was unmistakable.

"It's a big city." The corners of Inga's lips turned upward. "There are so many things to do there."

Mrs. Campbell arched a brow. "You been there?

"Several times, with my mother and her friends or with my mother and stepfather. We always took the train." A lightness filled Inga. "I loved the city every time we visited."

Shaking her head, the older woman walked into the entry hall. "All guests must enter through the front door. No men are allowed on the second floor." She gestured to the telephone on a marble-topped table. A stack of small papers and a pencil lay beside it. "You may use the telephone, but you must write down your calls and pay for them."

Inga marveled at the modern conveniences of electricity and telephones that seemed so prevalent in Laramie. She glanced up the stairs. "Who are your other boarders?"

"A secretary and a teacher. You'll meet them at supper." She started climbing the steps. "How do you make your money?"

Inga followed the woman's ample backside up the stairs. "I will begin teaching at the college in September. I hope to get a reporter position with a newspaper this summer."

"If the paper don't hire you, can you afford the rent?" The raspy voice that had been so friendly suddenly became grave. "It's $5 per week or $20 per month."

"Yes."

When they both reached the landing, Mrs. Campbell poked the button on the light switch, turning on the single bulb in the center of the hallway ceiling. A skeptical look pinched her face. "You'll have to pay for each week or month up front."

"I can do that. I opened an account with the bank yesterday."

"I require cash before you move in."

Inga sighed. The banker had warned her that Mrs. Campbell would not accept a check. "That's fine."

"The room that's vacant is my nicest one. Has a sleeping porch that's cool in summer. It was mine when my husband was alive." A momentary frown crossed her lips and her shoulders sagged. "He departed this life 'bout eight years past."

"I'm sorry," Inga said kindly.

After passing three doors, the landlady stopped and opened one. She raised her chin. "In here, we have a water closet, sink, and tub."

They walked to the end of the hall and Mrs. Campbell opened the door, revealing a large space with a tarnished brass bed. The white wallpaper with little pink roses and the white eyelet curtains projected a bright, airy feel. Even with a dresser, a clothes press, and a small writing desk and chair, there was plenty of floor space.

Inga loved it immediately, but she tried not to show how pleased she was for fear that the landlady might increase the rent. "You said there is a sleeping porch?"

"This way." Mrs. Campbell opened the door beside the desk.

Inga stepped into an appendage to the house with open windows on three sides. A cool breeze wafted through the small room furnished with a cot, a little table, and an easy chair. Inga stifled a smile. "This will do."

"You have to be sure you shut the windows whenever it looks like rain." Mrs. Campbell's voice had relaxed back into a friendly tone.

"I will," Inga promised.

They went back down to the dining room and settled all the details. Inga handed over the cash, then stood to leave. "I'll stop by the hotel and make arrangements to have my things delivered later this afternoon."

"Supper is at seven. Make sure you're moved in by then, Inga."

"Yes, ma'am."

The landlady grimaced. "Call me Ma or Mary."

"Yes, Mary."

"That's better. See you later."

Smiling to herself, Inga left through the front door.

C.J. Wakefield took one more look at the ledger, hoping to discover some available cash that had eluded him in his previous reviews of the journal. He found none. His chair creaked as he straightened. "Can we at least get tomorrow's edition of the paper out?"

"Didn't you hear me? We have a cracked type magazine on the linotype machine." His employee, Shorty, rubbed his hand over his bald head.

"Yes, but isn't there some way you could fix it temporarily?" C.J.'s gaze flitted around the sparsely furnished room. He cleared his throat. "Just to get us through a few more days."

Shorty frowned. "I suppose I could temporarily patch the press together, but you'll have to replace the part before long."

A knock sounded on the door. It opened just enough for his secretary, Homer Burrow, to pop his head inside. "Your 1:30 appointment is here."

Glancing at the small clock on the corner of his desk, C.J. noted she was five minutes early. "We'll be done here soon."

"Yes, sir." Homer disappeared and the door closed.

C.J. turned back to Shorty. "I'll telephone Cheyenne to be sure the part is in stock and they can ship it yet today."

"I'll do what I can to cobble together the type magazine so we can get tomorrow's edition cranked out." Shorty turned to leave.

"And I'll figure out some way to rustle up the money," C.J. murmured under his breath as he walked his employee to the door.

Inga stared at the plaque on the closed door. *C. J. Wakefield.*

Five minutes ticked past her 1:30 appointment time. Below the wall clock, the editor's secretary sat at a desk so small it barely held the typewriter and telephone. Inga caught his eye.

"Mr. Wakefield will come and get you when he's ready."

Inga nodded. "Thanks."

The smell of slightly burned printer's ink wafted through the room, irritating Inga's throat. She tried to re-settle on the hard, wooden chair, one of the two meant to provide seating in the waiting room.

She fiddled with her copy of the *Laramie Reporter.* She straightened the clippings of the four articles she had written for Cedar Falls papers and the copy of her piece in *The Chronicle* which she had brought with her. Refolding the newspaper, she read the ad again.

Help Wanted: Part-time woman reporter. Inquire at office of this newspaper.

The door opened and two men emerged. One was balding, short and stocky. The other was young and tall, with a thick shock of coffee-colored hair.

"Excuse me," the shorter man said, walking past her.

The handsome fellow grinned. His whiskey-brown

eyes glinted with golden highlights. “Come in, Miss Stryker.”

She returned his smile and followed him. Her knees had gone soft, so she concentrated on not catching her shoes on the hem of her skirt.

“I'm C.J. Wakefield.” He offered his hand as he would to a man.

She raised a brow. If she wanted to be accepted as an equal, she would have to get used to being treated as one. Clasping his hand firmly, she gave it a small shake. “Pleased to meet you. I'm interested in the reporter position in your ad.”

Gently, he held her fingers for a few moments longer than proper and then released his grip and gestured to another uncomfortable wooden chair. “Please sit down.”

While she did, he walked around the desk and seated himself. She slid the samples of her writing toward him. “These should give you an idea of my style and capabilities as a reporter.”

He sat back and perused her clips.

She swallowed and forced herself to breathe.

His brow furrowed. He frowned as he looked up at her. “These are all political topics and local issues.”

She nodded. “Yes, I wanted you to see the range of my experience.”

“But none of them relate to women's news.” He dropped her samples on his desk.

Inga blinked. “Sure they do. There are several about woman suffrage and one about women in higher education”

Mr. Wakefield shook his head. “Women's news. Who visited whom, women's club meetings, social events, weddings. Things ladies like to read about. That's why I advertised for a woman.”

She crossed her arms across her chest. “None of that holds any interest for me.”

“Then why did you apply for the position?” A note of irritation wove through his words.

She straightened her shoulders and lay her hands

in her lap. "Because I thought you wanted a journalist like Ida Tarbell at *McClures*, not a town gossip."

He chuckled. "Well, your writing shows potential. If you work real hard, you could become a pretty good women's reporter."

"And my skills as a journalist would wither away." She rose and snatched her clips from his desk. "I'm sorry to have wasted your time. And mine."

Clenching her teeth, she turned and headed for the door.

"If you change your mind, let me know soon," he called after her.

She marched out of the office.

In the warm sunshine, she began to quiver.

She would prove to Mr. C.J. Wakefield that she was more than just a town gossip.

C.J. appreciated the sway of Miss Stryker's skirt as she sashayed out of his office. It was nearly as alluring as her fiery blue eyes and captivating smile.

He returned to his desk and lifted from the bottom drawer the small stack of magazines his friend had sent him.

Opening the cover of the top issue, he withdrew the letter Nathan had sent and skimmed over the now-familiar words.

I hope this finds you and your family well and that your father's condition is showing improvement. Please give them my regards.

The Chronicle *is growing. Although I'm no longer looking for an investment partner, I am in need of an editor so that I may concentrate on the business of selling ads and marketing. The editor's responsibilities would include selecting articles and designing layouts as well as planning occasional themed issues and cultivating relationships with writers. I think you would be a strong candidate for the position.*

If at some point you're willing to consider giving up that daily rag of yours and come east, please drop me a line. We make a good team, and I think we'd both enjoy working together like we did on the college monthly.

C.J. flipped to the page with Miss Stryker's article and reread it.

She was a talented writer. If he could have afforded to hire her, he would have.

He sighed and tucked Nathan's note and the *Chronicles* back in the drawer.

For a long while, he studied the ledger. If he could drum up two or three more ads for the next two editions, he shouldn't have a problem paying for the part. Better get started.

On his way out of his office, he picked his top hat off the rack in the corner and donned it.

"Would you still be wanting the missus to report on the women's events?" Homer asked as C.J. passed through the outer office.

"For the time being."

"Thank you, Mr. Wakefield." The secretary smiled. "She'll be glad to hear it."

C.J. replied with a curt nod. "I'm going out. I'll be back in and hour or two."

A gossip column! Inga shook her head as she stepped into the Elkhorn Café. She took a seat next to a stack of newspapers presumably put there for customer use.

"Hello, miss." A red-haired, freckle-faced young man grinned. "Would you like a nice cold orange soda or lemonade?"

She smiled at him. "No, thank you. I'd like a cream soda and a dish of vanilla ice cream."

He nodded. "Right away."

She took the small mirror from her handbag and looked at her face. Red still tinged her cheeks. She took several slow breaths and schooled her features into a serene façade. Setting aside the copy of *The Laramie Reporter*, she slid *The Daily Boomerang* closer.

The young man set her order in front of her.

She glanced up and smiled. “Thank you.”

After a sip of soda and a spoonful of ice cream to soothe her throat, she returned her focus to an article about a treaty annexing the Republic of Hawaii to the United States signed in June. By the time she finished reading the front page, she had eaten all of her ice cream, and drank the last drop of her soda.

Checking her reflection again, she was pleased to see that the color of her cheeks had returned to normal.

The waiter approached with her ticket.

Inga straightened her hat, paid for her snack, and gathered her things. Standing with her best posture, she turned and headed toward the *The Daily Boomerang* office. Her determined strides propelled her one block over, bringing her to her destination more quickly than she had anticipated. She inhaled a long, slow breath and gazed momentarily at the mountains to the west. Some still had traces of snow at their peaks. She drew herself up to her full height, and opened the door.

She flashed her most winning smile at the man seated behind the reception desk. “Is Mr. Low in?”

The young man with the thin moustache and the large ears grinned back. “Is he expecting you?”

Inga kept her spine straight. “I'm afraid not. I just arrived in town yesterday.”

The man's grin faded and he cocked his head.

“My name is Inga Stryker. I'm a journalist,” she continued. “I've come to talk to him about writing for *The Daily Boomerang*.”

Staring at her, the man said nothing.

Inga cleared her throat. “Will you please ask if he will see me?”

The man stood, scurried to the door behind his desk, and knocked.

“Come in,” a deep, raspy voice called.

The man slipped inside and shut the door.

Muffled male voices drifted through the walls. Inga took a step toward the door and held her breath but couldn't make out their words.

After a few moments, the moustached man reappeared. “You may come in, ah, what was your name again?”

“Inga Stryker.” She strode though the doorway, nodding at the man behind the desk. “Thank you for seeing me, Mr. Low.”

The tall, rotund man stood. “Pleased to meet you, Miss Stryker. I understand you are interested in writing for *The Boomerang*.” His smile was welcoming. “Please have a seat.”

“Thank you.” Inga sat in the chair directly in front of him. “I brought some samples of my articles.” She set them on the desk.

He sank into his chair. One by one he read each clipping, saving the one from *The Chronicle* for last. His brows knit together as he studied it.

Inga watched for a clue to his reaction, but found none. She clasped her hands tightly together in her lap and caught her lower lip between her teeth.

Finally, the editor looked up. “These are very good.”

A breath escaped from her. “Thank you.”

“Your style lends itself to a weekly column.”

She grinned. “That would be perfect, since I’ll also be teaching at the university.”

“Is that so?” Mr. Low’s eyes widened. “And they’ll let you write for me?”

“As long as I show potentially controversial copy to them before I submit it to you.”

The editor frowned. “They want to censor the press?”

Inga shook her head. “It’s not that. They just don’t want one of their employees writing anything that will be detrimental to their relationship with the politicians. They wouldn’t care if a non-employee wrote it.”

His face softened. “I can see that.” He handed back her clips. “I will pay you commensurate with the reporters for one column per week. Some weeks, I’ll assign you topics. Others, you can choose your own.

We'll start with subjects that are not time-sensitive."

"Wonderful." Inga met and held his gaze. "Maybe I can write a few ahead this summer, so we'll have some in reserve."

A sparkle lit his eyes. "Good idea."

"Do you have any topics in mind?" She pulled a sheet of paper and pencil from her handbag.

"We'll introduce you on—" He consulted the calendar on his desk. "August sixth with 'A Newcomer's View of Laramie.' By then, I'd like to have two columns."

She scribbled notes on his directive.

"And sometime in August I'd like you to do a column on Ester Morris."

Inga wrote the unfamiliar name. "Who is Ester Morris?"

He tipped his head slightly to the left. "The first woman to hold public office. She was a Justice of the Peace."

Her pulse quickened. "I would be happy to. Does she live here in Laramie?"

"Cheyenne."

When she finished her notes, she looked up. "Do you have any objection to me writing articles for national magazines?"

"Like *The Chronicle*?"

She nodded. "Yes. And others, too."

"Not at all." He grinned. "Just mention in your biography that you write for *The Boomerang*."

Inga smiled back. "I'll do that."

The editor stood. "I look forward to working with you."

She stood, too. "And I with you. I'll have two articles to you by the end of next week."

Clasping her handbag, she forced herself to walk slowly from of his office. Once outside, she released the grin she had been holding back. She had found a home and landed a newspaper job on her first day in town. Her life in Wyoming was off to a good start.

Chapter Five

Laramie, Wyoming
July 10, 1897

Dear Moder,

I am very happy with my new living quarters. My room is much bigger and brighter than the one I had in Cedar Falls. And it has a sleeping porch!

Currently, I am working on my first weekly columns for a local paper, The Boomerang. I*t seems like a funny name for a newspaper in Wyoming, but it has been around for more than a decade. According to the accepted explanation, the paper was named after the first editor's mule.*

The streets here are still dirt, and the town does have a bit of a "wild west" look, but telephones and electricity are common. So far most of the people have been welcoming.

The town sits at the base of the Black Hills, and beautiful, tall peaks are visible to the west.

I have walked to the University several times. It's not far from my boarding house. I'll have a small office. There are far fewer students than attended the Normal School, and only a small faculty. Hopefully, it will grow in future years.

Please think about visiting in the fall, when the weather will be cooler for traveling.

With love,
Inga

Swabbing her forehead with a damp handkerchief, Inga rose from her small writing desk. She walked to the sleeping porch, although she was only wearing her chemise and drawers. Even with all the windows open, only a feeble, intermittent breeze lightened the heavy, sweltering air.

Finding no relief, she returned to her room, stepped into her old green skirt, and donned her lightest cotton blouse. Sniffing at her slightly wilted, slightly worn reflection in the mirror, she placed her wide-brimmed bonnet on her head. She picked up her letters and handbag and escaped into the outdoors.

Although the conditions were still hot, the faint breeze was less constrained and Inga felt the same way. She strolled at a leisurely pace to the milliner's shop, where the proprietor's husband, the postal clerk, had a small office.

She passed the buildings of her new hometown. The Kuster House, built in 1872, still served as a comfortable hotel. From the same vintage was the sturdy, brick Laramie National Bank. Although the hotel and restaurant associated with the railroad depot were only a few years older, Inga had found them much more elegant, but also more worn than these downtown structures. The depot had indoor plumbing, which the others did not. Indoor privies were rare in Laramie. Inga was thankful that Mary Campbell had installed a septic system similar to the one on her parents' farm.

Traversing the patchwork of planks, stones, bricks and cement, she missed the standardized wooden sidewalks of downtown Cedar Falls.

As she approached her destination, she spotted Mr. Low rounding the corner.

He lifted his straw hat then stopped in his tracks. "Good afternoon, Miss Stryker. How are your articles coming along?"

She paused. "I have nearly finished one about Wyoming being the first state with full woman suffrage, but am still adding impressions of Laramie to the other one."

"What has surprised you most about our town?"

Squinting to fend off the harsh mid-day sun, Inga smiled. "Two things. That the railroad arrived here as early as it did, and that some of the buildings in town are as old as early buildings in Cedar Falls. Until I began writing about the suffrage movement, I had assumed Wyoming was settled later than Iowa since it became a state much later."

He nodded. “A common misconception, but some of the state is still unsettled. Laramie was established early because it was initially the end of the line for the railroad. That’s also why we had electricity and telephones before many other towns.”

“Yes. It’s far more modern than I anticipated, and I appreciate the conveniences.”

“I look forward to reading your articles.” He touched two fingers to the brim of his hat. ”Good afternoon.”

“Good afternoon.”

Inga strode the rest of the way to the shop and stepped inside, grateful for the shade. She handed her letters to the clerk and paid for the stamps. As she placed the change in her handbag and turned to leave, she smacked directly into a solid figure who smelled of newsprint.

Taking a step back, she lifted her gaze and straightened her spine. “Excuse me, Mr. Wakefield. I didn’t realize you were right behind me.”

“I’m sorry, Miss Stryker.” A wide grin spread across his face. “I shouldn’t have been standing so close.”

Inga gave a dismissive nod. “Good afternoon.”

He didn’t move. “I saw you talking with the editor of *The Boomerang*.”

She arched a brow, but said nothing.

His grin faded. “You’re working for him, aren’t you?”

“Not that it’s any of your affair.” She lifted her chin. “But yes.”

“I thought as much.” His shoulders slumped. “Good afternoon, Miss Stryker.” He stepped toward the clerk and out of her path. “Did I receive a package from Cheyenne today?”

Inga strode back out into the sunshine and headed toward home, glad she would be writing for Mr. Low.

C.J. straightened, rubbing his grease- and ink-stained hands on an already dirty rag. Pressing his fingers into the cramp in his back, he massaged the clenched muscle. The type magazine on the linotype machine was finally fixed, not just cobbled together.

"I didn't think editors were supposed to get their hands dirty."

C.J. spun around. "Sis! What are you doing here?"

He reached out to pull her into a hug.

Ruth Wakefield stepped out of reach. "These are my going-to-town clothes. I don't want them stained."

He laughed. "Fair enough. To what do I owe the pleasure of your visit?"

"I had to go to Cheyenne to file papers." Her face flushed with excitement. "I've met my homesteading requirements. I finally own my land, free and clear."

C.J. pasted a smile on his face to hide his envy. "That's wonderful." He really was happy for her success. "Come upstairs while I clean up. Then we can talk."

He led her to his rooms above the newspaper office.

"I stopped in at the home place on the way to Cheyenne." She dropped her satchel on the floor. "Dad seems to be doing much better."

"Yes." C.J. agreed. "It's a relief."

"I'll make us a pot of coffee while you wash away that ink, or grease–or whatever." Ruth wrinkled her nose.

"You garden and raise livestock." C.J. grinned as he reluctantly started a fire in the cookstove. Even with his windows open, the room was already stifling. "You can't tell me you do all that without getting dirty."

"I won't." She poured water into the pot before he could claim the sink. She put a handful of coffee beans into the grinder and cranked. "How's your business going?"

Scrubbing his hands under the running water, cool from the well, he debated with himself about how to answer.

"It's good." He tried to force cheer into his voice, but thoughts of the linotype machine and the competition's acquisition of Miss Stryker muffled his enthusiasm.

Ruth poured grounds into the basket, replaced the lid, and set the pot on the stove.

C.J. rinsed his hands and splashed some water on his face. He blotted lightly with his towel, leaving some moisture on his skin. When he looked up, his sister was studying him.

She nailed him with her gaze. Her mouth was a grim line.

After a few uncomfortable moments, she asked, "Is that true? Are things that good?"

He inhaled a sharp breath. "Why wouldn't it be?"

"Because you look like you're a hundred years old. Your face is filled with worry wrinkles and frown lines."

The muscles in his back tensed, reigniting the cramp he'd been able to ease earlier. "If the linotype machine breaks down again, I'll have to close. I can't afford a new one. I'll try to sell out, but with two other viable newspapers in town and several more tenuous ones, that's a long shot."

Ruth's brows knitted together. "Dad would probably loan you money, if you ask."

"He already has." C.J. sighed. "I don't want to ask him for more."

She lay her hand on his arm. "What will you do?"

"For now, I'm hoping for the best. But I've also written to Nathan Bender to see if that position with *The Chronicle* is still available."

Her eyes widened. "You'd rather move to Philadelphia than find some other line of work in Wyoming?"

"If *The Reporter* goes bust, I'll need to make a whole new start."

Sitting across from Esther Hobart Morris in her Cheyenne home, Inga reached into her handbag for the set of questions she had prepared. At six feet tall, Mrs. Morris, was an imposing figure.

"I understand you had a birthday just a few days

ago," Inga began.

Mrs. Morris grinned. "Yes. I turned eighty-three."

"Well, happy belated birthday." Inga smiled and turned to her list. "Why do you think Wyoming passed the equality bill in 1869, when suffragists in the east have been unable to convince men to give them the right to vote?" Inga read from the page before her, pencil poised to note the response.

Mrs. Morris smiled. "Women on the frontier worked side-by-side with their men, pulling their weight. Many women, like myself, had to support ourselves and our families after our husbands died, so many men saw us as equals."

"What brought you to South Pass City, Wyoming?"

"After my first husband died, I remarried." She settled back in her chair. "John and I moved there to open a saloon. At that time it was a booming gold town."

"My brother Erik is now in the Yukon prospecting for gold," Inga said.

"I saw in the paper that they had a big strike up there." Mrs. Morris's tired eyes held a bit of a glint. "Was he one of the lucky ones?"

"I haven't had any recent news from him, but he hadn't mentioned a strike the last I heard." Inga looked down at her notes. "When were you first appointed Justice of the Peace?"

"In February of 1870."

Inga lifted her gaze. "Just after the equality bill passed?"

"Yes. I was appointed to fill the remaining term of James Sullivan. He resigned in protest *because* the equality bill passed." Mrs. Morris chuckled. "I finished out his term, but did not run for election."

Inga furiously scribbled notes. "Please tell me about your experience as Justice of the Peace."

"I was determined to prove that I could succeed in my appointed duties while carrying out my responsibilities as a wife and mother." Mrs. Morris straightened on her chair and leaned slightly forward. "I ruled on twenty-six cases, and not one was reversed on appeal."

"Why didn't you run for a second term?"

She frowned. "I liked the work, but with taking care of my home and family and helping my husband with the saloon, all the responsibilities just became too much."

Inga sighed. She continued asking questions until all she had prepared were answered.

The two conversed over cups of tea and cookies. Inga had brought a tin as a gift to thank Mrs. Morris for agreeing to the interview.

"Of course, I'll be writing columns for *The Boomerang*." Inga inhaled a breath. "But you've given me so much information. Would you mind if I also submit an article about you to a magazine called *The Chronicle*?"

Pink bloomed in Mrs. Morris's wrinkled cheeks. "I would be honored."

"If they publish it, I'll send you a copy," Inga promised.

As she rode the train back to Laramie, she sketched outlines for several *Boomerang* columns and one for a story to submit to *The Chronicle.* The magazine editor had published her article on suffrage. Hopefully, he would accept a profile about this remarkable woman.

The fall term began the third week of September, first with examinations and then with classes. Inga had been assigned to teach freshman and sophomore English in the College of Liberal Arts, along with first and second year English in the Normal School. The full professor was responsible for the upper level courses, while the instructor had the preparatory school classes and assisted the professor.

Inga gazed out at the sixteen students before her, each engrossed in writing the paragraph she had assigned. They were consolidated into a close group, leaving the other half of the desks vacant. She had learned each of their names by the end of September.

Huge windows flooded bright light into the space. Ornamental iron scrollwork supported the wooden desks. She pressed her lips tightly together to keep from smiling and glanced at the clock on the wall.

"Time is up," Inga said, breaking the silence. "Please place your papers on the corner of my desk as you leave the classroom."

One by one, the students filed by, leaving their assignments as directed.

A sturdy, brown-haired girl with plain features hung back as the others passed. When only she and Inga were left in the room, she stepped forward.

"Can I help you Miss Wallis?" Inga asked, as the girl laid her paper atop the others.

The girl cast her gaze downward, then up at Inga. "Did you write the article about Ester Morris in the new issue of *The Chronicle*, Miss Stryker?"

A flush of warmth tingled through Inga's body. "Why, yes I did." She smiled. "I didn't know it had been released."

"I happened to be in the bookstore when it was delivered yesterday." The corners of Miss Wallis's mouth tipped upward. "It was a very good story. I especially liked the part about how none of her decisions were overturned on appeal and how you used it to show that a woman can make as well-reasoned and legally correct decisions as men do. Maybe more so since none of hers were overturned when they were reviewed by men." She tilted her head slightly. "Do you know Mrs. Morris?"

"Only a little. I went to Cheyenne to meet with her."

"I enjoy reading items about brave women, especially when they are written by women. You and Ida Tarbell are my favorites."

Pride swelled in Inga's chest. "Thank you."

"I hope to be able to write well enough by the time I finish college to be published." Miss Wallis nibbled her lower lip.

"Work hard and practice writing stories in your spare time," Inga suggested. "Then set them aside for awhile. When you come back to them, evaluate them as though they'd been written by someone else."

"I'll try that." The girl clutched her hands together. "Thank you, Miss Stryker."

"Good luck."

The girl turned and left the classroom.

Inga gathered up the papers, then headed home to grade them. On the way, she purchased a copy of the new issue of *The Chronicle*. She wished she knew how readers, other than Miss Wallis, were reacting to her article.

C.J. waited in line to mail his letter. When his turn came, he completed his transaction and exhaled a heavy breath. As he headed for the door, he spotted Miss Stryker standing in line with her own letters to mail.

"Good morning, Miss Stryker."

She turned in surprise. "Mr. Wakefield."

"I didn't mean to startle you." He flashed her a wide grin. "I would have expected you to be teaching a class at this time of day."

"This afternoon." She lowered her lashes, and then peered up at him. "I was sorry to learn you are closing the *Laramie Reporter*."

He tilted his head toward her. His smile faded. "Are you really? After all, I was competition for *The Boomerang*."

She straightened to her full petite height. "Yes, I really am. I think it is good for a town to have several newspapers. Having more than one editor's slant on the facts helps prevent any one person from having too much influence on the public."

Earnest innocence filled her expression as she talked. Her lack of guile was her best feature.

"Well, you hold onto that lofty principle." He paused. "It might be the trait that makes your columns so engaging."

Her eyes widened. "You've read my columns?"

"Of course." He took a step closer to allow a woman

holding the hand of a small boy to pass by. "Businessmen always keep track of the competition."

She moved forward with the line. He followed.

"I especially liked your first impressions of Laramie." A small smile returned to his lips. "It was a delightful way to introduce yourself to the community."

Charming pink bloomed in her cheeks. "Thank you."

"And the one about Esther Morris."

Her blush darkened.

"It was interesting to read her story from a woman's perspective."

"My interview with her was one of the most thought-provoking I've ever conducted." She paused, her blue gaze resting on him. "Are you going to stay in town?"

He frowned. "No. I'm leaving tomorrow to go east and work with a friend."

Her expression went blank. She eased to the counter. It was her turn. "I wish you good luck in your future."

She handed her small envelopes to the clerk and set a large one down as she opened her handbag.

"Best of luck to you, also." He slanted a glance at the address on the larger mail piece. *The Chronicle.*

He flashed her a parting smile and strode out the door, wondering whether he or her submission would arrive in Philadelphia first.

The powerful November wind blew cold and strong. Acrid coal smoke from the locomotive wafted toward the platform outside the depot. Inga pulled the hood of her cloak closer around her face and turned toward the wall.

As the huge wheels screeched and the din of voices grew, Inga peeked around the black wool. When the engine came to a full stop, steam whooshed from the stack. She slid a glance to the left, where Tom, whom she'd hired to transport Sarah's luggage, stood beside his cart.

A thundering stampede of feet on wooden boards grew as passengers emerged from the train, and the pack of waiting people rushed forward to greet them. Inga held back.

Finally, from the back of the second passenger car, Sarah emerged. Pausing at the top of the iron steps, her brown curls tumbled in the wind. Inga slipped her arm from under her cloak and waved. Sarah grinned, waved back, and descended to the platform.

When they reached each other, Sarah dropped her satchel and pulled Inga into a hug.

"I'm glad you're here," Inga said.

Sarah released her. "Me, too. We have so much to catch up on."

The sun had dropped lower in the sky. "We can do that after dinner." Inga led her friend to the porter. "Sarah, this is Tom. He helps Mrs. Campbell around the boarding house. If you show him your luggage, he will transport it for you."

They made the arrangements, then set out on foot, chatting as they walked.

The aroma of freshly baked bread and Mary Campbell's savory beef stew greeted them when they stepped through the door.

Sarah closed her eyes and dramatically inhaled a breath. "Umm. My mouth is watering already."

Inga grinned. "Let's go upstairs and wash up."

By the time they were ready to go to the dining room for supper, Sarah's trunk had been delivered to Inga's room.

A few minutes before seven o'clock, the friends descended the stairs and took their places at the dining table.

"Ladies, this is my friend, Sarah Jefferson. We went to college together." Inga gestured toward the woman to her left with the graying reddish-brown hair. "Sarah, this is Bertha Rush. She teaches at the elementary school."

Sarah grinned. "I'm a teacher, too. I am a private tutor for two young children back in Cincinnati."

Bertha arched a brow. "And you're able to travel way out here during the school year?"

Mary set a plate of bread slices on the table and quickly returned to the kitchen.

Sarah's grin faded slightly, and she straightened on her chair. "I really don't work on a school year. I teach around the family's schedule. They were in France last month, and they're in England now. They'll be back in early December and we'll resume lessons then."

Bertha's eyes grew wide. "They're fortunate to have the opportunity to learn from travel."

Sarah's posture eased, and she leaned back in her chair.

"And this is Eliza Fagen. She is a secretary at the bank." Inga's gaze fixed on the petite woman with the near-black hair, who was about a decade older than herself.

"Nice to meet you." Sarah gave her a polite nod. Eliza nodded back, but said nothing.

Mary re-entered the dining room carrying a large tureen. She placed it in the center of the table and took her place at the end, near a stack of bowls. She filled each bowl with stew and passed them around.

As she did, Inga continued, "And this is Mary Campbell. She owns this house and is a wonderful cook." Inga grinned at her. "I have to be careful or I will no longer fit into my clothes."

"Welcome Miss Jefferson." Mary handed a bowl to Eliza. "We enjoy having guests here."

"This supper looks and smells delicious." Sarah dipped her spoon into the stew and watched the steam rise as she held it above the bowl. "I must confess, I know very little about cooking."

After the meal, the boarders retired to their rooms. Inga closed her door. She and Sarah sat cross-legged on the bed, facing each other.

"I really enjoyed your article about the first woman Justice of the Peace in *The Chronicle*." Sarah said. "I only wish she had been elected instead of appointed."

"I know." Inga grimaced. "But she showed a

woman can competently do what most people consider a *man's* job, and she is well-respected here in Wyoming."

"It was a good story, but it didn't specifically support woman suffrage."

"I did write a column on Louisa Swain, the first woman to vote in a general election here in Wyoming." Inga sighed. "But she has passed away so I couldn't interview her."

"That's interesting, but it doesn't counter the anti-suffragists. It doesn't do much to help the cause." Sarah leaned forward and took Inga's hands in hers. "I think living in a state where women are enfranchised has made you complacent."

Inga inhaled a sharp breath. She exhaled slowly, trying to expel the sting of her friend's remark. "Even when I lived in Iowa, not everything I wrote was in support of the cause."

"Are you going to the suffrage convention in Washington, D.C. next February?"

Inga shrugged. "I don't know."

"It will be the fiftieth anniversary of the first women's rights convention."

"Yes." Inga withdrew her hands and rested one on each knee. "But it's a long way to go in winter." She swallowed. "Maybe Rachel will go. Chicago is closer."

Sarah clasped her hands together in her lap and looked down at them. "It might be better if she didn't."

Inga gasped. "Why do you say that?"

"Mrs. Stanton has always believed white women should have had the vote before Negro men." Sarah rested an elbow on her knee and her chin in her hand. "I don't know for sure, but I think she felt abandoned when the 15th amendment did not include women. A lot of white women were angry."

"I can understand that, since the suffragists had worked closely with the abolitionists before the war and then afterward for universal suffrage." Inga pulled her unfocused gaze directly to Sarah. "But Negro women have contributed much to the cause."

"But I've been hearing a lot of talk about stronger opposition to woman suffrage, especially in the former Confederate states, if it includes enfranchising colored women." Sarah frowned. "White women might have a better chance of getting the vote if they campaign for it alone."

How could they even consider that strategy? Inga stared at her friend. "And you support that position?"

"I don't know what to think." Sarah lifted one shoulder. "If white women get the right to vote, we can push for the vote for our Negro sisters."

"Or it might never happen. That would be so unfair to women like Rachel." Inga narrowed her eyes. "How does Susan B. feel about it?"

"I haven't heard specifically, but I know she once said something about cutting off her arm before she would demand the ballot for Negro men and not women."

Inga worried her lower lip. "Well, I think votes for women should mean votes for all women."

She wasn't sure she could continue to support the cause if it didn't include women like Rachel.

CHAPTER SIX

November 12, 1897
The Chronicle
Philadelphia, Pennsylvania

Dear Miss Stryker:

I am pleased to inform you that we will be publishing your article, "The Importance of Education for the Future of America." Your arguments about the benefits to the country of increased public funding for education at all levels were compelling. And we were impressed with your points about higher education for women not only making direct contributions to society through their work in professions, but also indirectly through supplementing their children's education at home, contributing to a more competent population.

Enclosed please find a bank draft for purchase of this article.

As this will be your fourth article we have published, we would like to suggest additional topics for you to consider for your future stories.

1. *Women who are successful in professions where there are few women. As a university professor, you, yourself are one. But also include others like physicians, lawyers, and scientists.*
2. *Evaluation from a professor's perspective of the recently released book,* Dracula, *by Bram Stoker.*
3. *A cat or dog story like the ones you published in* Vogue Magazine.

Since you are not a staff writer, you are not obligated to write on these topics, and if you choose not to write on these subjects, it will not influence our decisions regarding future articles you may submit.

We look forward to reading your next article.

Sincerely,
C.J. Wakefield
Editor

Inga blinked. She reread the letter. Twice.

C.J. Wakefield. The C.J. Wakefield who had owned the *Laramie Reporter*? The C.J. Wakefield who only wanted her to write gossip? He was now an editor at *The Chronicle*? And he was buying her story.

But how did he know about her *Vogue* articles? And why would he suggest she write something like that for *The Chronicle*? That's not the kind of subject the magazine published. Was he toying with her?

Inga paced back and forth between her bedroom and the sleeping porch, trying to process this turn of events.

Maybe she should try sending her work to other periodicals. But the magazine had become a good market for her. And the idea of writing about women succeeding in occupations where they were rare held a strong appeal.

It might be worth submitting at least one more article to *The Chronicle's* new editor.

Even with the windows open, unusual early May heat pervaded the boarding house dining room. Inga blotted her forehead with her handkerchief.

"Have you heard from your brother?" Bertha asked, as she buttered her bread. Her hair clung to her cheeks, damp with perspiration. "Has he been sent to Cuba, yet?"

Inga shivered. "Poul—Paul never writes to me. All I know is from my mother's last letter. He's been in training and will go to Florida in early June." She paused. "I'm so worried about him."

"President McKinley should never have declared war with Spain." Eliza spat out the words as though they were as distasteful as the idea of war.

"No politics at the table," Mary scolded, as she returned to the dining room. She carried a platter of sliced, cold roast beef leftover from last night.

Eliza shot her an irritated glare, but said nothing more.

The bowl of canned peaches was passed, then the bread, the butter, the meat, and the cheese.

Mary filled the glasses with iced tea.

Everyone ate in silence.

Bertha was the first to speak. "Did you hear from *The Chronicle* about your article on women in professions?"

Inga nodded. "They are going to publish it."

"Congratulations." Eliza smiled. Her crisply pressed white blouse was unbuttoned at the collar.

Mary grinned. "Must be that new typewriter."

"I sent it in before the university offered us the machines." Inga chuckled. "And I'm still learning how to type."

"I think it was nice of the college to give you a chance to buy it at a reduced price." Bertha punctuated her words with a single nod.

Inga cut her slice of cheese in half and placed a piece on her bread.

Eliza's gaze focused on Inga. "What are you working on now?"

"The story of how suffragists won the vote in Colorado." Inga smiled. "When the term ends next month, I'm going down to Denver to meet with several of the women who worked for the cause."

Mary's dark gaze fixed on Inga. "I thought you meant to keep your room through the summer."

"I am. I only plan to be in Denver for a week. Then I'll come back here to write the article."

Mary spooned more peach slices into her sauce dish.

"Then the magazine wants me to do an article on women homesteaders and ranchers." Inga paused. "So I'll need to find some such women to interview."

"I know a few." Eliza offered. "They come into the bank."

Inga brightened. "If you give me their names and addresses, I'll write and ask if they'll agree to be interviewed."

"I know some, too," Mary said.

"Wonderful. With the help of you ladies, this might not to be as hard to write as I thought." Inga lay a hand on her chest. "And the editor has a sister who homesteaded. He's coming to visit her this summer and has promised to introduce me to her."

"Would that be Ruth Wakefield?" Mary asked.

"Yes." Inga turned to her. "Do you know her?"

"She's very smart," Bertha chimed in. "And very determined."

Mary frowned. "But she can be a very difficult woman."

An ache rose in the back of Inga's throat. She did not relish interviewing another difficult woman.

"I'm so glad it worked out that we could meet, even if only in passing." Inga nearly shouted to be heard above the rumble and screeches of trains coming in and out of the rail yard around the corner.

From across the table, Rachel smiled. "It's good to see you again."

As they waited for the waiter to bring their sandwiches, Inga glanced around the dark, noisy café. The room was small, with yellowing wallpaper. Odors of oil and tobacco smoke permeated the air. Customers occupied most of the tables. "What a coincidence that we're covering similar stories in different states."

Rachel covered her smile with her long, slender fingers. "Isn't that what we write about?"

Inga shrugged. "Not always. But I was impressed with the suffragists I've interviewed so far. They were able to convince hundreds of men and women to support enfranchisement. They worked tirelessly."

"So did the women I spoke with in California." Rachel took a sip of water. "But they were not successful."

"Susan B. said that was because of the liquor men and the movement's association with temperance." Inga inhaled a sooty breath. Her throat burned. "And that not all counties were organized."

"Yes, but some of the leadership may be rethinking that." Rachel frowned. "You weren't at this year's convention."

Inga winced. "Did Susan B. say something else?"

The waiter carefully set Inga's plate before her, then dropped Rachel's on the table with a thunk.

When rude behavior like his had happened in the past, Rachel had told Inga to ignore it. Shooting a glare at his retreating back, she pinched her lips together.

Rachel leaned forward. "Not directly. But in conversations off the podium, there were discussions of the fact that populations of the four states with full suffrage are mostly white Protestants. And the southern chapters are segregated."

"But from the start, the cause embraced all women." Inga protested. "And abolition."

"Things are changing. And not for the better." Rachel ran her fingers over the collar of her wine-red blouse. "I can feel it."

Thoughts of Inga's last conversation with Sarah flooded her mind. She pushed away the memory. "It can't be that bad."

"Oh, Inga." Rachel exhaled a heavy sigh. "You live in a cocoon. You're a white woman. You have plenty of money. You live in a state that already has suffrage, where many white men respect the white women and mostly treat them as equals, or nearly so. The rest of the country is *not* like that."

"Then move to Wyoming."

A small smile curved Rachel's lips. "It wouldn't be the same for me as it is for you."

She nodded toward the waiter.

Inga's heart grew heavy. Although she hadn't given it much thought, there were only a few Negroes in Laramie, most of whom were domestics or laborers. She took a bite of her chicken salad. It tasted like dust. The only local Negro she knew by name was Suzy Parker, the brothel owner, and Inga had never met her. She no longer had an appetite.

Rachel leaned forward until her chest rested against the table. "I'm sorry, Inga. But it's true. You are well-educated, but not experienced in the world. Come visit me in Chicago. I'll show you what my life is like there."

Inga lifted her chin. "I've been to Chicago. Several times. Shopping with my mother or with my whole family."

"That's downtown Chicago." Rachel rolled her eyes, but her tone was sympathetic. "It's very different in the neighborhoods."

Pressure built in Inga's temples. She massaged them with her fingertips.

"What're you doin' eatin' with a nigger?" A red-faced, bald-headed man stood at the corner of the table closest to Inga. His small, round eyes shot daggers at Rachel.

Inga blinked. She straightened her spine. "She's my—"

"Lady's maid," Rachel interrupted. The muscles in her jaw tensing. "Ain't that right, Miz Stryker?"

Inga could only nod.

The man's posture relaxed a bit. "Well, you shouldn't be eatin' with your help, young lady." A veiled threat wove through his words. "It makes niggers like that get uppity."

"Yes, sir," Inga whispered through clenched teeth.

He perched his top hat on his head and walked away.

When the café's door had closed behind him, Inga pinned her gaze on Rachel. "Why did you say that?"

With a curled lip, Rachel shot a fleeting glare toward the door, then met Inga's gaze. "To keep you from getting beaten, and me from getting killed."

With its yellow and orange flowered wallpaper and heavy oak table, The Wakefields' dining room was cheery and comfortable. A large fireplace with marble tiles and an oak mantel was centered on the wall opposite the window. A similar configuration graced every room Inga had seen in the sprawling ranch house.

She took a breath and leaned back on her chair. "That was delicious, Mrs. Wakefield. I ate much more than I should have."

"Naw." Mr. Wakefield, a big, burly man with a kind face, grinned at her from his place at the head of the table. "You're such a tiny little thing. A good meal won't hurt you."

"Dad." The editor's sister scolded. "Really!"

Inga chuckled.

"So, Ruth." C.J. turned to his sister. "How about I pick up Miss Stryker tomorrow morning and bring her out to your place? We should arrive by late afternoon."

"No."

C.J. flinched. "What do you mean 'no?' You promised to let Miss Stryker visit your homestead and complete her interview."

Inga gritted her teeth.

Ruth crossed her arms over her chest, then leaned forward and rested her elbows on the table. She winked at Inga.

Inga cocked her head as she returned Miss Wakefield's gaze.

"Let's go sit on the north porch," Mrs. Wakefield said. "It will be cooler there, and we might even catch a breeze."

"I would be happy to help you with the dishes," Inga offered, rising from her chair.

Mrs. Wakefield waved as if to swat the idea away. "Don't worry about that, dear. Ruth and I will take care of them later." She turned to her husband. "Why don't you take them on out? I'll be there with some lemonade in a few minutes."

He led the way to a wide, roofed verandah with six white-painted wooden chairs. Touching the back of the one in the center, Mr. Wakefield said, "Why don't you sit here, Miss Stryker?"

Inga settled into the chair. "Thank you."

The Wakefield siblings sat on either side of her.

Inga shifted in her seat.

"Drat, Ruth." C.J. raked his fingers through his thick, dark brown hair. "You promised to let Miss Stryker visit your place and interview you for her article."

"And I will." Ruth grinned at Inga. "But I will pick her up tomorrow morning and take her home with me, if that's okay with you, Miss Stryker."

Her brother frowned.

Inga rested her back against the wood. "That's fine with me." She smiled. "And please call me Inga."

"And I'd like it if you would call me Ruth."

"I will. And I look forward to learning about your homesteading experience."

"Make sure you bring old clothes. Trousers if you have some." Ruth turned to her brother. "You can pick Inga up on Wednesday morning and take her home."

C.J. groaned. "That will mean I have to leave at midnight."

"Use your head, son." Mr. Wakefield admonished. "You can take my tent and go out on Tuesday. You can camp in Ruth's yard overnight and bring Miss Stryker home in the morning."

Early in the morning, Inga was waiting on the front porch with her packed satchel. On a chair sat her handbag and a box containing cinnamon rolls that Mary had made for breakfast, along with a large hunk of cheese and a bowl of grapes.

Ruth pulled her wagon up to the boarding house just as the chirping birds called forth the first rays of dawn.

Inga slung her canteen filled with water over her shoulder. She waved then picked up her box and handbag.

Dressed in trousers and a calico shirt, Ruth hopped down from the wagon seat, tethered the horses to the hitching post, and started toward her. "Looks like you're ready for the trip."

"I think so." Inga smiled. "Just need to put this in the wagon, then go back and get my satchel." She glanced toward the porch.

"I'll get it." Ruth bounded up the walk.

Inga proceeded past the horses and tucked her things under the seat, careful not to disturb the rifle lying there.

Moments later, Ruth deposited the satchel in the back of the wagon. "Climb up."

Inga clambered onto the seat, trying to keep her skirt from hitching above her knees. She smoothed it down before sitting. Ruth untied the team and joined her.

"Was that cinnamon I smelled when I passed you?" Ruth asked.

"Yes. Mrs. Campbell thought we would need sustenance on the way to your place." Inga's mouth watered.

Ruth tossed her braid back and laughed. "My mother thought the same thing. There's a basket behind the seat also filled with food and a jar of cold tea. Or at least it was cold when I left her house."

Inga smiled. "We'll dine like royalty on this journey."

As the sun peeked over the horizon, the birds sang in full chorus. Cool morning air washed over her face as they passed through town. The soft thuds of the horses' hooves meeting the dirt streets and the squeak of the wheels punctuated the easy sway of the wagon as she settled in for the long ride ahead.

"Why did you decide to become a homesteader?" Inga asked.

"Because I like working the land. And caring for animals."

"And you couldn't have done that on your parents' ranch?"

"I could have. My father would have paid me like a ranch hand." Ruth grinned. "But then I would have had to do things *his* way."

Inga nodded. "Is that why your place is so far away from your parents'?"

"No. That was determined by the land that was

still available for homesteading. The best parcels and those closest to the towns had already been claimed."

They chatted as they rolled over the bumpy trail, weaving through a maze of towering hills and around rocky outcroppings. Along the way, Inga saw only a cabin and a two-story farm house, each at the foot of a massive hill.

When they came to a cluster of trees beside a stream, Ruth pulled off the path. "Let's have those cinnamon rolls."

She jumped down from the wagon and tied the reins to a tree branch. Inga climbed to the ground and retrieved the box and her canteen from under the seat.

Ruth spread a blanket in the shade and they sat down. Inga handed her the open box. "Help yourself."

Ruth and Inga each selected a roll.

"You know I wasn't trying to flatter you yesterday when I told you I enjoy reading your articles." Ruth kept her eyes on the trail. "After C.J. closed his paper, I started subscribing to *The Boomerang*. I have to pick them up with my mail when I'm in town, so I often get several weeks' worth at a time. And I look forward to issues of *The Chronicle* when you have pieces in them."

People were reading her articles and enjoying them. Inga's cheeks warmed. "Thank you."

With furrowed brow, Ruth turned to face Inga. "But I hope the one you're working on now won't be only about me."

"It won't." Inga lay her hand gently on Ruth's arm. "I've already spoken with a woman farmer down by Cheyenne and another who ranches east of Laramie." She moved her hand back to her lap. "There are far more women working the land than I realized. My mother operated a produce business when I was a girl, and after my father's death, she ran the whole farm until she married my stepfather. They still operate it together."

"Sometimes I think it would be nice to have a husband to help with the work," Ruth said wistfully.

"But most of the time I like being able to do things the way I want them."

Inga sighed. "I understand. I worked very hard to earn my master's degree, and I love teaching at the university. But I also love writing for the newspaper and the magazine. Some weeks it's all I can do to take care of my room at the boarding house. It would be impossible for me to take care of a home. Or livestock. Or a husband."

"That's too bad." Ruth frowned. "Because I think C.J. is quite smitten with you."

Smitten? With her? They'd barely had a civil conversation.

Inga's breath caught. She stared at the trail ahead of them.

Still shocked by Ruth's revelation, Inga followed her through the pasture to a large, rocky hill, one of many that stood on her land. This one had a nearly vertical side facing Ruth's cabin.

"This is where I lived when I first moved out here. I use it as a shelter for my cattle now." Ruth gestured at a large opening. To one side, a door, a small window and a stovepipe were visible. She strode to the door and opened it.

Inga stepped into a dark, damp room.

Ruth lit a lamp. "I keep this area to work in."

It was a small space with a table, a chair, and some shelves with halters, calf buckets and other familiar farm equipment. Wooden timbers supported a rough-hewn board ceiling.

Inga studied the structure. "Where did you learn how to build this?"

Ruth chuckled. "A high school friend with a mining company helped me design and build it.

She removed three wooden bars from a second door and opened it.

Inga walked to the threshold and gazed into the dark cave-like space. Ruth walked in. The lamp illuminated more and more space, with timber supports neatly lining the center.

"This is huge!"

Ruth laughed. "When I lived here, there were only two small rooms. We enlarged it to hold most of my cattle herd. At least for now."

"What was it like to live underground?"

"Surprisingly comfortable. It faces south, so there weren't winter winds blowing in." She turned and led the way back to the small room. "I wouldn't want to live here forever, but it was an acceptable place to start."

"You're a stronger woman than I am, Ruth Wakefield."

Even though Inga had lived in a small cabin as a young girl, she wasn't sure she would ever be able adjust a home that was little more than a cave.

Inga perused Ruth's one-room log cabin. Although the structure had appeared small from the outside, the interior was surprisingly spacious.

Pencil in hand, paper in front of her, she sat across the dining table from Ruth, adding to the notes she'd written about their conversation on yesterday's trip to the homestead. "Your home reminds me of the one we lived in before my father died. It was a little bigger than this, but it was divided into three rooms and a nursery addition. It always seemed so crowded with my parents, my three brothers and me, and our housekeeper. With just the two of us here, your place feels very large."

Ruth grinned. "My parents think I should put up some dividing walls, but as long as I'm the only one here, I like it this way. Especially since I was living underground not that long ago."

"Well, it's much bigger than my room, even with the sleeping porch. I like your home, too." Inga gazed at the corner with shelves filled with books. "You must like to read."

"It's my favorite hobby." Ruth chuckled. "I often indulge in a new book, a magazine or two, and a newspaper when I'm in town. And of course, C.J. sends me issues of *The Chronicle*."

Inga sighed. "I imagine you get snowed in out here in the winter."

"I do." She gestured toward a ladder built onto one wall. "That's my escape route in case I can't get out one of the doors. I would have to break a hole in the roof. I haven't put a door up there because I'm afraid rain might leak in around it. Luckily I haven't had to escape." She gestured to the cupboards and cabinets it the kitchen area. "And all of those are filled with canned goods, dried meat, flour, and other supplies."

Inga scribbled more notes for her story.

"Want to help me feed the chickens and gather the eggs?" Ruth asked, when Inga finally looked up.

Inga grinned. "Sure. That was one of my earliest chores, so I should be pretty good at it."

"You've been *pretty good* at all of the work we've done today." Ruth smiled back. She rose and picked up a basket. "It's been nice of you to help. And I've enjoyed having you here."

Inga rose and followed her hostess to the coop. Ruth picked up a bucket of cracked corn.

"It's been fun for me to spend this time with you," Inga said. "It's felt like having a sister closer to my age than any of my half-sisters. I always wanted that when I was a child."

"Me, too." Ruth handed the basket to Inga, and dumped the cracked corn into the long, low trough.

Inga carried the basket to the wall of nest boxes in the hen house. The once-familiar odor of chicken dung greeted her, and she wrinkled her nose. Carefully, she plucked the eggs from the compartments and gently placed them in the hamper.

When Inga emerged from the structure, Ruth was carrying two pails of water from the well. "I thought we'd pull some carrots and pick some tomatoes to have with the rabbit for supper."

"Sounds delicious."

Ruth set down her buckets and took the basket Inga held out to her. "I'll put this in the root cellar."

She returned and led Inga to her large garden. The

sun was on its downward arc, and a steady wind blew. An occasional distant cluck or moo carried over the subtle whoosh of moving air.

"Do you ever worry about living alone out here? So far away from neighbors and town?"

Ruth met Inga's gaze. "There's always the possibility of broken bones, rattlesnake bites, robbers, and so much more. The risks are in the back of my mind all the time. I think this awareness makes me more careful. Whenever I have a small accident or a near disaster, it really bothers me for a few days."

"You're very brave."

Ruth snorted. "Hardly."

Inga brushed away a little soil and checked the crown of a growing carrot to see if it was ripe for pulling. "Do you do a lot of canning for winter?"

Ruth's shoulders sagged. "Yes. I've done some this year, but need to do lots more."

"When I was growing up, I used to help my mother and her friends every summer," Inga said. "If you'd like, I could come out again for a few days and help you."

Ruth's eyes widened. "Really?"

"Of course." Inga plucked a large, red tomato from its vine. "But we'd need to do it before the fall term starts."

The thuds of hooves trotting along the trail carried on the breeze. Inga turned to see two horses pulling a black surrey.

Ruth burst out laughing. "He's certainly trying to impress you. I can't believe he talked my father into letting him bring Dad's pride and joy way out here." She put a hand on Inga's shoulder. "Dad must really like you, too."

Inga picked up the basket of vegetables, and they walked to the cabin.

"You can unharness your horses and put them in the small corral by the stream," Ruth told her brother.

He rolled his eyes and pursed his lips. "Good afternoon to you, too." He turned to Inga. "Good afternoon, Miss Stryker."

She nodded. "And to you."

Even though he wore denims and a work shirt with the sleeves rolled up, his dark hair was neatly combed and his face clean-shaven.

She glanced down at her dirty cotton trousers and worn calico blouse, embarrassed for him to see her this way. "Would you like me to wash the vegetables?"

"That would be good. Use the lighter bucket." Ruth brushed the dust off her shirt. "We'll use the other one to wash up. Charles James, take care of your horses, and you can start a fire in the cooking pit."

He winced.

Inga swept her gaze from him to Ruth.

A wicked glint sparkled in her eyes. "If you want to annoy him, use his full name."

"Mom sent molasses cookies and a chocolate cake." He grinned. "You girls had better be nice to me."

Ruth winked at Inga. "Mom must like you, too."

Mr. Wakefield shot his sister a quizzical glance.

Inga walked into the cabin and fetched the bowl and small brush. She returned to the rough-hewn bench sitting against the outside wall, assembled everything she needed to prepare the tomatoes and carrots, and set to work.

Once a strong fire was burning in the hole in the ground, Ruth placed the grate atop the bricks that surrounded the opening. She placed the rabbit she had shot and dressed earlier this afternoon on to cook.

"We'll roast the carrots when the meat is closer to being ready. Slice the tomatoes and put them on this." She handed the plate to Inga. "We'll eat them raw."

Mr. Wakefield came up behind Ruth with a broad smile lighting his face. "Has my sister been treating you like a slave?"

"Not at all. She's been the perfect hostess."

"But she's had you working ever since I got here."

"It's been a nice change of pace from my usual daily life."

When supper was ready, they sat around a rustic outdoor table in the shade.

"I really like this spot." Inga tipped her head back to allow the cool breeze brush over her face. "It's so shady and the fresh air is energizing."

Ruth smiled. "A picnic."

"Did Ruth give you good information for your story?" Mr. Wakefield nabbed one of the rolls his mother had sent home with his sister.

"Very much so." Inga turned to her hostess. "I have a few more facts to add. Then I'll let you review them to see if they are accurate, and make sure you'll be comfortable having the information in the public."

Mr. Wakefield raised a brow. "Do you always do that for the people you interview?"

"Not with public figures. Only with private citizens whose names I include in my articles." She nailed him with her gaze. "You wouldn't want your magazine to be sued for defamation, would you?"

He broke eye contact and looked down at his plate. "Of course not."

Ruth grinned. "I think you've met your match, C.J."

Inga smoothed a wrinkle from her brown skirt. She sat on the carriage seat next to Mr. Wakefield as he drove the pair of horses toward Laramie. Dust blew in the incessant wind and the team kicked up more. She kept her mouth closed.

"Will you have your article ready before I leave for Philadelphia on Saturday?" he asked.

"I'll try, but I still have to write up the information Ruth gave me and add an introduction and a summary paragraph or two." She tucked a wayward strand of hair that had escaped from her braid under her bonnet.

"What topic are you going to work on next?"

"I haven't decided. When I was having lunch with a friend in Denver, a disturbing incident happened." She held her hand a few inches from her mouth as a barrier to the dust. "A rude man came up to us and called Rachel a 'nigger.' She pretended to be my maid. Before he left, he told me not to eat with 'the help.'"

"You have a Negro friend?" The pitch of his voice rose on the question.

"Yes. We went to college together." Inga lifted her chin. "Does that bother you?"

"Not at all. I was just surprised."

A pair of tumbleweeds rolled across the path ahead of the horses. "I haven't been able to find an approach to write about the situation."

He shrugged. "Maybe that means you shouldn't."

Her chest tightened. "Why do you say that?"

"Because there is no good way to talk about it without offending the bigots, and if you do that you might create a reaction that would put their lives in danger."

Inga chewed her lower lip and clasped her hands together in her lap. "I wouldn't want to do that."

"We liked your piece on Colorado suffrage," he said gently. "Maybe you could write another article like that."

"Maybe." She turned so she could see his face. "How do you feel about the enfranchisement of women?"

"I support it." He shot her a wry grin. "How could I not, with a sister like Ruth. She's smarter and tougher than I am. Always has been."

"She is remarkable." Inga grinned, too. "And I'm pleased that you support giving women the right to vote, Mr. Wakefield."

"The two of you already have it." He shifted in the seat. "And, you can call me C.J."

Inga shook her head. "I don't think that would be proper."

He straightened. "Why not? You're friends with my sister, and I'm not that much older than you."

Inga leaned away from his scolding tone. "But you are the editor of *The Chronicle*."

He shrugged. "You can address me formally when you're writing to me at the magazine. But when you're with me or my family here in Wyoming, you can call me C.J., and I'll call you Inga when we are together socially. Do you think we could do that?"

Inga gazed out over the heads of the horses and sighed. "I suppose."

But the informality made her uncomfortable. If his sister was right about him being smitten, Inga wanted to keep as much distance from him as possible.

Chapter Seven

October 9, 1898
The Chronicle
Philadelphia, Pennsylvania

Dear Miss Stryker:

I am pleased to advise you that we are impressed by your article, "Women Who Work the Land." We will be publishing it in our November issue. Enclosed please find the bank draft.

We look forward to your next submission.

Sincerely,
C.J. Wakefield
Editor

Below the formal letter, the editor had scrawled a personal note.

Ruth wrote me that you helped her with the bulk of her vegetable canning. She very much appreciated your help and so do I. She is lucky to have you for a friend.

I also enjoyed our ride back to town. When I'm in Laramie over the Christmas holiday, I would like to see you.

C.J.

Inga glowered at the last line. It seemed too forward. But then, she'd ridden all the way back to Laramie alone with him. And, she had agreed to call him C.J.

She set the page to the side of her writing desk, and opened the letter addressed with Rachel's neat, but tiny, penmanship.

Dear Inga,

I was talking with Ida today, and she mentioned that next year's NASWA convention will be held April 27-May 3 in Grand Rapids, Michigan. Since it will be in the spring this year, and we shouldn't have to travel in snow, I am hoping that you can come to Chicago for a brief visit, and we can take the train to

Grand Rapids together.

Inga frowned. The university would still be in session. She scanned through the remaining news about Rachel's personal life.

I am being courted by a very handsome man who works as a porter at the Palmer House hotel. His name is Herman Ansel. I do not know if seeing him will lead to marriage, but he is personable and I enjoy his company.

The brief paragraph caught Inga's attention.

"I thought you vowed never to marry," Inga murmured to herself.

She set Rachel's note on the side of the desk opposite C.J.'s.

Sighing, she stood and walked over to her satchel and pulled out the stack of essays she had collected from her students this afternoon. She returned to her chair and set down the papers.

Her gaze slid over C.J.s scrawl. She had not yet decided on a topic for her next submission. Moder's last letter mentioned that after the war ended Paul's outfit had been sent to Cuba to keep the peace.

There had been plenty of stories in newspapers and periodicals about combat experiences, but very little, so far at least, about peacetime Cuba. If only Inga could get her brother to correspond with her regularly. That was unlikely, so she needed to come up with something else.

She pulled a list of possible topics from her top drawer.

Annie Oakley might be a good subject. Somewhere Inga had heard that the famous sharpshooter had offered to serve in combat along with some female friends. And to bring her own guns and ammunition. Maybe Miss Oakley would agree to give her opinions about women fighting with the military.

There was only one way to find out. Inga would write to her as soon as she finished grading papers.

As the train pulled into the Laramie station, Inga slipped the draft of her article into her satchel.

Hopefully, Miss Oakley's response to her final set of questions would be waiting for her now that she was back from Christmas in Iowa.

The train screeched to a stop. Inga stood and bundled her cloak around her. Picking up her belongings, she exited the train.

Snow flurries sparkled in the crisp air as she made her way through the other arriving passengers to the corner of the platform where Tom waited.

"I have only the little trunk this time. Do you remember what it looks like?"

"Yes ma'am." He pulled his wool cap down over his ears. His gaze fell to the bags in her hands. "Do you want me to take those for you?"

She handed the valise to him and pulled the baggage slip from her pocket. "I'm going to make a stop on my way home." She gave the slip to Tom. "Please leave them outside the door to my room. I'll pay you when I get to the boarding house."

"Yes ma'am." A shy smile tipped the corners of his mouth. "A man stopped by the boarding house asking for you. Twice."

Her eyes widened. "Who?"

"I don't know." He set her valise on his cart. "Sorry."

"That's all right. Thank you." She turned and headed toward the boarding house. Had her visitor been Mr. Wakefield? Luckily, she had missed him. She wanted to avoid the awkwardness seeing him would cause.

She scurried inside the stuffy warmth of the milliner's shop. After standing by the heating stove for a few minutes, she opened her post office box and pulled out two envelopes. Miss Oakley had responded. The other letter was from Sarah. She slipped them into her handbag.

"Inga!" a familiar male voice called.

She whirled around but closed her eyes. She really didn't want to talk with him.

When she opened her eyes, he was heading toward

her.

"Good afternoon, Mr. Wakefield."

"It's C.J., remember? I wasn't sure if I'd get to see you before I left for Philadelphia."

She clutched her handbag. "I just got back from Cedar Falls. I haven't even been home, yet."

He smiled. "Did you have a nice Christmas?"

"Yes." She kept her expression bland. "And you?"

"Very nice. Ruth was here, but she's gone back to her place." His dark gazed rested on Inga's face. "She said she knew you were going to be with your family, but she was sorry to miss you."

"I'm sorry, too."

"Are you working on another story for the magazine?" His voice had subtly shifted to a more professional tone.

"Yes. I hope to finish it before classes resume."

He leaned closer. "Have dinner with me tonight, and you can tell me all about it."

"If I do that, Mr. Wakefield—"

"C.J."

"C.J." She wracked her brain for an excuse. "If I do that, I won't have that time to write."

"Then let me take you to dinner when you finish." He grinned. "That way you can save your postage and have a free meal."

"We'll see."

"Please." His grin faded. "Ruth's told me a lot about you, and I'd like to get to know you better."

Inga took a step backward. Somehow, she would have to find a way to avoid C.J.'s advances without compromising her friendship with Ruth.

"If I finish my article tonight, I'll have lunch with you tomorrow."

It would be better to meet with him in broad daylight.

C.J. studied his appearance in the bank window. He slid his hand over his hair to smooth the strands that refused to lie flat. He straightened his collar. Somehow, he needed to persuade Inga to allow him to court her, even though she didn't seem willing to even be friends.

He strode to the Gem City Cafe, trying to calm his nervous stomach. Although he had only been able to convince Inga to have lunch with him, he was treating her to one of the best restaurants in town. Turning the final corner, he spotted her approaching from the opposite direction. She was bundled in her black cloak, her hood up. Anxiety clogged his throat.

"Hello, Inga."

She gave him a curt nod. "C.J."

Reaching the door before she did, he held it open and followed her inside. The host took their wraps and then seated them.

Delighted to be sitting across the table from her, he set down his menu and watched her study the list of foods. Finally, she looked up and met his gaze. Her blue dress enhanced her lovely blue eyes.

"Did you find something that looks good?" He choked out the question.

She placed her menu on the table. "The chicken sauté with vegetables, please."

A waitress in a black dress and white apron poured coffee into china cups. He gave her Inga's order and his, then turned to Inga.

"Have you finished the article?"

"Yes. I brought it with me." She leaned toward her satchel on the floor.

"You can give it to me after we finish our lunch."

She straightened.

"For now, just tell me the title."

"I called it *The Woman Who Volunteered For Combat.*"

"A woman in combat?" He ran his hand across his chin and down his neck trying to figure out what she might have written.

"Before the war, Annie Oakley volunteered to serve in combat." Inga paused. "I wrote about that, and her."

"I thought that was only a rumor."

She smiled. "It's not. She sent me the text of the letter she wrote to President McKinley."

Inga was full of surprises. He shook his head. "I'll look forward to reading it."

She took a sip of her coffee.

He searched his mind for another topic.

"I sent a note to your sister, asking her to visit me next time she comes to town." Inga broke the silence.

"Mom said the two of you are becoming close friends."

"I hope so," Inga said, wistfully. "I like her and enjoy discussing literature with her. She's very well-read."

He leaned forward. "I worry about her. All alone out there in the middle of nowhere."

Inga clasped her hands together on the table. "So do I. But she likes her life there."

His chest warmed. Her obvious affection for his sister touched his heart. And made him jealous. If only she developed a similar fondness for him.

"Why is it that you like her so much, but you're standoffish with me?" He tried to keep his tone light.

She parted her lips, but then flattened them. Pink colored her cheeks.

"Is it because I didn't hire you on the day we first met? I wanted to, you know." He rushed on, suddenly wanting her to understand. "But I couldn't afford it."

She tilted her head. "I don't think that's it. After all, at *The Boomerang*, I have the exact position I was seeking."

"Then what?"

She shrugged. "Maybe it's because I have more in common with Ruth."

He reached across the table and lay his hand on hers. "Maybe we have more in common than you think."

She withdrew her hand and rested it in her lap.

Clearly, she wasn't ready to be courted.

The tender green of spring had burst forth in the fresh leaves on the trees and the yellows and purples of wildflowers. Inga held the reins as the horse trotted steadily along the trail back to Laramie.

She would be a day late in returning the sulky she had hired, but she had enjoyed the extra day she spent with Ruth. And, it was much more pleasant to be traveling in today's sun than it would have been to slog through yesterday's rain. Luckily, the shower had been heavy enough to settle the dust but too light to make the trail unduly muddy.

Inga adjusted the brim of her bonnet forward and inhaled the heady scent of damp spring earth. Securing the reins between her knees, she stretched her arms up and out, reveling in the fleeting sense of freedom.

An hour later, she had unloaded her belongings and taken the rig back to the livery. Her room and sleeping porch were stuffy and warm so she opened all the windows. After collecting the letters needing replies, paper, pencils, pens, and ink, she packed them into her satchel. She carried it and her writing desk down to the shady front porch.

Both Sarah and Rachel had sent missives chastising her for missing the NASWA convention in Michigan, but each focused on a different aspect of the convention.

Inga reread Sarah's words first. Her friend had been offered a position working with Mrs. Shaw, and she planned to begin her new duties in early July. But the emphasis of Sarah's message was on words from Elizabeth Cady Stanton's letter to the meeting.

'It is a sad reflection that the chains of woman's bondage have been forged by her own sires and sons. Every man who is not for us in this prolonged struggle for liberty is responsible for the present degradation of the mothers of the race. It is pitiful to see how few men ever have made our cause their own, but while leaving us to fight our battle alone, they have been unsparing in their criticism of every failure.'

Inga sighed. For some time, Mrs. Stanton had been making similar complaints. Now, with her age and infirmities, it was not surprising that she would be frustrated and angry. Inga was so lucky to have men in her family and even Mr. Wakefield – C.J. – who supported the cause.

Sarah ended with:

Over the past year or so, you've published interesting and well-written stories about strong and successful women in The Chronicle, but only the one about the Des Moines meeting and the one about Colorado suffrage have promoted enfranchisement. I implore you to use your growing platform in support of the cause.

Inga tapped her pencil against her chin. It was true. Since she had moved to Wyoming, she had lost some of her fervor for the suffrage movement.

She exchanged Sarah's letter for Rachel's. Rachel still worked for *The Conservator.* Her beau was still courting her, although she was hesitant to wed him or anyone. She feared that marriage might spell the end of her career.

"I know just what you mean," Inga murmured.

In her description of the convention, she focused on one of Susan B.'s comments.

'Only one generation has passed (since passage of the 14th and 15th Amendments) and yet nearly all of the Southern States have by one device or another succeeded in excluding from the ballot-box very nearly the entire negro vote, openly and defiantly declaring their intention to secure the absolute supremacy of the white race, but there is not a suggestion on their part of allowing the citizens to whom they deny the right of suffrage to be counted out from the basis of representation.'

Rachel concluded her letter with:

Lottie Wilson Jackson tried to introduce a motion to condemn segregated transportation. It was tabled. I feel as if we are moving backward instead of forward. I fear that some of our leaders would support repealing enfranchisement of Negro men if it meant giving the vote to white women. The right to vote for white women should mean the vote for all women, and all men. Please do all you can to support this moral point.

Inga scratched her head. If she didn't know better, she would have thought her friends had attended two separate conventions.

A few months later, with her notes spread out over her bed, Inga checked the facts in her article. Detailing the states that still had not passed legislation giving married women some control over their earnings and their property required close attention. It had been a subject she had thought about ever since her father had demanded control of the proceeds of her mother's produce business. Unfortunately, it had taken Inga more than a year to collect the information she needed, and out of frustration, she had all but abandoned the project. Until she had received the letters from Sarah and Rachel this spring.

The topic wasn't exactly suffrage, but it did relate to women's rights.

A soft knock broke her concentration.

"Inga?"

She opened the door.

Bertha stood there, a smile on her face. "There's a young man waiting downstairs to see you."

Quelling her impatience at the interruption, she asked, "Who?"

"You'll see." Bertha's smile widened.

"I'll be right down." Inga went back into her room and checked her reflection in the mirror. Her skirt and blouse were wrinkled due to the humid July heat. The outfit would have to do. She slid her hands over her head, smoothing her hair back to the knot at the nape of her neck.

Inhaling a deep breath, she closed her door and started down the front stairs.

At the doorway between the entry and the parlor stood Paul. His hair had been bleached blond, his face a tanned bronze. She flew down the rest of the steps and wrapped her arms around him.

She stepped back to take a better look at him, a hand on each of his arms. He wore a crisply-ironed shirt, slightly wilted from the heat, and trim denim trousers.

He grinned.

She felt as if she could burst with joy. "You should have told me you were coming!"

"It was a spur of the moment decision."

"I can't believe you're here." Inga caught a glimpse of Bertha. She was sitting on the sofa watching them, a skirt she'd been hemming in her lap. In the summer, she took in sewing to earn rent money.

Inga took Paul's hand and led him into the parlor. "Bertha, this is my brother, Paul."

The older woman looked up at him. "We've already met."

Paul nodded politely.

"How long are you going to be in town? Do you have a place to stay?" Inga had so many questions.

Paul laughed and touched a finger to her lips. "I'll be here for two or three days, and I have a room at the hotel not far from the train depot."

Inga couldn't stop smiling. "Wait here."

She rushed to the kitchen, where Mary was snapping beans.

"My brother is here. I'd like him to be my dinner guest tomorrow night and maybe the night after."

Mary grinned. "Of course." She wiped her hands on her apron. "Introduce me to him."

Inga led her into the parlor. "Mary Campbell, this is my brother, Paul Stryker."

Paul nodded. "How do you do?"

"So pleased to meet you." Mary sobered. "What would you like for dinner tomorrow?"

"Oh, ma'am." He chuckled. "Anything will be fine. After more than a year of military food, all home cooking tastes good."

"Do you like pie?"

Inga could almost see her brother's mouth water.

"Yes, ma'am."

"Peach or rhubarb?"

Paul heaved a sigh. "Either is fine, but I love peach."

Mary rubbed her hands on her apron again. "Peach it'll be."

Paul lowered his gaze to the floor then raised it to Mary. "Thank you, Mrs. Campbell."

Mary returned to the kitchen.

Inga took her brother's arm. "Let's go outside where it's cooler and talk."

On the porch, they sat in adjoining seats. "We'll have to go to a restaurant for dinner. Mary requires a day's advance notice for guests."

"That will be fine. I saw several on my way here."

Inga settled back on her chair. "So how are Moder and Halvor? I haven't see them since Christmas, and they were planning to visit Erik this summer."

"They're fine." He frowned. "They should be in the Klondike by now."

He seemed more reserved than usual. Inga studied him. "Is something wrong?"

"Not really. It's just hard to be home with them." He drummed his fingers on the arm of his chair. "They make me feel like a child. Moder keeps asking me what I plan to do with my future, and Halvor offered to hire me to help with the farm work."

"I understand exactly what you're going through." Inga clasped her hands in her lap. "I don't want to sound like Moder, but do you know what you're going to do when you leave here?"

His fingers stilled. "When I was in Florida, one of my buddies told me all about Yellowstone Park. I'm going out there to have a look at it."

"I wish I could go with you." She turned to face him. "One of my fellow professors visits there every summer. He says it is awe-inspiring."

"You can come along, if you want." He leaned toward her, his lips slightly parted. "I would enjoy having your company."

Inga swallowed. "I can't. I have to write some articles for *The Chronicle* before the fall term starts.

As a matter of fact, I'm hoping you'll let me interview you about post-war Cuba."

The muscles in his jaw tightened. "There's not much to tell."

"Sure there is. I'll ask you a bunch of questions."

He clenched his hand. "Do you have to use my name?"

Inga studied the fine lines around the corners of her brother's mouth. "Not if you don't want me to."

"I don't." He raked his hand through his hair. "I'll answer your questions, but you have to promise to come visit me if I decide to stay in the Yellowstone area."

Inga wanted to know why he didn't want his name mentioned, but she knew not to push him for an answer.

She grinned. "It's a deal."

C.J. stared at the table near the front window of the Kuster House Dining Room. At first he couldn't believe that the woman in the pink blouse sitting across from the handsome blond man was Inga. But there she was, gazing fondly at her dinner companion.

He shouldn't be surprised. Not once had she returned any of C.J.'s expressions of affection. Still, she hadn't mentioned seeing another man.

He ran a shaky hand through his hair.

"I'd like the table over by the window," he told the *maître de*, finally. If C.J. had to eat his dinner in distress, Inga should be upset, too.

He followed the host to the front of the room. When he reached the table where she sat with her gentleman friend, he feigned surprise. "Inga! I didn't expect to see you here."

Her eyes widened. Then she broke into a smile. "C.J., I didn't know you were in town."

The blond man frowned.

"Paul, this is my editor, C.J. Wakefield." She tilted her head in his direction. "C.J., this is my brother, Paul Stryker."

"Your brother." C.J. relaxed his posture and

managed a grin.

Paul stood and offered his hand. C.J. shook it.

"Would you care to join us?" Inga asked.

Her invitation caught him by surprise. His heartbeat drummed in his chest. "I would, thank you."

The host pulled a place setting and laid it on the end of the Strykers' table.

C.J. seated himself.

"I'm interviewing Paul for an article on post-war Cuba," Inga told him.

Her brother shifted his position. "Anonymously."

"If that's what you want," C.J. agreed. He didn't want to antagonize Inga's brother. "It should be a good subject. There's been more than enough on the war itself."

The waiter brought the Strykers' food and took C.J.'s order.

"Where are you staying?" C.J. asked.

"In this hotel," Paul replied.

"So am I." C.J. turned to Inga. "I'll be in town tomorrow, and then I'm leaving for my parents' ranch."

Inga raised a brow. "Is Ruth going to be there?"

"I don't know yet."

"Ruth is C.J.'s sister." Inga told Paul.

"She owns a ranch of her own." C.J. took pride in saying that.

Paul's eyes widened momentarily. "Good for her." He paused. "Can't say I've ever had much interest in farming."

C.J. nodded. "Me neither."

The waiter delivered C.J.'s meal of roast pork and trimmings and took the plates Inga and her brother had finished with.

They discussed the similarities and differences in their childhood experiences and C.J.'s work at the magazine. Each had a dish of ice cream for dessert.

When they had finished, C.J. and Paul walked Inga to her boarding house.

"Good night," C.J. said, his gaze lingering on her

face for several moments before he and her brother left for their hotel.

Riding by C.J.'s side on the trip to Ruth's farmstead, Inga realized she was becoming more comfortable each time they made the trip together. And his kindness to Paul three days before had shown her a side of C.J. she had resisted acknowledging until now. She was glad she had invited him to join Paul and her for dinner.

And there was no denying that C.J. Wakefield was a handsome man.

"Your brother is an interesting fellow." C.J. slowed the team.

"He said the same thing about you." Inga studied the particularly bumpy section of the trail looming before them. "I wish he could have stayed longer in Laramie."

The day was hot, and she was glad C.J. had paid extra to hire a carriage with a roof to shade them from the relentless Wyoming sun. The carriage pitched left and right as the wheels traversed the uneven earth. Inga slid back and forth on the seat with each lurch, bumping against C.J. then against the end of the seat. She clutched the rail.

"He invited me to go with him to Yellowstone Park." She paused, thinking about the undercurrent of sadness she had sensed in her brother, despite his cheerful demeanor. "Maybe I should have."

"Why do you say that?" C.J. slipped his arm around her waist, and held her in place next to him. She shivered, despite the warmth washing through her.

"He seems..." She searched her mind for an adequate descriptor. "Adrift. Without a plan for the future."

"He told me that he's been having a hard time since his unit was mustered out of the service." A note of concern tinged his words. "He'd gotten used to being told what to do every minute of the day."

Although they had passed the rough section of the

trail, C.J. kept his arm around her.

She considered his words. "Except he told me that he didn't like our parents telling him what to do."

"I think he's trying to find a purpose for his life."

"Yes." Inga sighed. "I suspect something happened in Cuba that he didn't tell me about."

"He didn't say much to me about his time there."

When they reached the small stand of trees beside the creek, C.J. withdrew his arm and guided the team off the trail. "I'm getting hungry. How about you?"

Inga shrugged. "I could eat."

He hopped down from the seat and secured the reins to a branch. Then he rounded the team and helped Inga to the ground. She strolled to the stream, now barely a trickle.

"It'll probably dry up by August," C.J. predicted. His chocolate brown gaze rested on her.

She met and held it. "I think it was entirely parched when I passed it last fall."

C.J. lingered at her side for a moment before returning to the carriage. He tossed a faded quilt to the ground and opened the hamper, revealing food and delicacies his mother had sent.

Inga unfolded the quilt and spread it in the shade. She retrieved their canteens from under the seat, then eased herself down to the coverlet, wishing she had worn her trousers instead of a skirt.

C.J. sat down beside her on the quilt. He pulled cloth-wrapped packages of biscuits and cheese and handed them down to her. "Would you prefer a plum or a peach?"

"Plum, please."

The breeze rippled through his thick coffee-brown hair as he selected a plum for each of them. Inga wondered if it felt as soft as it looked.

"Your article about women's property rights was very compelling." He handed her a plum and set his beside his canteen. "I sent it off with a note to work it into the next issue if possible. There are still several states who are going to take it up in their next legislative sessions."

"I know." Inga noticed that C.J.'s strong, straight nose was showing the early pink effects of sun exposure. She cast her gaze on the biscuits and selected one. "I fear the story might no longer be timely."

"If we can get it into one of the next few issues before the holidays, the timing should be about right."

They ate in silence for a few minutes.

"I brought my notes and my story about Cuba with me. I'll work on it tonight so you can take it back with you in the morning."

"I look forward to reading it." C.J. grinned. "Now that I know Paul, the information will be more meaningful." He bit into his plum.

Inga tasted hers, allowing the sweetness to slide over her tongue. As her bites got closer to the pit, the sweetness mixed pleasantly with the more tart, tighter flesh of the fruit. When she finished eating, she stood. "Just don't let your friendship with him color your editorial objectivity."

She ruffled his thick brown hair, finding it even softer than she had expected, then stooped to pick up the cloths with the remaining biscuits and cheese. She carried them to the hamper and nestled them so they would remain wrapped.

C.J. brought the canteens and returned them to their place under the seat.

Inga picked up two corners on a shorter side of the quilt and shook off the crumbs. Grinning, he picked up the corners at the opposite end, and together, they neatly folded it.

She set it in the back of the carriage, smoothing the fabric.

She turned. He stood behind her, arms open.

Hesitating for only a moment, she took a step toward him.

Drawing her into an embrace, he whispered in her ear, "I really like being with you. I like you."

Her knees turned to jelly. She clutched his shoulders for support.

He trailed gentle kisses from her ear, across her cheek. His mouth claimed hers.

So much for editorial objectivity.

She reveled in his firm lips, sweet with the taste of plum. Her thoughts spun, and her body grew warm.

He deepened the kiss.

Inga lost herself in a swirl of sensations she had never experienced before.

When he finally pulled his lips from hers, she was reeling. He held her close for a few more moments before releasing her, then helped her into the carriage.

He joined her on the seat, sitting so close that they were touching. Inga did not pull away.

C.J.'s embrace had felt natural. The taste of his kiss burned in her mind, sparking a tingle of the awareness that was still fresh and exhilarating. To her surprise, his affectionate advances seemed genuine and right. How could this be?

Inga folded the last of her summer blouses and placed it in the crate. Bracing for the November cold, she carried the box to the sleeping porch, where they would stay until spring.

She paused to watch big, fluffy snowflakes floating past the windows.

It had been four months since C.J. had gone back to Philadelphia. Although she kept busy with her teaching and her writing, thoughts of him had become more of a distraction than she would have liked. He threatened to interfere with the careers she had worked so hard to attain.

A shiver shook her body. She hurried back to the relative warmth of her room and closed the door. Smoothing the creases of her warmest undergarments, she situated the rest of her winter clothing into the clothespress.

The pile of papers on her desk drew her gaze. She sighed and pushed her musings about C.J. to the back of her mind. What had possessed her to assign her literature students to write short fictional stories?

Perhaps, the assignment had something to do with having Miss Wallis in the class. The young woman's writing had improved, but she still had difficulty supporting her points in her compositions. Her style might better lend itself to imagined prose.

When Inga's professor at Oberlin had given her class the same assignment, he had said it would help them to better appraise classical literature. Inga had hated the work.

Now, on the other side of the assignment, she still hated it. Had her professor felt the same way?

She blew a breath upward, riffling a few strands of hair hanging over her forehead. With the back of her hand, she brushed them away from her eyes.

Sighing, she sat down and began to work.

Halfway through the first paper, someone tapped on her door.

"Yes," she called.

"You have a visitor." Mary's voice carried through the door.

Inga swiped her palm across her forehead. She had been hoping Ruth would come for a visit, but this was not a good time.

Inga placed her pencil on the page she was reading. "I'll be right down."

Standing before the mirror, she fastened all the little buttons on her jacket and straightened her skirt. Closing the door behind her, she walked down the hall. She stopped short at the top of the steps. At the bottom of the staircase, stood C.J. Heat radiated from her head to her toes.

His letters had not mentioned stopping in Laramie on his way back from Seattle.

With her heart fluttering, she descended the steps. Glancing into the parlor, she saw both Bertha and Eliza sitting there. She frowned. The last thing she wanted was an audience.

"Good morning, Mr. Wakefield." She slanted her eyes toward the eavesdroppers. "I didn't know you were in town."

He nodded. "I'm sorry to stop by without notice, Miss Stryker. Laramie happened to be on my way back from Seattle." He winked. "I got in last night and leave tomorrow afternoon, but I wanted to meet with you about future articles we might be looking for."

"I'm so sorry, but this really isn't a convenient time. I have a lot of papers to grade, and I need to work on my lessons for next week." Inga pressed her fingertips to her temples.

"Perhaps we could discuss your articles over dinner," C.J. said. "You have to eat, so meeting then would not take you away from your work much longer than you would be anyway."

Inga fiddled with the top button on her jacket. "All right. I'll bring along the piece I'm working on to see what you think of it."

He took her hand in his, gave it a brief squeeze, and then released it. "I will come by for you at six o'clock."

C.J. leaned forward. Inga sat across from him. The candlelight reflected in her blue eyes, adding a warm glow to her gaze.

"We'll be sending a bank draft for your Cuba article as soon as I get back to Philadelphia. You did well describing the heat and the palm trees. Hopefully, it will help our readers feel warm when they read it in the middle of winter." He chuckled.

She smiled. "I hope Paul will like it."

"Is he still in Yellowstone?"

"I don't know." She lifted a shoulder. "He hasn't written to me, and my mother hadn't heard from him when she last wrote me."

C.J. frowned.

The waiter brought a bottle of wine. The short, stout man adeptly removed the cork and handed it to C.J. He sniffed it and nodded. The waiter poured a splash of wine into C.J.'s glass. He swirled it and took a tiny taste. After consideration, he nodded again. The man filled both their glasses.

Her attention shifted from her wine to C.J.

He smiled. "You are a very special lady. I wanted to give you a special night."

She lowered her lashes momentarily, then met his gaze. "Thank you."

His smile broadened.

"Did the Seattle meeting you wrote about in your last letter go well?" she asked.

"So-so. I was trying to hire a new staff writer, but he didn't want to come to Philadelphia." He frowned. "But he agreed to write an article a month for us – sort of like you."

She tipped her head to one side. "That's not so bad, is it?"

"No, but it means we don't have a reporter to send to Washington D.C. if something comes up while our other man is away on assignment." His smile faded. "Which means that I'll have to go."

Throughout their meal, they discussed the articles Inga had planned and the latest news about their families. When they finished, C.J. escorted Inga to the carriage.

Their breath turned to frost as they walked. The third-quarter moon hung low and bright in the sky. He helped her into the carriage and tucked the musty buffalo skin around her. After untying the horses, he climbed up beside her.

"That was an extraordinary dinner," she whispered. "Thank you."

Shaking the reins, he started the horses moving along the street. He inhaled a deep breath. The air seemed so much fresher here than in Philadelphia.

The team kept moving straight ahead.

He slipped his arm around her shoulders. "It's a lovely night. Look at all of those stars."

"They always seem brighter when it's cold." She snuggled against him.

He pulled her close.

Only the soft thuds of hooves broke the stillness.

Suddenly, she jerked upright. "You missed my street."

He eased her back. "I'm taking the long way. I want to spend a little more time with you."

The horses kept their slow pace.

At the edge of town, he halted the team so the moon lit her face. He turned, taking both of her gloved hands in his. His heart hammered against his ribs.

"Inga. From the first day we met, I have been bewitched by you. As I've gotten to know you better, my feelings for you have only grown. I love you."

Moonlight shimmered in her eyes.

"Will you please do me the honor of becoming my wife?"

Her eyes widened. She bit her lip. Her gloved fingers stiffened in his.

She dropped her gaze to the joined hands. "Oh, C.J., I'm sorry." She cleared her throat. "I can't."

The words came out on a whisper.

His muscles tensed. "Don't you love me?"

"Yes, but—" her voice cracked.

He tightened his grip on her hands. "I know you'll need to finish your contract with the university. We can wait until next summer."

"But you'll expect me to move to Philadelphia."

"Ye-es."

"I moved here because women are enfranchised." Her voice quavered. "I want to vote in next year's general election."

A chill slid through his bones, stealing his breath. "We can marry next Christmas."

She pulled her hands free. "I worked hard to earn my master's degree. I want to use it." She paused. "And I want to continue to write."

He forced air into his lungs. "You can continue to do all that after we are married. You proved that in your article about Ester Morris."

"But she only did it for less than a year."

He heard her swallow.

"And maybe I'm not as strong as she is."

He leaned toward her, laying his hand on her arm. "You're stronger than you think."

Tears slipped down her cheeks. She shifted away from him. "Please take me home."

CHAPTER EIGHT

March 1, 1900
Washington, D.C.

Dear Inga,

I missed seeing you at the NAWSA convention here in the nation's capitol. It would have given you a lot to write about. Susan B. turned leadership over to Carrie Chapman Catt. You should do a story on Susan B. and her long fight for women's right to vote.

Mrs. Catt has invited me to work with her on The Woman's Journal *in the coming year. I have accepted and will be moving to New York in June. I am very excited by the prospect of working on the mouthpiece of our organization, although I can't help thinking that you would be more suited to the task than I.*

I was interested to learn that you will be interviewing Theodore Roosevelt this summer. Be sure to ask why he did not include woman suffrage in his thesis on "Equalizing Men and Women Before the Law." If you come east to meet with him, stop by and see me.

Your concerns about continuing to submit articles to The Chronicle are legitimate, although the reason made me smile. For as long as I've known you, you've said that having a successful career was more important to you than having a husband. My only concern is that your letter sounded as if you were more torn between the choices than you expected to be.

I guess we'll know for sure if your editor can separate his personal and professional life when you hear back on the story you sent in. If he can't, you should have enough credibility from those they have published already to be accepted by Century *or* McClure's. *I'll be waiting on pins and needles to hear how it comes out.*

Lovingly in Friendship,
Sarah

C.J. gritted his teeth as he read the article Inga had submitted, determined to give it an unbiased review. Andrew Carnegie was funding libraries around the United States. He had been establishing them in Scotland and the Pittsburgh area for years, but now Cheyenne, Wyoming was going to get one.

'*When asked why he had decided to focus his philanthropy on libraries, Mr. Carnegie stated that the rich should give so the poor can improve their own lives as well as the communities in which they live...*'

C.J. sighed. He shouldn't have sprung marriage on Inga. They hadn't really been courting. They had only exchanged a few letters and one kiss. Obviously, she had spent less time obsessing about it than he had. Now he had bungled everything. She hadn't even penned a personal note on her formal submission letter.

Drat! Once again, he'd lost his concentration. He would have to re-read the article. His first impulse was to reject it out of hand. Just as she had rejected his proposal. But he couldn't deny that her story was interesting, and well-written.

Dropping the manuscript on his desk, he stood and walked to the window. Philadelphia in late March was so dreary. Dark wisps of coal smoke drifted across the cloudy gray sky. Even in the dead of winter, Laramie had never felt as dismal.

Glancing around the barren white walls of his small office, he frowned. He would have to marshal his patience.

"Are you woolgathering again?"

Nathan Bender's voice jerked C.J. out of his reverie. He inhaled a deep breath to clear his head. "Just considering the new submission from Inga Stryker."

Nathan grinned. "About the article or about the girl?"

That was the problem with being friends with the

boss. He knew C.J. too well. "Both," he admitted. "What can I do for you?"

"You know that *The Chronicle* is growing faster than I had expected." Nathan dropped onto the visitor's chair.

C.J. took his seat behind his desk. "That's a good problem to have, isn't it?"

"Yes, but we're outgrowing the space we have here." Nathan swept the small room with an assessing gaze. "You need a larger office, and I'd like to bring on a few staff writers."

"Big plans." C.J. smiled at his friend. "Are you sure you can afford to make those changes so fast?"

"We'll phase in the staff writers, but we need to find a larger building now so I can purchase more modern equipment."

"I'll look forward to that."

Nathan tapped the desktop. "Is that Miss Stryker's new story?"

"Yes." C.J. ran his fingers through his hair. "I haven't finished it yet."

"May I?" Nathan picked up the pages. "I always enjoy reading her work."

C.J. watched him peruse the article.

"This girl is good." He set the manuscript back on the desk. "We should bring her to Philadelphia so she can write for every issue."

C.J. stifled a grin. "She wouldn't come."

Nathan raised a brow. "How do you know?"

"She's made it clear she wants to continue teaching at the university."

A slow smile spread over Nathan's face. "Well then, you'll have to work on her the next time you go home."

"I'll try." He would. If she was in Philadelphia, he might have a better chance of winning her over.

"And buy this article. I'm not an admirer of Carnegie, but maybe the publicity can help more small towns get free libraries if their leaders know they can apply to him for the money."

"I'll draft a letter to her right away." C.J. allowed his stifled grin to bloom. "And I'll plan a trip to Laramie at the end of April."

Inga relaxed back into her office chair, glad to be in the warmth of the small room. The winter had been exceptionally snowy, and she had been glad for the arrival of spring. An unexpected cold had settled upon Laramie overnight, and a thick fog had enveloped the town in a cold, damp blanket this morning.

The cheerful yellow walls gave her office a comfortable ambiance. A four-shelf bookcase on the wall beside the door was nearly filled with textbooks and literature she had accumulated over the years. Many of them seemed like old friends as she'd read them repeatedly.

Sighing, she glanced at the essays from her Composition and Rhetoric class lying on her desk. She picked up the top paper and read. Obviously, Mr. Bacon had not researched very deeply into the historical period in which *Wuthering Heights* had been written. His assumption that modern factors influenced Emily Bronte would be almost comical, were it not threatening to cause him to fail the course.

Inga's gaze drifted to the window. The world outside had brightened, and the fog had been replaced by an overcast sky. She stood and walked over to have a closer look. The trees were adorned in feathery white, where the foggy mist had frozen, delineating each barely-budding twig and branch.

She dragged her attention back to the essay in her hands.

"Knock. Knock."

The words drew Inga's attention to Ruth Wakefield. She stood in the open doorway wearing a navy blue skirt and a polka-dot blouse. Inga didn't remember ever seeing her friend so dressed up. She looked pretty.

"Come in," Inga welcomed her. "You're all dressed up. You look nice."

"Ya, well...thanks." Ruth shook her head. "I

brought you a surprise." She angled her body half in and half out of the office. Her gaze flitted between Inga and the hallway. "I hope you won't mind."

"A gift?"

C.J. stepped into view. "Hello, Inga."

Surprise hitched her breath. She grasped the back of her chair. "C.J."

"I really liked your Carnegie story. I hope you've received the bank draft."

She froze at the determined look in his eyes. Heat rose from her chest to her face. She shifted her weight from foot to foot. "Yes, I have. Thank you."

Ruth moved to her brother's side. "We would like to take you to dinner tonight, if you're free."

Inga glanced at the pile of essays on her desk. "I was going to stay here to grade my students' papers without interruption."

"And we're already interrupting that plan." Ruth's voice carried a compassionate note. "I'm sorry."

"Don't be. If the truth be told, I was daydreaming." Inga managed a small smile.

"Then how about you come out to my place for the weekend? I promise to leave you alone until your work is done. I'll get mine done, too, and when we're finished we can ride out to the pasture. The wildflowers are beginning to bloom."

Inga sighed. "It sounds lovely. Hopefully, the spring weather will return soon."

"I can come out and pick you up on Sunday afternoon." C.J. brightened. "*The Chronicle* is moving, and we're making some structural changes I need to talk with you about."

"Changes?" She worried her lower lip. "So you're no longer going to be my editor?"

She glanced down at her clasped hands, then back up at him.

The corners of C.J.'s mouth lifted. "That's not going to change. And I look forward to your next article."

The worry that he might not purchase more of her articles dissolved.

"I've been corresponding with Miss Susan B. Anthony," Inga said. "I'll put the information into a story when the term ends."

Ruth rested a hand on her hip. "How about we take you to dinner? I'm starving, and we can finish this discussion over a nice meal."

Inga hesitated. "Okay, but I need to drop off the essays and let Mary know to put my supper in her icebox."

"We can have it on the way to my place tomorrow," Ruth suggested.

Inga cocked her head. "We'll see."

On Sunday, Ruth and Inga carried the mashed potatoes and roast chicken to the small table inside his sister's cabin. C.J.'s mouth watered at the tantalizing aroma. In Philadelphia, he rarely cooked for himself except to fry bacon and eggs or warm leftovers from a meal at Nathan's house or a restaurant. But he could make a good pot of coffee, and he already had one brewing on Ruth's stove.

"Hope this rain lets up soon so the trail isn't too muddy for your trip back to town," Ruth said as she placed a basket of biscuits on the table and took her seat.

"It should be fine unless this drizzle turns into a downpour." C.J. snagged a biscuit and slathered it with butter.

Ruth gave his wrist a gentle tap. "Hey! Wait for our guest."

C.J. winked at her. "I'm your guest, too."

Inga set a bowl before each of them and sat down next to Ruth. "Sorry. It took me longer to section these oranges than I thought it would."

"Well, they're worth it." Ruth smiled at her. "What a treat to have fresh oranges."

"My mother sent me a case for my birthday. She doesn't want me to get scurvy." Inga took the bowl of potatoes C.J. passed and dished a dollop onto her plate. "These are the last of them."

C.J. studied the fruit. "Where does she get oranges

in Iowa?"

Inga smiled. "She orders them from Florida."

"You'll have to get the address, C.J., so you can order a case for me next Christmas." Ruth passed him the platter of chicken.

He selected a thigh and drumstick before handing the plate to Inga.

"I'll order one for you." Inga flashed her sweet smile at Ruth. "It's the least I can do in return for all the hospitality you've shown me."

A rosy pink bloomed in his sister's cheeks. "You'll do nothing of the sort. You've more than made up for it with all the planting and canning you helped with last summer."

"I'm sorry to say I won't be much help with the planting this year." Inga gave her an apologetic look. "I'm going to New York to interview the governor and to see a college friend. And I promised my mother I'd stop in Cedar Falls on the way back."

C.J.'s mouth dropped opened. He closed it, staring at Inga. "You're going to interview Theodore Roosevelt?"

"Yes. He's accomplished many good things for New York, and he's an author." Inga grinned. "I'll send my weekly columns about my trip to *The Boomerang*, and I might be able to get two articles for *The Chronicle* out of the interview."

Ruth sighed. "Sounds like you'll be gone for a big part of the summer."

"The first half, anyway." Inga's face tightened in a pained expression. "I'm sorry."

"Between the growing size of my herd and the bounty of my garden, I really need to hire a hand to help me work the place." Ruth fluttered her eyelashes at C.J. "Unless you want to come back to Wyoming and be my hired hand."

"Sorry," C.J. drawled. "You know I went into publishing because I didn't want to work on a ranch."

"I should be back in time to help with the canning," Inga offered.

"We'll be in our new offices by then." C.J.'s pulse quickened. "You should make a stop in Philadelphia to see our new digs and drop off your Roosevelt articles."

Inga shook her head. "Going that far south would be out of the way, and I want to get home in time for Ruth's summer harvest. Besides, the mail will probably give you a faster delivery."

"Distances between cities are shorter in the East than out here," C.J. argued. "It would only take a day or two. Have you ever been to Philadelphia?"

"No." Inga leaned back in her chair, arms crossed at her chest. "I have never seen your current offices. I don't need to see your new ones."

"There's a lot of history in the city. Benjamin Franklin had his printing business there." C.J. tried to make Philadelphia sound enticing. "The Declaration of Independence and Constitution were both written only a few blocks from our building."

Inga dropped her hands to her lap and straightened.

C.J. stifled a grin.

"You should go," Ruth said, leaning forward. "It sounds very interesting."

"See." C.J. allowed his grin to break through. "Ruth can spare you for a few days. I could show you around, and you could write an article or two about the city and, maybe, its history."

Inga tilted her chin down, and wrinkled her nose. "You're there all the time. You could write those articles."

His forays into writing for the magazine had been soundly rebuffed. C.J.'s stomach tightened. "You're a far better writer than I am. Nathan bought your stories before I became editor. Even though we were friends, he didn't buy any of my articles. In his rejections, he said I was far better as an editor, and he kept offering me the job I have now."

Inga pursed her lips. "I'll try to work Philadelphia into my schedule."

"Let me know when you will arrive. I'll pick you up

at the train station and take you to meet Nathan," C.J. said. "The magazine will book a hotel room, and pay your expenses while you're in town."

And he would plan an agenda that would give him plenty of time alone with her.

Two months later when Inga arrived in New York on the train from Albany, Sarah was waiting on the platform.

Inga worked her way through the crowd to her friend's side. "I'm so glad you're here. The towns I'm used to are so much smaller than this."

"This is a great city." Sarah pulled Inga into a hug. "There's always something new and lots of things to do." She stepped back and threaded her arm through the crook of Inga's elbow. "Come, now. Let's claim your trunk. I have a surprise for you."

They secured the services of a porter, who placed Inga's luggage on his cart.

Sarah led the way to an automobile, parked in a line of horse-drawn cabs and horseless vehicles. She released Inga's arm and grinned. "Your carriage awaits you. Or us, actually."

Inga stared suspiciously at the metal contraption. "I've seen a few of these in person and dozens in photos, but I've never ridden in one."

The porter and driver wrestled her trunk into the back of the cab. Inga tipped the porter, and he handed her into the back seat. She hoped there wouldn't be rain since the vehicle had no roof. The driver helped Sarah in on the other side before taking his seat at the steering wheel.

Moments later, he pulled into the moving traffic.

"I'm amazed at how smooth and quiet this ride is." Inga did not know what words to use in talking about horseless carriages.

"I just love these electric cars." Sarah removed her hat and tossed back her brown curls. "They don't make much noise and they don't add foul smells to the street. My beau is teaching me to drive, and I hope to have one of my own someday."

Inga laughed. "That will be nice for you, but I don't think it would be very functional on the rutty roads and trails of Wyoming."

"Then you should move to New York." A hopeful look settled on her friend's face. "You should get an interview with Sam McClure. He already has one woman on his magazine's staff."

"You forget. In Wyoming, I'll be able to vote for president and my representative in November." Inga's mood sobered. "Besides, my writing is no match for Ida Tarbell's."

"I've heard that she is against woman suffrage." Sarah wrinkled her nose. "Too bad you can't replace her. You underestimate your talent."

"If I was to come east, I could probably get a staff position at *The Chronicle*." Inga considered the idea for a moment then dismissed it. "But I don't want it. I'm happy with my teaching and submitting articles I choose to write."

The cab jolted to a stop.

Other carriages and automobiles had also halted. Horns blasted. Drivers shouted.

"Well, after you vote in November, I hope you'll consider coming to New York. You could teach and work with Carrie and me in your free time."

Inga waved away a pesky fly. "When would I be able to write?"

"You could write for the cause." Sarah leaned toward the driver. "Why are we still stopped?"

"I'm sorry, miss," he said over his shoulder. "There is a traffic block up ahead."

Sarah sighed and sat back in her seat.

Inga perused the unmoving vehicles and the pedestrians weaving around them. "Does this happen often?"

"More often than anyone likes."

The odors of wood and coal smoke, horse manure and rotting food drifted around them. The cab was parked in the shadow of a building. Only faint breezes worked their way between the many structures lining the street. The effect was stifling, despite the mild late-June temperature.

Sarah turned toward Inga. "Did you even consider writing a story about Susan B.?"

Inga smiled. "I wrote one before I left for New York. It's sitting with *The Chronicle* editor now. When I get to Philadelphia I expect to learn if they want to publish it."

Finally, they reached Sarah's building. The driver secured a small cart from the manager and delivered Inga's trunk to Sarah's apartment. She tipped him handsomely, closed the door behind him, and she led Inga to a sitting room. A tray with cups and a plate of cookies sat on a marble-topped table between two upholstered chairs. Wordlessly, a young woman dressed in a maid's uniform placed a teapot on the tray, then left.

"Please make yourself comfortable." Sarah gestured to one of the chairs. "I'll pour the tea."

"Thank you." Inga swept her gaze over the opulent surroundings as she sat down. "This place is beautiful." She turned to her friend. "Does NAWSA pay you enough to afford this?"

"Oh, no." Sarah handed her a steaming cup perched on a dainty saucer. "My father bought it so my parents would have a place to stay when they come to the city. My mother fills it with her cast-off furnishings when she redecorates their house in Cincinnati."

"It's lovely." Inga took a sip, nearly burning her tongue.

"It also puts me in the vicinity of wealthy women that the Association is courting to support woman suffrage."

Inga tilted her head slightly. "With donations?"

"Yes, but many have given money for years." Sarah flashed a conspiratorial grin. "We're trying to get them more actively involved in our organization. They can be very influential."

"And that's your job?"

"I also help to form new suffrage groups. I speak in opposition to anti-suffrage arguments and meet with state officials. And, I write for *The Woman's Journal*." She winked. "But not as well as you write. You should move to New York and take over that task. You could live here with me."

Inga laughed. "I'm happy teaching and writing as time permits."

Sarah picked up the plate of cookies and offered them to Inga. "I'm sure the association would hire you, if you change your mind."

"I won't." Inga cradled her saucer in one hand and reached for a cookie with the other. "Have you heard from Rachel lately?"

Sarah chewed a bite of gingersnap for a long while before answering. "I haven't seen or heard from her since the convention."

She took a sip of her tea without looking up.

"Did something happen?"

Sarah shifted in her chair. "Not exactly."

She was obviously uncomfortable, and Inga didn't want to pry. Taking a bite of her cookie, she waited. Hopefully, her silence would prompt an explanation.

Finally, Sarah set down her cup. "Well, there was a private discussion about how southern white men would never support woman suffrage if it gave the vote to colored women." She cleared her throat. "The white men there are making efforts to keep colored men from voting. And some of the older women said they regretted supporting abolition and the vote for Negro men, because if Negro men hadn't gotten the ballot, white women probably would already have been granted suffrage."

Inga's heart thudded. "Were you and Rachel part of that conversation?"

Sarah's lips thinned. "I was. Rachel wasn't, but I think she overheard part of it. We argued about the subject later."

Inga surmised from Sarah's tone that she had sided with those in favor of confining suffrage to white women. Had she really taken such a bigoted position?

Was the cause driving a wedge between her friends? Inga didn't know for sure, but she wanted to avoid pushing her hostess into a conversational corner.

"She didn't mention that in either of the letters I've received from her since the convention, but she's going to try to be in Philadelphia for a few days while I'm there so we can get together." Inga took the last bite of her cookie, chewed and swallowed it, then continued, "She said she'd send a note for me in care of *The Chronicle*, telling me if she was able to meet me."

"Speaking of *The Chronicle*, how was your interview with our governor?"

Inga blinked. "Mr. Roosevelt was very interesting. I only hope I can do him justice."

"What's he like?"

"He's a whirlwind. He goes to the office early and works non-stop into the evening. But when he goes home, he leaves his work behind to be with his family." Inga shook her head. "I don't know how he does it. I was exhausted after the first day. He has a close relationship with the press, one that you and the organization might do well to emulate."

Sarah's brow furrowed. "How does he do it?"

"I think he has developed friendships with many of the reporters. And he's very open with them." Inga smiled as she recalled their conversations. "And he was more forthright with me than I expected. He answered my questions in great detail. Even with my shorthand, I could barely keep up."

"So, what does he consider his biggest accomplishments?"

"One is definitely the revision of the laws regarding tenement housing." Inga tucked a wayward strand of hair behind her ear. "He went into some of those dwellings and saw large families living in single filthy rooms. Sometimes the whole family, including little children, worked from dawn to dusk in those squalid conditions, rarely seeing the light of day."

Sarah shrank back. "That's horrible."

"He said he had no idea the situation was so bad until he saw it for himself. His reforms prohibit those conditions." Inga paused. "He gave me so much material on this, and his experiences as Police Commissioner that I started a story on this subject alone."

"What else did he talk about?"

"His efforts to conserve many thousands of acres of state land for preservation and public use." Inga's chest warmed as she recalled how excited she was to learn of these policies. "I'd like to expand on this, as it's a câuse near and dear to my brother Paul's heart."

"The legislature hasn't always been that supportive of him." Sarah picked up the plate and offered Inga another cookie. "What does he regret most?"

Inga shook her head. "That's hard to say. He mentioned that the legislature wouldn't pass a bill to make employers liable for the safety of their workers, but he was able to get some limits on working hours for state employees, women and children, and a few safety laws were enacted."

Sarah nodded. "Lincoln Steffens has an article about him in *McClure's* suggesting that the Republicans nominated Roosevelt for vice president to neutralize his power."

"Mr. Roosevelt isn't very happy about the nomination. He sees it as a do-nothing office, but he plans to campaign vigorously for their ticket." Inga recalled his frustration as he spoke about his political party. "I don't plan to focus on politics in any of my articles. I'm trying to decide if I can do a story on his labor-related efforts alone."

"Everything you write about him now is likely to become political." Sarah teased. "Sounds like you could spend the whole summer writing about him."

Inga pursed her lips and considered the idea. "I could if *The Chronicle* agrees to run the articles as a series. But *The Boomerang* is a Democratic newspaper. I'm not sure how they'll feel about my writing articles about a man on the Republican ticket.

I dread letting them know about the magazine stories when I get home."

"Good luck." Sarah caught her lower lip between her teeth. "I was hoping to convince you to do a piece on the anti-suffragist arguments and why they aren't true. I could supply you with materials on both sides."

"You should write one yourself." Inga nodded her encouragement. "You have the information you need and you know what you want to say."

"But I work for the association, so I have a lot less credibility than you do as someone who is independent." Sarah implored. "Will you do it?"

"It's the kind of topic I can work on when the fall term starts." Inga swallowed back her irritation at her friend's brashness. Sarah was dedicating her time and talent to winning woman suffrage. It was a cause they both believed in, even if Inga no longer felt the urgency she had a few years ago. "Send your information with me."

"Great. I've got more ideas for you to help the cause, but I'm starving." Sarah stood. "Let's go down to Herald's Square. There's a great restaurant called Keen's that I want you to try. And tomorrow, we can go to a play." She grinned. "By the end of your visit, I plan to entice you into writing a whole series of articles in support of suffrage."

"I don't really need to be persuaded to support the cause, but in the meantime, I'll enjoy your bribes." Inga was willing to write a series, although she couldn't imagine that *The Chronicle* would publish more than one or two stories promoting votes for women.

Chapter Nine

July 1, 1900
En route to Philadelphia

Dear Moder,

If my penmanship appears a bit rough, it is because I'm on the train. I'm sorry if this letter is hard to read.

My interview with Colonel Roosevelt went well. He was very cooperative, and I have more material than I can use. He didn't know of Paul, but made me feel very proud of him for being willing to fight for our country.

New York City was fascinating. Sarah took me to see two plays, three museums, and many fancy restaurants. We rode in horseless carriages and relaxed in her parents' luxurious apartment.

Although our visit was pleasant, I felt a bit of tension growing between us. Some in the Suffrage Association are considering abandoning Negroes if it means the vote for white women can be secured. Although she sometimes hedges when she's talking with me, I think she supports this position. She said she and Rachel argued about it. Sarah doesn't seem to recognize that she is betraying Rachel. Or maybe she's embarrassed to admit it, even to herself.

I am still anticipating that Rachel will be able to meet with me in Philadelphia. I'm eager to speak with her, although I fear I may be caught between my two friends. Were you ever in a situation like this with Mrs. Cook and Mrs. Holden? How I wish I could discuss this with you before I see Rachel. At least we can talk when I stop by on my way back to Wyoming.

Looking forward to seeing you and the family.

Love,
Inga

C.J.'s pulse raced as he ushered Inga into his new

office. She walked straight to the window.

He smiled. It was his favorite feature of the room.

"What an exceptional view of the river. And the city." Her voice was soft. "Much better than the one from my hotel."

"I'm sorry about that," C.J. said. "Next time I'll reserve a better room for you."

She shook her head and turned toward him. "Oh, no. My accommodations are fine, and I appreciate having you accompany me around the city, since this is my first time here."

"My pleasure." C.J. grinned. "And I know what you mean. Compared with Laramie, Philadelphia can be quite overwhelming."

The hint of a smile curved her full petal-pink lips as she perused the room. "Your office is lovely."

A flash of pride rushed though him. "Please, sit down." He put his hand on the back of the new upholstered chair.

"This is very different from your office in Laramie." She ran a hand over the brocade fabric before seating herself.

"*The Chronicle* has grown quite successful. I was fortunate to have taken my position here when I did."

She raised a brow. "And you've had an important role in that success."

"Speaking of our success, I reviewed your article on Susan B. Anthony." He moved behind his desk and sat on his padded chair. "It—"

The telephone rang.

Inga flinched.

C.J. swallowed a chuckle. He had reacted the same way for days, until he got used to the sound. "Excuse me." He picked up the receiver in one hand and the mouthpiece in the other. "Hello."

"Mr. Bender is here." The voice of Elmer Tibbets, C.J.'s secretary, came through the line.

"Please send him in."

The door opened immediately, and Nathan strode directly to where Inga sat.

C.J. stood. "Miss Inga Stryker, this is our publisher, Nathan Bender." He gestured to his friend. "Nathan, Miss Stryker."

The boss held out his hand. C.J. cringed. A gentleman always waits for a lady to offer her hand first, but Inga accepted it politely.

"I've been wanting to meet you ever since your article on the Des Moines suffrage convention." He paused. "And C.J. tells me you've written a masterpiece on Miss Anthony."

Pink bloomed in Inga's cheeks. She looked straight at Nathan. "I appreciate your willingness to publish pro-suffrage articles."

He scooted the wooden side chair next to Inga's and perched on it. "We don't want to become a voice for the cause. However, we support the vote for women – at least C.J. and I do – and we don't mind printing occasional pieces to that effect."

Inga frowned. "Sometimes, I think the stories would be more effective if they were written by men. Mr. Wakefield could write one."

She flashed C.J. a smile.

"C.J.'s a lot better editor than he is a writer." Nathan shot him a quick glance, but returned his attention to Inga. "Besides, it would be better if our editor didn't take a public position on the matter."

C.J. hated that Nathan was evaluating his writing skills in front of Inga, but he agreed with his boss's policy of personally staying away from political issues.

Inga clasped her hands in her lap. "I suppose."

Nathan patted her arm. "He also said you're writing an article on Theodore Roosevelt. Too bad you couldn't have come in June for the Republican Convention."

C.J. gritted his teeth. He didn't like seeing Nathan touch Inga, no matter how innocent that touch might be.

"I wish I could have, but it didn't work out with the university's schedule. I might have been able to attend, but I would have been cutting it close."

"C.J. said he offered you a staff position here, but

you refused." Nathan's tone had gathered more authority. "I hope you will reconsider."

"I won't." She lifted her chin and faced him. "As I told Mr. Wakefield, I like my teaching position and want to continue it as my primary employment."

"I can pay you more than the university pays you."

C.J. wished Nathan would stop trying to push Inga into accepting a position. His method and timing were making her uncomfortable, and less likely to be persuaded later by C.J's subtler approach.

She shifted in her chair. "But, I also receive payment for the articles I write for your magazine and *The Boomerang*."

Nathan's posture stiffened. "We could meet that, too."

C.J. knew his boss hadn't planned on offering that much money.

"Even so, it's far more expensive to live in Philadelphia than in Laramie." The tone of her voice had gathered a level of authority that matched Nathan's. "Besides, I like teaching."

"Maybe you'll reconsider in the future."

She tilted her head without conceding. "Perhaps. But I doubt it."

The room fell silent. C.J. rubbed the back of his neck.

"Say! Did C.J. show you our printing operation?"

C.J. smiled at the pride with which Nathan spoke. They felt the same way about their operation.

"Yes, he did." Inga's features softened. "Very impressive."

"All of our equipment is the most modern design. Publishing has made huge strides in the last decade or so." He stood. "It's been a pleasure to meet you Miss Stryker, but I must excuse myself and get back to my work."

"The pleasure was mine." Inga's tight smile belied her words.

Had Nathan even noticed?

He walked to the door then turned back. "C.J.,

please stop by my office when you're finished here."

"I'm going to take Miss Stryker to lunch and show her around the historic district before I take her back to the hotel," C.J. told him.

"Tomorrow will be fine." Nathan strode out of the office.

C.J. expelled a breath. "As Nathan said, I was impressed with your Susan B. Anthony article and will be buying it."

Inga relaxed back into her chair. "Thank you."

"And tonight, I'll read the Teddy Roosevelt article you gave me this morning." He tapped the pages that lay on the side of his desk. "If I like it, we'll discuss the possibility of the series you mentioned." He stood. "I'm feeling a bit peckish. Are you ready for lunch?"

She smiled and stood too. "Very much so."

He started around the desk, but glimpsed the envelope on the corner. "I almost forgot." He picked it up and held it out to her. "This came for you."

She took the envelope and studied it. "It's from my friend Rachel."

"I hope it's good news."

"So do I." She gazed up at him then back at the handwriting. "I'm counting on meeting with her while I'm in town."

She slipped the missive into her handbag, unopened.

Wasn't she curious to learn what her friend had written? Or didn't she want to discuss it with him?

Inga stared at the massive red brick building C.J. had brought her to. Independence Hall. A shiver of awe rippled through her. Tipping her head back, she studied the square steeple topped with a cupola and a smaller cupola with a spire atop it. On either side of the Hall were brick additions. A statue of George Washington stood in front of the structure.

This was the spot where the United States of America had been conceived and birthed. And she stood where the signers of the Declaration of Independence once walked.

The knowledge was almost beyond comprehension.

"Want to go inside?" C.J's voice broke through her overwhelming sensation of reverence.

"Could we?"

"Sure. The city operates it as a museum." C.J. took her elbow. "I have an idea for a series of articles you could write."

Inga's breath caught. "About what?"

"Next year will be the one-hundred-twenty-fifth anniversary of the Declaration of Independence. You could do a series of articles based on the landmarks here in Philadelphia, our July Fourth celebration, and maybe work in some material about the founding fathers."

As a first generation American, Inga felt a reverence for their audacity, their foresight and their wisdom. She wasn't sure she could adequately convey the importance of the people and places that had brought this country into being. "But I don't expect to be back here next summer."

"I know. But you could write the stories this year, and we could hold them until next spring." He released her arm and held open the heavy wooden door. "If necessary, we could update them and print one per month leading up to Independence Day."

Inga pursed her lips as she stepped into the illustrious building. The entry was flanked by staircases leading to the second floor. The woodwork and fireplaces were in the classic eighteenth century style. Straight ahead, in the vestibule leading to the back door, stood the Liberty Bell. The building was not as deep as she had expected. "I'm not sure I can do justice to the enormous significance of the events that happened here."

"But you could convey how inspirational a visit to these important landmarks can be." He carefully closed the door behind them. "And relate those feelings to the monumental actions of a few common men."

She stood rooted to the floor and glared at him.

"Common men? I think they were extremely uncommon."

"Then write about the qualities that made them exceptional."

"What if the articles end up sounding like travel advertisements for Philadelphia?"

"Then we'll have plenty of time to make revisions." He chuckled. "Although a little promotion of our notable city wouldn't hurt."

She was humbled by his faith in her ability to write such a momentous series. "I'll make notes when I get back to the hotel tonight, and give it some thought."

They strolled through the ground floor rooms – rooms where the Declaration of Independence and Constitution had been written – studying the paintings and the placards. The building had served as the first Capitol building, with the House of Representatives meeting on the first floor and the Senate meeting upstairs. The significance of these hallowed rooms made her feel privileged to have the rights she enjoyed, including the right to vote as a citizen of Wyoming. All women deserved to have that same right, wherever they might live in this great country.

On a wooden platform in the tower vestibule, the Liberty Bell hung from a metal structure in the shape of a wishbone. Her pulse quickened as she approached it.

"It really does have a crack in it." Inga stared at the bell, trying to memorize every detail.

"I was surprised the first time I saw it," C.J. said. "As a kid, I had pictured it bigger."

When they had walked through the entire building, Inga sighed. "I'm definitely going to come back and take notes. There is so much here. I'll never remember it all."

"I notice new things every time." C.J. took her elbow and led her outside.

An affection for the city was budding inside her. "I'm so glad that Philadelphia has preserved all this history."

"Would you like to go back to your hotel and rest before we go to dinner?" he asked in a tone indicating that sharing the meal was a given.

Although she was tempted, his presumption annoyed her. This afternoon, they'd quickly grown comfortable with each other. She needed some distance to recover her priorities before she reconsidered his marriage proposal and impulsively agreed to accept *The Chronicle's* job offer.

She shook her head. "I'd like to go back to my hotel, but I don't feel much like dining out. I want to make notes for the historical articles, finish my second Roosevelt story, and read Rachel's letter."

He frowned. "Aren't you going to eat?"

She shrugged. "I'll have a sandwich sent up to my room."

"Are you sure?"

"I am." She flashed him what she hoped was a charming smile. "Besides, you need time to read my first Roosevelt article so we can discuss the possibility of running a series."

She wanted to keep their interactions focused on business as much as she possibly could. Already, she felt herself drawn to him with an attraction she feared she might not be able to overcome.

Alone in her hotel that evening, Inga read Rachel's letter. A smile formed on Inga's lips. Her friend would be arriving in town early tomorrow morning.

Since before the Civil War, Philadelphia has had a large, well-established Negro community, and I have some relatives there. Ida has arranged for me to stay for a few days with some of her friends, a doctor and a nurse. They have a telephone and you may call me at their number, which I have noted below.

I hope all will work out so that we may meet.

Inga gathered her notes and the draft of her second article on Theodore Roosevelt and arranged them on the writing desk.

Glancing at the folded letter, Inga's thoughts returned to her friend. She could only hope Rachel would arrive safely.

"Your article about Theodore Roosevelt made me see him from a whole new perspective." C.J. smiled at Inga, who sat across the desk from him the next morning. "I look forward to reading your next one about him."

She reached into her handbag and pulled out several sheets of folded paper, smoothed them, and handed them to him. "It's still mostly a rough draft, but if you like it, I will polish it while I'm here in the city."

"Now that Mr. Roosevelt is Mr. McKinley's running mate, we could run your articles as a series in August, and September, and maybe even October, if you have enough material for a third article." He set the new pages beside the other story. "What's *The Boomerang* going to think about us running a series about the Republican?"

"I don't know. He wasn't the nominee when I told them I planned to interview him." Her lips thinned. "I just hope that they won't mind since he's not the presidential candidate. I don't look forward to telling them, and I certainly won't write any columns for them about him."

"Well, for your sake, I hope Mr. Low will keep an open mind."

"So do I." Her gaze met his. "I'd like to use your telephone, if you don't mind."

"Is it business-related?" Allowing non-employees to use the telephones was against company policy, except in emergency situations.

"No. I want to make arrangements to meet my friend tomorrow."

In a tangential sort of way, he could argue this was an emergency. Or maybe that she was like an employee since they published so many of her articles. "Yes, but don't be too long."

The corners of her mouth turned slightly upward.

"Thank you."

She pulled a slip of paper from her handbag.

"I'll give you some privacy." He picked up the draft of the new story and stepped into the outer office.

"Did she kick you out?" A wide grin lit Elmer's shiny face.

"Only temporarily." C.J. perched on the corner of the secretary's desk and perused Inga's new article. The writing was rougher than her usual products. Still, it was much better than he could have done.

Inga appeared sooner than C.J. had expected. "Did you get everything arranged?"

She shook her head. "No. I left her a message. I hope you don't mind that I said she could reach me at this number at five o'clock this afternoon."

Elmer opened his mouth, but closed it without saying anything.

"That's fine." C.J. shot him a pointed glance. "As long as you'll let me take you to dinner."

Her gaze fell to the pages in his hands. "I really should work on that story."

He held them out to her. "It doesn't need a lot of work, just a little refining."

She folded the pages and slipped them into her handbag. "Thank you. Now I'm going back to Independence Hall and make notes for that series of articles you want."

C.J. stood. "I'll escort you."

"That's not necessary." She smiled. "You showed me the way, and it's only a couple of blocks."

He wanted to insist, but he had come to recognize the same independent streak in Inga that he'd long known in Ruth. Self-reliance was important to Inga, and he would be better off respecting it than challenging it. "But you'll let me take you to dinner."

She sighed. "If you insist."

The chandeliers cast a soft warm glow in the wood-paneled room. Aromas of food, perfume, and tobacco smoke mingled in the air. Inga nestled back into the soft, leather upholstered chair and studied the steak and potato on her plate. This meal, a staple in her diet when she was growing up on the farm, had become an indulgence now that she was an adult. Her mouth watered.

"I was surprised that you had time to revise your Roosevelt article," C.J. said. "Did you get enough material for your patriotic series?"

She cut into the juicy meat on her plate. "I think so. I spoke with several docents and made notes of topics, like the framers of the Declaration of Independence. And I have the names of several museum officials I can correspond with if I need more details."

"That's good." He paused. "We won't begin publishing the series until after the first of the year, so there's no hurry."

"But I'd like to write them while the information is still fresh in my memory. After I finish the final Roosevelt story, I'll move on to those. There should be time while I'm at Ruth's to help her can, so I'll be ahead when the school year starts in September."

C.J smiled. "That sounds like a good plan."

They ate in silence for a while. As more time passed without C.J. initiating conversation, Inga's muscles began to tense. She took a sip of water.

"Are you going to be back in Laramie this summer?" She felt confident that back in Wyoming she could enjoy his company and still resist accepting his job offer or another marriage proposal.

He raised his gaze. "I'm not planning on it."

He picked up his knife and cut off another bite of steak.

A surprising pang of disappointment tightened Inga's chest. Just as she was becoming more comfortable with him, he seemed to be pulling back. Had her rejection of his proposal somehow affected his attitude toward her? Or worse, interfered with his relationship with his family?

Hopefully not.

She stole a glance at him. He seemed intent on

attacking his steak.

Returning her attention to her meal, she discovered she no longer had much of an appetite.

"I'll probably be back for Christmas. Or maybe Thanksgiving." His tone was matter-of-fact. "I don't really like to travel to Wyoming in the winter."

They fell into an awkward silence as he finished his meal. Inga forced a final bite of potato into her mouth, then set down her fork.

C.J. leaned forward. "Did you and your friend make arrangements to meet for lunch?"

Inga forced a smile and settled against the back of her chair. "Yes. She suggested a restaurant a few blocks from Independence Hall, so I'll be in familiar territory."

"Would you like me to arrange a cab for you?"

She swallowed. "No, thank you. I can walk."

He took a sip of water. "Be careful. Just because you and I accept Negroes as equals doesn't mean everyone in Philadelphia does." A concerned expression darkened his face. "Remember that incident you told me about when you met Rachel in Denver?"

Inga's stomach clenched. She nodded.

"A similar incident could happen here."

His words sent a cold shudder through her.

Inga watched the door of the café. Although C.J. had obviously tried to be discreet, she had spotted him following her. His expression of concern touched her deeply, nearly bringing her to tears of relief after last night's worries.

"I'm glad Mr. Barnett stationed me in Washington for *The Conservator*," Rachel said. "I like living in familiar surroundings and being close to my family."

Inga smiled. "I'm happy for you, but what about your suitor?"

Rachel dropped her gaze to her plate then looked back up at Inga. "Herman's moving to Washington next month. He has secured a job at the Willard

Hotel. The owners are expanding and remodeling it." Her eyes sparkled with happiness. "We're planning to marry in October."

Marry! Inga's fingers flew to her mouth. "Oh Rachel! That's wonderful. I wish you all the best."

"I'm elated." She paused. "I was worried about balancing my work and a family, but Ida does it with six children, so I think I can manage it."

"You'll be fine," Inga reassured her. "You're one of the most organized people I know."

"Coming from you, I take that as a compliment."

The waiter brought their sandwiches and refilled their glasses of iced tea.

"What about you? Do you have a beau back in Wyoming?" Rachel asked.

Hesitating, Inga took a sip of her tea. "Not really. I don't think I could manage teaching, writing columns, and a family."

"Will you be coming to next year's NAWSA convention?" Rachel's hopeful gaze bore into Inga. "It's going to be in Minneapolis in late May to early June."

"I don't know. It's closer than the recent ones, but it comes at an inconvenient time." Inga picked up her glass but didn't bring it to her lips. "It's near the end of the term. The seniors will be preparing and giving their oratories, and there's preparation for final exams."

Finally, she took another sip.

Rachel's countenance fell in disappointment.

"The January time frame, like the one in Des Moines, is a lot easier for me."

"I was so hoping you'd be there." Rachel pursed her lips. "I think there is going to be a move to segregate the Association. I was hoping you'd come and, if not speak out against it, at least expose that it is happening."

Inga set down her glass then concentrated on Rachel. "Sarah mentioned something about that when I was in New York."

"I think she supports it." Rachel's shoulders drooped. "She's gotten in with the group that is willing to kick Negro women to the curb if whites can gain the vote. Did you get that impression?"

"Sadly, yes." Inga replied. She'd begun to understand the magnitude of the rift between her friends and it saddened her.

"Do you agree with her?"

"No, Rachel. I don't."

"But you don't feel strongly enough about the issue to come to the convention and fight for it." Accusation hardened Rachel's words. "Since you've been in Wyoming, you've written a few articles on the cause but your soul has lost its fire."

Inga drew back as if she'd been slapped. She didn't know whether she felt ashamed, embarrassed or angry.

For many long minutes, she contemplated what Rachel had said.

"I'm sorry to say you may be right." Inga finally met Rachel's relentless gaze. "I know I have full suffrage, and I'll be able to vote for president in November. I'm ashamed to admit it, but I no longer feel the same hunger I did when I was younger."

Rachel broke eye contact and studied her plate.

"But I still believe in the cause of woman suffrage." Inga gently placed her hand on Rachel's arm. "And, I'm still a member of the association. I'll write to the leaders and implore them to continue fighting for the vote—for all woman."

Inga stood before her cheval mirror and studied her reflection. She really didn't want to attend tonight's party, but the university's president had made it clear that all faculty were expected to put in an appearance.

If only she had stayed a week longer in Cedar Falls with her family.

She smoothed a wrinkle in her deep blue silk skirt. Thankfully, the Ivinsons' home was only a few blocks west of the boarding house, so she hadn't needed to hire a carriage.

She donned her hat and gloves, picked up her small reticule, and descended the stairs.

"Good night," she called to Eliza and Bertha, both of whom were sitting in the parlor.

"Good night," they said in unison.

"Have a good time," Bertha added.

Inga flashed her a sham smile and walked into the afterglow of the sunset.

She ambled down the sidewalk, watching other guests arriving as she neared the imposing three-story Victorian mansion. Events like this were awkward, with so many people she didn't know. With the city leaders, the university president, and the upper crust of Laramie's society in attendance, Inga always felt as if she and the rest of the faculty were on display.

Inga rounded the block to the entrance and climbed the steps to the grand front porch, where a small group of guests stood talking.

A uniformed servant greeted her at the massive front door and directed her toward her host and hostess, who stood near the base of the grand curved stairway.

"Good evening, Mrs. Ivinson. Mr. Ivinson." She nodded to each in turn.

"Miss Stryker, so nice to see you." Mrs. Ivinson smiled warmly.

"Thank you for inviting me." Inga mustered a smile she hoped was equally warm. "Your home looks lovely."

"How nice of you to say so." Her hostess's gaze swept the room. "I enjoy decorating with mums and other autumn flowers and fruits."

"It's a pleasant time of year," Mr. Ivinson said looking past Inga to an arriving group of guests.

"That it is," Inga agreed. With the small talk over, she turned toward the parlor.

Spotting a cluster of people that included President Smiley and some of her fellow professors, she strolled toward them.

"Miss Stryker, so glad you could make it."

President Smiley gave her an approving nod.

"Isn't this a grand house?" gushed Louise Morey, a fellow English professor.

"Yes, it is," Inga agreed.

Their conversation covered the upcoming term, a few notable incoming students, and hopes that the nice weather would hold through the fall, before the group began to disperse.

Piano notes drifted through the air. Whoever was playing was quite expert, several cuts above Inga's level of proficiency.

Inga wandered in the direction of the music. The pianist was a young Negro girl. Inga watched in awe as her fingers floated over the keys. She'd heard tales of this prodigy, Carrie Burton, but had not previously heard her play.

"She's very good, isn't she?"

Inga startled at the sound of a male voice.

Beside her stood Mr. Low, the *Boomerang* editor. She hadn't even heard him approach. "Masterful."

"It's surprising to see so much talent in someone like her."

Inga's skin prickled and she turned to face him. Had he meant someone so young? Or did he mean a Negro girl? Inga wasn't sure and she didn't want to become entangled in a heated public discussion, so she chose not to ask. "I hope she'll have the opportunity to continue developing her gifts and use them to her advantage in the future."

"Perhaps you can do a brief column on this party and mention the entertainment."

Inga clenched her jaw. It sounded as if he expected a gossip piece like those C.J. had initially offered to let her write. "Isn't your women's reporter here tonight?"

"She's in Denver." He scowled. "Shopping for winter."

"I'll put something together." Something focusing on this talented young pianist and minimizing the guest list. Probably not at all what he expected.

But if he decided to publish it, she'd be sure to send a copy to Rachel. Hopefully, she would see the story as evidence of Inga's belief in including all women, equally, here in the Laramie community.

Chapter Ten

October 18, 1900
Laramie, Wyoming

Dear Rachel,

Best wishes to you and Herman on your marriage. I'm sorry I was not able to make another trip east this fall for your wedding. I have sent a gift to celebrate your union, and it should arrive shortly after this letter. Next time you write, please tell me all about your ceremony and reception.

My editor at The Boomerang *was not happy about the articles I wrote about Theodore Roosevelt, but he did not fire me. He said he hoped few of his subscribers would actually read* The Chronicle, *but he let me know my days might be numbered at the paper if he gets a lot of complaints. I'm going to stay away from writing about political figures for awhile.*

As the election approaches, I am becoming more and more excited about casting my ballot. I have to admit I am torn about who would make a better president. Bryan supports woman suffrage, and if I still lived in Iowa, that position would win my vote. But if I still lived in Iowa, I would not have been allowed to cast that vote. Now that I have the vote, I look at the improved economy and my strong favorable impression of Roosevelt, and think I might need to look at broader issues, like Bryan's often bigoted ideas about Negroes. For me, the decision has become quite a conundrum. I would like to use my voting privilege to advance the cause of woman suffrage, but not at the expense of increased suppression of Negro rights.

My friend Ruth will be coming to town to cast her ballot, and we plan to have dinner at a nice restaurant to celebrate. As winter approaches, I worry about her all alone out on her homestead. She has been looking for a ranch hand, but to my knowledge, she has not found anyone she considers suitable.

Last summer, I told Sarah I would write an article countering anti-suffrage arguments, and she has sent me some material. If there are any points you want me to include, please send them along. Also, do you want me to mention the bigotry that is infesting the movement, or do you think that would exacerbate the situation? I'm going to put the piece together later next month and mention my voting experience.

I'm enclosing a clipping of an article I wrote about a very talented young pianist who played at a party I recently attended. She is a lovely girl with an enormous musical gift.

My classes are going well this term. I look forward to the second term, other than the fact that it occurs entirely during the winter. Winters here seem very harsh, mostly because of the unrelenting winds. Supposedly, Laramie is in the center of a "bowl" of hills and mountains, but they don't serve as much of a windbreak.

Take care and be happy.

Lovingly in friendship,
Inga

Inga filled out her ballot for all of the offices, except president. She hesitated. Even though she had studied the party platforms and researched the personal positions and writings of McKinley and Bryan, she was still torn.

Thoughts of her mother and half-sisters flooded her mind. And Sarah. And Rachel. And Etta. And Jess's mother and sister. They should all be filling out ballots today, too. But they weren't.

The responsibility weighed heavy on Inga. She didn't like Bryan's bigoted attitude toward Negroes, but current efforts to gain woman suffrage included all woman. She would do all she could to keep it that way.

Inga cast her vote for William Jennings Bryan.

When she stepped outside the polling place, Ruth was waiting. "So, was it worth the move to Wyoming?"

"It was." It was all Inga could do to refrain from asking Ruth who she voted for, but that didn't seem proper. "Besides, I like it here. But, I didn't realize how responsible I would feel to choose the right people for the future of our community and for our country." She swallowed. "I hope I made the right choices."

"I know what you mean." Ruth sobered. "It's like making sure we hire the candidates who are most qualified to do the things that government is supposed to do."

"And now we have to wait to see who wins." Inga sighed. "I'll stop in at the Boomerang office first thing in the morning to get the results."

Ruth took Inga by the arm. "Let's take a stroll down by the river. Then we can go for an early dinner."

As they walked, they talked of the coming winter, the end of the university's term, and Ruth's preparations for her livestock.

"What articles are you working on for *The Chronicle*?"

"I'm working on one about voting for the first time." Inga gazed out at the white-capped mountains of the Snowy Range. "And I've been doing research for a series C.J. wants me to write relating to next year's hundred-and-twenty-fifth anniversary of the Declaration of Independence. I have two of them in rough draft form."

"He's quite taken with you." Ruth stopped before they crossed Grand Avenue. "And not only as a writer." She nailed Inga with her gaze. "How do you feel about him?"

Inga froze. "I feel like we've talked about this before. Did he put you up to asking?"

"No. But when we're together he talks about you all the time, and he mentions you in every letter. He cares deeply for you, but you rarely mention him." Ruth's gaze burned into Inga. "He's my brother and I love him." Ruth finally blinked. "I don't want to see him hurt."

Inga studied her shoes while she organized her thoughts. "I don't know what to say. He's my editor, my boss, so I feel like I should keep a professional distance between us." She looked up at Ruth. "But I find I like him. I enjoy being with him. It's as if I have a war going on inside myself." Tension built in Inga's temples. "I'm afraid that if I fall in love with him – or with any man – I'll lose my career."

"Oh, Inga. It's not like you're employed by *The Chronicle*." Ruth slipped an arm around her shoulder. "Besides, C.J. would never try to prevent you from pursuing your teaching or your writing."

"C.J. is a wonderful man." Inga hung her head. "But I'm afraid I can't engage in my profession and run a household and do both well, even if I love a man."

"C.J. is very considerate." Ruth's voice softened. "I'm sure he would hire people to help you around the house."

Inga sniffled. "But he's in Philadelphia. I'm here. If I go to Philadelphia, I won't be able to vote."

"That's a most difficult obstacle. I don't have an answer for that." Ruth moved her arm from Inga's shoulder and clasped her elbow. "Let's eat."

They crossed the street and entered the Johnson Hotel Café.

Inga removed her hat and gloves and set them on the chair beside her. "Have you found a hired hand to work on your homestead yet?"

"Not yet." Ruth settled herself on the chair across the table. "I ran an ad in *The Republican*, but none of the men I talked to worked out."

"You should have run it in *The Boomerang*," Inga teased.

Ruth grinned. "Maybe so."

Inga glanced around the room. The hour was early, and most of the tables were unoccupied.

"How shall we celebrate the election?"

"I think I'm going to indulge." Ruth pursed her lips.

"In what?"

"Oysters!"

Inga wrinkled her nose. "I've never developed a taste for them."

"But you need to order something extravagant."

Inga tapped her fingers against her lips. "Ice cream."

Ruth chuckled. "I might have to order that, too."

By the time they had enjoyed their cold, creamy vanilla dessert, dusk had fallen.

Pulling their wraps close, they walked down First Street to Thornburg. When they rounded the corner, Inga tipped her head against the wind and picked up her pace.

"I think that might be the last ice cream I have before spring." Inga raised the volume of her voice to be heard over the relentless frigid air blowing in her face. "I'm glad to have had that last cup of coffee."

Ruth pulled her collar closer around her neck. "If this keeps up, it won't take us long to acclimate to winter."

"I have to admit, even after three years, I haven't acclimated to the gales that plague us here." Inga shivered beneath her cloak. "I think we should move the bed in from the sleeping porch. We'll be a bit crowded, but we'll both be warm."

"That sounds good."

As they reached the end of the block and crossed the street, a shadowy male figure approached them.

Every nerve in Inga's body snapped alert. She was glad to be accompanied by Ruth.

As the distance closed between him and the women, a sense of familiarity engulfed Inga. She squinted.

"Inga?" he said, as they met at the corner.

Inga hadn't seen or heard from Jess Holden since she had rebuffed his proposal back in Cedar Falls. She cringed. "Jess, what are you doing here?"

"Looking all over for you."

Inga turned to her friend. "Ruth, this is Jess Holden. His parents' farm was just up the road from my parents' place. Jess, this is my friend, Ruth Wakefield. Let's go to my boarding house and talk where it's warm."

Jess fell into step behind them. They traversed the final blocks in silence.

Inga hoped he hadn't come to Wyoming to renew his efforts to court her, but she couldn't think of any other reason he would be here.

When they entered the parlor, Eliza looked up from the book she was reading. "You found them."

Jess nodded. "Yes, thank you."

"I see you two have met." Inga said.

Ruth removed her cloak and hung it on the rack in the hallway.

"What are you doing in Laramie, Jess? And on election day. Didn't you vote?" Inga didn't try to hide her exasperation.

"No. I didn't. I came today 'cause I knew you'd be in town for the election." He unbuttoned his sheepskin coat. "I wrote to the Land Office and asked if there are still lands available to homestead in Wyoming. There are. I thought if I claimed some land close to Laramie, you might feel different 'bout me since you can vote here."

She wouldn't, even if he moved next door. "But I haven't heard from you since I moved!"

"I thought it'd be a good surprise." His posture slumped. "But the land still available for homesteading is pretty far away."

"I got one of the last plots within a day of Laramie." Ruth's soft, gentle voice carried a note of sympathy.

"What are you planning to do? Go back to Cedar Falls?" Inga asked.

"I don't know yet." Jess ran a hand through his brown hair. "I shipped all my things here and I have some money, but not enough to buy much land. I might try to find work as a ranch hand."

Ruth inspected him up and down. "I'm looking for someone to help on my place. If you're interested, you'll need to decide if you can work for a woman.

Where are you staying?"

He stared at her with surprise. "At the Globe Hotel."

"I'll meet you in the lobby tomorrow morning at eight o'clock." Ruth's brusk tone commanded attention. "We'll talk for a while, and I can figure out if you're the ranch hand I'm looking for."

Inga could hardly believe what she was hearing. Jess didn't see women as equals, let alone bosses. And he could be stubborn. Ruth would have her hands full if she hired him, and Inga would tell her so when they were alone tonight.

The warm, moist, cinnamon-scented air of her mother's kitchen reminded Inga of many happy Christmases in her childhood. She had always enjoyed helping to prepare the special meal before everyone went to church. Goose and pork roasted in the large oven, while the apple and pumpkin pies cooled on the counter. Mrs. Jensen stood at the sink peeling potatoes.

Inga stirred sugar into vinegar, while her mother sliced cucumbers.

"I'm so glad you could come for Christmas," Moder said. "With Erik, Poul, Anesa and Karoline all away, it's hard to get into the proper spirit."

"I miss them all, but especially Erik." A small smile curved Inga's lips. "Being out of the country, he seems so far away. And I'd love to meet Katie."

"She's a sweet girl." Moder slid the slices into a bowl. "Brigitte is unhappy with you for introducing Jess to your friend. She blames you for his decision to stay in Wyoming."

"He came out with the plan to homestead there." Inga tossed the dressing with the cucumbers. "If he had done that, he would have stayed anyway."

Moder wiped her hands on a towel. "She doesn't think he would have gone through with it, and she doesn't like having him so far away."

"I'm surprised to hear that Brigitte has become so

provincial." Inga placed the bowl into the icebox. "I'll admit, I didn't think it was a good idea for Ruth to hire him, but she seems to be happy with his work. And it's given her more flexibility to get away from her ranch than she's had since she began homesteading."

"Do you think they'll marry?"

Inga lifted her shoulders and held her hands palms up. "I have no idea. Ruth hasn't said anything to indicate she's attracted to him, but who knows what can happen with the two of them way out on her place alone? Even if she lives in the cabin and he stays in the sod house."

"Do you think they'd be a good match?" Moder handed Inga a dishtowel. Mrs. Jensen had set the pot of potatoes on the stove, ready to boil when they returned from church, and was now washing the dishes they'd used in preparing the meal.

"Ruth would be good for Jess. She's smart and a hard worker." Inga picked up an empty bowl. "I'm not sure how good it would be for Ruth. I'll be interested to see if he's still working for her when winter's over."

"You think she might fire him?"

"Jess likes things his own way. So does Ruth. And it's her ranch." Inga set the bowl on the kitchen table. "If he starts trying to boss her around, that will be a problem, especially since the land in Wyoming is quite different than Iowa's farmland."

Moder dried the butcher knife and slipped it into the drawer. "What article are you working on now?"

"C.J. wants me to do a series on the founding of our country. Next year is the one-hundred-twenty-fifth anniversary of the Declaration of Independence." Inga picked up the knife her mother had used to cut the cucumbers, now washed and lying in the rinse water. She ran her towel over the blade then the handle. "I've been working on those articles all fall."

"C.J.?"

Inga raised her gaze. Her mother was watching her with an arched brow.

"Mr. Wakefield. My editor. Ruth's brother." Inga

grinned. "He introduced me to her when I was working on my Women of the Land piece."

Moder sighed. "I think you mentioned that Founding Fathers series when you stopped here on your way back from Philadelphia."

"I'm working on my fourth article, now. It's about Benjamin Franklin."

"How many do you plan to write?"

"C.J. wants six." Inga hung her towel on the rack near the stove.

"Sounds like you have a good start." Moder placed her towel next to Inga's. "Why don't you go upstairs and change your clothes for church before Uncle Peder and his family get here?"

"I will. Thanks." Inga left the kitchen and climbed the stairs to her childhood bedroom.

Although Moder enjoyed redecorating the downstairs rooms, she had left the children's bedrooms pretty much as they had been. Inga was thankful that her mother had kept the violet-and-daisy wallpaper Inga had picked when the house was built. Her white-painted iron bedframe and Dresden Plate quilt in shades of purple had been hard to leave behind when she went to college. Now, whenever she visited it welcomed her home. She loved the sweet, comfortable ambience of her childhood space.

Inga shrugged out of her skirt and blouse and tugged the front laces of her corset. She didn't cinch it too tight, as she wanted to be able to enjoy dinner after they returned from Christmas Eve services. Carefully, she donned the fashionable blue silk dress she had purchased especially for Christmas.

From the floor below rose a clatter of feet and clamor of voices. Uncle Peder and his family must have arrived. Inga checked her appearance in the mirror and patted a curl back into place. Satisfied, she inhaled a breath and headed down to see them. As she descended the stairs, Uncle Peder's ten-year-old daughter, Elizabeth, rushed into the hall.

"Inga! Inga! Hurry quick." Her brown curls

bounced and her blue eyes shone brightly. "We brought you a present."

"A present?" Normally, the family did not open gifts until after they finished dinner. Puzzled, Inga took the hand her cousin offered.

Elizabeth led her into the parlor.

Inga smiled at her family members. She dropped Elizabeth's hand.

Standing near the fireplace, talking with Uncle Peder and Halvor, was C.J. Wakefield.

C.J. stared as Inga floated into the room. He diverted his gaze for a few moments, but couldn't resist the temptation to watch her. She wore a dark blue dress, which brought out the summer-sky blue of her wide eyes. From her tiny waist, the skirt flowed to the floor, skimming over her slender hips.

He swallowed to ease the tension coursing through his limbs and forced a smile.

After a brief pause, she strode toward him. "How did you get here?"

Glancing at her uncle, C.J. replied, "I came with Peder and his family."

"Let me rephrase my question. What are you doing here?"

The conversations in the room quieted, and everyone was watching them.

"When I got to Des Moines, we learned that a blizzard had closed the tracks west of Omaha." He inhaled a breath. "I telephoned information in Cedar Falls. The operator said she knew your family and put me in touch with your uncle."

"Since he would be unable to make it to Laramie, I invited him to join us for Christmas." Peder's blue eyes twinkled. "And I picked him up at the depot yesterday. I thought he would be a nice holiday surprise for you."

Heat rose from C.J.'s chest, creeping up his neck. Inga looked surprised, but he couldn't tell whether or not she was pleased.

Her gaze shifted to her uncle. "It *is* a surprise. Or,

more accurately, a shock." Her chest rose and fell with a sigh. She turned her attention back to C.J. "Have you met everyone?"

His taut muscles eased a bit. He scanned the room. "I believe so."

"Inga has a beau. Inga has a beau," taunted Peder's youngest daughter.

Inga's half-sister Ella giggled. She, her brothers, and Peder's children sat at a table with a Parcheesi board to the right of the fireplace.

C.J. suppressed a grin. Although he rather liked the idea that her family might think of him as Inga's beau, she wouldn't like it.

She blushed and pivoted slowly toward her cousin, a tight smile on her face. "Mr. Wakefield is not my beau." Her voice was calm, controlled. She smoothed her skirt. "He is my editor at *The Chronicle*."

"The two aren't mutually exclusive," Peder said quietly, but with a twinkle in his eyes.

She glared at her uncle. "They are in this case."

Her words were less vehement than C.J. had expected. Perhaps, he could nudge her in the direction of accepting his suit.

Mrs. Hansen strode into the room, now dressed in a fashionable skirt and jacket. She was petite like her daughter, and C.J. appreciated her welcoming friendliness.

"I think we're ready to leave for the church now," Peder said. His gaze swept the room and landed on his wife, Charlotte.

Smiling, Inga's stepfather approached her mother and took her arm. "You look lovely, my dear."

"Everyone get your wraps," Peder directed. "The carriages are waiting."

Peder grinned at C.J. "Ella, you can ride with us. C.J., you and Inga can go with Anna's family."

C.J. glanced at Inga. She was smiling. He took that as a good sign.

In the Hansens' festively decorated parlor, C.J.

joined in as Inga's sizable family sang familiar Christmas carols. Inga accompanied them expertly on the piano.

After a reverent rendition of *Silent Night*, Peder asked, "Are your fingers tired yet?"

Charlotte moved toward the piano. "I can take a turn playing."

Mr. Hansen and Peder eased the decorated tree into the middle of the room. The younger children encircled the tree, joining hands. The adults and older children formed a circle around the youngsters. Inga held one of C.J.'s hands. Her mother held the other. He exchanged a glance with Inga. She grinned.

Charlotte struck up the refrain of *Deck the Halls* and the revelers sang the words while they skipped and danced around the tree. When the song ended, the family talked and laughed. Notes of a melody C.J. hadn't heard before rose from the piano. Everyone held hands again and the others sang in a language he did not recognize. Even the younger children seemed to know the words as they circled around the tree.

When the song ended, C.J. turned to Inga. "What was that one?"

"It's a Danish carol about Christmas lasting until Easter." She explained. "It's one of three Danish tunes that are part of our tradition."

After two more English and two more Danish numbers, Mrs. Hansen clapped her hands together. "Okay, everyone. We're going to take a break. Charlotte and I will serve some refreshments on the buffet. Then we'll invite you into the dining room."

"Do you need help?" Inga asked.

"No, thanks, dear." Charlotte smiled. "You have a guest to entertain."

C.J. could have hugged the woman. He patted his pocket and felt the small square box.

Peder and Mr. Hansen moved the tree back into place, then Peder clapped his hand on C.J.'s shoulder. "You can help us move the gifts in from the sitting room."

A smidgen of jealousy wormed its way through C.J. Inga's family clearly cherished these long-standing traditions. His family confined Christmas celebrations to a nice meal and opening gifts. It wasn't that anything was wrong with the simple practices. His parents were good people, loving and kind to their children. He considered his childhood happy. But, in comparison to what was happening around him, it had been staid and formal.

"Refreshments are ready!" Mrs. Hansen called from the entry to the dining room.

The younger children scampered to the buffet.

"We'd better get in line." Inga winked at him. "Before the best treats are gone."

Plates of candies, cookies, and pastries interspersed with bowls of fruit and popcorn balls, topped the full length of the sideboard. On the end of the table stood a pitcher of eggnog, a coffee pot, and bottles of wine and spirits.

"Your mother and Peder's wife must have been busy for a week," C.J. said to Inga.

"I'm sure Mrs. Jensen, my mother's cook, and Aunt Charlotte's cook helped a lot."

They filled their plates, and Inga led him to the settee in the parlor. They settled in to indulge in the sweets.

C.J. took a bite of the pastry with frosting and nuts on top. The taste of sweet almond burst in his mouth. Chewing slowly, he savored the delicious flavor. He gestured to the remainder of the piece with his fork. "This is delicious. What is it?"

"Kringle."

His brows drew together. "What?"

"Kringle. It's a Danish pastry." Inga delicately swept a crumb from her lip with the tip of her tongue. "It's my mother's specialty."

He relished the last bite.

"I'm glad you like it." Mrs. Hansen appeared as if on cue. "I'm going to put you in Greg's room with my nephew. We'll set up a cot in Torsten's room for Greg."

C.J. nodded. "Thank you for putting me up, ma'am. I'm sorry to have come uninvited."

"You're more than welcome, Mr. Wakefield." She cast a motherly smile his way. "We like to meet our children's friends."

"It's very kind of you."

After indulging in the goodies, the family opened their gifts. Within minutes, a riot of wrapping paper and ribbons had been strewn around the room.

Without a word to anyone, Inga left the room and climbed the stairs. C.J. glanced at the others. No one else seemed to have noticed. He considered following her, but doubted her family would approve.

"What did you think of our Christmas Eve?" Ella plopped down next to C.J.

"Very enjoyable." He grinned.

"Inga's a good piano player, isn't she?"

"Yes, she is."

"But, I'm better." She hopped up abruptly. "You'll see." She rushed off toward her cousins.

C.J. shook his head. He hadn't spent much time around girls her age since his school days. And he hadn't thought much about what it would be like to raise children. Now, the thoughts gave him pause. In light of his intention to court Inga, he should seriously consider both subjects.

And he would. Later.

Inga glided down the stairs. She carried a small bundle tied with red ribbon.

C.J. stroked his jaw. What had she brought?

Smiling, she approached him. "I forgot. I have a gift for you."

She held the present toward him.

As soon as the package was in his hands, he knew what it was. He grinned.

After untying the ribbon, he removed the wrapping. He gazed at the stack of papers he held.

"There are three of the independence-related articles you want, and one on my experience of casting my first vote." She brushed a strand of hair from her face and tucked it behind her ear. "I hope you'll like them."

She had written the pieces he had requested. He rose and gave her a quick hug. "I'm sure I will."

To his surprise, she didn't pull away nor did she stiffen, even though they were in full view of her family.

"Ruth wrote that the two of you went to the polling place together." He gritted his teeth to keep from touching her again. "How did you find voting?"

"It was a great honor." Her expression became solemn. "I felt it as an ominous responsibility to pick the right candidates for the right reasons."

Mrs. Hansen strode up to them. "Ella's going to play for the dancing. I was hoping to get Greg to take a turn on the piano, but he didn't want to."

"I haven't heard him practice once since I've been home."

"That's why he doesn't want to perform." Inga's mother sighed. "It's nice that you can keep up your skills at your boarding house."

"I could probably use a piano at the university, but it's convenient to have one where I live."

Mrs. Hansen patted Inga's shoulder. "You're lucky, my sweet."

Not long after Mrs. Hansen had left them, notes of a familiar waltz filled the room.

Inga turned to him. "Do you dance?"

"Yes, but not well." He laid the pages on the marble-topped table and held out his hand. "Shall we?"

She took it, and together they glided around the room. The Hansens and the Jorgesens did the same. The cousins paired up and waltzed among the adults. C.J. relished Inga's slender form in his arms. She smelled faintly of roses.

The couples changed partners at the end of each tune, but he returned to Inga for the last two dances.

"Is there somewhere we can be alone to talk for a few minutes?" he whispered over the final strains of *After the Ball.*

"Not really." She leaned away and her gaze met his. "Well…I suppose we could use the back stairs."

That didn't sound very romantic, but at least it might be private.

She led him through the kitchen to a door. Behind it was a staircase he hadn't known existed. The stairs were dimly lit and much narrower than the ones in the front hall. She sat on a step. He eased himself down beside her.

"I have a gift for you, too." He reached in his pocket and pulled out the box.

"Oh, C.J., no." She drew back against the wall.

He took her hand and lay the gift on her palm. "It's not what you think."

She remained still, and he could barely make out her features.

Gently, he placed his hands over hers. "Open it."

Her fingers shook as she slowly lifted the lid. She reached forward, pushing the door open wider, allowing more light in. He could barely make out the filigree setting and the sterling silver chain of the necklace he had so carefully selected.

She released a pent-up breath. "It's lovely."

"Like you." He watched as she outlined the stone with her slender finger. "It's an amethyst. Your birthstone."

"I love it." Her voice was barely audible. "But you shouldn't have."

"Inga, please let me court you. I promise not to pressure you into marriage. I'll wait for you to tell me when you're ready." He paused. "I just want a chance to win your hand."

She inhaled a raspy breath.

"Will you give me that chance?"

Her breath rushed out on a sigh. "Yes."

He could hardly believe his ears. Although he wanted her to hold up her hand and swear that she meant it, he smiled. "Let me put the necklace on you."

Her soft hair brushed his hands as he fastened the clasp.

Inga glanced out the train window at the shadowy, snow-covered landscape rushing by. The last vestiges of pinks and reds were fading into the dusk. The foggy glass pane was no match for the fierce Nebraska cold. Neither was the coach's heater. She shivered beneath her cloak.

Bedside her, C.J. was studying one of the articles she had given him. She tried to force her focus back to the book open in her lap, John Dewey's *The School and Society*. Concentrating was hopeless. She stole a glance at her handsome beau. Beau. The thought gave her pause.

His thick dark-brown hair obscured all of his profile except his aquiline nose and strong chin.

Her chest fluttered as though a swarm of butterflies was trapped there. Although he hadn't pressured her to move to Philadelphia, he had made it nearly impossible to suppress her attraction to him.

C.J. turned to face her. "Are you losing interest in your book? I have some magazines in my satchel."

"No." Inga shook her head. "With all of the conversations around us, I'm having trouble concentrating."

"I really like this story about casting your first vote." He lifted the papers he was holding. "You've done a good job of reminding us how important it is to take the responsibility of selecting government officials seriously. I'm thinking about running it now and repeating it before the 1904 election."

"Will Mr. Bender approve of that?"

"We've done it before when an old story takes on new relevance."

"If you decide to do that, I'd like to have a chance to revise it before it's published."

"Of course." He slipped the article into his satchel. "Did I hear you tell your mother that the second term begins right after New Years?"

"Yes."

"That's too bad." He frowned. "I'm going out to see Ruth on the second, and I was hoping you could come with me."

"I'd love to see her, but there's always so much to do before classes start."

"Since I'm getting home so late, I thought about skipping my visit to her so I could spend more time with you." A rueful smile curved his lips. "But you've expressed reservations about her new hired man, and I want to see first hand how he's working out."

Inga rubbed her temple. "I hope it's going well. I feel responsible for introducing them."

His smile faded. "But she hired him after you told her how you felt."

"Let me know what you think after your visit."

"If you come to the depot to see me off, I will." He laid his hand over hers. A startling spark shot through her.

She drew in a quick breath. The warmth of his touch was a pleasant intimacy. "When does your train leave?"

"The afternoon of January fourth. I'm not sure exactly what time."

"That's Friday." Disappointment and relief pushed and pulled within her like the ebb and flow of the tide as she considered the first separation of their courtship. "I have to teach rhetoric on Friday afternoon until 2:30. I'll be there to see you off if class is over in time."

She leaned her head against the back of the seat. Guilt niggled at the edges of her mind. Being courted by this handsome man might well lead to giving up her career. She had already betrayed her vow to dedicate herself to the pursuit of woman suffrage. Her friends had been right. Living in Wyoming where she could vote had weakened her resolve.

When she was back in Laramie, alone in her room, she would have to imagine the future that might lie ahead and decide what she wanted to do with the rest of her life.

CHAPTER ELEVEN

January 18,1901
Philadelphia, Pennsylvania

Dear Inga,

Philadelphia seems cold and bleak, although we have not had nearly the snow that the west has had. So maybe it just seems dreary because I left my heart with you in Wyoming. But I am cheered that you are allowing me to carry on this long-distance courtship.

I was heartily disappointed that you were not able to see me off, but you had warned me of the possibility. I greatly appreciated the farewell letter you left for me at the depot, and I am buoyed by your expressions of pleasure about our time together.

Your friend, Mr. Holden, seems to be getting on fairly well with his duties on Ruth's homestead. Ruth said he had some difficulty taking direction from her at first, but after he was responsible for the death of a newborn calf, he has been more compliant. I hope she's right.

She invited him to dine with us one evening, and he spent much of the meal hinting that she should cook three meals for him every day, and even that she should invite him to stay in the cabin on bitterly cold nights. She makes light of the situation, but holds firm.

I confess, I was hoping he might be a good match for Ruth, but after meeting him, I understand your reservations about his attitude toward women. At least she's no longer all alone out there.

Although I promised not to mix personal messages with business in my letters to you, I want to tell that we are accepting and buying all of the articles you sent back with me. However, payment for the patriotic pieces will come as they are published.

Nathan has assigned me to work with a group planning the Independence Day festivities here in the city, in addition to my editorial duties. I had hoped to spend time in Laramie this spring, but now it looks like I won't be able to do so until late summer. I hope you will provide me the consolation of frequent letters.

The hour is late and I must close.

Yours faithfully,
C.J.W.

"I really appreciate your help." Ruth funneled stewed tomatoes into canning jars on the table next to her stove. "Now that it's August, my vegetables are starting to pass their peak."

"My mother would have been happy to lend a hand. And my stepfather wouldn't have minded working in your garden when they were here last week." Inga sliced another fresh tomato in half, then in half again.

"I didn't want to intrude on your visit. They don't come to Wyoming that often." Ruth frowned. "Besides, it keeps Jess busy when he's not checking on the cattle."

Inga dropped the quarters into the pan with the other tomatoes that were currently boiling. She bit her tongue. She'd already expressed her misgivings, and Ruth had rebuffed them. Inga didn't have to deal with Jess, and she didn't want to argue with Ruth.

After giving the pot a stir, Inga moved another bowl of freshly-picked tomatoes to the counter where she was working.

"Are you planning to get together with your college friends this summer?" Ruth asked.

"I think that is definitely a thing of the past." Inga sliced another tomato. "Rachel is married and busy with her life in Washington, D.C. She wrote that some of the NAWSA meetings in southern states have been banning Negro women from attending. She holds Sarah and the women she has been working with in the organization responsible for allowing it to happen." She sighed. "And, even if they were willing to meet, Sarah is busy planning her elaborate society wedding for November."

"November. Are you going? Maybe the three of you could get together then."

"I suppose it might be possible, but I don't like the idea of travelling to New York at the onset of winter. And the fall term will be near its midpoint." Inga sighed. "Besides, I think each is a little put out with me for defending the other. And both feel I've abandoned the suffrage cause."

"Have you?"

"Not entirely. But I confess, my passion has waned." She peeled and quartered another tomato.

"Is that why you agreed to allow C.J. to court you?"

Inga stopped wielding her knife and considered the question. "I suppose it might have had something to do with it, but as long as he is in Philadelphia—"

The sound of hoofbeats and squeaky wheels reached them through the open window.

"I think he's finally here!" Ruth cried. She set down her funnel and ladle, then dashed to the door.

Inga wiped her hands on a towel and rushed to join her friend.

Indeed, a carriage driven by C.J. was pulling into the door yard.

Jess came running from behind the new shed he was building. He carried a rifle.

Ruth scampered across the distance to her brother, reaching him just as he hopped down from his seat. He secured the reins to the hitching post, then drew his sister into a bear hug.

Inga strolled toward them, restraining her impulse to break into a run. He released Ruth and took both of Inga's hands in his.

She smiled. "Hello, Mr. Wakefield."

He kissed the fingers of her right hand and then her left. "Have I been too long away from you?" He grinned. "It's C.J., remember?"

Her heart fluttered. "C.J."

His dark eyes sparkled. "I'm so happy to see you again."

"And you remember my hired hand, Jess Holden."

Ruth's words tore Inga's attention from C.J.

Still holding Inga's hands, he nodded to Jess.

Jess nodded stiffly. "Mr. Wakefield." He turned to Ruth. "If you'll excuse me, I'll get back to building."

"Of course." She shifted her gaze to C.J., then to Inga. "Let's go inside and get out of the hot sun."

"Where would you like me to put the horses?" he asked.

"They can go in the east corral. It has shade." Ruth inclined her head toward the wooden gate. "Turn them over to Mr. Holden and come join us."

"He's busy with your barn." C.J. released Inga's hands.

"Not that busy." Ruth rolled her eyes. "And, the building is going to be a stable."

"I want to give the horses water before I turn them loose."

"Suit yourself." She touched her fingers to Inga's arm. "Come with me."

They returned to the cabin while C.J. tended the team.

By the time he rejoined them, they had finished packing jars with the last of the tomatoes they had picked that morning.

"I pitched the tent and put my things inside, except for the supplies I brought to earn my keep." He grinned at his sister and set a large crate on the dining table.

Ruth unpacked fresh peaches, plums, and a pineapple. Below were tins of herring, sweet nuts, crackers, and assorted delicacies.

"You are very generous," Ruth said. "You must tell me what of this you would like for dinner."

"How about the pineapple for dessert?" C.J. stroked his clean-shaven chin. "Other than that, please make whatever you had planned."

After a late dinner of green peppers stuffed with scrambled eggs and topped with bacon, crusty fresh-baked bread, and the remainder of stewed tomatoes, Ruth prepared the pineapple and divided the chunks into three bowls. They savored it as the women caught

C.J. up on the happenings in and around Laramie.

"This is such a treat!" Inga exclaimed. "Thanks for bringing it. We never have pineapple at the boarding house." She forked her final bite-sized piece into her mouth.

"For me, too." He speared his last chunk.

Through the open window, she gazed at the pink-streaked sky, heralding dusk.

C.J. stood and held a hand out to her "Let's go for a walk."

Inga shook her head. "I need to help Ruth with the dishes. We have all the canning equipment as well as what we used for dinner."

"Go on." Ruth swept her hand toward the door in a whisking motion. "You've worked hard enough today."

Inga stood and cleared her plate and silverware to the counter. "Not any harder than you."

Ruth moved in front of the table and stood with her feet apart and her hands on her hips. "And I have to pack up some leftovers to take to Jess. You two go on."

The amusement in her eyes belied her stern tone.

"Okay." Inga grasped the strong hand C.J. offered and walked with him into the twilight.

A brisk gust riffled through her hair, dislodging a strand. C.J. reached up and tucked it behind her ear.

She smiled, happy to have him with her again.

"Have you given any thought to moving to Philadelphia next summer, after the school year is over?" C.J. spoke in a gentle, but earnest voice that touched Inga's heart.

"Not really." Inga sighed. "I haven't seen any indication that Pennsylvania is likely to adopt woman suffrage."

"But you would be closer to the Suffrage Association's headquarters."

"That's not going to earn me the right to vote." Her jaw tensed involuntarily. She forced it to relax.

"Nathan really wants you to take a position on staff."

Inga tipped her head to catch C.J.'s gaze. "Is he going to move *The Chronicle* to Denver? It's a good-sized city and Colorado has given women full voting rights."

"We've just moved into our new building. He's not going to want to leave."

"Neither do I."

C.J. frowned. "So voting is more important to you than being with me."

"You promised you wouldn't pressure me." She gave his hand a gentle squeeze. "Maybe you could consider coming back to Laramie."

Inga clutched her portfolio to her chest as she opened the door to *The Boomerang* office.

"Miss Stryker!" Her student who'd been working at the paper greeted her with a big grin. His good humor and eagerness to learn had endeared him to her. "I thought you already turned in your column for next week."

She returned his smile. "I did, but I'm dropping off the rest of September and the first week of October so I don't have to worry about them as the fall term starts."

"Did you hear the news?" The question flew out of his mouth on a breathless wave.

Inga tipped her head to the side. "What news?"

"President McKinley was shot today at the Pan-American Exposition." He rubbed the back of his neck. "The boss is putting together a story for tomorrow's paper."

Inga's breath left her. She forced air back into her lungs. "Is the president dead?"

His mouth now formed a grim line. "He wasn't when the report came in."

"Thank you for letting me know."

Upon her return to the boarding house, Mary handed Inga a note.

Call C.J. Wakefield right away.

"Did he give you a telephone number?" Inga wondered if he was calling about the president.

"It's on the back."

Inga turned it over.

"You can use the telephone in the kitchen if you pay for the long distance call when the bill comes," Mary offered.

"I will. Thank you."

Carrying the note number-side up, Inga hurried to the kitchen. She gave the handle a crank and reached the operator immediately. Reading from the paper, she gave her C.J.'s number in Philadelphia.

C.J. answered right away.

Inga's heart fluttered at the sound of his voice through the line.

"I called to tell you the president has been shot," he blurted as soon as she had identified herself.

"I know. I was at the *Boomerang* office soon after they learned the news." She moved closer to the mouthpiece on the oak, wall-mounted telephone.

"There's not much information on his condition yet, but in case he doesn't survive, we'll want an article on Roosevelt and what we might expect from him as president." His tone was formal, businesslike.

Inga scratched her head. "I have no idea how to get in touch with him. According to the paper, he's speaking at an event. In New England, I think."

"You won't need new material. Just put the relevant information from your previous stories together in a new way."

"That seems like cheating."

A deep-throated chuckle through the receiver tickled her ear. "It's done all the time."

"But not by me." She stiffened. "Can't you just rerun one of the articles I wrote last summer?"

"Oh Inga." He had adopted a tone of over-taxed patience. "There's nothing wrong with reorganizing the material and giving it a different slant. And you might find something in your notes that you didn't use."

She sighed. "If the president survives, you won't need it, right?"

"No, but if he dies, we'll want it right away. We'll be holding space for it in the issue we're getting ready to print." He paused. "Nathan is already working on a memorial tribute."

"If I have to do this, it will only be a page or two."

"That's fine. I'll plan on two and fill in with an advertisement or cartoon, if necessary."

Inga shook her head. "A cartoon doesn't seem very tasteful."

"It will be something related to Roosevelt's military service. It won't make fun of him."

The line went silent for a few moments.

Had they had lost their connection? Finally, C.J. spoke. "You don't have much faith in my judgement, do you?"

She took a step backward. Her chest tightened. "Of course, I do. You're a wonderful editor. That's why I submit all my stories to you."

"That's good to hear, especially since I've been sorely missing you since I got back to Philadelphia."

A small smile played at her lips. "I miss you, too."

"I like talking on the telephone much better than writing letters. It's good to hear your voice."

"Yes, but I do look forward to your letters." She twisted the cord connected to the receiver around her finger.

"I'll keep writing them, too. But I'd like to call you once a week. Would you like that?"

"Yes." Warmth surged to her cheeks. At least he couldn't see her blush through the wire.

"Since today is Friday, how about I call you next Friday evening?"

"I'll look forward to it."

After they said their 'good-byes,' a sense of loss washed over Inga. She stood in the kitchen for a few moments before going to tell Mary about the president.

For the next five days, Inga carefully scoured *The Boomerang* for news of President McKinley's condition. Dutifully, she pulled together her previous articles on Roosevelt and her notes. She created an outline for a story, but didn't start writing.

On September eleventh, she stopped in the newspaper office and spoke with her editor.

"Did the articles I dropped off last Friday meet with your approval?" she asked, as she sat across the desk from him.

He gazed at her from behind his wire-rimmed spectacles. "They are fine. And I appreciate having them so early."

"I will try to get more to you before the term starts." She folded her hands in her lap. "At least enough to get us through October."

"I will look forward to them." He leaned toward her. "Are you planning to do any pieces on McKinley?"

She straightened. "I wasn't. I don't have any information on his medical condition, and that's what people are most interested in now."

"I think you're right about that." He relaxed back into his chair. "I was going to ask you to write something about T.R. in case he became president. But our most recent report indicated that yesterday McKinley was improving so well that T.R. left to join his family on vacation."

"That's encouraging news." Inga smiled with relief. "My editor at *The Chronicle* has asked me to prepare the same kind of piece for the magazine. I've outlined it, but with what you just told me, I'll put it aside."

"If the situation changes, I'll telephone you. Then I'll want a short column on T.R. for the next day's paper." He smiled wryly. "So, you might want to pen something in the next day or two, just in case."

Inga sighed. "It seems like a waste of time, but I'll put something together for you today."

Reluctantly, Inga worked on the two articles. The thought that writing them might somehow negatively affect President McKinley's outcome crossed her mind from time to time. She mentally kicked herself for the superstitious thinking.

She pulled the final page off the typewriter roller, carefully separated the carbon copy and laid it aside. Picking up the other two originals of the story for *The Chronicle*, she collated and placed them neatly on her desk.

After washing her hands of the carbon residue, she joined the other boarders in the dining room for dinner.

She turned to Bertha. "How are things going at your school?"

"My new class of pupils is very intelligent, but not well-disciplined." She brushed the back of her hand across her forehead.

Eliza turned her attention to the teacher. "You say that every year. Do you think it is because they were not well-managed by their last teacher or because they have not yet settled down from their summer break?"

"Probably some of both. But smarter children can be more devious than their less intelligent peers." Bertha laid her napkin in her lap. "Usually, that also means—"

The ring of the telephone interrupted her explanation.

"That they'll learn quickly how to behave," Bertha finished.

Mary appeared in the doorway. "It's for you, Inga."

"Me?" Who would be calling her? It was only Thursday. C.J. said he would call on Fridays. Inga stood and walked to the kitchen.

"It's your Philadelphia editor." Mary handed her the receiver. "Don't be too long. I'm going to put the food on the table now."

"I won't." Inga tightened her grip on the telephone. "Hello."

"I'm sorry to interrupt your dinner." C.J.'s voice carried a more serious tone than the last time they had spoken. "We just got a report that the president has taken a turn for the worse."

Inga's hopes fell. "What happened?"

Mary walked past, carrying a bowl in each hand.

"Apparently, he developed a serious infection, and he's not likely to recover. Nathan didn't have many details when he called, but he has assigned a writer to go to Washington to get more information."

"That's terrible." Inga leaned against the wall.

"Have you written your article?"

She stepped closer to the phone so she could speak into the mouthpiece more easily. "Yes. I finished it this evening."

"Good girl." The relief in his voice was palpable.

"Don't say that to me. You're not my father." She surprised herself with the sharp edge in her voice.

"I'm sorry. I was just pleased to hear you have something ready." A mix of confusion and contrition wove through his words.

"I apologize for my testiness." Inga glanced behind her to make sure she was alone. "Your news took me by surprise, because I was told only two days ago that he was doing so well that the vice president went on vacation. And your 'good girl' comment hit me the wrong way."

"Yes, I heard that too. I think the worsening of his condition was quite unexpected."

The line was silent. Mary passed by with a platter in one hand and a bowl in the other.

"Can you send your article in tomorrow's mail?"

Inga swallowed. The implication of C.J.'s news weighed heavily on her.

"Yes. I'll post it in the morning when I stop by *The Boomerang* with my column."

"Thank you." His tone softened. "I'm sorry to be the bearer of bad news."

"I appreciate knowing what to expect." Moisture collected in her eyes. Although she hadn't voted for this president, she hated the idea of his life ending this way.

"I wish I could be with you."

"Me, too." Tears spilled down her cheeks.

"You'd better go have dinner. Good night."

"Good night." She echoed. Her appetite was gone.

After hanging up the receiver, she leaned against the wall and took a series of slow, deep breaths. She swabbed her damp cheeks with the sleeve of her blouse before rejoining the group in the dining room.

"Did the president pass away?" Mary asked solemnly.

Inga's vision blurred. "No, but he is on his deathbed."

Inga ran her fingers over the hem of the linen tablecloth. The Johnson Hotel Café was surprisingly empty for so early in the evening. Perhaps the townspeople were preparing for the upcoming Thanksgiving holiday.

A little more than two months had passed since President McKinley had died. Although President Roosevelt had continued his predecessor's policies for the time being, Inga was amazed the country had already moved on to preparations for their traditional celebrations.

The table was not directly under the exposed-bulb light fixture that hung from the ceiling, so the illumination cast shadows on the planes of C.J.'s handsome face as he sipped his wine. A shiver of excitement rippled through her chest.

"I was hoping you would come east for your friend's marriage in New York so I could have seen you earlier this month." He set his wine glass back on the table.

Inga lowered her gaze. "It didn't work out with my teaching schedule."

"And you didn't want it enough to ask permission to be away."

She looked up, catching his wry smile.

"I suppose you're right." She dropped her hands back into her lap. "I guess I didn't feel comfortable with all the decadent activities Sarah was planning around her wedding."

"Both parties come from well-known, wealthy families." C.J. shook his head. "Their ceremony was written up in most of the eastern papers."

"I don't envy her being so much in the limelight,"

Inga said with a sigh. "But she seems to enjoy it."

"She lives in a different world from Laramie."

Inga sipped her wine. "Along with my regrets, I sent her a letter suggesting that the NAWSA should contact President Roosevelt about supporting woman suffrage." She fiddled with the stem of her glass. "When he was in college, he wrote a paper supporting equality in marriage. So far, he hasn't supported giving women the vote, but he's much more likely to be convinced than McKinley was." She returned her hand to her lap. "But the idea was probably lost on her in all the hoopla, so I'll mention it again after the first of the year."

"She'll probably get caught up in New York society," C.J. suggested. "Her husband's family will expect it, so it will be interesting to see if she continues her activities in pursuit of the ballot."

"Maybe I should write directly to Mrs. Catt." Inga frowned. "But I doubt she'd remember me from the Iowa convention."

C.J. chuckled. "I'd wager she knows you from your articles in *The Chronicle*."

Inga doubted it.

"My mother said you've agreed to come for our Thanksgiving celebration. You can ride with me out to their place tomorrow if you like." He grinned. "I'd enjoy your company."

Inga smiled at his enthusiasm. "I have to teach tomorrow. Besides, Ruth is coming to town to check on her order for winter provisions. She's going to spend the night with me, and I'll ride with her to your parents' house on Wednesday. I've arranged to pick up my contribution to the Thanksgiving feast first thing Wednesday morning."

"That's one benefit I see of her hired man," he conceded. "She's not as tied down as she was before."

"I'll admit it's working out better than I expected." Inga shrugged one shoulder. "She told me she's going to let Jess go to Cedar Falls for Christmas. It's really nice of her."

C.J. scowled. "Are you going to travel with him?"

"I'm not going home this year." Inga inwardly cringed at the thought of her first Christmas without her family. "My parents and younger siblings are going to South Dakota to be with my oldest half-sister."

He tipped his head and held her gaze. "Would you consider coming to Philadelphia for Christmas?"

Her pulse quickened as she savored the invitation. "That might be fun, but I can't afford to be so far away in case a winter storm halts the trains."

"Are you going out to Ruth's place, since her hired hand will be away?"

"No. I'm staying at the boarding house." She caught her lower lip. "Mary has agreed to let me host Christmas dinner for students who are away from home and staying in Laramie for the holiday. Eliza and Bertha will both be with their families." She clasped her hands together and unclasped them. "As long as I help with the majority of the cooking." She paused and dropped her gaze to her plate then raised it. "I'm going to invite your parents and Ruth when I see them on Thanksgiving."

"And me?"

Her breath hitched. "I thought you were going to be in Philadelphia."

"I was."

His sheepish grin amused her.

"But I can probably get away." He picked up his empty wine glass, but set it down again. "After McKinley's death, we scrambled to change much of our October issue so we had material from that issue for November. And we have material for November and December that we can move back."

The waiter appeared and refilled their wine glasses. "Your meals will be here soon."

As he left, C.J. continued. "If I buckle down and get the next two issues ready in a few weeks, Nathan should be willing to let me take time off." He leaned forward. "If he does, am I invited?"

Inga chuckled. "I think you just invited yourself."

C.J. relaxed back on his chair as the waiter delivered their dinner. While they dined, Inga spoke of her classes this term and happenings in Laramie. C.J. told her about stories in upcoming issues of *The Chronicle* and the details of Philadelphia's celebration of the one-hundred-twenty-fifth year of the Declaration of Independence.

When they had finished, he escorted her to the hired carriage.

Inga took his hand and stepped up to the seat. "You're lucky to have so many connections from having grown up near Laramie."

"Yes." He released the reins and walked the horse back from the hitching post, then climbed in beside her. "Especially a friend who owns a livery." He gave the reins a shake and the carriage jolted forward. "But it works for him, too. He trusts me to return the rig and care for the horse, so he gets paid and I save him work."

"Well, I appreciate it." She inhaled a breath of chilly air. "Although I don't live far from downtown, it would be a cold walk home tonight."

"My dear." He shifted closer to her on the seat. "Maybe we should have walked to get you acclimated to the approaching winter."

"I get plenty of chances to habituate to the changing seasons walking to and from the university each day." She feigned indignation, but fell short of the effect she had hoped for.

"We could help you by taking the long way to the boarding house."

She pressed her lips together. The last time he had taken her 'the long way' he had proposed. Was that his intent tonight? After the pleasant evening they had shared, she wasn't certain how she would answer.

"It's such a beautiful, clear night," he continued. "I thought we could leave behind the lights of town and do some star-gazing."

She shivered, partly from the cold but mostly from his romantic suggestion.

He took the road toward Ruth's place, but stopped when the town appeared only as points of dim light behind them, and no homesteads were visible. A faint spicy scent of sagebrush carried on the crisp air. Gradually, her eyes became accustomed to the dim moonlight.

C.J. hopped down and secured the reins. He came to Inga's side and helped her to the ground.

They strolled away from the carriage, holding hands.

Above them, a canopy of constellations shone bright in the dark sky. He wrapped an arm around her shoulders. With the other, he pointed to the North Star. "There's the Ursa Major. And Ursa Minor."

"And Pisces, Andromeda, and Cassiopeia." She gestured in the general direction of each.

He whipped around to face her. "You know the constellations!"

"Yes." She smiled. "After Halvor married my mother, he used to take us children outdoors on clear nights and point them out." The memory warmed her heart.

His teeth flashed white in his wide grin. "My father did the same thing."

She liked the idea that they had this childhood experience in common. "It's good to learn such things about the natural world as a child," she observed. "Sometimes, as an adult, I feel as if I've always known them."

"Someday we'll pass this knowledge on to our children."

The wistful note in his voice touched her heart, but she braced for the question she was not ready to answer. The mention of 'our children' was quite presumptuous—

Without warning, he claimed her lips with his and wrapped his arms around her shoulders.

The suddenness startled her but she didn't pull away. She slid her arms around his waist.

Heat radiated from her chest to the top of her head and the tips of her toes.

Teasing her lips apart with his tongue, he deepened the kiss. He tasted vaguely of wine and the chocolate cake they had shared for dessert.

Her knees weakened. She clung to him for support and allowed her thoughts to dissolve into the delightful sensations rippling through her. He crushed her to him, the buttons of their overcoats clinking together. She feared she might swoon.

Abruptly, he broke the kiss.

"It's time to take you home." His raspy voice whispered, his breath tickling her ear. Holding her upper arms, he took a step back.

Wishing she could stay in his embrace forever, she nodded. "It's getting late and I have to teach in the morning."

On the trip home, they spoke of the upcoming Thanksgiving holiday, Inga's plans for her Christmas party, and other innocuous topics.

When they reached the boarding house, he hitched the horse to the post and escorted her inside.

He gently brushed his gloved fingers over her cheek. "I'll look forward to seeing you Wednesday."

Her gaze met his. "Thank you for a perfect evening."

When he had left and she was snuggled in bed under her warm blankets, she replayed the evening in her mind. She could no longer deny that she loved C.J. Wakefield. But, was she ready to give up the career she had worked so hard for to marry him?

After Thanksgiving dinner, Inga, Ruth, and Mrs. Wakefield washed and dried the dishes while C.J. and his father went outside to finish the evening chores.

"That was a wonderful dinner. Thank you for inviting me." Inga handed the dried plate to her hostess and picked up the bowl Ruth had just rinsed. The fading scents of roasted turkey and cinnamon still hung in the air.

"No need to thank me." Mrs. Wakefield smiled. "You and Ruth helped a lot with the cooking."

"But we do need to thank *you* for the cases of oranges and grapefruit." Ruth grinned at Inga. "Your gift gave me a chance to tell C.J. what to get me for Christmas."

"I was going to have a case of oranges sent to him as well." Inga ran the dish towel over the bowl one last time and set it on the counter. "But now that he's coming here, I don't think I will. I'm not sure how well they would travel back to Philadelphia."

"I'm so grateful for you invitation to Christmas dinner." Mrs. Wakefield turned to Inga. "Since C.J.'s here now for Thanksgiving, I wasn't expecting to have him home again so soon—"

The door burst open. C.J. and his father entered the kitchen with a gust of cold air.

Mr. Wakefield walked straight to the cookstove.

"The wind is very strong and cold tonight." C.J. removed his gloves and shrugged off his old coat, letting it drop to the floor. He sat on the low radiator under the window.

"Feels like snow might be on the way," Mr. Wakefield said.

Inga's gaze cut to him. "I hope it holds off long enough to get back to town before it starts."

"And for me to get back home." Ruth's brows knit together. "Is it okay with you if we leave first thing tomorrow morning, Inga?"

"Yes, of course."

"Or, you could wait and go back with me on Saturday." C.J. grinned, his expression hopeful.

It was tempting. They would have time alone on the trip to Laramie. Since she had arrived at the Wakefields, they'd only had a few private moments. Enough for a brief kiss. Her heart fluttered.

She gave him a soft smile. "Thank you, but I have papers to grade and lesson plans to review this weekend. I'll be going with Ruth tomorrow."

His expression showed his disappointment.

"Is there anything left of those pastries you brought, Inga?" Mr. Wakefield asked.

Ruth shifted her gaze to her mother. "I think there

are a few pieces."

"Do you want it tonight or for breakfast tomorrow?" Mrs. Wakefield picked up a cake pan covered with a dish towel.

"Tonight!" C.J. stood and crossed to the icebox. "Maybe with some warm milk."

Ruth took the pitcher her brother held out. "With chocolate in it."

Mrs. Wakefield heated the milk, added sugar, and shaved chocolate into it while Ruth set out the kringle and dessert plates.

"My men really like this pastry. Thank you for bringing it," she said. "You'll have to give me your recipe."

Inga smiled at her. "I'd be happy to. It had been a while since I made it, so I'm glad it turned out well."

Ruth poured the hot chocolate into mugs and set them on the table.

Everyone took their seats. C.J. sat beside Inga.

Not used to snacking after dinner, Inga delighted in the sweet chocolate.

"I'll be in town Saturday night so I can catch my Sunday morning train." C.J. set down his fork and turned to her. "Would you like to have dinner with me?"

The memory of their star-gazing sent warmth from her chest to her cheeks. "That would be lovely. Thank you for asking."

Beneath the table, his hand found hers, setting off sparks of awareness.

Saturday night could not come soon enough.

Chapter Twelve

Washington, D.C.
December 2, 1901

Dear Inga,

Thank you for your letter inviting us to come for Christmas. If I could wish us to Wyoming or anywhere removed from our life here, I would.

Herman's brother was lynched in Kentucky because he insisted on being allowed to vote last year. It was a shock to us because he was always mild-mannered, and we wouldn't have expected him to stand up for his rights. We were devastated, but proud.

As soon as we received the news, Herman went to Memphis to be with his family. He asked the authorities if they knew who had done the lynching. They said they didn't and gave the impression that they would do nothing to bring the men to justice. (No surprise.) The next night, Herman was severely beaten by white-robed and masked Ku Klux Klan men. He remained at his brother's house for two months until he was able to travel. I am thankful he is back and alive. My sister-in-law, along with her baby and toddler, accompanied Herman home. When she and her children returned to Memphis, my sister-in-law didn't feel safe there. They are staying with us for now. Ida has been helping make arrangements to move their things here, since she still has contacts in Memphis.

Ever since the Supreme Court's Plessy v. Ferguson decision, many states and cities have enacted 'separate but equal' laws (which are usually anything but equal) and requirements for passing tests on obscure questions or paying poll taxes to discourage black men from voting.

And, of course, NAWSA is moving in that direction as well. Negro women are being excluded in many places, especially in the south, so large numbers of them are continuing their effort through Negro women's clubs. Things have changed so much since the Iowa convention that you probably wouldn't recognize the organization if you decided to become an active member again.

I feel as if our country is moving backward instead of forward in the area of race relations. It would be good if our new president would take steps to improve the situation. He did invite Booker T. Washington to dine with him at the White House, so I'm cautiously optimistic.

I'm sorry to send you such a bleak letter, especially with Christmas approaching. I hope your dinner goes well, and that you'll have a joyous holiday.
Lovingly in friendship,
Rachel

In the week since Inga received Rachel's letter, she had been able to think of little else. A vague nausea overcame Inga at the thought of a lynching. How horrible for Rachel to learn that someone in her family was hanged for trying to exercise his legal right to vote. And to have the crime go unpunished added to the horror.

On top of that, the assault on her husband would probably also go unpunished. Inga's anger flared again. What has happened in our country? It is supposed to be governed by equal justice under our laws.

Inga sighed. If Rachel was here, she would point out the naiveté of those ideas, but Inga couldn't help what she believed.

Poor Rachel. She was most likely supporting her recovering husband and his brother's family on her salary alone. No wonder Inga hadn't heard from her friend in over a year.

Inga had ordered a case of oranges to be sent to Rachel as she did every Christmas, but she ached to do more to help her friend. But what?

One evening, when Inga took a few minutes away from grading term papers to work on her shopping list for Christmas dinner, a solution occurred to her. She would send Rachel a crate with all the fixings for the menu Inga planned to serve that could safely be shipped to Washington, D.C.

Pleased with her solution, Inga returned to the assignments her students had turned in.

What if Rachel considered the gift to be charity? The thought yanked Inga out of the paper she was reading. Pondering the question, she put the report aside and stood. She took the back stairway down to the kitchen.

Mary sat at the sink, peeling potatoes.

"A friend I invited for Christmas will be unable to come to Wyoming." Inga walked to the counter so she could see Mary's face. "I would like to send her the ingredients to make a similar dinner."

"How are you going to do that?" Mary stopped peeling and met Inga's gaze.

"I thought I'd ship canned meats, fruits, and vegetables so she can make a meal similar to the one we'll be having. And I'll also send pickled herring and crackers." Inga paused. "Although I don't know if she likes them."

Mary shook her head. "I'm not sure if I'll like them, either."

"It's a Danish tradition I grew up with." Inga smiled. "You don't have to eat them." Her smile faded. "I would appreciate it if I could use the kitchen this weekend to make bread, kringle, and cookies to send along."

"That'll be fine." Mary resumed her peeling. "And you'll be making everything again for Christmas here?"

"Yes, and tomorrow I'll check train schedules and transport requirements. And I'll try to find a small trunk to ship everything in so it will really be a surprise."

The dining table in the boarding house had been

stretched to its full length by the addition of leaves. Two appended smaller tables reached into the parlor. All fourteen guests, Mary, and Inga were seated together, cheerfully conversing as they dined.

Ruth and Mrs. Wakefield had contributed glazed carrots and a dish with onions and cheese. One of the female students had made a German fruit bread called stollen, another had provided a British fruitcake. Three of the men brought bottles of wine, and another provided a box of chocolates. Along with the menu Inga had planned and prepared with Mary's help, there was more food than sixteen people could eat.

"What a wonderful feast!" Mrs. Wakefield exclaimed as the meal was winding down.

Ruth grinned. "All the better since we didn't have to prepare it."

Inga smiled, but she couldn't help wondering for the dozenth time if Rachel and her family were enjoying a similar meal. "Let's retire to the parlor and sing carols."

"Betsy, Florence, Ida, and I will do the dishes while you do that," said Nancy, who had not contributed food.

From the surprised look on the other girls' faces, Inga surmised that Nancy had not discussed the plan with her cohorts. But after all the cooking, baking, and dishwashing of the past two days, Inga wasn't going to argue. "Is that all right with you, Mary?"

"Yes, but I'll help." Mary grinned. "Or at least supervise."

"Thank you." Inga's gaze drifted over the women. "All of you."

"We'll leave the breads," Mary said. "And when we're finished, we'll put the desserts on the table along with clean plates."

C.J. made a noise that sounded like a fake groan. "I forgot about dessert."

Inga fixed her gaze on him. "Maybe we'll have to enjoy some dancing to work off the meal." She stood.

"But we'll start with carols."

She led the way to the parlor and seated herself at the piano, where she had placed her old sheet music. Her mother had taught her to play these songs. A pang of homesickness came over her. Suppressing it, she sat down and played the introductory notes to *Hark! The Herald Angels Sing.*

As she progressed, the others joined in. C.J. and his father sang harmony, with clear, strong baritones.

O Little Town of Bethlehem, Silent Night, Away in a Manger. By the time she got to *Deck the Halls*, she realized the women in the kitchen were singing along.

She kept playing until she had exhausted the supply of carols, concluding with *Jingle Bells.* The women who had done the dishes joined them. Throughout, the guests wandered in and out of the dining room, snacking on the various desserts.

"You said there is going to be dancing?" Betsy asked, her gaze resting on C.J.

"If you'd like to." Inga also gazed at C.J.

"Oh, yes," Betsy cooed.

Inga fought down a pang of jealousy.

"C'mon, boys." Mary gestured them to her. "Let's move these tables out of the way."

While they moved the smaller tables out of the room and eased the dining table away from the wide doorway with the pocket doors, Inga switched her carol sheet music for waltzes and polkas.

After she had played several pieces, the men rotating through the female partners, Florence tapped Inga on the shoulder. "Would you mind if I play for awhile?"

"I'd love it." Inga stood and flexed her fingers.

Florence sat down on the stool, played a few scales, then picked up the next sheet on the pile of music.

C.J. moved to Inga's side. "I'm so glad she offered to play."

Notes of the *Peacock Waltz* rose and C.J. took Inga in his arms. Mr. Wakefield partnered with his wife. One of the students invited Mary, another paired with Ruth.

Pulling Inga close, C.J. rested his cheek against the crown of her head. He smelled of soap and pine. She relaxed and enjoyed the warmth of his closeness.

"I'm not sure if we'll get any time alone today," he whispered above her ear. "But I'll be back in town Friday to catch a Saturday train. Have dinner with me."

"Of course." She smiled into his shoulder. Although she missed sharing Christmas with her relatives, she had enjoyed the day. C.J., his parents, and Ruth had been so kind that Inga was beginning to feel as though she was part of their family.

C.J. was pleased that Inga was wearing the necklace he'd given her last Christmas. The memories of sharing the holiday with her family brought a smile to his lips.

Holding her in his arms, he knew she was the woman he wanted to be with for the rest of his life. Unfortunately, it was nearly impossible to court her with almost two thousand miles between them. He drew her closer, sending a jolt of awareness through his body.

Apparently, she shared the feeling, because she nestled her head against his shoulder.

Had this been a public ball, they would have had to maintain an appropriate distance. Perhaps they should have done so here, too, since some of Inga's students were present. But Inga hadn't pulled away, so she must not be worried about what they thought.

If only he had thought to bring mistletoe.

His parents waltzed past. So did Ruth, in the arms of a student. A couple of the students had paired up to dance. Laughter and conversation of the others wove through the piano notes.

The pianist finished the waltz and began a polka.

"Shall we get some refreshments?" C.J. asked.

Inga smiled. "Yes. A sip of cider sounds good right now."

He took her elbow and they made their way around

the dancers to the dining room. She poured them each a glass of apple cider. He snagged a cookie with sugar and a pecan on top.

The brunette flirt, who had been staring at him most of the day, sauntered up to the spread of desserts. Her eyelashes fluttered as she gazed at him.

C.J. tensed. He forced himself to bite into the cookie and washed it down with cider.

"Are you going to dance with anyone besides Miss Stryker?" she asked. Her coquettish smile irritated him.

He glanced at Inga. Her lips were a thin, grim line.

"My sister again, maybe, if she insists." C.J. forced a grin. "Otherwise, no. I am courting Miss Stryker and have no interest in partnering with anyone else."

The student raised a brow.

Inga blushed. She had told him that she wanted to keep their association a secret. After today, the students would have been speculating anyway. C.J. munched on another bite of cookie.

The girl turned to Inga. "Are you engaged?"

"Not that it's any of your business." Inga's glance flitted to C.J., then back to the student. "No, we are not."

But if C.J. could convince her to accept his ring, they would be after Friday.

Festive candles and evergreens with red bows adorned the restaurant tables. Across from Inga, C.J. discreetly pulled a needle from a bough and bent it. The needle did not break.

"See?" Inga smiled. It was nice to be right. "It's fresh. It wouldn't be this fragrant if it was dry."

C. J. shook his head. "I didn't expect the proprietors to replace the decorations, now that Christmas is past."

The waiter cleared away their dishes and headed for the kitchen.

"That reminds me." She reached for her handbag and removed the envelope. "I have something for you."

She handed the article across the table. "I meant to

give this to you on Christmas."

He tucked the envelope into his inside coat pocket. She had expected him to at least look at the title.

"It's about the temperance movement," she offered.

He raised a brow. "For or against?"

"I tried to give arguments on both sides, so I think it comes off neutral."

His gaze locked on her. "Are you personally for or against it?"

Inga shrugged. "As I was writing the story, I realized I don't feel strongly one way or the other." She picked up her glass and regarded the rich dark liquid. "I would miss wine, though."

"So would I." He grinned. "Not to mention bourbon and brandy."

She chuckled. "Are you a secret lush?"

He laughed, too. "No, but I enjoy the occasional libation." He tipped his head to the left. "What are you going to write about next?"

"Lynchings." She tried to keep her voice quiet. Although the room was not crowded, there was an older couple at a nearby table.

C.J.'s eyes widened. "Why did you choose that subject?"

"Rachel's brother-in-law was lynched for voting." Inga told him about her friend's letter.

"You're writing about him?" He rubbed his chin. "A Negro."

"Not just him, and I'm not mentioning his name. But I found an article about one in Omaha in the early 1890's that I remembered hearing about. And, there have been several lynchings of whites in Wyoming, including a husband and wife about a decade ago." Her voice was rising. She cleared her throat and lowered her volume. "My point is that we profess to believe in the rule of law, but lynching is a lawless act."

His shoulders rose and fell. "Sounds pretty controversial, but we'll take a look at it when you send it in."

She clenched her teeth. Sometimes C.J. and Mr. Bender could be too safe in their decisions. *The Chronicle* could become even more successful if they were willing to publish more provocative articles, like those that regularly appeared in *Mc Clure's*.

The waiter appeared with the check and a coffee pot. "Would you care for coffee?"

C.J. caught her gaze.

She shook her head.

"No, thank you," he said.

The waiter left.

"Are you ready to leave?" C.J. asked.

"Yes."

He came around to help with her chair. "Are your fellow boarders back, or will we have your parlor to ourselves?"

"Eliza will be back Monday. Bertha after the first of the year." Inga stood. "Mary usually spends evenings in her room or the kitchen, so we should have it to ourselves."

C.J. paid the check and retrieved their wraps. When they were properly bundled against the cold, he escorted her to the waiting buggy and helped her into it. He untied the horses and joined her on the seat. Before starting the team moving, he reached behind the seat and retrieved a clump of something leafy that Inga couldn't identify. He held it to the ceiling of the carriage, over her head.

"What's that?" She squinted, trying to identify it in the dim streetlight filtering into the cab. "Mistletoe?"

"Mistletoe," he said at the same time. "You know what that means."

She swallowed. "Here? In front of the hotel?"

He looked left, forward, and right, exaggerating the movement. "There's no one around, so I'll settle for a quick one here. But you have to promise me a proper kiss later."

Her heartbeat quickened.

"I promise," she murmured as his lips met hers, filling her with warmth.

A few minutes later, C.J. halted the horses in front of Inga's boarding house. He held the reins under his foot in case the horses took a notion to move.

Once again he pulled out the mistletoe.

"You don't need that." Her voice was quiet. She eased closer to him. "I already promised you a proper kiss."

Her face was mostly in shadow. Too bad the night wasn't brighter. He slipped off his gloves and positioned a hand gently on each of her cheeks. She shivered under his touch, although his fingers were still warm. He leaned toward her until their foreheads met.

"I love you, Inga Stryker," he whispered.

"And I love you."

He barely heard her words over the pounding of his heart. It was the first time she had said them.

His mouth claimed hers. She tasted vaguely of wine, but sweeter.

Heat surged through his core. He nibbled at her lips until they parted, allowing him to deepen the kiss. The tightening in his groin began to ache.

Reluctantly, he drew back.

"We'd better go inside." His voice came out hoarse. He cleared his throat. Clutching the reins, he eased himself out of the cab. The cold air smacked him in the face. As he secured the horses, he realized he'd left his gloves in the cab.

Moving slowly to compose himself before they went into her boarding house, he returned to the driver's side.

"Need your gloves?" Inga asked, holding them up.

"Yes, thank you."

Before putting them on, he patted the cube in his pocket. Finding it secure, he walked to the passenger side and helped Inga down.

He escorted her into the entry hall and helped her out of her cloak, hanging it on the rack. She strode into the parlor and switched on the lamp, sending a subtle green light through the stained-glass shade. He draped his coat over a hook and joined her in the room.

She took his hand and led him to the sofa. He waited until she was seated.

Still clasping her fingers, he knelt, gazing up at her. "Inga, I love you and I want you to be my wife."

Her eyes widened. She shifted her position.

"I know you don't want to leave Laramie, and I've sprung this on you." He swallowed. "But even so, I want you to think about the possibility of marrying me. We could be like a ship captain I know and his wife. He goes out to sea for a month or two at a time, then comes home for a few weeks." C.J. rushed on before he lost his nerve. "I could come back here every month or two, and you could come to Philadelphia for summers. When you're ready, you could come to live with me permanently." He swallowed again. "Or we can have a long engagement. I just want you to be mine."

Her chest rose and fell, but she kept her liquid gaze locked on his. His knees trembled.

"Oh, C.J." She choked on the words, laying her hand on her chest.

He pulled the velvet box from his pocket and opened it to reveal his grandmother's diamond wedding ring. "Please, Inga." He held the ring toward her. "Please accept this ring and promise to marry me someday."

A tear slipped down her cheek. "Yes. I promise."

The next morning, Inga strode into the jeweler's shop on C.J.'s arm. She hadn't slept a wink last night, but nonetheless, energy and excitement filled her this morning.

C.J.'s proposal had surprised her, but her acceptance had surprised her more. Still, she did not regret her answer. They had time. He had said that. And, in her sleepless hours, she had decided that as long as the university had no objection and they didn't have children, she and C.J. could manage the separations their respective jobs required. After all, her great-grandfather had been a ship captain. Like C.J.'s friend, he and his wife had lived apart much of the time, but Moder had always spoken reverently of their marriage and tried to replicate it with her second husband, Halvor.

"My grandmother's ring is too large for my fiancée's finger," C.J. said, handing over the velvet box that held the ring.

Warmth spread into her cheeks even though she liked the sound of 'my fiancée.' And she had been very moved to learn that the ring had belonged to his beloved grandmother.

The jeweler's gray moustache wiggled as his grin widened. "So, congratulations are in order." He turned to Inga, his eyes twinkling. "Best wishes to you, Miss Stryker."

She removed her gloves and gave him a demure smile. "Thank you, Mr. Converse."

"I've known your intended from his boyhood." He tipped his head in C.J.'s direction. "He's a good man."

Inga chuckled. "Did he pay you to say that?"

The jeweler guffawed. "You've got yourself a pistol here, C.J. Good for you."

He turned back to Inga. "I need to measure your finger, young lady."

She held out her hand.

"Did my repair to the clasp on your necklace hold for you?" he asked, slipping the tape around her finger.

"Yes. It has been fine. Thank you."

He made a note of her size. "Shall I measure you for your wedding band, C.J.? While you're in town."

C.J. shrugged. "I suppose."

He held out his hand.

Flustered by the reality dawning on her, Inga turned to the jeweler. "It might be a while before we actually wed."

He shot her a benign smile. "I'll keep his size on file until we need it."

She drew in a steadying breath. "Thank you."

"I'll have your engagement ring ready on Monday. You can pick it up, then."

"I will, sir." She slid her hands into her gloves and picked up her handbag.

When they were back outside on the board sidewalk, C.J. turned to her. "My train leaves in a little more than an hour, and I have already checked in my bags." He paused. "I'd love to have you see me off, but if it's too cold, I'll walk you back to the boarding house."

Inga considered her options. She wished he wasn't leaving so soon. "The wind isn't bad today. I'd be happy to see you off."

Side by side, they strolled toward the depot.

As they approached Kleeman's confectionary, C.J. picked up the pace. "Let's stop here. I want to get some snacks for the train."

"Good idea," Inga agreed. "I want to take some sweets home for Mary as a thank-you for her help with the Christmas celebration."

After choosing from the array of candies, C.J. paid the bill. Inga slipped her box into her handbag.

They left and proceeded toward the depot.

"Valentine's Day is on Friday this coming year," C.J. said as they walked. "I was thinking we could meet in Omaha or Denver or Cheyenne for the weekend."

Inga raised a brow. "Why?"

"Because we can spend more time together and try new restaurants." He lowered his voice. "People won't know us and gossip about us."

"By then, people here will know we're engaged." She lifted her chin. "I'm not sure I'd want to do anything that would create gossip."

"Everything we do here is talked about, and often embellished," he argued. "You know that."

She did. Eliza and Bertha often asked her to refute or verify tales they'd heard. She nodded. "I wouldn't want to go farther than Cheyenne. I'll have to teach the following Monday, and since it will still be winter, I don't want to be stranded far away."

"Cheyenne, it is." He stopped and turned to face her, wearing a wicked grin. "We could pretend we're married." His eyes flashed. "No one there will know the difference."

She put a hand on her hip. "I would know."

His grin became sheepish. "We could get married secretly. I could make arrangements with a Justice of the Peace. No one here would have to know."

She shivered, finding the suggestion enthralling. "I like that idea."

Chapter Thirteen

January 25, 1902
Laramie, Wyoming

Dear Rachel,

Thank you for your note. I'm glad you enjoyed your Christmas dinner. Mine was pretty successful, as well, although I don't think inviting the students was one of my better ideas. I probably won't do it again.

Since your previous letter, I haven't been able to get the subject of lynchings out of my mind. I have written to Mrs. Wells Barnett for information and have been collecting newspaper pieces on them. My editor is skeptical about such an article for The Chronicle, *but I think I can write a compelling story if I include cases of both Negroes and whites. There was a couple here in Wyoming who were lynched without a trial, most likely by owners or employees of big cattle outfits who wanted their land and cattle.*

My Boomerang *editor won't publish anything I write about lynchings. He warned me to be careful of how I word the Wyoming part, as the men who own those cattle ranches are very powerful. And ruthless. But I am determined to produce something so compelling that* The Chronicle *will publish it.*

I might have some extra influence with the magazine editor, as I am now engaged to him. We have not set a wedding date. I thought I was in no hurry, but now that we've made the commitment, I find myself becoming impatient. C.J. is a good man, and I really like his family, so I am happy with the betrothal. My mother, however, is ecstatic. I think she had given up hope that I would ever marry.

Speaking of magazines, your letter mentioned you were going to meet with the editor of the new (or new to me, at least) Colored American Magazine. *I hope it went well. Did she offer you a position?*

Most likely, I will spend some of my summer in

Philadelphia. I hope we can get together while I am there.
Lovingly in friendship,
Inga

A dusting of fresh snow gave the depot and its Cheyenne surroundings a clean, crisp aura—a cold, but perfect setting for a very special romantic weekend. C.J.'s worries about an impending blizzard had been unfounded.

In the last rays of daylight, he spotted Inga as she stepped off the train. Even in her dark cloak, she looked like a petite princess, with her erect posture and her blond curls peeking out around her hood.

Picking his way through the others who were meeting passengers, he waved to her.

She caught his gaze and smiled, sending a spark of electricity through him.

He still had a hard time believing that she had agreed to become his wife. Tomorrow.

"Happy Valentine's Day, my one, true valentine." He wrapped an arm around her shoulders and gave her a quick hug.

"And Happy Valentine's Day to you." Her blue eyes sparkled in the light from the depot.

"Did you have a pleasant trip?" he asked, taking her satchel and shepherding her toward the depot.

"Yes." She slipped her hand through the crook of his arm. "It was still snowing in Laramie when we left."

"It stopped here about half an hour ago." He escorted her through a door held open by a railroad employee. "Did you check a bag?"

"Yes."

They moved toward an empty space near the wall. She reached into her handbag and retrieved her claim ticket.

He set down her satchel and held out his hand. "I'll collect it, and we'll get you checked into the hotel."

When Inga had settled into her room at the Inter

Ocean Hotel, C.J. knocked at her door. She answered, wearing a fresh dress in emerald green. "Would you like to have dinner or go to the theatre and catch a bite afterward?"

She pursed her lips while considering her options. "Let's go to the theatre."

After helping her into her cloak, he took her arm, and they walked down the stairs and into the night.

"I've brought along an article for you." Her voice was uncharacteristically tentative. "It's the one about lynchings."

C.J.'s muscles tensed. He forced his jaw to relax. "How did it turn out?"

"I think it's general enough for your *Chronicle* subscribers." She sighed. "But I hope they'll find it interesting. And that it will make them think about how awful and unlawful lynchings are."

Her words ran through his mind as if a printed subtitle. "Awful and unlawful?" He grinned. "Did you think of how that would look on the page, with awful, being the last part of unlawful?"

She chuckled. "I was just describing the story. I don't think I wrote those words together in the text." She paused. "If I did, you have my permission to revise it."

"Thank you," he said with exaggerated politeness. "Even though I'll be your husband, I'm also still your editor."

"I know." Her tone was pensive. "And I'm still not sure how that will work."

He gave her elbow a gentle squeeze. "We'll figure it out together."

Inga was glad that C.J. had suggested a restaurant close to the hotel after the play. She had gotten up early to be sure everything was packed and ready to go after she finished teaching her morning classes. They only reason she had agreed to come on a Friday was because her afternoon was free.

But the hour was late, and she was tired. She didn't feel much like eating. Butterflies had been swarming in her stomach all day.

C.J. set his fork on his now-empty plate. From across the table, he studied her. "You're very quiet tonight. Are you feeling all right?"

Inga managed a small smile and clasped her hands together in her lap. "I'm fine. It's just been a long day."

He frowned. "I was afraid you might be getting cold feet."

So was she, but she didn't want to admit it. "I'm not."

"Good." His facial muscles slackened.

"In the seven weeks of our engagement, I've thought through all the options and possibilities in as rational a way as I could, given that I love you." She took a calming breath. "I came to realize that you're very important to me. Maybe the most important part of my life."

He was staring at her, his eyes wide.

She lifted the corners of her mouth upward. "And not just because you're my editor. It was quite a revelation."

"You're very important to me, too," he said in a hoarse voice.

His words warmed her. "That's good since we're going to be husband and wife."

"I've made an appointment with the Justice of the Peace for ten o'clock tomorrow morning and with a photographer for half past one in the afternoon." His gaze didn't waver.

She smiled. "I'll be ready."

Her thoughts darted to her handbag, where she had tucked the box with his wedding ring into the bottom. When she had gone in to the jeweler's shop to order it, Mr. Converse had confided that C.J. had already purchased a band for her. She had asked him to match it as closely as possible, but to make it wider and masculine-looking. He had created a work of art. She hoped C.J. would think so, too.

"Have you told your parents?"

His grave expression struck her as humorous. She stifled a smile. "No. My mother will be furious that we've kept this secret, but I'm not ready to tell her. At least not yet."

His eyes widened. "Are you sure? We could call her tomorrow when it's done."

"No. I'll be living like—how did you put it?—a sea captain's wife. No one needs to know." Inga allowed her grin to break through. "She'll want us to have a church ceremony and party at their home."

"We can do that sometime next summer, maybe."

Inga shrugged. "Or maybe in a year or two. Have you told your parents?"

"No." He fiddled with his fork. "They'd want us to get married in their church and have the marriage published in the paper."

He seemed as nervous about their plan as she was. Maybe they shouldn't go through with it. "I feel bad about keeping our wedding from Ruth."

"Me, too." He looked up at her. "Maybe we could tell her next summer."

"I'd like that." Inga held his gaze. "And, I'd like to tell the college president in confidence. In case of rumors."

C.J. gazed at his bride as she repeated the vows the Justice of the Peace read. Blond and petite, she was wearing a dusky-blue dress, with a sailor-style collar trimmed in white lace. Matching white lace trimmed the skirt. Her hat was a feminine version of a blue top hat, with white flowers around the brim.

The outfit not only displayed her trim figure, but it reflected her discreet sense of humor. She had latched onto the idea of being like a ship captain's wife and her fashionable apparel subtly reflected that fact.

He was glad he had purchased a new suit for the occasion.

The Justice leaned toward C.J. and whispered, "Are there rings?"

"Yes," C.J. replied. Inga nodded.

"Mr. Wakefield, slip the ring on her finger and

repeat after me, 'With this ring I the wed.'"

With shaking hands, C.J. did so. Inga's fingers were icy cold.

"Miss..." The official looked down at the paper he held. "Stryker. Please do the same."

She reached into a hidden pocket in her skirt and produced a ring. As she slipped it on his finger, she vowed, "With this ring, I thee wed."

The ring hitched on his knuckle. He helped her slide it into place.

"By the authority vested in me by the state of Wyoming, I now pronounce you man and wife." The justice's official voice echoed softly off the walls of the nearly empty wood-paneled chamber.

A smile broke across Inga's face, so warm it melted C.J.'s heart.

"I'm sorry to hurry you, but we need to sign the marriage certificates, so I can move on to my next appointment." The justice moved to an oak table where a series of papers were spread. The couple he had brought in to witness the ceremony joined him.

C.J. took Inga's hand and led her toward the small group. When all the legal papers were signed, the justice shook C.J.'s hand. "Congratulations, Mr. Wakefield." He nodded to Inga. "Best wishes, Mrs. Wakefield."

Mrs. Wakefield. C.J. liked the sound of that.

Pink bloomed in her cheeks. "Thank you."

The older woman witness slid three marriage certificates into a large envelope and handed it to Inga. "I hope you'll be very happy."

C.J. hoped so, too.

"Thank you." Inga flashed her bright smile to the stranger, then to C.J.

Pride and love swelled his chest.

How he wished they would have more than just one day together before they'd have to part tomorrow.

Later that afternoon, Inga relaxed into the overstuffed chair in her hotel room. She leaned her head back and closed her eyes. Inga Wakefield. How long would it be before she could use her new name openly? Or wear her lovely new wedding band? Maybe years if they continued their ship captain arrangement for that long.

She removed her shoes, then rose and slipped off her bodice and skirt. She unbuttoned her blouse and loosened her front-laced corset. After removing all but her drawers and chemise, she donned a clean blouse and a loose-fitting skirt. Still barefooted, she curled up on the chaise and picked up the novel she had begun on yesterday's train ride.

A knock sounded at the door before she had even read a chapter. C.J. entered the room, carrying his trunk, his valise resting on top. He set them in the corner, then crossed to Inga.

"I took the marriage certificate to the front desk and explained that I was moving my things into your room since it is larger than mine."

Still attired in his new, gray-pinstriped suit, he unbuttoned his jacket and vest, and carefully draped them over the back of a straight chair. "I also ordered dinner to be delivered in a couple hours."

"That sounds wonderful." She smiled and scooted over to make room for him.

"You look comfortable, my beautiful wife." He claimed the spot she had made for him. "As soon as I receive the photographs, I will send one to you." He took her hands in his.

"Thank you." She gave his fingers a gentle squeeze. "I will look forward to seeing the rest in the summer."

His heartbeats quickened. "I suppose we could tell everyone they are our engagement pictures. Then we could have them sent to you. That wouldn't disclose our secret."

"It's better if they go to you." She sighed. "Fewer questions."

"I'll still be calling you every Friday, so if we decide to tell our parents I can bring the ones we got for them when I come back at Easter." He could hardly wait to tell their families. "If you like, I can bring all the pictures so you can see them."

She considered the idea for a moment. "No, I don't want to risk them being damaged." She grinned. "Besides, they'll give me a reason to go to Philadelphia next summer."

He blinked. "Are you saying that your husband isn't reason enough?"

By his tone, she wasn't sure whether he was joking or not.

She slipped a hand from his and gave his shoulder a playful push. "I'll be spending the greater part of the next few months with only your photograph. By June, I'll be ready to be with the flesh-and-blood you again."

The cold wind blew across the platform outside the Cheyenne depot. Memories of last night's consummation of their marriage helped ward off the chill. Inga was tempted to exchange her ticket for one to Philadelphia and call the university tomorrow to resign. But she couldn't leave the president in a lurch in the middle of the term.

She gazed at C.J.'s handsome face, memorizing every line and plane so she could conjure him in her mind while they were apart. Her chest ached.

He took her hands in his. "I'll call you Friday."

The train whistle blasted out the call for all passengers to board.

A repressed sob strangled her goodbye. All she could do was nod.

He gave her a quick kiss on her forehead.

She blinked back her tears, but one trickled down her cheek.

He picked up her satchel, then took her elbow and escorted her to the railcar.

"I'll see you in about five weeks." He handed her onto the step and pushed her case up so she could reach it.

"Farewell." She choked out the word. "I love you."

A sad smile crossed his face. "I love you, too, Mrs. Wakefield."

She turned and rushed inside before she broke into tears. Finding a seat by the window, she searched the crowd on the platform until she found C.J. She waved.

He waved back.

Her breath fogged the glass. Tears blurred her vision.

When she had agreed to marry and live as a sea captain's wife, she hadn't realized how hard parting with her husband would be.

The conductor came through the car, collecting tickets. When he reached the end of the row, he called: "All aboard."

Moments later, the train lurched forward, moved smoothly for a bit, then lurched again. The metal-on-metal sound of the wheels rolling over the rails was loud, and the movement settled into a gentle sway.

She rested her head against the cold window pane.

Her new husband had been a patient lover, gently guiding and responding to her at every turn. He had been careful to take precautions to prevent conception. Never had she imaged how marital relations could deepen her love for C.J. to the extent that they had.

Before leaving the hotel, she had tucked her wedding ring back into its velvet box and nestled it into the bottom of her handbag. She removed the handles from her arm and, through the heavy fabric, felt to be sure that the small box was still there. When she got back to her room, she would hide it and her copy of their marriage certificate for safekeeping in the secret compartment of the trunk her mother had given her.

She sighed and looped the handles back over her wrist.

Staring through the glass into the darkness, she tried to concentrate on her lecture plans for tomorrow. She felt numb.

Hopefully their separation would become easier over time.

C.J. brought the team to a halt near a small stand

of trees. The weather had grown warmer than he had expected for a late-March Saturday. And there had been much more traffic on the road to his parents' ranch than he had anticipated, probably because of tomorrow's Easter holiday.

He took Inga's hands in his and studied every inch of her.

"When you come to Philadelphia in the summer, we can buy a home of our own." C.J. kissed her fingertips. "I've already been looking at the types of houses that might be available and that we can afford."

Her gaze focused on his face. "Are there bigger apartments in your building?"

"I really don't want to continue living directly above work. There are a few openings on the upper floors, but they have only two bedrooms and we would still be renting. I think we should buy a home."

She shrugged and shifted her position. "You'll be the one living in it for the foreseeable future. Don't you want to be close to *The Chronicle*?"

"But you'll be there in the summers." He gave her a quick kiss on her cheek. "We can find something close to a streetcar line."

She chuckled. "I've been considering myself the one who's living as a ship captain's wife, but maybe it's really you."

He stared at her for a moment before laughing. "I guess we both are. You're here waiting for me in the fall and winter. I'll be in Philadelphia waiting for you in the spring."

The horses took a few steps forward. C.J. released her hands and pulled back on the reins until they halted then wrapped the leather straps around the rail in front of him.

"Are you thinking we should get a house in Laramie, too?"

After considering the question, he shook his head. "If we do that, we'll have to announce our marriage."

She frowned. "I don't want to do that, yet."

"It will mean we won't have anywhere in town to be alone." He put his hands on her cheeks. "Shall we tell Ruth? We could use her place to get a day or two alone together."

"Maybe. Will you be back again before I come to Philadelphia in June?"

"I'll try, but I can't promise." He drew her face to his and kissed her full pink lips. "You know we'll have to tell people there that we're married if we're going to live together."

She nodded. "I know. And I'm looking forward to being able to wear my wedding ring in public."

"Me, too." Heat surged through him. He wanted so much more than a kiss, but it wouldn't do for them to arrive at his parents' place looking disheveled.

The next day, Inga reveled in sharing Easter with her new family, although they didn't know yet that's what they were.

"Your engagement photograph is very nice." Mrs. Wakefield held a plate of biscuits toward Inga.

She took the dish and passed it on. She'd had two already. "Thank you."

"I'm surprised you went to Cheyenne to have it taken." A hint of accusation laced Ruth's words. She shifted her gaze from Inga to C.J. "Especially since you've known Fred Frick for a long time."

C.J. shrugged. "I thought there might be less gossip this way."

He bit into the biscuit he had selected.

Ruth shot him a skeptical glance, but said nothing more on the subject.

Inga caught her gaze. "I've been meaning to ask you how Jess is doing"

"Surprisingly well." Ruth grinned. "After two years, he's catching on to the routine so I don't have to spend so much time supervising or showing him how to do things."

"I'm glad to hear it." Inga released a breath she hadn't realized she was holding. "I've always felt responsible for you hiring him."

Ruth brightened. "You might be surprised to know that he has come around to supporting woman suffrage."

Inga's eyes widened. "Really? How did you convince him?"

"I offered him your articles on Theodore Roosevelt and *Boomerangs* that I had finished reading. He refused them." She paused. "I asked him how he would know who to vote for in the next election. He admitted that I know more about potential candidates than he does. And not only that I know more about those running for local offices, but I know more about the races for president and representative than he does because I read the papers." She rolled her eyes. "And he said I should just tell him who to vote for."

"That sounds like Jess."

"So I told him that you and many other women are also well-informed, and that you should have the same right to vote that I do." Ruth grinned. "To my surprised, he agreed."

"Congratulations." Inga chuckled. "I'm impressed with you, but disappointed in Jess's lack of interest."

Ruth and her parents discussed cattle, the winter weather and its effect on livestock. They talked over prospects for planting in the spring.

Thanks to the warmth of the Wakefield's dining room mingled with the satisfaction of having eaten a good meal, sleepiness engulfed Inga. She fought it, knowing that soon she would be plunged into freezing temperatures and relentless winds. After last night's light snowfall, daylight had revealed a crisp, sparkling landscape. Beautiful, as long as she was inside the ranch house looking out.

She sighed. "That was a wonderful dinner. Thank you for inviting me."

"You can ride back to town with me," Ruth offered.

Inga's gaze flew to C.J.

"I was going to take her," he replied.

Inga settled back on her chair.

"But if she goes with me, it will save you a trip,"

Ruth argued. "You can spend more time with Mom and Dad before you have to go back East."

C.J. scrubbed his hand over his face. "Yes, but I want to spend some more time with my—my—fiancé." He was blushing. "I won't get to see her again until summer."

Ruth grinned. "Sorry, I forgot that I will probably see her again before you do."

C.J. grimaced. "Rub it in."

"Children, children," Mrs. Wakefield admonished in an amused tone. "That will do."

Inga smiled.

"Son, you should marry the girl so you can spend your life with her," Mr. Wakefield said.

Every muscle in Inga's body tightened.

C.J.'s eyes grew wide. He coughed. "We only got engaged at Christmas."

"You could at least set a date." Mrs. Wakefield's demeanor had become more serious.

Inga's throat felt thick. She inhaled a breath. "We'll talk about it."

The driver of the electric cab delivered Inga to *The Chronicle*'s headquarters. C.J. met them at the door and helped the cabbie lug her large trunk into the elevator. She cringed. Her wedding photo, the silver bar her mother had given her, and two gold bars which she had purchased with the savings from her salary as a professor and her writing income were hidden in the secret compartment. They were heavy, and she feared the release mechanism might be damaged.

When the elevator door opened on the fifth floor, Nathan Bender stood among her smaller trunk, satchel, two crates, and valise.

He grinned. "Welcome, Mrs. Wakefield." He gestured to her luggage, which encompassed half of the hallway. "When I offered you a staff position, I didn't think you would actually be moving into your office."

"As soon as we purchase a home, we'll take this

stuff there." C.J. set down his end of the trunk and tipped the cabbie.

Inga turned to Mr. Bender. "I will leave the large trunk in my office, in case I have to go back and teach for the fall term, but we'll move out the rest."

"How did your boss take it when you told him you weren't going to renew your contract?" he asked.

She sighed. It had been a difficult conversation, because she loved teaching and President Smiley knew it. In the end, she had shared in confidence that she and C.J. were wed. "He was very professional. He wished me well at my new position, and said he would do his best to find someone to take my place before the fall term begins."

Nathan picked his way out of the maze of cases. "Do you think it likely that he will?"

"I think so."

Nathan gestured to the luggage behind him. "How much of this stuff can you fit into C.J.'s small place while you look for a house?"

"We can take up as much as she would have been able to fit in a hotel room." A surprising note of defensiveness wound through C.J.'s words.

Nathan's brow furrowed. "You know, you'll need to have a telephone in your house, since we'll no longer be able to run upstairs to reach you when we need to."

C.J. took a step closer to Inga. "We're planning on it."

"Good." Nathan's grin returned. He nodded to Inga. "I'm glad to have you here. Now C.J. won't have to be leaving so often. You can keep your things in your office for as long as you need to." He turned to C.J. "Both of you can take the next few days off to find a house. I'll try not to bother you unless an emergency comes up."

"Thank you," Inga and C.J. said in unison.

C.J. unlocked the door, and together they moved her things into her new office. The room was smaller than C.J.'s, but it had a desk with a typewriter that appeared to be new. In one corner was a filing cabinet.

On the wall across from the door, a good-sized window let in enough light so that, in the afternoon at least, she wouldn't need to turn on the lamp.

C.J. closed the door. "At least Nathan put you on the same floor as my office." He strode across the room and took Inga in his arms. "I tried to get him to move Adams down here, so you could be right next to me, but he wouldn't do it. Said we both might be too distracted."

"He might be right." Inga nestled into him, wondering if that explained the tension she had felt in the air between C.J. and Mr. Bender.

After a quick dinner across the street, Inga and C.J. carried her satchel and small trunk upstairs. His apartment wasn't much more than a large room. A room the size of a large closet adjoined with a toilet and washbasin. When he'd lived here alone, it had seemed just fine. After all, he didn't cook, and the community shower down the hall had been convenient enough. But now that his wife was here, his place seemed tiny.

She pulled a chair out from the table and set her satchel on it. "It will be nice not to have to go down the hall to use the water closet."

He stared at her as she pulled toiletries from her case. Light from the ceiling fixture danced on her blond hair. "I still can't believe you've agreed to live in Philadelphia, but I'm happy to have you here."

Her back still to him, she shrugged. "Mr. Bender's job offer and your letters about potential tutoring positions convinced me that I could pursue my career here." She turned to face him, grinning. "It didn't hurt that I found it very hard to say goodbye and to live apart after your Easter visit." Her grin faded. "I warned you that I'm not as strong as my great-grandmother."

He took a step forward and wrapped her in his arms. "You're stronger than you think. Look at what you've done, leaving a comfortable home in the boarding house, and a position you are familiar with, to move here to the unknown. I remember how hard it was when I came to work for Nathan—almost five years ago, now."

She pulled back enough to look up at him. Her blue gaze ignited heat in his chest that quickly radiated through his body. "Yes, but back then the magazine was new, and its future was uncertain."

"I was more worried about living in a big city." He kissed her forehead. "I had never done that before."

"But I have you to help me through that part." She snuggled back against him.

"I'll do my best." He kissed the top of her head. "I have four houses lined up for us to look at tomorrow, and you can chose the one you like best. All are close to streetcar lines, so it will be easy for us to get around town."

"Is there one you like best?" she asked.

"The streetcar row house. It's relatively new and large enough for our future family." He smiled. "And we could afford to purchase it without a mortgage."

"You know, since women are disenfranchised here, I'll have to become active in working for the cause again." She hated that she sounded almost apologetic.

He nodded. "I assumed as much, and I've already talked with Nathan about you needing the flexibility to do so."

"I hope neither of you will be bothered by my involvement."

He stroked her back. "We think it might give us some scoops on what the movement is up to."

"Whenever I can, without compromising the effort."

"Fair enough." He kissed the top of her head again.

"We're going to have to tell our parents soon that we're married," she murmured against his shoulder.

"When we move into our new house, we can tell them," he said into her hair, relishing the faint scent of roses. "Then we can give them our new address and telephone number."

"Good idea. I'll call Uncle Peder and arrange a time

for Moder to be at his house so we can talk." She pulled back and began unbuttoning the jacket of her travel outfit.

His heart pounded.

"Good idea." He echoed her words because he couldn't think of any of his own.

Tentatively, he reached out his aching fingers to unfasten the rest of her buttons.

For a moment she appeared puzzled. Then her smile slowly built.

When her jacket hung open, she reached out and unbuttoned his jacket.

It was all he could do to keep from grabbing her, tearing off her clothes, and satisfying his growing ache. But he held himself in tight rein.

They had the rest of their lives to be together. And the rest of their lives would begin tonight.

Chapter Fourteen

July 2, 1902
Philadelphia, Pennsylvania

Dear Sarah,

I am now in Philadelphia, permanently working for The Chronicle. *My article about lynchings will be in the next issue. Mr. Bender thinks it will be the most controversial story I have written and possibly one of the most controversial they have published, so we'll see what the response will be.*

Although I hated leaving Wyoming and teaching at the university, I am in love with C.J. Wakefield. We were married in February. (We are calling my parents tonight, and his parents tomorrow to disclose the secret.) Our original plan was to keep the wedding quiet and live apart most of the year, but after parting at Easter, I realized I wasn't strong enough for repeated separations.

We have purchased a row house not far from the magazine's offices. It is three floors, but very narrow—just one room wide on each floor. It will be large enough for when we have children, but I fear it will be too big for me to take care of, especially if I work five days each week at the magazine. I guess we could close off the third floor, since we don't yet have furniture for the first two. We are in the process of unpacking our things, but are sleeping in C.J.'s apartment until we purchase a bed.

Now that I live much closer to New York, I hope we will be able to get together more often than we have since college.

I am enclosing one of my newly-printed calling cards, with our new address and telephone number.

Hope to see you soon.
Lovingly in friendship,
Inga

Inga chewed her lower lip as she sat in one of the new cane-bottomed dining chairs, waiting for the telephone to ring. C.J. sat beside her holding her hand.

Secretly marrying had seemed like a good idea at the time, but she hadn't considered what it would be like to reveal the secret. She dreaded telling her mother, especially since her half-sister, Anesa, had run away three years ago and married Paul's friend from the army.

Although she hadn't disclosed to her uncle the reason she wanted to talk with Moder, Inga suspected he might have guessed when she told him she was calling from Philadelphia. Had he and her mother speculated when they'd set the date and time for the call?

C.J. pulled the watch from his pocket and clicked open the case. "Should be any minute now."

She frowned, staring down at the wedding ring she now wore with pride. "I know."

He gave her hand a gentle squeeze. "We've rehearsed this. It will be fine."

She pasted on a smile. "I sure hope you—"

The ring sounded.

She started, then picked up the receiver with a trembling hand.

"Hello." Her voice sounded timid, even to her.

"Hello, Inga," Moder's voice sounded tinny through the wire. "Is everything all right?"

Inga inhaled a deep breath. "Yes. I have some good news to tell you." She glanced at her husband. "C.J. and I are married."

"You're what? When?"

Inga grimaced. "We married in February—the day after Valentine's Day." Her words came out in a rush. "We didn't tell anyone since we thought we would be living apart for a long time, and I wasn't sure how people at the university or my boarding house would react."

"Did they find out and dismiss you?" Annoyance tinged her mother's voice. "Peder said you're in

Philadelphia."

"No." Inga sighed. "I decided I didn't want to live apart from my husband. I've taken a staff writer position at *The Chronicle*."

"What about your teaching?"

"I may do some tutoring for college students when the fall term starts, if I have time." The tension in her chest eased.

"Did you marry in a church?"

Again she tensed. She knew how important a church wedding was to her mother. "No. A Justice of the Peace married us in Cheyenne."

The phone line went silent.

"Moder?"

"I'm here." Her voice sounded weary. "I'm happy for you, my sweet. And I wish you the very best."

"Thank you." Inga went on to describe their new home, furniture shopping, and her agreement with the university.

"Will you be back for a visit this fall?" Moder asked.

Inga glanced at C.J. "Probably not until December. We'll spend Christmas with you and New Year's Day with the Wakefields, if that works for you and Halvor."

"That will be wonderful. We'll look forward to it."

"So will we." Inga smiled at C.J.

"Inga? I have a favor to ask of you. Or you can consider it your Christmas present to me."

"What?" Inga's muscles tensed again.

"Will you and C.J. agree to remarry in the church?" She paused. "Or in my house with the pastor officiating? It would mean a lot to me."

Inga's mother had always regretted having only a civil wedding to her father, but Inga hadn't considered how she felt about it. "I'll discuss it with C.J."

After giving her mother their new address, Inga ended the call.

She turned to her husband. "She wants us to have a religious wedding when we go at Christmas. How would you feel about that?"

He hooked a lock of her hair behind her ear. "I wouldn't mind. If that's what you want."

She caught and held his gaze. "Do you think your parents and Ruth would come?"

He frowned. "I doubt it." Then a chuckle escaped him. "But they might want us to do the whole thing all over again when we get to Wyoming."

Inga was thankful for the restaurant's warmth. The late September morning had been cool, and her office was chilly since the boilers in the building were not yet being fired up. Nathan had said he wanted to be sure there wouldn't be a late-season heat wave before starting the furnace.

"I'm not sure how I'll ever be able to keep up my house, with working at the magazine and getting more involved with the suffrage movement." Inga watched as Rachel tore off a piece of her dinner roll and spread it with butter.

"Are you planning to hire a housekeeper?" Rachel asked before popping the bread into her mouth.

"I guess I haven't thought seriously about it." Inga shrugged. "Mostly the idea comes to me when the hour is late and I still have cleaning to do or dishes to wash."

Rachel smiled. "Well, if you decide you want to hire someone, I'd like to recommend my cousin. My aunt—the one I stay with when I come to Philadelphia—has a daughter who would be good. She has worked alongside her mother, who cooks and cleans for a prominent family here in the city."

"How old is she?" Inga set down her fork and dabbed her mouth with her napkin.

"She's seventeen, I think." Rachel pressed her lips together. "Maybe eighteen. She graduated from high school last spring, and she wants to earn enough money to go to college."

Inga tipped her head to the side. "So she won't want to keep the job indefinitely."

"No." Rachel frowned. "But I'm sure she'll help you

find a replacement. Maybe her sister, who is three years younger."

"I'll talk with C.J. about it tonight." The more Inga thought about having someone to help with the house, the more she liked the idea. "Would she want to stay at our house or just come in for the days?"

Rachel shook her head. "I don't know. I think my aunt stays where she works a couple nights each week and comes home the rest of the week, but I'm sure Minnie will do whatever you want her to."

Inga's anticipation built as they discussed the topic. "How would I get in touch with her for an interview?"

"You need to talk to C.J., and I probably should talk with Minnie before offering her services." Rachel smiled wryly. "Before I leave for Washington tomorrow, I'll drop you a note and tell you if she's interested. If she is, I'll give you her address."

"That will be perfect. I'll talk with C.J. as soon as I get back to the office." Whether or not they hired Minnie, Inga was now determined to find a housekeeper.

Rachel rested her utensils on her plate. "Have you been getting involved with NASWA again?"

Inga sighed. "I haven't yet as all my free time has gone to furnishing and getting settled into the house. But I have been corresponding with Elizabeth Cady Stanton, or rather with her daughter, for an article I'm working on."

"She's kind of fallen out of favor with the movement, you know." Rachel frowned. "Mostly because of her views on Christianity, I think."

"Yes, but my story is broader than suffrage. Her views on women's equality and women in the workplace have certainly influenced my thinking." Inga shifted her position on the chair. "The work of Mrs. Stanton and her cohorts helped to pave the way for working women like us."

"I suppose." Rachel pursed her lips. "But enslaved women have always worked."

Inga blinked. Heat rose into her cheeks. "You're right. Do you think that resulted in both Negroes and white people being more accepting of Negro women working than white women?"

"Maybe. But white people mostly accept Negro women working in menial jobs." Her jaw clenched. "And I think that is also true of Negro men working outside of Negro neighborhoods."

Inga rubbed her forehead. "I'm sorry to say I haven't given it much thought. When I think of Negro women, I mostly think of those I met in college, like you, and others I know about from the cause, like Ida Wells-Barnett."

Rachel flashed her a benevolent smile. "That's because you don't know many of us."

"I know." Inga smiled back. "You once told me that I've lived a sheltered life. Moving to Philadelphia has shown me how right you were. I hope living here will broaden my perspective."

Rachel sobered. "I hope it won't make you cynical."

"Well, if you see me becoming cynical, point it out to me. I don't think cynicism is a good trait in a journalist." Inga opened the case of her watch pin and checked the time. "Oh dear. Time flies when we're together. I probably should get back to work."

"What time is it?"

"A little after two." Inga snapped the watch case closed. "Do you want to stop in and see my office?"

"Thanks, but no. I need to get going or I'll miss my three o'clock appointment."

"Next time you're in Philadelphia, then." Inga stood.

So did Rachel. "We'll plan on it."

"Your memorial article about Mrs. Stanton was very nice," Moder said, as she adjusted Inga's collar.

"I didn't write it as a memorial." Inga perused her familiar childhood bedroom.

With all her mother's redecorating, she still had changed little in here. "I knew she wasn't doing well, but I didn't expect her to pass before the article was published. When she did, I made a few changes and C.J. did some rearranging to get my story into the next issue."

"Well, it was very nice." Moder tapped Inga's shoulder. "Turn around so I can fix your hair."

Inga studied her image in the cheval mirror as her mother adjusted her hat and her curls. The dusty rose color of her new dress accentuated the red in her cheeks that was left from her nausea and vomiting earlier in the morning. She would have to dab on a bit more powder. Hopefully, she wouldn't faint from lack of food during the ceremony, but her stomach was still queasy, so she dared not eat.

"You did tell the pastor that we've been legally married since February, didn't you?" Inga asked.

Moder stepped back. "Yes. He said he would mention it and say you were now renewing your vows in the eyes of God."

"And you told him to take references to 'obey' out of my vows?"

Moder patted her shoulder. "Yes, dear."

Inga inhaled a cleansing breath. "I wish we had planned the wedding for the afternoon."

"I would have." Moder put her hands on her hips. "If I had known you were with child."

Inga closed her eyes momentarily. "We only knew for sure when I saw the doctor the day before we left. We had been taking precautions, so we thought I must have contracted some illness. It was quite a surprise."

"And a happy one." Moder grinned. "I'm so pleased that you have come home in spite of your condition."

"Remember, you promised not to mention my condition to anyone until after we leave."

"I won't." Her smile didn't waver. "I think Halvor suspects, but he won't say anything." She checked her own reflection in the mirror. "Did I tell you that Erik plans to move his family back to this country when their baby reaches school age? He thinks the schools will be better here than in Dawson."

"That will be nice. Perhaps our children will have a chance to know each other." Inga patted a light dusting of powder on her face.

Moder looked her up and down. "Are you ready?"

"I think so." Inga cast her gaze around her childhood bedroom. A sense of calming familiarity settled over her. She nodded.

"Give me a few minutes." Moder started toward the door. "I'll send Halvor up and tell Charlotte to get ready to play the Wedding March."

She left.

It seemed rather anti-climactic to have the piece played. But Moder had put a great deal of thought and effort in planning and preparing for today's ceremony, and she was so excited to be holding it on *Julaften*. She and Halvor had decorated the Christmas tree and decked the mantels with evergreens and candles. With the dinner afterward, she was recreating a tradition from her early days in this house – having friends, neighbors, and relatives all together for a meal.

A knock sounded.

"Come in."

Halvor stepped inside. He broke into a grin. "You look beautiful." His gaze was tender. "It's hard to believe our sweet little angel is a grown woman."

Inga chuckled. "It's been a long time since anyone has considered me a sweet little angel."

"Not true." Halvor held the door open and gestured for her to go through. "I'll always hold in my heart the image of the angelic, blue-eyed wisp of the girl you were as a child." He joined her in the hall. "Even though I know you've grown into a fine young woman."

They paused at the top of the steps.

"I hope C.J. will make you as happy as your mother has made me," Halvor said in a low voice.

Inga smiled. "And that you have made her."

Greg stood at the bottom of the staircase. He turned toward the parlor and raised a hand.

As the Wedding March began to play Halvor

escorted her slowly down the stairs, past the guests, and to her designated spot. He took her hand and placed it in C.J.'s.

Her husband smiled and gave her fingers a gentle squeeze.

The pastor guided them through the service and declared them 'husband and wife in the eyes of the Lord.'

C.J. led her to the entryway, where they greeted each of the guests as they passed into the dining room and parlor.

Before joining the others, C.J. gave her a peck on the cheek. "Now that we're doubly married, you'll have to stay with me forever."

A week later, C.J. stood at the alter, waiting for his wife to join him for their third wedding. While three marriage ceremonies felt excessive, they had pleased themselves and both sets of parents so the repetition was worth it.

His father was escorting Inga down the aisle. C.J. winked at his sister, who was standing up for them as the maid of honor.

C.J. turned and smiled at Inga as his dad offered her hand to him. She had been a good sport, despite her daily fit of nausea. C.J. gently clasped her fingers and they stepped forward to the preacher.

Once again, she had insisted that the word 'obey' be omitted from the vows, and C.J. had required that the date of their original nuptials be mentioned.

She wore the same dress she had for the service at her mother's house, but Mrs. Hansen's housekeeper had cleaned and pressed it so nicely that the garment looked like new. Once again his bride looked beautiful, but she had told him last night that she would not wear the outfit again until after their baby was born.

The preacher mentioned his full name.

C.J.'s head jerked up. Instead of listening, he had been allowing his thoughts to wander.

He stole a glance at Inga. Her lips were tightly closed, as if she was trying to suppress a smile or a giggle. The vision of them both dissolving in laughter flitted through his mind. He swallowed to prevent that from happening.

Finally, they recited their vows and the service ended. C.J. led his bride back up the aisle and down into the church basement, where the reception was held.

"Your parents must have invited everyone in town," Inga whispered as they made their way to the spot his mother had designated for greeting the guests. "I saw Mary, Bertha and Eliza sitting together and some of the faculty from the university."

"Ruth probably helped with the invitations," C.J. replied.

When they were in place, his parents and sister joined them as everyone else offered their congratulations and best wishes. When the last person cleared the line, his mother led them to a tall cake with white frosting. Inga's mother had called it royal icing. For the second time in a week, they made the ceremonial cutting before some of the church women stepped in to slice and distribute the dessert. His father and several other men from the church filled the flutes with champagne for adults and sarsaparilla for the few children in attendance.

The well-wishers toasted the couple, and finally C.J. and Inga were seated with family members.

"Are you holding your own?" C.J.'s mother asked Inga.

"I'm fine." Inga said, although she looked tired. "Thank you for scheduling this in the afternoon."

C.J. wished his wife could have rested between the ceremony and the reception.

"You're welcome, dear." His mother gave Inga the doting smile that she had flashed to her ever since they'd told his parents that she was with child.

Ruth's eyes widened. "Are you—?"

Inga put her index finger to her lips and nodded.

Mom shushed Ruth.

"We'll talk about it later," C.J. said, fixing a bite of cake on his fork.

"Okay." Ruth broke into a grin. "I have some news."

Everyone at the table focused on her. "Jess asked me to marry him right after Christmas."

Inga's eyes widened.

C.J. nearly choked, pinching his lips to avoid spewing crumbs across the table.

His mother looked skeptical. "Did you accept his proposal?"

"No." Ruth shook her head. "At least not yet."

His father's jaw tensed. "Are you sure he's not just trying to get his hands on your property?"

"He's not." Ruth lifted her chin. "He said the ranch should remain in my name, but he's looking at buying forty acres adjoining my property."

"I mean no offense, but," Inga said with a grin. "He probably just wants to move out of the sod house and into your cabin."

Ruth chuckled. "I wouldn't blame him for that. But the land he's looking at has a house on it. Even nicer than my cabin."

"Are you considering his proposal?"

C.J. was glad his wife had asked the question. His sister seemed to be taking it better from Inga than she would have from him.

Ruth tipped her head. "I'm thinking about it, but I'm not in a hurry to give him an answer."

"Let us know what you decide." Inga sighed. "I miss you since I moved to Philadelphia."

"I miss you, too." Ruth reached across the table and patted Inga's hand. "I'll write to you if you promise to answer my letters."

"I promise." Inga exchanged a glance with C.J. "We have a telephone in our house. We'll give you the number so you can call whenever you're in town and feel like talking."

Warmth filled C.J.'s chest. He was thankful that his wife and his family got along so well, and also that he had a similar relationship with her family. He hoped they could maintain those relationships despite living so far away. He wanted his children to know their grandparents.

"You did a splendid job of caring for the house while we were gone." Inga studied her new housekeeper after dinner, while C.J. carried the rest of their luggage upstairs. Unlike her cousin, Minnie Davis was not tall and slender. She was only an inch or two taller than Inga and a bit on the pudgy side, but Minnie had Rachel's quick smile and calm demeanor. "Do you have a bank account?"

"No, ma'am." Minnie looked down at her hands.

"If you want to save for college, I think it would be a good idea." Inga opened her handbag. "If you decide you want to open an account, I'd be happy to go along and help you get one set up."

Minnie finally met her gaze. "Thank you, ma'am."

"I'll pay you in cash today, but I prefer to use bank drafts in the future." Inga pulled bills from her purse. "They help me to better keep track of where my money goes."

"You got a 'count of your own?" Minnie's dark eyes widened. "Apart from Mr. Wakefield's?"

"Yes. We have allocated the household expenses between us, and your services will come out of my account." Inga counted out the bills to cover Minnie's salary. "If you would like, I will purchase a few dresses for you to wear while you're here. That way, you can save wear and tear on your own clothes."

Minnie tipped her head. "Uniforms?"

Inga grimaced. "If that's what you would like. I was just thinking about something easy to wash and iron. You can choose what you want."

A bright grin bloomed on Minnie's dark face. "Anything?"

"Within reason, as long as it's easy to care for." Inga smiled and handed the money to Minnie. "Have a nice day off tomorrow."

"I will, ma'am." She slipped into her cloak. "Good

night."

"Good night."

After Minnie left, Inga walked around her kitchen. It was spick and span, all the dishes washed and put away and the counters spotless. She felt light. Maybe it was only light at heart, but it was so nice to come home from their trip or from her job at the magazine to a warm meal and not have to clean up after cooking it.

The soft thuds of footfalls approaching broke into Inga's reverie.

"Are you sorry to have hired a housekeeper, so you no longer do things the way you want them?" C.J. wrapped his arms around her shoulders.

Inga leaned back against him. "Not at all. I was just thinking how grateful I am to be able to afford a housekeeper. My mother had help when I was growing up, and I'm not sure I could manage a home this big by myself, especially with all the time I spend at the magazine."

"What did Minnie say about spending nights here?"

"That she would like to spend three or four nights here each week so she doesn't have to travel to and from her parents' house every day." Inga sighed. "And maybe more in the winter."

"Are you going to reduce her pay to account for room and board?"

He swayed from side to side. Inga's eyes drifted closed.

"No. She's trying to save enough money for college." She leaned her head back against his shoulder. "Besides, we've discussed the fact that she'll have more work when the baby comes."

"If she's planning to go to college, she'll need to learn correct grammar." He kissed the top of her head, his warm breath tickling her scalp.

"I know. I'm sure Rachel's told her that I was a professor, so I'm hoping she will ask for help." Inga rested her hands on C.J.'s "Or maybe Rachel will convince her to go to Oberlin. I think they still have the preparation courses to get students ready for the higher-level classes."

"You could offer to help her." C.J.'s voice was soft, soothing.

"If I can figure out how to do it without offending her, I will. Or maybe I'll ask Rachel how best to approach the situation." A yawn overcame Inga. "I think I'm ready to turn in for the night."

He released her and moved to face her. He skimmed his hand over her cheek. "Let's go upstairs."

His lips caressed her eyelids, her nose, her cheeks, before claiming her mouth. The sleepiness that had enveloped her moments before now drifted away.

Inga lay back on the pillow with her eyes closed as Minnie read to her. Even with the windows open and the electric fan blowing directly on her, the heat and humidity of the city's early summer was stifling. Because of the swelling in her feet and the ache in her back, the doctor had sent her to bed two weeks ago to await the birth of her child.

"Double, double, toil and trouble," Minnie read. "Fire burn and cauldron— "

The doorbell rang downstairs.

Minnie lifted her head. "Shall I go answer the door?"

Inga shifted to a cooler spot on the mattress. "No, thanks. I think my mother's downstairs. She'll answer it."

Minnie returned to reading aloud.

A few minutes later, Inga heard footfalls on the stairs, then a tap on the half-open door.

Moder poked her head in. "You have a visitor."

She pushed open the panel. Rachel followed her into the room.

Inga grinned. "What a nice surprise!"

"I stopped by your office, and your husband told me I'd find you here." Rachel glanced at Minnie. "Was that *Macbeth* I heard when we were coming down the hall?"

"Yes." Minnie put a marker in the book and set it on the table in front of the window. She stood.

"Minnie's keeping me company on my rest breaks so I don't get bored with just lying here." Inga was delighted to see her friend.

"And Inga's helping me with the strange words and what they mean." Minnie smiled back, but covered her mouth with her hand, obviously self-conscious about her crooked front teeth.

"She helped me with that years ago when we were at Oberlin," Rachel said. "And she's Mrs. Wakefield to you."

Minnie took a step back. "But—"

"I asked her to call me Inga." Inga adjusted her pillows to prop herself upright. "When she finishes working here and goes to college, I hope we'll be friends."

Rachel shook her head.

Moder walked to the bowl and pitcher on the small dresser opposite the window. "When Inga was a child, we called our housekeeper by her first name and she called us by ours. It made us feel more like family."

"And years later, when Moder married Halvor, we became actual family." Inga chuckled.

"Our housekeeper was his mother." Moder brought a damp cloth to Inga and swabbed her face. "I'll go down and get you some fresh ice water."

"I can do that." Minnie took a few steps toward the door.

Moder raised her hand. "I'm sure Inga would rather you work on typing her story." She dumped the water from the bowl into the pitcher and started for the door. "I'll get the water and then make lunch."

Minnie looked to Inga.

Inga shrugged. "She's always liked feeling useful."

Rachel's gaze bounced from Minnie to Inga. "You've taught Minnie to type?"

"Yes, and she caught on really quickly." Inga shifted position, trying to get more comfortable. "If Wyoming is any indication, I think that typing might someday become a requirement in more colleges. I just don't know when."

"I still need a lot of practice." Minnie sighed. "I'll go down to the library and work on your story."

After she left, Rachel pulled her chair closer to the bed and sat. "Sounds like you've been working on a story, even when you're on bedrest."

"I'm trying to get enough articles ahead that I won't have to start collecting new material for a few months." Inga shifted again and gestured toward the stack of papers on her nightstand. "I have one more to finish before the baby comes."

"I hope I'm not interrupting your work."

"I was taking a break." Inga repositioned her pillows. "And it's so nice to see you."

Moder bustled into the room with the bowl and pitcher. She took a fresh cloth, dampened it and gave it to Inga. "I'll leave you girls alone so you can talk."

"What have you been working on?" Rachel asked.

"The one Minnie is typing is a short piece about Roosevelt shutting down the post office in Indianola, Mississippi for refusing to accept the postmistress he appointed because she is a Negro." Inga smiled and shook her head. "I'm so glad I interviewed him two years ago. It gave me so much background material. The woman responded to my inquiry with a lot of helpful information. He did this in January so my story isn't really timely, but I hope readers will find it interesting."

Rachel stared at Inga. "I hadn't heard about that. How did you find out about it?"

"*The Chronicle* keeps a writer in Washington who comes back for meetings once or twice a month." Inga shifted again to relieve the ache in her left hip. "He often gives me information on issues he doesn't think worthy of his attention, but his cast offs have turned into some good leads for me."

"How are you feeling about becoming a mother by now?" Rachel tucked her lower lip between her teeth.

"Right now, I just want it to happen soon. I'm very tired of this bed." Inga lowered her voice. "I'm much more accepting of the idea than I was before, but I worry about how a child will change my life." She caught Rachel's gaze. "How have you been able to avoid it?"

Rachel looked down at her clasped hands. "We haven't taken any precautions." She coughed lightly. "When Herman was beaten, his male parts were severely bruised. Although they are now healed, the doctor thinks something might have been damaged."

"Oh, Rachel. I'm so sorry." Inga reached out a hand to her friend.

Rachel clasped her fingers. "We've been helping to raise his brother's children. They still stay with us since their mother takes care of an elderly woman and spends most nights at her house."

"You've been so good to them."

"Having them with us has been a real blessing."

Inga's chest tightened. Rachel's stoic gratitude, rather than the anger she was entitled to, put Inga's selfishness to shame. When her baby was born, she would think of Rachel every day to remind herself how lucky she and C.J. were to be able to have children of their own.

C.J. paced up and down the hallway outside the closed bedroom door. He wasn't sure how much longer he could bear to hear his wife's groans and cries of pain.

When he had returned from the meeting on tomorrow's Independence Day celebration, his mother-in-law had only allowed him to see Inga briefly.

He removed his topcoat and loosened his necktie. Carefully, he placed them over the bannister before taking another lap around the corridor.

As he approached the closed door yet again, it opened and Mrs. Hansen popped her head out.

"Is the baby here?" Even to himself, the question sounded inane, as if he expected a stork to deliver it.

She shook her head as a pain-filled moan sounded

behind her.

C.J. flinched.

"Not yet, but soon." She made a shooing motion with her hand. "Go downstairs and make a kettle of hot water, then bring it up with a trivet. And gather a few clean towels, too."

He started to ring for Minnie but remembered they had given her today and tomorrow off for the holiday. He turned on his heel and flew down the hall and the stairs. In the kitchen, he built a fire in the cookstove and put a pot of water on to boil. While it was heating, he ran to the linen cupboard, grabbed a handful of towels, and delivered them to Mrs. Hansen. "Are these enough?"

"For now. Thanks." She took them and disappeared back into the room.

He hurried back downstairs to check on the water. Tiny wisps of steam began wafting from the kettle's spout. Frantically, he searched for a trivet.

From above came a blood-curdling scream mixed with a strangled moan. Then silence.

He dashed to the stairs. As he climbed the first step, he nearly stumbled. Righting himself, he released a huge breath.

Finding a trivet on the sideboard, he carried it and the kettle of hot water to the bedroom.

Mrs. Hansen opened the door, revealing his wife cuddling a towel-wrapped bundle. His mother-in-law took the kettle and trivet. Entranced, he drifted to the bedside.

Inga turned the infant so he could see the baby's red face. Bits of a white waxy substance clung to his skin.

"We have a daughter." Her skin. Inga sounded tired, but joy filled her voice.

Her mother added hot water to a half-full basin.

"Let me clean her up a bit." She moved to the opposite side of the bed and unwrapped the towel exposing a perfectly formed tiny girl, with the cord cut and tied.

C.J. stared in awe. "She's so little."

Mrs. Hansen stroked the infant with the wet cloth. "But she's strong."

The baby began to cry. Inga caressed the little one's pale, peach-fuzz hair.

His chest swelled with love for his wife and daughter.

"Have you two thought about a name?" Mrs. Hansen refreshed the cloth and returned to swabbing.

"We had talked about Susan for a girl." C.J. reached out and touched his index finger to one tiny fist.

Inga supported the baby's head and studied their daughter's face. "She's already letting us know she likes the blanket and not the bath. I think Susan fits her."

"I think Miss Anthony would be honored." Mrs. Hansen finished washing Susan and wrapped a clean towel around her. "What about a middle name?"

Inga looked up at him, her gaze filled with love. "What would you think about Ruth?"

Warmth filled his chest. He took his wife's free hand in his and brought it to his lips. "My sister will be very pleased."

Inga smiled. "You know what this means."

He kissed her hand again.

"What?" he murmured against her skin.

"Now I'm going to have to work even harder on behalf of woman's suffrage so that when Susan reaches majority, she'll be able to vote."

Her earnest words tugged at his heartstrings. He gazed at the tiny girl in her arms and tried to imagine his daughter's future. "Let me know what I can do to help."

Ten Years Later

CHAPTER FIFTEEN

January 12, 1913
Philadelphia, Pennsylvania

Dear Rachel,

I hope to see you in Washington in March for the Woman Suffrage Procession. Although I hate the idea of walking through the streets of the capitol in winter, I know Alice Paul and her Congressional Committee put in a great effort to organize the parade with the city, bands, floats and mounted brigades. It should be an impressive event, especially if everyone who pledged at last year's convention here in Philadelphia actually participates. After so many years of Anna Shaw's lackluster "be patient" (and do little) leadership, I feel obligated to support this new energy in the NASWA. I suppose I shouldn't complain since I haven't stepped up to challenge her for the presidency.

The Chronicle *is paying for my trip, as they expect me to write an article about the procession and one about Woodrow Wilson's inauguration. I'll be glad to see Taft go, but I can't say that I'm very excited about Wilson, either. After working for Roosevelt and the Bull Moose party, their second-place finish was a disappointment, especially since I was here instead of Wyoming, where I could have cast my vote.*

Susan wants to walk in the procession with me, and because she does, the younger girls do, too. C.J. opposes the idea, and I think I'm going to side with him. Because they're so young, it would be too hard to keep track of them and take notes for stories.

Looking at the calendar, I think I'll try to come in on the train on March 2 and leave on the 5th or 6th. Please let me know if one of those days will work for you.

Lovingly in Friendship,
Inga

Inga strode across the thick rug of the opulent hotel lobby to meet two of the women from the Philadelphia delegation. The liveried doorman held the door, and together the women strode out into the sunny, but chilly day and on to the designated meeting place for the Pennsylvania contingent.

"If this weather holds, it should be the perfect day for the procession," she said to her companions.

"We're so fortunate." Martha Scott slipped her arm through Inga's at the elbow. "March is such an unpredictable month. Too bad they didn't schedule this for May."

"Then it wouldn't be on the day before the inauguration," Inga said.

Martha had slipped her other arm through Emma Reed's, effectively linking the three of them together.

As they rounded the corner, a brisk breeze caught Inga's 'Votes for Women' sash, and it fluttered against her chest. She reached up and re-settled her hat.

"There seem to be a lot of men in town," Emma observed. "I know there are some men marching in support of suffrage, but I can't believe they all are."

"They're probably here for the inauguration, but came in early to see our parade," Inga said.

Martha squared her shoulders. "Then I hope our procession will convince them to champion our right to vote."

When they joined the Pennsylvania contingent, the leaders were already assembling the group into rows and columns.

"Caroline Katzenstein did a wonderful job of getting most of our members from Philadelphia to participate." Emma smiled.

Inga perused the crowd and found many familiar faces. "She certainly did."

Everyone lined up. They watched as the parade marshal, Inez Milholland Boissevain, riding atop a white horse, passed by on the cross street. Many cheered. Others, like Inga, stood solemnly and waited for other state delegations, a few dignitaries in automobiles, and a float to pass. Their leaders signaled for the Pennsylvanians to proceed, moving into their designated position. More units fell into place, following Inga's group.

Crowds of spectators lined the streets. Many waved and shouted encouragement. Others jeered.

While Inga walked, she wondered if Rachel had joined the march. She had agreed to meet Inga at the corner of the Treasury Building, near the end of the route.

One of the bands struck up a marching song. Inga smiled as she passed the by-standers along the route. As they approached the turn onto Pennsylvania Avenue, shouts rang out, and the sound of marching collapsed into muffled shuffling. Inga squinted, trying to see farther ahead, but there were too many women blocking her view.

"What's happening?" Martha shouted over the din.

"I don't know." Inga's chest tightened. Thank God she hadn't brought the girls.

"Remember, we're supposed to keep walking," Emma called. "No matter what."

Inga steeled herself and willed her feet to keep moving.

The Peace Monument came into view. This was their turn onto the main parade route. At the intersection, a mass of spectators had swarmed into the roadway.

Inga's pulse raced as her unit turned into the chaos. Moving forward, she perused the unfolding scene, searching for a pathway through the horde without making eye contact with any of the interlopers.

"Go back home where you belong," a man shouted somewhere ahead of them.

She and her companions were jostled from both sides.

"Stop nagging and go take care of your children," another male called.

"You're ruining American society!"

"All your marchin's makin' you ugly."

One of the hecklers shoved Inga. She lurched forward and struggled to maintain her balance.

The neatly formed lines of the Pennsylvania delegation degenerated into clusters of three or more, each attempting to make their way through the chaos.

"You're all a bunch of whores!"

"Who allowed all these depraved females in the streets?"

Forward they plodded, ignoring the insults.

"Why dirty your hands in politics?"

"Wilson will never give you the vote!"

Inga looked up to see a besieged policeman, attempting to keep a narrow path open for the procession. She nodded to him and shot him a small smile. He nodded back, then diverted his gaze.

"Get off the street!"

"Go home to your children where you belong!"

The women trudged forward.

"Perverts!"

From the right, a moustached man in a bowler hat darted toward Inga's row. His hand shot out, grabbing for her 'Votes for Women' sash. He missed, grazing her breast.

Her heart raced. She stepped forward and to the left to evade him. A few steps ahead, she spotted another policeman and caught his gaze.

The mustached man reappeared.

Inga's breaths came fast and shallow. She clasped her sash with her right hand to protect it.

"A woman's place is in the home!" The interloper lunged toward her, snatching at her sash. Missing, he hurtled into Inga.

With her other hand, she groped for something or someone for support. Finding none, she crashed to the ground.

A sharp, cracking pain shot through her arm. She shrieked and rolled herself into a sitting position, clutching her throbbing arm to her chest.

Emma turned around and hurried to her side, directing traffic around her. "Are you all right?"

Pressure built behind Inga's eyes. She shook her head. "My arm."

She cradled it tenderly, trying to prevent movement.

Emma leaned in close. "Can you get up?"

Inga held out her good hand and tried to get her feet beneath her. Unceremoniously, she plopped back down. An excruciating jolt shot through her arm.

"Officer, will you please help her up?" Emma called to the policeman, who had been watching the whole ordeal.

He turned away and remained planted in his spot.

Emma scowled. "Chivalry really is dead."

Inga cast a wary gaze around for the man who had collided into her. He was nowhere to be seen.

"If you would stay at home, nothing like this would happen!" shouted a man standing nearby. Sneering, he spit in Inga's direction, then turned away.

"We can do this." Inga slipped her injured arm between her sash and dress for support and pivoted onto her good hand and her knees. Another agonizing bolt stole her breath and she couldn't hold back her moan. She raised her torso upright and planted her right foot flat in front of her.

Emma placed one hand under Inga's right arm and the other around her waist. "Ready?"

Inga swallowed back the bile rising in her throat. "Yes."

While Emma lifted, Inga struggled to her feet. She inhaled a deep breath and expelled it. "Let's go."

With Emma's support, Inga straightened her spine and strode ahead. Glaring at the useless policeman as she passed, she made a mental note of the smirk on his face. It was a detail she wanted to be sure to include in her article.

"I'm meeting a friend at the corner of the Treasury building," Inga said as her destination finally came into view about forty minutes later. "You can leave me there if you want to finish the procession."

Her arm throbbed, but at least it wasn't bleeding. Nausea waved through her. The idea of leaning against the wall as she waited for Rachel grew more appealing with every step.

Emma dismissed the idea with a tisking tone. "You need medical attention. We'll find you a doctor or a hospital."

"Rachel lives here in town." The pain was causing Inga's whole body to tense. She concentrated on putting one foot in front of the other.

Emma guided Inga toward the sidewalk. "We're getting close. I can see some of the allegorical performers."

Inga lifted her gaze. The women in white had attracted a respectable audience. A movement near the building caught her attention.

"She's already here!" A surge of unexpected energy shot through Inga.

"Where?" Emma scanned the area and Rachel stepped forward.

"What happened?" Rachel cried when she reached them.

"A man shoved me." Inga gently cradled the arm in her sash. "I've injured my arm."

Still supporting Inga, Emma watched the conversation with a furrowed brow.

"This is my friend, Rachel Jones Ansel."

Emma's eyes widened.

"Rachel, this is my friend, Emma Reed."

"How do you do?" Rachel said, nodding in her direction.

Emma gave her head a barely perceptible shake. "Nice to meet you." She turned to Inga. "You still need medical attention."

"Do you want to go to the white hospital or to a doctor?" Concern wove through Rachel's voice.

The sooner Inga could get her arm treated, the better. "Which is closer?"

"The hospital is not far," Rachel said. "The only doctors I know well are in the Negro part of town."

Emma tipped her head forward. "Lead the way."

Rachel stepped to Inga's left.

"Did you decide not to march?" Inga asked.

"They wanted us to follow at the end of the parade. Behind the men, even." Rachel spat out the words. "Ida refused. She was going to join the Illinois group along the way. I think someone else was going to do the same with the New York unit."

"Good for them." Inga winced as they made an abrupt turn. She swallowed. "I'm sorry the NAWSA did that. I haven't yet met Alice Paul, but I would have expected better from her."

"Oh, Inga." Rachel gestured toward a side street. "After all these years, you're still giving everyone the benefit of the doubt. I wonder what Sarah will have to say about it."

So did Inga. The NASWA leadership deemed segregation to be the most expedient approach to pursuing the cause. It was so disrespectful of the contributions their Negro sisters had made through the years and continued to make in the face of discrimination.

"The last I knew, she wasn't coming. She mentioned having a social engagement that conflicted." Inga clenched her teeth against the pain.

"Have you known each other long?" Emma's tone betrayed her surprise.

"We went to college together at Oberlin," Inga replied. "It seems like a long time ago, now."

Rachel chuckled. "It was."

Emma perused the street. "I was hoping we could find a cab, but I don't see any."

Rachel frowned. "They are probably all waiting at the White House, since that's where everyone's supposed to end up."

They trudged on in silence.

"The hospital's in the next block, across the street. I think it best that we pretend I'm your lady's maid."

"Rachel," Inga protested.

"If we don't, I most likely won't be allowed to stay with you."

Silently, Emma watched the conversation.

When they entered the hospital, several other woman from the parade were seated in the dreary, sparse waiting area. Unidentifiable chemical odors hung in the air. They found three metal chairs together and claimed them.

Emma gasped. "Were they all injured in the march?"

A nearby woman dressed in yellow turned to Emma. "We were, and there are already seventeen others inside who were more seriously hurt."

"Seventeen plus four." Emma said aloud.

As she spoke, another woman limped through the entrance.

Moments later, a young woman in a uniform came through an interior door with a clipboard in hand. She surveyed the room and approached Inga. "And how can we help you?"

"Her arm is injured," Emma volunteered.

Wincing, Inga drew her arm from its makeshift sling. Her hand had swollen. She fumbled with the button at her cuff, now tight from the swelling.

"Let me help you, Miz Wakefield." Rachel deftly unfastened the button.

The nurse tried unsuccessfully to raise the sleeve. She pulled a scissors from an apron pocket and cut the fabric to the elbow.

Pain shot from her wrist to her shoulder as her arm slipped out of the fabric. Inga inhaled a sharp breath.

The swollen, reddened skin contrasted with the light green fabric beneath it

"That doesn't look good." The woman handed the clipboard and a pencil to Emma. "We need information about your friend. I'll see about the lady who just came in, then check to see if we have a room ready."

"But the others were here before me." Inga eased her arm into a less painful position.

"We had a telephone call to expect more patients, so we're treating the most seriously hurt first. For now, you are next in line."

"Will she need to stay here overnight?" Emma asked.

The woman shrugged. "We won't know until the doctor has a look at her."

She moved to talk with the newcomer.

Emma helped Inga fill out the information sheet. Her lips thinned into a tight line. "I wonder how long this is going to take."

"I'll stay with her," Rachel said. "If you need to leave."

"Well...," Emma said absently.

"I'll be fine." Inga didn't want to impose on Emma any longer. "Thank you so much for all your help and support. I hate to think what might have happened if you hadn't come to my rescue, especially since that policeman was of no help."

"There was an officer five feet from me when that cad tripped me and shoved my friend." The older woman on the other side of Emma leaned forward so Inga could see her. "She's inside. She hit her head on the curb and was bleeding and dizzy."

"I'm not sure what the police were doing there anyway," a woman across the room said. "They weren't much help."

"One group did try to keep a clear path open when we went through the turn," someone else offered. "I think they were outnumbered."

"Maybe holding the procession the day before the inauguration wasn't such a good idea," Emma said on a sigh.

"Emma, why don't you go back to the hotel and let the others know what happened?" Inga managed a fleeting smile. "If I stay here overnight, I'll ask the staff to telephone the hotel and give you a message. If they let me go back to the hotel, Rachel will see that I get there."

Emma stood and handed the clipboard to Rachel. "If I don't hear from you, I'll stop by your room later and check on you."

"Thank you." Inga flashed another brief smile. "For everything."

"It was a pleasure meeting you," Rachel said.

Emma nodded to her then focused on Inga. "Good luck."

Inga looked around the sickly green walls for a clock, but found none. Her arm throbbed.

Finally, a nurse appeared. She took the clipboard from Rachel and skimmed it. "Follow me, Mrs. Wakefield."

Inga's gaze shifted to Rachel. "Can Rachel come with me? I might need her help."

The woman glanced at Rachel and frowned. "I suppose."

They were shown to a small, windowless room with two chairs, a little table, a metal cabinet, and a metal cupboard on the wall above it. The walls were painted the same green as the waiting room. A chemical smell permeated the confined space.

"The doctor will be with you as soon as he can." The nurse set the clipboard on the cabinet, nodded curtly, then left them alone.

"You should have told her I am your maid," Rachel whispered so softly that Inga barely heard her.

"I couldn't bring myself to say that. I'm sorry to have used your first name," Inga whispered back. Then she raised her volume to a normal level. "I wonder how many other women were injured today."

Rachel shrugged.

"Do you think anything will be done about the police response to the violence?" Inga still spoke in a whisper.

"I doubt it."

"I definitely plan to mention it in my article." Inga kept her voice low. "And I'm going to write a letter to the editor of the *Inquirer*, and maybe one to the *Post*, to tell the public about today's happenings right away."

"I'll talk with Ida—"

The door swung open. The doctor entered, a nurse at his side. He picked up the clipboard. "Mrs.

Wakefield, I'm Dr. Olson and this is Nurse Smith."

The woman glared at Rachel but said nothing as she moved the little table to Rachel's left.

"How do you do?" Inga nodded to each in turn.

"Let's have a look at your arm." The doctor pushed the loose portion of the cut sleeve out of the way and took her arm, resting it on the table.

Inga winced.

As he poked and prodded, a yelp escaped her. She clenched her teeth to prevent another.

When he finished, he raised his gaze to meet Inga's. "You have a broken ulna. I can't feel a break in the radius, so if there is one, there is no displacement."

"That is good news," Inga said.

"However, there is a slight displacement in your ulna. I'll try to ease it back, then we'll apply a cast."

Inga cringed.

Without a word, the nurse left the room.

"We'll keep you overnight to make sure you don't have symptoms of other injuries," Dr. Olson said.

"I can't," Inga cried. "I need to be at tomorrow's inauguration."

"What you need, Mrs. Wakefield, is rest." He flicked a glance toward Rachel. "If you don't stay here at the hospital, your maid will need to keep an eye on you through the night. And you definitely should not get into the middle of the crowds tomorrow."

Inga bit her tongue to avoid arguing.

The nurse returned with a basin of water and a wad of heavy cloth strips. She took a jar labeled 'Plaster' from the cabinet and dumped a portion into the water.

While she mixed the concoction, Dr. Olson again held Inga's arm.

She sucked in a breath and steeled herself.

With strong fingers, he manipulated the painful area.

Inga cried out. She swallowed against the nausea washing over her.

"Got it." He reached for a long strip of dry bandage and wrapped it around her arm from wrist to elbow. The nurse soaked another fabric strip in the plaster mixture. The doctor applied it over the dry linen. Repeating the process with strip after strip, he built up a cast.

"If you are determined to leave, you must wait here for a quarter to half an hour for the plaster to harden," the doctor said. "It will take a day or two to dry out completely, so you must be careful not to allow the cast to be damaged."

"Thank you, doctor," Inga said.

"I'll get you a sling." The nurse picked up the basin and remaining bandages.

"Do you have a public telephone?" Inga asked. "I should contact my husband before he gets word I have been injured and starts to worry."

"Some of the other women are doing the same thing," the nurse said. "I'll come get you when it's your turn."

"We've arranged for cabs to take patients back to their hotels," the doctor said. "There should be one waiting outside for you when you leave." He held the door open, and they both left.

Inga turned to Rachel and whispered. "I'm sorry he assumed you were my maid."

"Why?" Rachel grinned. "You have a Negro maid."

"Yes, because you recommended your niece." Inga grinned back. "And we love Sadie like family."

"Thanks to you, members of my family starting with Minnie have gone to college who probably wouldn't have if they hadn't worked for you." Rachel sobered. "Not every boss tutors their maids in writing, arithmetic, handling money, and even typing. They are much better prepared for college than I was."

"It's a pleasure." Inga gently touched her finger to her cast. It was still damp. "You know I've always liked teaching."

"Yes." Rachel shot her a fond smile then glanced toward the door. "I'll go back with you to your hotel. Herman's working tonight so I'll go home with him."

After what seemed like hours, Nurse Smith returned carrying a folded cloth. "I'll put your arm in this sling." When that was finished, she said. "The telephone is available now. Follow me."

She led them to a small room with a telephone on the table. Inga sat in one of the chairs, careful not to bump her arm. Inhaling a steadying breath, she lifted the receiver then set it on the table so she could dial the operator.

When the female voice came over the line, Inga gave her the Philadelphia number. After a series of clicks and muffled voices, she was connected with C.J.

"Inga!" C.J. hadn't expected her to call. "How was the parade? Did you have a lot of marchers?"

"Yes. And a lot of spectators." She sounded tired. "Unfortunately, many of the spectators became disorderly."

He froze. "Disorderly how?"

"They swarmed the parade and assaulted the marchers." Her sigh hissed through the line. "The police did nothing to stop them."

Trepidation washed over him. "Are you all right?"

"I have a broken arm." She paused. "The doctor put a cast on it."

He closed his eyes. "I should have gone with you."

"Rachel is with me, and we'll be going back to the hotel soon." She cleared her throat. "I hope this injustice gets covered appropriately in the newspapers."

He bit back anger. "I'll speak tonight with one of my reporter friends at the *Inquirer*. This story needs to get out as soon as possible."

"They may already have more information than I do, but be sure to emphasize the failure of the police to take action to protect us." Inga's voice was tight.

"Do you want me to come down there and bring you back?"

"No. I'll be fine."

He wanted to see that for himself. "Are you sure

you'll be up to covering the inauguration tomorrow?"

"I'll be fine," she repeated more sternly.

"Telephone me tomorrow night and tell me how you are." He couldn't quell his concern. "I want to know that you are okay."

"I will." She sounded wistful. "Give the girls my love and kiss them goodnight for me."

"Sure thing," he said. "Take care of yourself, my love."

"I will. You, too. Good night." Her words rushed out. The call disconnected.

"Good night," he murmured into the dead line.

The day had been long. With her arm in a cast, Inga had found taking notes at the inauguration nearly impossible.

By the time she returned to the hotel, she was cold to her core. Her arm pulsated within the cast. Her whole body ached.

As she entered the lobby she forced a smile toward the man holding the door open.

Martha and Emma were talking with a small group of women next to a gold brocade sofa. Inga maintained her smile long enough to nod at them, then headed toward the elevator. She couldn't wait to remove her shoes and prop her arm on some pillows.

Drat! She'd promised to call C.J.

Abruptly, she changed direction and started toward the line of telephone booths.

Nearly colliding with Martha, Inga dropped her handbag and grabbed the other woman to keep from falling, turning her body to avoid landing on her cast if she fell.

Martha clutched Inga's free arm and helped her steady herself.

"I'm sorry." Inga took the handbag Emma held out to her. "I didn't know you were behind me."

"We've been watching for you," Emma said. "Some of the Association staff and several men who work for senators came by this afternoon. I told them what happened in the procession yesterday, and they want to speak with you."

"The Senate is considering hearings about the behavior of the district police," Martha added. "They might want you to testify."

"I hope they fire them all," Inga muttered, although today's events had been kept much more orderly.

Emma held out a piece of paper. "I have a number for you to call to arrange a meeting tonight."

Inga did not have a free hand to take it. She shook her head. "I need to call my husband. Why don't you call them and say I'll meet with them here at the hotel restaurant, if I can eat while they talk. I'm exhausted and famished."

"I'll do that and meet you here," Emma offered.

Inga nodded to the attendant and carefully situated herself inside the booth.

She reached into her handbag for the cash she would need to pay for her call and tip the attendant, then placed her call.

"Our parade made the left front page headline of the Washington Post, next to the article about the plans for today's inauguration. Our photographs were even the same size. I haven't read the articles, yet."

"So you were able to go to the inauguration?" C.J. sounded surprised.

"Of course. I told you I would." She caught her bottom lip in her teeth. She shouldn't have used such a snippy tone. She was glad to be talking with him.

The line went silent for a moment.

"You sounded so tired last night, I was worried about you," he said finally.

"I was, and I'm even more so tonight. I'm sorry if I sound short." She leaned her head against the side of the phone booth. "How are the girls?"

"They're fine. Doing their homework. Looking forward to having you home." He paused. "Are you going to feel up to traveling back tomorrow?"

"I think so, but I may not be leaving tomorrow." She paused. "The Senate is considering a hearing into the response of the District police. I'm meeting with some aids tonight. I may be called to testify."

"If you do, do you want me to come down to be with you?"

She sighed. "You don't have to if you can't get away. But if you can, I would love to have you with me."

"I'll speak with Sadie and Nathan tonight about the possibility," he said. "Telephone me in the morning and let me know what comes of your meeting tonight."

On Thursday afternoon, Inga sat beside C.J. in the Senate Hearing Room. A subcommittee of three Senators from the Committee on the District of Columbia, sat at the front of the room behind a massive wooden dais, conducting the inquiry. Senator Wesley Jones from the state of Washington presided.

C.J. scribbled notes as the Police Commissioner from the District read the orders issued regarding the suffrage parade.

Afterward, male witnesses and women who had marched in the parade were questioned. Most described a scene similar to what Inga had witnessed. A few of the men defended the police response, stating they were badly outnumbered and acting within their orders.

When Inga was called to testify, C.J. escorted her to her seat at the witness table. She lay a protective hand over her casted arm as she sat. He returned to his seat to continue taking notes.

Senator Jones asked her a series of questions to establish her identity, her participation, and the location of her unit in the procession. By the time he had finished with these preliminary questions, she had begun to relax.

"Where in your route did you first encounter the crowd?" the chairman asked.

"As we approached the Peace Monument, we began to see the congestion in the street," Inga replied. "We were taunted with disparaging shouts and jostled as we tried to make our way through."

"Did you see any police during this encounter?"

"I saw two officers in uniform."

The chairman cleared his throat. "Were you able to get their numbers?"

"No."

"Did they try to keep the crowd back?"

"One was trying to clear a path, but the other did not." Inga paused. "And he did nothing to try to stop the man who was grabbing for my sash."

"How close to that man was the policeman?" Senator Pomerene asked.

"Within arm's length. I believe."

The chairman raised a brow. "The policeman was not making any effort to keep that man back?"

"No. And when I was pushed to the ground, the policeman did not even attempt to help me up or keep me from being trampled." Inga kept her voice calm and even. "One of my fellow marchers from Pennsylvania had to help me up. The officer just stood there and smirked."

"Did you find the crowd under better control toward the end of the parade?"

"I didn't finish. I was in extreme pain, and I left the procession at the Treasury Building with two friends who accompanied me to the hospital."

Senator Pomerene folded his hands on the desk before him. "What did you find at the hospital?"

"Many other women from the parade were in the waiting room. I have since heard that between eighty and one hundred women marchers were being treated in the hospital yesterday."

"I see you have a cast on your left arm."

"The doctor said my ulna was broken."

"As I understand you, there would have been plenty of room for the parade to pass if the crowd had been pressed back to the curb," the chairman said.

"Yes. We could have maintained our formation of five abreast with an arm's length apart had the crowd not been in the street."

"That is all." The chairman dismissed her and called the next witness.

Inga returned to her place next to C.J. He gave her knee a gentle squeeze.

"You did very well," he whispered.

"Thanks." She sighed. The tension in her muscles eased.

When the chairman called for a brief recess, C.J. and Inga left the room.

"Are you sure you don't want to stay for the rest of the witnesses?" Inga asked, as her husband headed them in the direction of the doors.

C. J. shook his head. "You need rest for the trip back home tomorrow. When the hearing is over and the proceedings are printed, I can get a copy. It will be soon enough."

Inga grinned. "So you're going to write this article?"

He laughed. "I wouldn't want to deny you the satisfaction of putting your story into print."

CHAPTER SIXTEEN

September 21, 1913
Cedar Falls, Iowa

My dearest Inga,

Thank you for your letter telling me the doctor took off your cast. I'm glad your arm has healed nicely. Too bad you had it for most of the hot summer weather.

Halvor and I enjoyed our visit with you and your family. Your girls are so sweet and bright. I'm glad you're playing school with them like we did when you were young, and I had fun playing teacher with them while you were at work. Halvor enjoyed having them with us when we visited the historic sites.

Our train trip back home was pleasant. We spent a few days in Chicago before the final leg of our trip. I found Christmas gifts I think Helen and Elizabeth will like, but I'll need some suggestions for Susan. Sometimes she seems so grown up for her age, and I don't want to give her something that is too young for her.

We'd like to have you home for Christmas, and we'd be happy to host C.J.'s family, too, if that would help convince C.J. to make the trip. I know it's hard to get away, since the girls have to be back for school and winter weather is uncertain, but please consider it.

I hope you'll think about cutting back on your suffrage involvement. You are working yourself ragged, and I'm concerned about you. Since the Washington, D.C. parade, I worry about your safety.

In the next few days, I will write to each of the girls. I'll mail them on the same day, so hopefully, they will arrive around the same time.

Take care of yourself, my dear.
My love to you and your family.
Moder

C.J. drummed his fingers on his desk as he tried to concentrate on the article about President Wilson's vow to never attack another country. The writing was dry, and the arguments weren't clearly drawn. Someone would have to rewrite it before it was ready for the public, but the original reporter wouldn't want to share the credit.

And his wife had been gone from the office for more than two-and-a-half hours.

He flexed his aching jaw. Trying to relax, he stood and walked to the window.

His telephone rang.

He returned to his desk and picked up the receiver. "Wakefield."

"She's back," his secretary's deep voice boomed through the line.

Placing the handset back on its cradle, C.J. took a deep breath to calm himself.

"Thank you," he said quietly as he passed the secretary's desk on the way to Inga's office.

Her door was ajar. He gave a gentle knock and walked in as she hung her cloak on the coat-tree.

She turned and smiled at him.

He frowned. "Where have you been?"

She blinked. "I had lunch with Alice Paul. I told you I was going to last night, remember?"

"For two-and-a-half hours?" He fought to keep his voice quiet.

"I'm going to do a story on her and the Congressional Union." Inga paused. "She's considering demonstrations across the country for next May Day."

"Another suffrage article." He shook his head. "Three of your last four stories have been on suffrage."

She placed her hands on her hips. "Well, if you had let me take the girls to Vienna to cover the opening of *Pygmalion*, you would have had one less suffrage article. But you wouldn't, even though Mr. Shaw invited me after I did the article on him last year."

They'd argued about this before. C.J. tamped down

his irritation. "They're too young."

"Maybe Helen is, but Susan and Elizabeth would have gotten a lot out of it." Her eyes flashed and her voice rose. "I think Theodore Roosevelt was between their ages when his family spent a year abroad."

C.J. turned and pulled the door shut. "We're not the Roosevelts."

Her eyes narrowed. "What do you want me to write about?"

He wracked his brain for a topic before facing her again. "Not long ago President Wilson said that the United States would never attack another country. You could ask him about that and how he views the Mexican Revolution."

"He would never talk with me about that. He doesn't respect intelligent women, nor does he support woman suffrage." She paused, eyes narrowed. "But his daughters do. I could try to interview them."

C.J. exhaled an exasperated breath. "Don't you ever think of anything else?"

"In April both houses of Congress introduced the suffrage amendment, and Wilson has all but ignored it. I'm worried they'll start the same cat-and-mouse game that the Iowa legislature engaged in when I lived there." Her hands curled into fists. "Besides, when I came east, you promised to support my suffrage work."

His jaw tightened again. "I do."

"But I still can't vote." Her stare shot daggers. "And I want us women to win the right to vote before our girls grow up."

He swallowed against the irritation tightening his throat. "I want that, too."

"But you're not willing to work for it. I am."

"I don't object to your involvement in the cause." He searched for a way to make his point without further infuriating her. "But I can't let it take over *The Chronicle*."

"I'll find another subject for the next story." Her tone carried a steely edge. "But if we don't get the vote here in Pennsylvania before Susan is grown, I'll take the girls and move back to Wyoming."

His breath left him. "Without me?"

"I hope you would come with us." She smiled sweetly.

The implication of her words washed over him. "I don't like the idea of having to start my life all over again."

Stifling a yawn, Inga stepped off the train from Highland Park, Michigan. It had been a long week, working with a photographer, interviewing executives and workers, and watching finished automobiles being turned out at an amazing pace. All she wanted to do was to get a cab to take her home, see the girls, and get some sleep.

Covering this event had meant missing the NAWSA conference in Washington, a detail that still annoyed her, but Nathan and C.J. had insisted. She would have to contact Emma next week to get the details.

Token in hand, she headed toward the baggage area.

"Mrs. Wakefield!"

She spun in the direction of the familiar deep voice.

C.J. walked toward her.

She smiled, her heartbeat racing. "What are you doing here?"

He stepped forward and gave her a quick hug. "I thought you'd get home quicker if I picked you up."

"It's a nice surprise. Thank you. I wasn't looking forward to securing a cab." She paused. "Is there a reason I need to get home quickly?"

"Not really. The girls are eager to see you." He hesitated. "Elizabeth has a cold. She stayed home from school with Sadie today."

Inga's head began to ache. "Is she better tonight than she was this morning?"

"She seemed about the same to me at lunch time. I assume she's improved after an afternoon in bed." He nodded toward the luggage that had arrived on the cart. "I'll get your suitcase."

She handed him the token. He retrieved her bag and they went home.

As soon as she was inside the door, she hurried up the stairs.

"Mama! Mama!" Susan and Helen came running to the landing.

She gave each girl a kiss on the cheek. "I want both of you to tell me one thing about school today, and then I need to go check on your sister."

"I made a be-u-ti-ful decoration for our Christmas tree at school." Helen's rosy face glowed with pride.

"We got our parts for the Christmas program." Susan smiled. "I got the biggest one."

"Wonderful. I can't wait to hear more, but now I need to check on your sister." Inga stood. "You girls get ready for dinner."

She inhaled a deep breath and walked into the room that Elizabeth shared with Helen.

The lamplight cast a soft glow on her sleeping daughter. At her bedside, in the shadows sat a welcome friend.

"Minnie!" Inga whispered. "What are you doing here?"

Elizabeth coughed, a congested, croupy sound. She stirred, but did not awaken.

Minnie stood, took Inga by the arm and walked her to the corner farthest away from the bed. "Sadie was worried about Elizabeth's fever. She wanted a doctor to check on her, but you were out of town, and she couldn't reach Mr. Wakefield to call your doctor." She paused. "So she called me. I hope you don't mind having a Negro doctor treat her."

Inga threw her arms around Minnie. "I'm just glad she called you. You're one of the best doctors I know."

Minnie hugged her back, then stepped out of the embrace.

Inga tiptoed to her daughter's bedside and gently touched the back of her hand to Elizabeth's cheek.

"She's still very warm," Inga whispered. She looked to Minnie.

"Her fever was a hundred and one when I took it just before she fell asleep." Minnie sighed. "It was a hundred and three when I got here."

Inga tread softly back to the corner where Minnie still stood. "I'm so glad Sadie called you. Don't let me forget to pay you before you leave."

Minnie waved dismissively. She looked toward the bed. "We gave her a cool bath, and we've been pouring steaming water into pans on the radiator. She's cooler, and her cough seems to be loosening up. Right now, she seems to be resting comfortably," Minnie continued. "I told Sadie to check on her through the night and keep refilling the pans with hot water."

"I'll work out a schedule to take turns," Inga said. "And I'll have my husband set up a cot for Helen in Susan's room."

"You go downstairs and eat." Minnie took a step toward the chair. "I'll stay with her until you finish."

Inga smiled weakly. "Thank you."

She went downstairs to find dinner already on the table and the family seated.

"I wasn't sure if you were going to eat, so I asked Sadie to go ahead with dinner." C.J. flashed Inga a sheepish smile.

She sat in her usual place. "That's fine."

C.J. sobered. "How's Elizabeth doing?"

"Minnie has gotten her fever down a little and she's resting better." Inga turned her focus to the girls. "Dr. Minnie says that Elizabeth needs to be in a room by herself so you girls don't get sick too, so for now Helen is going to have to sleep in your room, Susan. Daddy will set up a cot tonight."

Inga smiled at her housekeeper, who was helping Helen dish roast beef onto her plate. "I know Dr. Minnie told you to check on Elizabeth through the night, Sadie, but I'll sit with her half and you can take the other half."

Sadie smiled. "Yes, I'll do that."

Inga caught C.J.'s gaze. "I'll let Moder know we

won't be coming to Cedar Falls for Christmas. I don't think the long trip in cold weather would be good for Elizabeth."

By the time spring rolled around, Elizabeth had fully recovered, and against C.J.'s better judgement, Inga had once again become active in the suffrage cause. He watched as his wife pinned on the new 'Votes for Women' sash she had bought for the May Day demonstration and parade.

"At least, you'll have decent weather," he observed.

"Are you planning to meet me in Washington Square when the march is over?" Inga asked as she finished stitching the bottom of the ribbon to her skirt. She tied a knot and cut the thread.

"I want to go with Mama!" Elizabeth skipped across the parlor to stand between her parents.

He stiffened. After the violence in the procession in Washington, he didn't want his daughters involved.

Inga smiled at her. "It's a long walk, and you won't be able to stop along the way."

Elizabeth straightened to her full height, which now reached to Inga's shoulder. "I can do it."

"Me, too." Susan put down the book she was reading and came to join her sisters.

"Me, too." Helen jumped up and down.

C.J. caught Inga's gaze and gave his head a small shake.

She narrowed her eyes.

"I want to vote when I grow up, and I'm willing to march for it." Susan glowered at her father. "And this is the first parade here in Philadelphia."

She seemed far more grown up than normal for her ten – eleven in July – years. But then, she had participated in family discussions of the topic almost since she could talk.

"Me, too," parroted her younger sisters.

Inga glanced at the girls and then back at C.J. "I know Susan can handle the route."

"So can I." Elizabeth looked from him to her

mother. "And I asked first."

"Maybe." Inga lifted a shoulder.

C.J.'s jaw tightened. "She's only seven."

Elizabeth stamped her foot. "Eight!"

He smiled at her. "Sorry, eight."

"Can you walk the whole way without stopping or complaining?" Inga asked.

Although C.J. knew the circumstances would be far different from those at last year's parade in Washington, he worried for his girls' safety.

"Yes, Mama." She nodded solemnly.

"Are you sure, Lizzie Bear?" C.J. put a little threat in his tone.

She smiled at him sweetly. "Yes, Daddy."

"Me, too!" Helen shouted.

"You are definitely too young." He shot Inga a 'don't contradict me' glare.

"But I wanna to be in the parade, too." Helen pouted.

"When you're older." Inga smiled at her, then looked up at C.J., a glint in her eye. "Unless Daddy wants to join the Men's League this morning. Then he could carry you on his shoulders."

Inga winked at C.J.

"Will you, Daddy? Will you?" Hope radiated in Helen's small face.

"No, baby. Not today." He reached to pick her up, but she twisted out of his range. "But we can stand by Washington Square and watch the finish line."

She burst into tears.

Inga patted Helen's head. "Afterwards, we can go to the Wanamaker store to get new coats for winter and hear the organ play. I want to support them since Mr. Wanamaker gives us a discount on supplies we need for our local suffrage headquarters."

An automobile horn honked outside.

"That will be Miss Reed," Inga said.

She kissed the top of Helen's head and gave C.J. a peck on the cheek, then shepherded their older daughters toward the door. "We'll see if she has room for us." She tossed a quick glance at C.J. "If not, you and Helen can drop us off at Rittenhouse Square."

He scowled at the door as it closed behind them. "Come on, baby." He swept Helen into his arms and headed for the garage. "Let's get us each a doughnut before the parade starts."

Inga approached Washington Square holding hands with Susan and Elizabeth. Throughout the march, they had behaved perfectly, and even seemed honored to be involved. She gave their fingers a gentle squeeze. "We're almost there."

"You girls did very well," said Martha, who had been marching to Susan's right throughout the route. She grinned at the girls.

Susan held her head high. "Thank you."

Elizabeth did not reply. Since she probably hadn't heard Martha's message over the noise of the crowd, Inga relayed it to her younger daughter.

Still holding Inga's hand, Elizabeth skipped a few steps ahead, grinning broadly. "Thank you, Mrs. Scott."

"You're both welcome." Martha raised her voice loud enough that Inga was sure Elizabeth heard her.

Elizabeth fell back into the line.

About thirty steps later, they reached the end point. Inga gathered the girls in her arms and gave them a hug. "I'm so proud of you both."

"Can we march with you next time?" Susan's wide eyes and serious expression touched Inga's heart.

"I don't know when or where the next march will be, but if things work out, I'd be happy to have you girls with me." Inga straightened.

Susan threw her arms around Inga's waist. "Thank you, Mama."

"Let's go find Helen and your father." Inga scanned the area, but was unable to see above the heads of the people surrounding them.

Turning into Washington Square, they headed toward the old drinking fountain for horses. They walked slowly through the crowd of marchers who were also looking for loved ones or conversing in small groups.

"Can we get ice cream before we go home?" Susan asked.

"We'll ask Daddy when we find him."

"Mama! Mama!" Helen's voice came from the left.

Inga turned to see her youngest riding above the throng on her father's shoulders. She guided her older daughters toward them.

Elizabeth nearly glowed with pride. "Mrs. Scott said we did good."

"Did she, now?" C.J.'s mouth tightened into a grim line.

Inga looked up at Helen. "Were you a good girl for Daddy?"

She nodded enthusiastically. "Yes. And we had doughnuts."

Inga raised her brows. "You did! You're a lucky girl."

She winked at C.J.

His mouth softened a bit. He set Helen on her feet.

"Can we please get ice cream before we go home?" Susan's earnest tone seemed disproportionately serious for the subject of her question.

All the eyes focused on C.J.

"Don't you think that would spoil your dinner?" he asked somberly, but his lips quivered, as if he was trying to avoid smiling.

"No." Elizabeth stepped forward and took his hand.

"I'm hungry now, and I heard Mama tell Sadie to plan on a later dinner," Susan said in a needy tone. "Please."

"Please," Helen echoed.

C.J.'s gaze fell on Inga.

She shrugged a shoulder and smiled. "It's up to you, Daddy."

He looked from daughter to daughter to daughter.

Finally, his posture relaxed. "Okay, we'll get ice cream." He turned to Inga with a glint in his eyes. "But only if your mama says 'please.'"

A chuckle burst from Inga. She grinned. "Please."

C.J. lit a fire in the fireplace to chase the winter chill from the parlor. Although he had enjoyed their Christmas trip to the west, he was happy to be home. Now that the girls had gone to bed, Inga was curled up on the sofa, reading a book.

He sat down next to her and rested his arm around her shoulders. She looked up and smiled before returning to her book.

After a few minutes, she slipped her bookmark between two pages and closed her book. "The holidays were nice. I'm glad we went west since we didn't go last year." She snuggled against him. "But I'm glad to be back home."

"So am I." He held her close. "Maybe we should stay here for the holidays next year."

"It's tempting. But our parents aren't getting any younger." She looked up at him. "And it's good for our girls to get to know their cousins on both sides."

"Yes. Even if we invited everyone here, I don't think Ruth and Jess would come." C.J. rested his cheek against the top of her head. "They wouldn't want to be this far away from their place in winter when the weather can turn deadly for their cattle."

"I'm not sure I'd want everyone here at one time, anyway." She sighed. "We'd be very crowded."

"Besides." C.J. kissed her hair. "Our parents like their traditions."

"Maybe we could invite one brother or sister's family at a time. In the summer when the children don't have school," Inga mused. "We could show them around the historical sites." She grinned. "I know I was impressed the first time I saw them."

He gave her shoulders a gentle hug. "I think that was one of the reasons I was able to convince you to move here."

She shrugged. "You might be right."

"Are you sorry you gave up teaching to write for *The Chronicle*?"

"Not as much as I thought I would be. It helped

that I was able to tutor Minnie, and now Sadie. And I love playing school with the girls." Her lips curved upward. "It's made me understand why my mother always played school with my brothers and half-sisters and me."

"It's because they learned so much from 'playing school' with you that Susan and Elizabeth were able to skip grades. They're so smart." He lightly kissed her cheek. "Like their mother."

"Because we've been given the opportunity to learn."

They sat in comfortable silence for a while.

"What story are you working on for the magazine?" he asked idly.

"Something for the May issue about Mother's Day, now that President Wilson has declared it a national holiday." She paused. "And I've been corresponding with some of the survivors from the *Titanic* to find out what their lives are like for the three-year anniversary of it sinking in April. I'm hoping to arrange to meet with one or more of them."

"Three years. It doesn't seem like it's been nearly that long." He considered the heart-breaking story she had written shortly after the tragic disaster. "Maybe we could use a few excerpts from your original piece."

"Maybe." She tensed under his arm. "Carrie Catt is going to take back the leadership of NAWSA this year and hopefully, patch up some of the rifts that tore the group apart under Anna Shaw." Inga pursed her lips. "I haven't written a suffrage article in more than a year. Do you think I can do a story on Carrie now that it's 1915?"

"It's been more than a year since we ran a suffrage article." C.J. had expected her to lobby for one sooner. "I think that might be all right."

C.J. thumbed through the latest issue of *The Chronicle*, hot off the press. He turned to Inga's story about Carrie Chapman Catt. He'd had no idea about the years she'd spent caring for her husband before his death, her international experience, or her role in founding the Women's Peace Party. And Inga had handled it all masterfully. Without overtly bugling support for the suffrage cause, she'd managed to argue the merits of women having the vote.

He walked straight to his wife's office and knocked on her door.

"Come in." Her voice sounded stronger than it had when they'd arrived at work this morning.

Upon entering, he found her reading a newspaper.

"Do you think President Wilson will take back his declaration of neutrality now that the Germans have sunk the *Lusitania*?"

He took a step backward. "What prompted that question?"

"The headline says that Secretary of State Bryan has resigned over the protest the president lodged with Germany and his failure to warn our citizens against traveling on British ships," she said without looking up. "One letter to the editor states that he should hold true to his word, another argues that we should join the side of the British."

"I'm becoming inclined to agree with the latter." He took the chair across from her desk and waited for her to finish reading. Watching her, he was relieved to note that color had returned to her cheeks.

Finally, she set down the newspaper. "To what do I owe the pleasure of this visit?"

He handed the magazine to her.

She glanced at the contents page, then turned to her article. After skimming it, she looked up and smiled.

"I didn't edit it, if that's what you were worried about." He grinned.

She lifted her chin. "I wasn't worried. I expect you would have told me if you'd made changes."

"You appear to be feeling better. Are you?"

She nodded. "Yes, thank goodness." After folding the newspaper, she held it out to him. "Want to trade this for the magazine?"

"Sure." He took the paper from her.

"What would you think of my doing an article about the Justice Bell? Maybe for the October issue?" She tipped her head. "So it comes out right before the Pennsylvania referendum."

"Maybe." He would discuss it with Nathan this afternoon. "What are you working on now?"

"I've been contacting some of our Olympic athletes to get their reaction to the 1916 Berlin games being cancelled, and to find out their future plans." She shrugged. "I'm not sure if there will be enough there for a good story, but if there is I might plan on gathering the information to write an article for early next year."

"I'm sure they're disappointed." He stood. "I'd better go so you can get back to work. I'm glad you're feeling better."

Inga leaned over the toilet and retched until nothing more came up, leaving her feeling exhausted. After flushing, she sat on the edge of the bathtub. This was the fifth day in a row she'd woken up sick.

A light tap sounded at the door.

"Can I help you back to bed?" The concern in C.J.'s soft voice came through the oak.

She stood, recovering her balance before walking over to open the door. "I would appreciate it."

"Tomorrow I'll take you to see a doctor." C.J. wrapped his arm around her waist, giving her welcome support as he escorted her back to bed.

"I don't need a doctor." She sat on the edge of the mattress. He sat down beside her.

"I'm worried about you." He put his arm around her shoulder. "And I want to be sure what you have is not contagious. I wouldn't want the girls to get sick."

She rested her head on his chest. "They won't."

"How do you know?" he murmured against the top of her head.

"Because I'm expecting." She wished she could muster some enthusiasm for the idea, but at this moment she couldn't.

"Really?" He pulled away, jaw dropping.

She nodded then wished she hadn't.

"That possibility had occurred to me, but I didn't want to get my hopes up." His eyes shone bright. He smiled. "How long have you known?"

"I've suspected for about a month, but this morning I'm sure." She swallowed.

"Maybe we'll have a little boy." His wistful tone touched Inga's heart.

She managed a weak smile. "For your sake, I hope so."

"Lie down and rest." He stood. "Would you like me to bring you some tea and toast?"

"Not right now. Maybe in an hour or two."

"I'll tell Sadie to let you rest and bring you some tea later."

Inga lay back down. "Thank you."

At C.J.'s insistence, she spent Sunday and Monday in bed.

By Tuesday, she felt stronger than she had in a week. He agreed that she should return to work for a few hours, but said he would take her home at noon.

"It's hard to believe the girls will be going back to school soon," C.J. said as they approached the *Chronicle* building.

"I think they're looking forward to it, even though only Susan admits it." A brief, sharp twinge in Inga's side caused her to inhale a sharp breath as C.J. held the door open for her.

She tried to ignore the cramp clenching her abdominal muscles as she approached the elevator.

C.J. pushed the call button, then turned to her. His brows knit together. "Are you all right? You're very pale."

"I'm having pains in my stomach." Fighting tears, she rested a hand on the offending area. "I don't think—"

The elevator door opened. The operator smiled his usual smile. "Good morning."

C.J. wrapped his arm around her waist. "Let me help you to your office, and I'll get you some water."

The hot, stale air in the closed compartment was stifling. She could hardly catch her breath. The elevator car began to whirl. She swayed.

He tightened his grip on her. "Hold on."

A lightheadedness fogged her vision.

Her knees gave out and all went dark.

Her head throbbed. Her limbs felt too heavy to move. Something was wrong.

"Does she need to go to the hospital?" C.J. asked, his voice wavering.

"I don't think so. The bleeding seems to have stopped, for now at least. But she needs to remain there for a while," a man said softly. "Then take her home and put her to bed. If the bleeding starts up again, I'll want to check on her. But if it's profuse, take her straight to the hospital."

Pressure built in her temples. She opened her eyes.

C.J. was at her side. Holding her hand.

"She's awake!" His face was splotched with red. He was looking at her with puffy eyes. She was lying on the sofa in C.J.'s office.

Dr. Price stood a few feet away. His open medical bag lay on a wooden chair next to C.J.

She lifted her head slightly, but felt as though a lightning bolt had struck her forehead. Her skirt was bunched up around her waist and blood-stained newspapers covered her legs. A sickly metallic smell engulfed her.

The doctor came to her side.

No. It couldn't have happened again.

"C.J." She thought she'd said his name, but she'd barely heard the sound.

Her husband leaned closer to her face. "How do you feel?"

She tried to lick her dry lips, but no moisture came. "Dreadful. What?"

His gaze flew to Dr. Price.

C.J. gently stroked her cheek. "I'm sorry, Inga," he said in a choked voice. "You've lost the baby."

Lost the baby. Sob after sob escaped her.

Chapter Seventeen

September 10, 1915
Philadelphia, Pennsylvania

Dear Sarah,

Thank you for your kind invitation for my family and me to visit you and your family for New York's suffrage march on October 23. I regret we will be unable to join you for the event.

We will be having our own parade and ceremony here in Philadelphia the day before, October 22, to welcome the Justice Bell. My girls are excited to have the opportunity to see it. Dr. Shaw's 'Yellow Suffrage' automobile is also scheduled to appear in our procession. Is she planning to have it participate in yours?

Congratulations on convincing your husband to join the Men's League. I have been unable to persuade mine to sign up. He and his employer still feel they need to be seen as neutral, or at least as not actively supporting the cause.

In addition to the Carrie Catt article that just came out, I have received permission to do an article on the Justice Bell. I've spoken with Mrs. Ruschenberger about her decision to finance it. The story will come out after Pennsylvania's referendum on woman suffrage on November 2. I'm hoping the piece will have a happy ending.

All my best to you and your family.

Lovingly in friendship,
Inga

After the procession, C.J. followed Inga and his daughters as they worked their way toward the Justice Bell.

"It looks just like the Liberty Bell!" Elizabeth cried, as they neared the front of the crowd.

Inga smiled. "But there is one big difference. Can

you tell what it is?"

All three girls solemnly studied the bell.

"It doesn't have a crack," Susan said after a few moments.

"That's right." Inga shot a glance at C.J.

He winked.

"There's another difference." Inga's gaze floated from girl to girl. "The bell can't ring, yet."

"Why not?" Helen asked, an endearing pout on her lips.

"Because we women can't vote, yet." Inga said it with barely a hint of frustration.

"When will it ring?" Helen asked.

Elizabeth glared at her sister. "When women can vote, dummy."

"Elizabeth!" Inga and C.J. scolded at the same time.

She hung her head. "Sorry."

"Your question was a good one, Helen," Inga said in her teacher voice. "We don't know for sure. We hope that women in Pennsylvania will be able to vote after the men cast their ballots on November second."

"Do you think that will happen?" Susan's focus on her mother did not waver. "I want to be able to vote when I'm twenty-one."

C.J.'s chest tightened. It was hard to believe that was only nine years away. And if women weren't granted suffrage by then, Inga would insist on moving back to Wyoming.

"I don't know if that will happen." Inga's eyes shone with unspilled tears, but her voice remained even. "Many of the older women I met when I started working for the cause spent their whole lives trying to win the vote. They have now passed away, never having had the chance to vote. I'm very sad for them."

She looked up at C.J. and then back to the girls. "I don't want that to happen to you." She folded her arms. "When I lived in Laramie, I could vote. Grandma Wakefield and Aunt Ruth cast their ballots in elections just like the men do. Do you remember when we read about the Boston Tea Party?"

"The colonists threw tea into Boston Harbor," Elizabeth said.

"It was one reason we had the Revolutionary War," Susan added.

"Because England made the colonists pay taxes, but they couldn't choose–vote for–people to represent them in the government." Inga smiled. "I'm proud of you girls for remembering."

His daughters all grinned, their faces aglow.

Inga's smile faded. "Well, I work very hard, and I have to pay taxes, but I don't get to vote for people to represent me."

C.J. saw her chest rise and fall with a breath. He'd always known she was passionate about suffrage, but until now, he hadn't thought about woman suffrage in terms of taxation without representation.

"I have to rely on Daddy to vote in a way that takes care of my needs. Sometimes he has different needs than I do, so we each need to be able to vote for people that represent our own needs." She shot him a glance.

He nodded, ashamed he had never even thought of her interests when casting his vote.

She shifted her focus back to the girls. "That's why, if we don't win the right to vote in the next few years, I think we should go live in Wyoming."

The girls' eyes widened. Susan gasped.

"We won't be leaving anytime soon, but I want you to consider the idea." Inga straightened.

C.J.'s stomach tightened.

She took a step back. "We should move out of the way so other people can get a better look at the bell."

The referendum had been defeated.

Inga closed her office door. She could no longer hold back her sobs. Over the last months and years, she and so many of her friends had worked so hard for suffrage in Pennsylvania.

She dropped into her desk chair and scanned the newspaper column. The words blurred as she blinked to make out more details.

A determined tap sounded. Had she missed a previous one?

She sniffed in a breath and wiped her tears away with her handkerchief.

Another knock.

She swallowed a threatening sob and called, "Come in."

Her voice was more unsteady than she would have liked.

C.J. entered the room and closed the door behind him.

"Oh, sweetheart." He hurried over, stood behind her chair and wrapped his arms around her. "I'm so sorry it didn't pass."

Another sob escaped her.

"New York's didn't pass either." C.J. offered this information in a way that sounded like it was a consolation prize, but it only deepened her despair.

"Carrie Catt worked very hard on the New York effort." She narrowed her eyes. "I think this shows we need to pursue a national amendment. If we have to wait for each state to pass suffrage, it'll be a hundred more years before all women in the United States win the right to vote."

"If it makes you feel any better, forty-nine percent of the voters in Pennsylvania supported it."

His soothing voice annoyed her. She drew a ragged breath. "It doesn't make me feel better. We still haven't won." She swallowed. "I fear we'll never win suffrage since we have to depend on men to vote it in."

"With each referendum, it gains more support." He rubbed her back, but his touch wasn't comforting.

Clenching her teeth, she fought to keep her voice measured. "I guess this just means we'll have to redouble our efforts."

The following August, Inga attended a meeting of the newly formed National Women's Party in Colorado Springs, Colorado. Although the referendum in Pennsylvania had failed, Inga wanted to learn the general thinking of women who currently had full suffrage, and whether or not they would be willing to support their sisters from states where the right to vote had not yet been won.

From there, she took a train to Laramie to rejoin her family in their visit to the Wakefield ranch. At the depot, she disembarked from the stuffy passenger car, scanning the crowd for C.J.

"Inga!" A female voice called. "Over here."

"Ruth!" She grinned and started in the direction of her sister-in-law.

When they reached each other, they hugged.

"What a nice surprise!" Inga couldn't stop smiling.

"I thought this would give us more time to talk," Ruth said, wiping the perspiration from her face.

"How are C.J. and the girls?" Inga asked.

"The girls have been running wild with my children on my folks' ranch." Ruth grinned. "It reminds C.J. and me of when we were growing up."

Inga laughed. "The same thing happens to me when we're on the farm in Iowa."

"Let's get your luggage and then have a cool drink. Maybe some ice cream."

"Sounds good."

They gathered Inga's suitcase and stowed it in the back of a newer model Chevrolet.

"Is this yours?" Inga asked.

"No." Ruth chuckled. "I have a well-worn truck that contends with the nearly non-existent roads out my way." She gestured for Inga to get in then took the driver's seat. "This is Dad's pride and joy. He thought you should be chauffeured in style."

Ruth drove to a nearby café. Inga welcomed the breeze created by the moving car.

The café had a host of fans circulating the air. They were seated near one of them.

"This was a good choice," Inga said as the waiter came and took their order.

"So tell me." Ruth planted her elbows on the table and rested her chin in her hands. "How was your meeting?"

"Very good. They decided not to make a presidential endorsement, and to oppose all Democratic congressional candidates, because the party has been in power and they have failed to pass a federal suffrage amendment."

"I confess I'm a bit confused about all the suffrage organizations." Ruth frowned. "I guess I haven't been following the cause as I should have."

"Why would you?" Inga patted her hand. "If I was still living here, I wouldn't be all that interested either."

"So are they all part of the NASWA?"

"The Congressional Union started out as a Committee of the NASWA, but after the 1913 march in Washington, they became more independent and split off in 1914." Inga placed her napkin in her lap. "Last December, they made one last attempt at reconciliation. It failed."

Inga sat back as the waiter delivered their root beers.

Ruth leaned forward after he left. "So which one is the Woman's Party associated with?"

"The Congressional Union." Inga sighed. "The Woman's Party is made up of women from the twelve states where they have the vote, so primarily those in the west. The CU is made up of those of us still trying to win enfranchisement. They're complementary."

Ruth's brow furrowed. "So what's the difference between NASWA and the Congressional Union, if they both represent disenfranchised women?"

"Carrie Catt believes patience will eventually bring us progress. Since she took over the NASWA again this year, she's made it more active than it was under Anna Shaw. Carrie believes in concentrating on the states."

Inga paused while their ice cream was delivered.

"Lucy Burns and Alice Paul have a more national focus." Inga picked up her spoon. "They're both Americans, but they worked for suffrage in England, and they're willing to use more radical methods, like parades and pickets to make their points." She put a spoonful of the cold, creamy treat into her mouth. It slid down her throat, leaving a cool trail.

Ruth watched as Inga ate. "And which group are you with?"

Before answering, Inga took a sip of root beer to buy time. "So far this year, I've been trying to associate with both. Since I'm a journalist, they've both tolerated me and neither have made any loyalty demands." She met and held Ruth's gaze. "I don't know how much longer that can last."

C.J. glanced out the window at the gray November day. He and Inga needed to settle on a date to leave on their trip west for the holidays. He felt like Scrooge as he set Inga's suffrage article on the corner of his desk, but he had no choice but to reject it.

He trudged down the hall to her office. Her door stood open. He tapped on the frame and walked in.

She sat in her chair, back to the desk, staring out the window.

He cleared his throat. "Are you okay?"

"Inez Milholland Boissevain passed away." Her voice was flat.

He walked over and placed a hand on her shoulder. She leaned her head against his arm.

Maybe this wasn't the best time to discuss her article.

"I want to do a story on her." Her tone carried a determined note. "Is that okay with you?"

He hesitated. Since it would likely be more of a memorial piece than a political one, Nathan would probably find it acceptable. "Would you be willing to swap it for the one on the Woman's Party?"

She sighed. "I suppose. Ever since she led the Washington parade in 1913, I've thought she would be a good subject. I should have written about her when I could have interviewed her."

"But you knew her." He gave her shoulder a gentle squeeze. "And you know of her work. You have enough information to compose a nice tribute."

Finally, she looked up at him. Her eyes were dry, but their puffiness belied the fact that she had been crying. "She was only thirty. Her passing has made me realize how much she has done for the cause, and how little I've done in comparison."

"You've done quite a lot considering you have a job and a family."

She inhaled a long breath. "I think I'm going down to Washington to participate in the demonstration during the president's annual address to Congress."

"That's only a little more than a week away!"

"I know." She met his gaze. "I'll do it in memory of Inez."

"But it's dangerous." He moved in front of her, towering over her in an effort to convey the risk. "It's only been a month since the women demonstrating against Wilson in Chicago were attacked by a mob."

"If women in the east could have voted, Wilson wouldn't have won this year's election." Her eyes narrowed. "Unfortunately, we couldn't. It's time we stop begging men for the vote and start demanding it."

He took a few steps backward. "But you might be hurt." He softened his voice. "Think of the girls."

The muscles in her face tensed. "I am thinking about them. I'm thinking about their future. I want them to have the right to vote."

"But what about your time with them right now?"

She frowned. "It's a necessary sacrifice I'm willing to make."

He jammed his hands into his pockets. "At what cost to you? And to our family?"

As President Wilson delivered his annual address to Congress, Inga stood silently with fellow demonstrators, holding their suffrage banner. The next morning, before returning to Philadelphia, she met Rachel in front of the Washington monument.

"So you're abandoning the NAWSA for the Congressional Union?" Rachel asked as they strolled toward a nearby café. "Even after Mrs. Catt set up the 'Suffrage House' as headquarters for more intense lobbying efforts?"

"I think they realize that Alice and Lucy have made great strides in getting suffrage back into the national conversation, and they don't want to be left out. But, since Carrie made a deal with the president to put the suffrage efforts on hold once the country becomes involved in the war—and we know things are moving in that direction—the Association will again become a do-nothing organization." Inga couldn't keep the annoyance out of her voice. "I don't think we should let up on our pressure. We've made a lot of progress with more western states enfranchising women."

"But she says it will give American women a chance to show their patriotism." Rachel gestured toward the street they were looking for. "While our men will be fighting for freedom in Europe."

"I think it's every bit as patriotic to fight for our rights here at home." Inga drew in a breath of chilly air. "It seems a travesty if Wilson agrees to fight for the democracies abroad, while the rights of our own citizens are being denied."

"I see your point of view," Rachel allowed. "The same can be said about suppression of the rights of Negro men to vote."

"I know, and I share your frustration with the situation." Inga focused on the buildings ahead, trying to identify the one they sought. "Once war is declared, I plan to do an article on the topic."

"But you might make some of your readers mad."

"I don't care if I make them mad, as long as I make them think." Inga lifted her coat collar against the cold. "I want them to acknowledge the truth, if only to themselves."

"Good luck."

At the corner, Rachel turned to the right. Inga followed.

"What are you working on now?" Rachel asked.

"A tribute to Inez Boissevain," Inga said. "I've been struggling to show her courage without putting her memory on a pedestal."

"There's going to be a memorial service for her at the Capitol."

Inga nodded. "I found out when I got into town yesterday."

"Are you going to come back for it?"

"I'd like to, but it's going to be on the twenty-fifth." Inga sighed. "We're going to Iowa for Christmas. How about you?"

"I'm torn." Rachel frowned. "I associate her with the segregation in the 1913 parade. I don't know if she had anything to do with it, but she led the march."

"I still can't believe how pervasive bigotry has become in the movement." Inga sighed again. "You were right in Denver when you said I was naïve. I've learned so much since then."

Rachel flashed her a small smile. "Are you going to do an article about that woman who was elected to represent Montana?"

"Jeanette Rankin. I hope so." A small surge of energy rippled through Inga. "I've written her a letter asking to meet with her when she gets here."

"I never thought I'd live to see a woman in Congress." Rachel's dark eyes shone.

"It is amazing." Inga grinned. "I wonder if she intends to 'clean the nation's house' as Inez would have said."

Stopping at the door to the café, Rachel shook her head. "I don't envy her. She'll be far outnumbered by all those men, and I don't expect they'll be kind."

Inga sobered. "But, hopefully, she'll be a beacon for change. I expect we'd have far less corruption and far more compassion if this country wasn't run only by white men."

C.J. placed the plan for the February issue on the corner of his desk and stood. Still tired from the Christmas trip to Iowa and Wyoming, he reached his arms over his head and stretched.

He shrugged into his heavy coat and hung his scarf around his neck. Plucking his hat from the top of the rack, he walked out of his office. His secretary had already left.

The hallway was nearly empty as he strode to Inga's office.

The door was ajar. She was scribbling notes. He tapped before stepping inside. "Ready to go home?"

She looked up and nodded.

"What are you working on?" he asked, as she stood and put on her coat.

"Jeanette Rankin has agreed to meet with me, and she sent some biographical information." She buttoned up and placed her hat on her head. "I was just drafting a response."

"So you'll be going to Washington to interview her?"

"Yes, but not until she's been sworn in and has a little experience in the House." She wrapped her scarf around her neck.

"Darn. I was hoping you might be able to cover the inauguration and interview her on the same trip." He held the door and closed it behind them.

"I refuse to cover the inauguration. Since President Wilson won re-election, he's become more condescending than ever toward suffrage." A current of anger ran below her words. "Yesterday, he rebuked the women who presented the resolutions that were passed in Inez's memory."

"Where did you hear about this?" He pinched his lips together.

"I had lunch with Emma Reed, remember? I told you this morning."

He nodded.

"She's been working regularly at the local headquarters," Inga continued. "Alice Paul and a group of women who had met with the president picketed the White House today."

"Do you think that's a good idea?"

She tipped her head. "I believe that keeping up a

visible presence in the nation's capitol is what has brought the cause back into the national limelight."

Pulling his coat around him, he fastened the buttons. He didn't mind the suffrage movement being in the 'limelight' as long as his wife didn't become the face of it.

A few months later, Inga strolled from the Capitol to the National Woman's Party headquarters in the Cameron House on Lafayette Square. May had always been one of her favorite months, and today's sunny warmth with a gentle breeze reaffirmed that opinion. Flowers bloomed. Leaves fluttered.

Her interview with Jeanette Rankin had gone well. Although Inga had the urge to skip along the sidewalk, she kept her steps brisk and dignified. Once inside the door, a grin spread across her face.

"Hello. May I help you?" A young woman Inga didn't know greeted her.

"I'm Inga Stryker Wakefield." She smiled at the stranger. "I'm meeting Emma Reed here."

"Inga Stryker." The woman blinked. "I thought your story about Inez Milholland was lovely."

Pressure built behind Inga's eyes. "Thank you. She was a very special woman."

The other woman cleared her throat. "I'm Mary Ingrahm. I believe Miss Reed is in the kitchen."

Inga thanked her and walked back to the kitchen.

Emma greeted her. "How did your interview with Miss Rankin go?"

"She's amazing." Inga set her handbag on a stool. "It will be good to have her voice in the House now that the suffrage amendment has been reintroduced in both houses of Congress."

"NASWA has criticized her vote against entering the European war." Emma set the coffee pot on the stove. "Did she say how she feels about that?"

"When I asked, she shrugged it off." Inga pulled mugs from the glass-doored cupboard. "She said she's always been a pacifist, and her constituents knew it when they elected her. She wasn't happy with the

Selective Service Act that just passed."

"I'm not either." Emma frowned. "My brother falls within the ages of men eligible to be drafted."

"I'm sorry to hear it." Inga gave her friend a quick hug. "All of mine are over thirty, so I feel fortunate."

Emma turned away and retrieved a pitcher of cream from the refrigerator. She set it on the counter beside the mugs.

"I've heard from some of the women here that the male representatives have been giving her a hard time." She pressed her mouth into a thin line.

"It's true, but she doesn't want me to say anything about the situation." Inga had decided to honor Miss Rankin's request. "She fears that mentioning their behavior will exacerbate it."

"She's probably right."

The pulsing sound of the percolating pot grew louder. The roasted nutty aroma of coffee filled the room.

"Are you still planning to stand with us at the White House gate tomorrow?" Emma asked.

"Yes." Inga nodded. "C.J. was angry about it when I left. I hope he'll be over it by the time I get home on Friday."

"Mama, I want to take the trousers you helped me make when we were out at Grandma's house, but they're in the laundry," Susan said, entering the kitchen through the back stairway. "I wore them on the hike with the Scotts last Sunday."

Inga raised a brow. "And you forgot to put them in the laundry on Monday?"

Susan hung her head. "Yes."

"I can run a quick load or two through the washing machine today," Sadie offered. "And if the weather stays clear, everything will be dry and pressed in time to pack for your trip."

Inga smiled sadly. "I don't know what we're going to do without you this fall, Sadie. You've spoiled us."

"I'll be working with Ada all summer. She'll be

ready to take over in the fall." Sadie glanced around the kitchen. "Besides, I'm still gonna be here in town, so I can come help her when I'm not in classes."

"Like Minnie did," Susan added.

Inga gazed at her daughter. "I'm surprised you remember that."

Susan lifted her chin. "I remember everything."

Chuckling, Inga shook her head. She couldn't look at Sadie or she might burst out laughing.

"Well, I do," Susan said haughtily.

"Okay, Miss Elephant, who never forgets...." Inga swallowed back a giggle. "You and your sisters should collect the clothes that need to be washed right away and bring them to Sadie. I'll check mine and your father's. Then I'm going to finish my article so I can give it to your father when he comes home for lunch."

Susan frowned. "I was hoping we could play school this morning."

"I know it's your turn to pick our language for today." Inga patted her daughter's shoulder. "I won't forget before this afternoon."

"Since I'm going to skip a grade this fall, I want to be sure I know my French."

"You know you can stay with your current class if you want to." Inga studied her daughter's reaction.

"No, I want to skip."

"Maybe one day a week we could speak only French." Inga suggested. "That would help keep you in practice."

Sadie smiled. "It would help me be ready for college, too."

"Let's do it." Susan grinned for a moment, then sobered. "What about when we're in Iowa and Wyoming?"

"I don't know about Wyoming, but we can plan on it in Iowa," Inga said, recalling playing school with her mother years ago. "It will be fun to see how much French Grandma Anna remembers."

Later, she was proofreading her typed final draft when she heard C.J.'s footsteps coming down the hallway. Surprised, she skimmed more quickly, finishing as he entered the library.

"Have you seen this morning's paper?" He sounded almost breathless, as if he'd run home to share some news.

Was something wrong? Were they going to have to delay their trip? "No." She kept her tone calmer than her racing heart belied. "I've been working on my article and waiting for you to bring home the newspaper."

He handed it to her. "Two of the National Woman's Party pickets at the White House were arrested when the Russian diplomats came in yesterday."

Inga's brow furrowed. "Who? For what? The women just stand there silently. It's their First Amendment right. They've done it for six months without being arrested."

"Maybe it's become too much of an embarrassment for the president."

Inga stood. "It's meant to be. Since when is embarrassing the president against the law? He often does it himself."

"Miss Burns and another young woman."

Inga opened the paper and quickly scanned the article. "Miss Morey from Boston was the other one arrested."

"It looks like they were released without charges," C. J. said.

Forcing herself to inhale a calming breath, she picked up her article and thrust it into his hands. "After lunch, I'm going down to local headquarters so I can find out what is going on."

Early in the afternoon, Inga walked into the Eastern District of Pennsylvania offices in the Hale Building and found Emma Reed positioned next to a telephone at a desk just inside the door.

"What's going on down in Washington?" Inga tapped the story in the newspaper she'd brought along. An identical issue lay on the desk.

"Miss Katzenstein said that the District of

Columbia police chief went to the Woman's Party headquarters day before yesterday and told Alice Paul that the women had to stop picketing."

Inga pulled a pencil and paper from her handbag. "On what grounds?"

Emma's gaze fixed on the items in Inga's hands. "Are you going to write a story about it?"

"Not now, but possibly in the future." Inga made note of the date and Emma's name. "We're getting ready to leave for Iowa and Wyoming, but maybe when I get back. What reason did he give to stop picketing?"

"None, except that if they didn't stop, the pickets would be arrested." Emma inhaled as though to fortify herself. "Miss Paul pointed out that the law hadn't changed and the party's lawyers had advised them of their legal right to picket. But yesterday the police arrested Miss Burns and Miss Morey anyway."

Inga jotted notes. "What were the charges?"

"According to the person Miss Katzenstein talked with, the women were held at the police station for hours, then told they had obstructed traffic on Pennsylvania Avenue and were released."

Inga scribbled notes in her personal shorthand. "Were they in the street?"

"Of course not." Emma's face tensed. "They were standing by the fence as usual."

"So how were they obstructing traffic?" Inga held her pencil at the ready.

Emma shrugged. "I wasn't there."

"It sounds like a trumped-up charge. Maybe they did it to scare the women." Inga scratched another note. "What's the plan going forward?"

"I'm not sure, but I know there are pickets at both the White House and Congress today." Emma frowned.

"Have you heard if they've been arrested, too?"

"Not yet." Emma pulled open a drawer and withdrew a notebook. "Can we count on you to take a turn with the picketing?"

Inga swallowed. Her heart pounded at the thought

of being arrested. “Ask me again when I get back home at the end of the summer.”

Chapter Eighteen

Philadelphia, Pennsylvania
September 2, 1917

Dear Moder,

I'm very worried about what's happening in this country. In our nation's capitol, the First Amendment rights of women are under siege. Week after week small numbers of women stand quietly with banners protesting the administration's policy toward woman suffrage, and week after week they are being arrested on the manufactured charge of 'obstruction of traffic.' They aren't obstructing anything, although the crowds that come to watch or taunt or even attack the brave women may be guilty of the charged offense.

Even when the pickets are assaulted, the police do nothing to protect them. Instead, they arrest the women, not the assailants. And the women are being sentenced to the District Jail and the Occoquan Workhouse. It's a frightening direction for our government to take—a government most women had no say in electing.

We are criticized as 'unpatriotic' for calling the president 'Kaiser Wilson,' but his authoritarian efforts to suppress women's rights have earned him the title. Especially when he could convince Congress to pass the Susan B. Anthony Amendment. The Senate Woman Suffrage Committee is discussing a bill now. Unfortunately, the House Judiciary Committee will likely table it, like they have all the other suffrage measures.

The arrested suffragists have repeatedly pointed out that they are being jailed for political reasons, not for breaking laws. Meanwhile, American men are fighting in Europe for political liberty that is still denied to women here at home. The pickets have elected to serve the jail sentence rather than pay the unjust fines the court imposed.

I hope all is well with you and the family, and that your harvest is bountiful. We enjoyed our visit with you this summer, and the girls are still talking about the cats. C.J. and I are discussing getting them one for Christmas, but I fear each daughter will want her own.
With love,
Inga

"Thank you for calling with this." C.J. hung up the receiver and finished sorting the photographs of wreckage the darkroom had sent up an hour ago. Although the pictures accurately recorded the damage, they fell short of conveying the feeling of despair of those whose lives had been destroyed in an instant.

When he finished, he walked down the hall. The door to Inga's office was open, so he stepped inside.

She was pounding away on her typewriter keys with her usual concentration.

"Is that your story on the Matoon tornado?" he asked.

She held up a hand momentarily, then returned to typing.

A few minutes later, the clicking stopped. She yanked the sheets of paper and the carbon from the roller and set them down. Her gaze lifted to him. "No." She reached to the far corner of her desk and picked up a different small stack of papers. "Here it is. Did you get your photographs of the devastation developed?"

"Yes." He accepted the article she offered. "It was convenient that we could stop there on our way home from Iowa."

She smiled wryly. "And that you insisted on buying a new Brownie camera before we left for Wyoming."

He grinned. "That, too."

She held out another set of pages. "And here's my piece on the Espionage Act that was passed in June."

"Thank you." He paused. "How was your interview

with W.E.B. Du Bois this morning?"

"Very interesting." Inga's eyes sparkled, as they always did when she talked of subjects that interested her. "I got the information I needed from him for my article about the National Association for the Advancement of Colored People, but he was telling me about the Silent Protest he helped organize."

"What is that?" C.J. squared the set of papers in his hands. "Is it like the suffrage protests?"

"A little." She leaned back in her chair. "They held a demonstration in New York in July to bring attention to the deaths of Negroes in the East St. Louis riot along with lynchings in Texas and Tennessee."

He dropped onto the chair across from her and she leaned toward him.

"I mentioned Rachel's brother-in-law's death in Memphis," she continued. "And he said he remembered reading my long-ago article on lynchings. He was very complimentary."

C.J. shifted his position. They had quibbled over whether or not lynching was an appropriate subject for *The Chronicle*. "That was a good one, even though we did have some criticism."

"I will be going up to Boston on Tuesday to interview Moorfield Storey about serving as the founding president of the NAACP." She straightened. "I'll be home Tuesday night."

"Is he that white attorney you mentioned?"

She nodded. "From the information I've found on his career, he should be an interesting man to talk with."

He glanced down at the two articles he held. A prickle of uneasiness climbed up his spine. She was pressing herself to get ahead in her work. Why? Hopefully if he started talking about suffrage, she would tell him.

Swallowing back his foreboding, he turned his thoughts to the reason he'd walked into her office. "Our contact in D.C. called a few minutes ago. The House of Representatives has created a Woman

Suffrage Committee."

Her eyes widened. "If the suffrage bill reported out by the Senate Woman Suffrage Committee last week passes the full Senate, does that mean it will bypass the House Judiciary Committee?"

"That's the speculation."

Inga scowled. "Senator Jones' visit to the Occoquan Workhouse and his report of ill treatment of suffrage prisoners spurred the Senate's committee to action, but I feel sorry for the women held there."

Even though he couldn't believe the situation was as bad as the Senator had described, he was relieved his wife wasn't among them. "Well, at least suffrage is finally beginning to progress through Congress."

A genuine smile spread over her face. "The pressure from the pickets is finally bearing fruit."

He slumped against the wooden chair's back. "So maybe they can stop protesting soon."

Her smile vanished. "Only when the Susan B. Anthony Amendment is passed by both houses of Congress and signed by the president. Until then, the cause needs more workers, since the police keep putting the women in jail."

He felt as though she had kicked him in the stomach. "You're not going down to protest at the White House."

"Not yet." Her eyes narrowed. "But Emma Reed is. For now, I'm going to take her place answering phones at the local headquarters."

"For now?" He had known she was committed to the cause when he courted her, but he hadn't expected she would put the suffrage effort ahead of their marriage, their children. "How will it look if you end up in jail?"

"The same as it does for those who have already been in jail." A muscle in her jaw twitched.

"But how will it affect our family? The girls?" he asked, already knowing her answer.

"Hopefully, it will affect the girls and me by securing the vote for us." She glowered at him. "When

I agreed to marry you and come to Philadelphia, you promised to support my work for the cause and do whatever you could to help."

Every muscle in his body tightened.

"You haven't even joined the Men's League to show your support." Her voice sounded as taut as he felt.

"And you know why. Nathan and I need to be seen as neutral."

"A convenient excuse." She trembled with anger.

He clenched his teeth to keep from saying anything that would make their situation worse. The suffrage movement was driving a wedge between them. He didn't want to set it deeper.

"But I'm no longer making excuses." Her volume was low, her tone icy. "From now on, I'll do whatever the Party needs me to do until we win the right to vote."

C.J. frowned. She'd already had her arm broken in service to the cause. He hated to think what could happen if she joined the picket lines.

A week later, C.J. watched from the hallway outside his office as Miss Katzenstein strode toward the elevator. Not a good omen. There was only one person on this floor that she could have been meeting.

Returning to his desk, he tried to concentrate on the final layout for the tornado article. After rearranging the photographs several times, he slid the materials to one side.

The telephone rang. Dread stole over him. A second ring.

He lifted the receiver to his ear. "Wakefield."

"Mrs. Wakefield is here," his secretary said. "She would like to speak with you."

"Okay." C.J. spoke into the mouthpiece. "Send her in." His gaze darted to the door.

Inga walked into his office and set several papers on his desk. "Here's the National Association for the Advancement of Colored People article."

"Already?" C.J. asked.

She tucked a stray strand of hair behind her ear. "I

had most of it finished by the time I got back from Boston yesterday."

"What are you going to work on next?" He slid the article closer.

She caught her lower lip between her teeth and walked to the window. He studied her straight posture, her slim frame her beautiful face. She was still as lovely as ever. But something had changed, a poignant resolve seemed to infuse every facet of her being.

His gaze followed hers as she looked out at the dreary gray drizzle. Rivulets of water streaked the glass.

She crossed her arms. "I'm going home to pack."

He couldn't breathe. He gulped in air.

"Where are you going?" He knew the answer, but he asked anyway.

"To Washington. To help out at the National Woman's Party headquarters." Her halting speech reflected her nervous expression. "I'll be staying there."

"But you won't be picketing." He infused authority into his words.

"Emma Reed is going to orient me to answering the phone and making calls to families of women who are arrested." She dropped her arms to her sides.

"But you won't be picketing," he repeated forcefully.

She reeled around to face him. "C.J., I can't promise that I won't eventually move to that."

He stood and approached her. "But it's dangerous. What if you're sent to jail?"

A fleeting smile crossed her lips. "If I am, I expect you to get an attorney and appeal my sentence, since I promise I won't do anything illegal."

How could he stop her? He couldn't. She was his wife and he loved her. Her convictions made her who she was. He swallowed his argument. "When are you leaving?"

She straightened her posture. "Tomorrow morning.

On the train."

"I hate what you're doing, but I admire your courage." He enfolded her in his arms, suppressing his fear for both their sakes. "You'll need to tell the girls."

She inhaled an audible breath. "I'll tell them after supper tonight."

"Promise me you'll be careful." He kissed the top of her head. "No more broken arms."

"I promise."

That evening, Inga insisted that the whole family, including Ada, remain at the table after they finished eating.

"Tomorrow morning, I'm going down to Washington to help in the suffrage work," Inga began. "I'm not sure how long they'll need me." She turned to Ada. "Will you be able to stay nights here for the duration, or shall I contact my mother and ask her to come and help out?"

Concern strained Susan's young face. "How long will you be gone?"

Inga shrugged. "It could be days or weeks." She didn't want to scare them, but she wanted to be truthful. "Or maybe months."

Helen's gaze implored her. "You're going to be home for Christmas, aren't you?"

Bile rose in Inga's throat. Missing the holidays with her family would break her heart, but now she had to do her part for woman suffrage. "I hope so."

"Are the police going to put you in jail?" Elizabeth looked as though she might burst into tears.

Glancing at C.J., Inga inhaled a steadying breath. "I hope not." Jail was what she feared most. "But I don't know for sure."

"Oh, Mama. No." Helen jumped up, ran to Inga, and threw her arms around her mother's neck. "Don't go!"

"I have to." Tears stung Inga's eyes as she wrapped her arms around her sobbing daughter. "We're making progress toward winning the right to vote. We can't stop now."

"I can stay for a while," Ada offered quietly. "And Sadie'll probably help. Maybe even Minnie." She paused. Her gaze slid to C.J. then back to Inga. "But if ya want your mama to come help, it'll be okay."

"I'll send her a note tomorrow and let her know what's happening." Inga turned her attention to C.J. "I'll tell her you'll call if you need her."

His expression remained neutral, unreadable.

"Can we go down on the train to visit you?" Elizabeth asked.

Inga gave her daughters a reassuring smile. "We'll see."

"Your mama is very brave to fight for what she believes in," C.J. said, his voice solemn. "We'll all need to be brave and strong here at home so she won't have to worry about us."

Inga could have kissed him. And she would when they were alone. She wanted to show him how much she loved him and appreciated that he was her husband.

He had come through for her when she'd needed him tonight.

The next morning, Inga's stomach churned as C.J. drove her to the train station.

After they checked her suitcase and picked up her ticket, he walked her to the platform. The screech of arriving trains and the smell of grease bombarded her senses.

"It's nice to have you here." She grasped his hand in hers. "You don't often see me off when I'm leaving on work trips."

He gave her fingers a gentle squeeze. "I didn't realize you wanted me to. I will from now on."

"Oh, C.J., I wish I knew what was going to happen." She clung to his arm. "No matter what, I'd feel a lot better if I could expect and plan for it."

"You've proven time after time that you're a strong woman and can rise to any occasion." He wrapped his arms around her and gave her a quick hug. "I'm sure you will this time, too."

A small smile played at her lips. "Except that I didn't do well the last time we were apart for months."

He kissed the top of her head. "I'll call you every night."

The conductor shouted for the stragglers to board.

"I'll look forward to it." She walked toward the passenger car, clasping his fingers until the very last minute.

She boarded and found a seat in the crowded coach. Carefully, she stowed her satchel at her feet, trying not to disturb the young man in the adjacent seat. He nodded at her and she returned the silent gesture. He engrossed himself in his newspaper.

When the conductor had completed his duties and moved to the next car, she settled back and closed her eyes.

She'd gotten very little sleep last night. Her body tingled with the memories. After fifteen years of marriage, she still loved her husband as much as ever.

The train shuddered and lurched forward with a squeal. Her eyes opened until the train fell into its familiar rocking rhythm. She lowered her lids again.

The next thing she knew, the man beside her was gently shaking her arm. "We're comin' into the capitol."

She roused and glanced out the window as they rolled past houses and commercial buildings.

"D'ya have business in the city?" the man asked.

She nodded. "Yes."

It was much easier than trying to explain her reason for coming. She lifted her left hand to cover a yawn, making certain her wedding ring was clearly visible. "And you?"

"I'm meeting with my congressman to see if he can git me out of the draft." The man's jaw tightened. "My daddy's dead and my mama needs my help in runnin' the farm."

A wave of compassion washed through Inga.

"I wish you the best of luck." She momentarily

placed her hand on his arm.

Thoughts this young man facing the horrors of war put the less dangerous possibility of her going to jail in a proper perspective. She would keep the comparison in mind whenever her fear raised its ugly head.

That afternoon, Inga arrived at the National Woman's Party headquarters.

"Thank you so much for coming to help." Alice Paul led Inga into an office with a desk, chair, and a cot in the corner. A telephone and typewriter sat on the desk. The mouth-watering aroma of beef and herbs wafted through the air.

Alice seemed so young to have accomplished so much and shown such strong leadership capability. She gestured toward the empty wall. "You can stow your things here."

"If you're hungry, help yourself to food in the kitchen." Alice offered. "I'll have Emma show you what to do after you're settled."

"My husband wants to call every night." Inga glanced at the phone on the desk. "I've given him this number, but I can tell him not to."

"As long as he waits until after dinner and you don't talk too long, it should be fine." Alice smiled. "And I imagine your daughters will want to talk with you, too."

Tears stung behind Inga's eyes. "Thank you."

"I'll see you later." Alice left the room and headed up the stairs.

Inga situated her suitcase under the cot. She placed her satchel on top and pulled out her stationary, envelopes, and stamps, then placed it beside the suitcase.

She sat at the desk and penned a letter to her mother. Moder had always supported the cause, but how would she feel about Inga leaving her family?

Inga looked up to see Emma standing before her.

She frowned. "I'm sorry that you're the person

Caroline sent. I know it will be hard for you to be away from your children."

"It is." Inga swallowed against the knot in her throat. "But I want to fight for the vote now so they won't have to."

A sad smile curved Emma's lips. "I have a beef stew simmering on the stove. We can fill bowls and come back here to eat."

They each dipped up soup and snagged a slice of bread and an apple. After setting their lunches on opposite corners of the desk, Emma got them each a cup of coffee.

"We eat well here," she said. "The women who have served time in jail say that the food there is inedible. We want everyone to be well-nourished in case they are arrested."

Her tone was joking, but Inga suspected there was more truth than humor in her words.

The telephone rang.

"Answer 'National Woman's Party,'" Emma instructed.

Inga did as she was told, then paused, listening to the voice on the other end of the line. "Just one moment." She covered the mouthpiece with her hand. "It's for you."

Emma closed her eyes for a moment, then reached for the receiver. "This is Emma Reed." She paused. "Hello, Mother."

"I'll step out so you'll have some privacy," Inga whispered.

Emma cupped her hand over the mouthpiece as Inga had done. "That'll be a first."

Inga picked up her stew and spoon and walked to the kitchen. She lingered, slowly eating her soup. When she finished, she set her bowl in the sink.

Emma popped her head in the doorway. "All done. You can come back, now."

Inga followed her back to the office.

"She called to make sure I am still here." Emma took a bite of stew then opened the middle drawer on the right hand side of the desk and pulled out a few papers.

"Have you told her you'll be picketing?"

"Yes, but not when." Emma set the papers next to Inga's apple. "That's why she called."

Inga glanced at the top sheet on the stack.

"Those are the women who are picketing today." Emma stirred her stew. "And underneath are their information sheets. If they are arrested, you'll need to let their contact persons know."

"Do the contacts usually know the woman is picketing?"

"Sometimes. Oh." Emma reached back into the drawer. "I forgot to have you fill out one." She held out a mimeographed form.

Inga smiled. "I haven't used a mimeograph machine since I was teaching in Wyoming."

"Well, if you know how to use one, you're a step ahead of most of the volunteers here."

Inga skimmed the form and began filling in the blanks. There was no turning back now. If she was called upon to picket, she would risk going to jail.

Chapter Nineteen

Washington, D.C.
October 18, 1917

Dear Moder,

Thank you for your letter.

It's hard to believe I've been here in Washington for almost three weeks. The first weekend C.J. brought the girls, and we stayed together in a hotel. Last weekend, I went home and spent two days with them. I miss them so.

I'm not sure what we will do this coming weekend. So many women have been arrested and sentenced to jail that our numbers of volunteers are dwindling. Some who have returned from serving their sentences have complained that conditions at the Workhouse are abominable. I feel so sorry for those still held there.

On October 6, Alice Paul and ten others were arrested for standing silently at the White House and charged with 'obstructing traffic.' They were released on bail and returned to court on October 8. Refusing to make a plea, Miss Paul pointed out that they do not recognize themselves as subject to the court, since they cannot vote so have no part in making the laws under which they are charged. To everyone's surprise, the judge suspended the women's sentences and returned their bail.

Three days ago, four of the released women were arrested again for picketing, and this time each were sentenced to a $25 fine or six months in prison. This seems to me an excessive penalty for standing in silent protest in accordance with the First Amendment. Of course, the women refused to pay the fine since they didn't commit a crime. Their sentences were suspended 'for the time being.' We're not sure what that means.

Lucy Burns and some of the other imprisoned

suffragists petitioned to get the government to treat them as political prisoners. It seems appropriate as the women's only real crime is disagreeing with the officials on the issue of woman suffrage. Their petition was smuggled out. Not only did the D.C. commissioners reject it, but word has it that the women were placed in solitary confinement.

In my wildest imagination, I never would have conceived that the United States President and Congress would allow law-abiding citizens to be treated so grievously for exercising their rights to free speech. If this situation is not rectified, what will become of the country's honor?

I send wishes for a happy Thanksgiving to you and the rest of the family, and I pray fervently that we suffragists will have something to be thankful for in relation to the cause.

Love,
Inga

Inga was mimeographing forms when Alice came to the door. Inga stopped cranking and allowed the machine to go still.

"The Antis have a new slogan, or at least one I hadn't seen before." She wore a wan smile on her tired face. "'You do not need a ballot to clean out a sink spout. A handful of potash and some boiling water is quicker and cheaper.'"

Inga rolled her eyes. "How insulting."

"Have you heard from any more volunteers for tomorrow's picket?" Alice moistened her cracked lips with the tip of her tongue.

"Only one. I'm sorry there aren't more." Inga picked the fresh copies from the tray and placed them in a neat stack on the table.

Alice's shoulders slumped. "Even if I go, we still need one or two more sentinels for the White House gate tomorrow."

Inga's heartbeat shifted into high gear. "But *you* can't. Your case from October sixth is still open. If you're arrested again, they'll punish you with a six-month sentence."

Alice rubbed the back of her neck with her hand. "If that's what happens, so be it."

Inga sighed. "But with Lucy still in jail, who will run the party?"

"We have a lot of capable women." A tired smile curved her lips. "You, for instance. And Emma. But I'm leaving Doris in charge this time. Besides, Lucy should be back soon."

"But you need pickets." Pressure built in Inga's temples. "I should take my turn."

Alice's wide-set, dark eyes flashed. "No. You have children still in school."

Inga dropped her argument. She missed her daughters so much. When C.J. called tonight, she would be sure to speak with each of the girls for a few minutes.

"Good luck," Inga called to Alice and a small contingent of picketers as they left headquarters. The air was crisp, and Inga pulled her collar closer around her neck as she stood outside the door.

Alice led the way across the square and to the west gate of the White House, carrying a large sign that quoted President Wilson's own words, 'The time has come to conquer or submit, for us there can be but one choice. We have made it.'

One of Inga's Philadelphia cohorts, Dr. Caroline Spencer, proudly clutched one that read, 'Resistance to tyranny is obedience to God.'

Sighing, Inga went inside.

"I don't like it that Alice is going out there today," Emma said.

Inga nodded her agreement. "I fear her defiance of the officials will enrage them, and they'll take their revenge on her."

"Now we wait to see what happens."

Inga stepped behind the desk. "I'll type those letters requesting donations."

Emma pressed her lips into a thin line. "Let me

know right away if you hear anything."

"They've been arrested and taken to the District Jail," Inga told the small group of women gathered around the dinner table.

The telephone rang. Emma rose and hurried into the other room to answer.

Everyone sat in silence.

When Emma trudged back to the table, her eyes were red and puffy. Her lower lip quivered, but no tears fell.

"Their hearing is Monday." Emma reclaimed her chair. "They broke a window at the jail."

"What?"

"Why?"

"I don't know," said a woman Inga didn't know. "When I was there, the air was stale, but the place is cold, so they may regret it if the officials don't fix the glass soon."

Inga shivered at the thought. She rose. "I'll telephone Mr. Malone and make sure he knows about the situation. He'll probably need the weekend to put together a defense for Alice and the others."

Emma sighed. "If they'll let him."

On Monday, Inga sat in the jam-packed spectator section of the courtroom, waiting for the hearing to begin. Conversations buzzed around her, so many that the words blurred into background noise. Cigar smoke, body odors, and acrid perfumes filled the stuffy air.

The tenor of the room changed as guards marched the prisoners into the chamber. There were more than had been arrested on Friday.

A bailiff called for order.

As the crowd quieted, Inga caught the words "... Judge Mullowny presiding."

While the legal ritual of opening the hearing progressed, Inga studied Alice. With dark circles under her eyes and her pale complexion, she looked as though she hadn't slept at all. Or maybe she was ill.

Still, like the other women, she sat with her back straight and her head held high.

From his perch on the dais, the judge leaned forward. He cleared his throat. "Will the prisoners stand and be sworn?"

Not one of the women stood. They remained silent.

Inga cringed inwardly.

Mullowny glared at the defendants. Then he turned to the lawyer representing them. "Will they speak on their own behalf?"

Rose Winslow, an attractive young woman with dark hair and eyes, got to her feet. "We have broken no laws in the expression of our First Amendment rights." Her voice quivered a bit. "So we are confused."

The judge's expression tightened.

"You sentence us to jail for a few days, then you sentence us to the workhouse for thirty days, then sixty, and then you suspend sentence." Her voice became stronger and steadier as she spoke. "Sometimes we are accused of carrying seditious banners, then of obstructing traffic. How do you expect us to see any consistency in the law, or in your sentence?"

Mullowny's lip curled. Red infused his cheeks. "You ladies seem to feel that we discriminate in making arrests and in sentencing you." His tight, menacing voice sent a chill through Inga. "The result is that you force me to take the most drastic means in my power to compel you to obey the law."

Beads of sweat formed on the judge's forehead. "You are all hereby sentenced to a fine of $25, or in lieu of the fine, six months in the Occoquan Workhouse."

Inga gasped, as did the other observers around her. Six months! She stared at Alice, who remained stoic.

"Those of you who have previous offenses shall pay an additional $5 fine or you shall serve an additional 30 days."

One by one, each woman refused to pay her fine.

The proceedings were brought to a close. Inga felt

as though she had turned to stone. She remained in her seat as the onlookers dispersed.

Reporters tried to interview the prisoners as they were led from the courtroom.

Several of them encircled Alice. Inga hurried toward them.

Alice lifted her chin. "We are being imprisoned, not because we obstructed traffic, but because we pointed out to the president the fact that he was obstructing the cause of democracy at home, while Americans are fighting for it abroad."

C.J. waited on the platform as the arriving passengers got off the train. He'd been surprised when Inga called yesterday, saying she was coming home for a few days.

Finally, he spotted her and waved. She smiled and headed toward him.

Her hair was pulled back from her face. Without make-up, she looked pale and tired. She carried only a small satchel and her handbag.

When she reached him, she raised up on her toes and gave him a chaste kiss on the cheek.

"Do you have any luggage?"

She shook her head and handed her satchel to him. "I have to go back next week. And I'll take some winter clothes."

C.J. winced. "Can't you at least stay until Halloween? The girls have been invited to two different parties."

Inga began walking toward the exit. "Do we know the parents of the children hosting them?"

C.J. caught the open door before it closed. Inga passed through it to the street.

"Yes." He took her arm and guided her toward their parked automobile. "I've already told the girls they can go."

She stopped abruptly. He walked two steps ahead before realizing she wasn't beside him.

"If they aren't going to be home, why do I need to

be?" she asked.

Heat rose under his collar. "I thought we could have a nice dinner alone. Just the two of us."

She grinned. "You always know the perfect bribes to..." A moment passed. "Convince me."

His heart pounded in his chest. Placing his hand on her elbow, he started them moving again. "So you'll stay?"

"I'll call D.C. next week and make sure they have enough staff to cover until the weekend."

She stopped by the passenger side of their auto. "Emma's coming back here to see her parents the first weekend in November."

C.J. opened the door, and Inga slid into the seat.

When they reached home, the savory aroma of roasting pork greeted them. Inga removed her coat and hung it in the hall closet. He did the same.

"I have some articles for you." She reached for her satchel, which C.J. had placed on the console. "I didn't feel right about using the party's typewriters for them, but if you like one or both, I'll type them."

"Let's go into the library," he suggested. She led the way. He followed her into the room and closed the door.

Opening her satchel, she pulled out a handful of papers. She separated them into two stacks and lay them on the desk.

C.J. hoped to start on a neutral note. "What did you write about?"

"One is stories about men who have registered for the draft, what they think about going to war, and what they will leave behind if their numbers are drawn." She frowned. "One was called up, so I had the chance to get his feelings about that."

C.J. perched on the corner of the desk. "That should be interesting. What's the other one about?"

She squared her shoulders. "Monday's trial of Alice and the other protesters, the unduly harsh sentences, and Lucy Burns' rationale for their being political prisoners."

He wished she'd sit down, but it was clear she

wanted to stand her ground for this discussion.

He steeled himself. “Nathan said the president has made it known that he doesn’t want newspapers and magazines to give coverage to the protesters.”

“We suspected as much.” Inga wrapped her arms around her chest. “First he wants to curb our right to peacefully picket by having us arrested on trumped-up charges. Now he wants to close in on freedom of the press.” Her eyes narrowed. “He has no respect for the First Amendment.”

“That’s what we thought, too.” C.J. waited for her expression to relax. “Nathan also wants you in the office on a regular basis after Christmas break.”

She inhaled a breath so deep that the fabric of her blouse pulled tight. “But I’m already several months ahead of my article deadlines. I don’t have to be in my office to write.”

C.J. stiffened. “I know. But he’s giving you plenty of notice.”

“Maybe I should give up my staff position and go back to submitting my stories freelance.”

He could barely hear her words as a knock sounded at the door.

Inga walked across the rug and opened the door. All three girls stood in the hallway.

“May we please come in?” Susan asked.

“Of course,” Inga said without even looking at him. She hugged each daughter as she entered the room. “I’m so glad to see you.”

“Are you going to be home for good now?” Susan shifted her feet.

“No, sweetheart.” Inga hugged her again. “But I hope to be here for a week.”

“Are we all going to the masquerade ball on Saturday?” Elizabeth held her hands together as if she was praying. “Please?”

Inga’s gaze flew to C.J. His stomach clenched. His daughters had been so excited about the invitation. He should have mentioned it on the way home. “I was going to bring it up at dinner.”

"A masquerade ball?" She smiled at Elizabeth. "That sounds like fun."

"What do you think, Daddy?" Susan asked.

C.J. relaxed. "I think we should start planning our costumes tonight. Then you girls can wear them to your Halloween parties, too."

"Are you going to be here for Halloween, Mama?" Elizabeth reached for her mother's hand.

"I hope so, sweetie." Inga brought her daughter's fingers to her lips. "I'll call headquarters first thing next week and ask."

Helen stuck out her lower lip in a pout. "Why do you have to go back to Washington?"

Inga reached to embrace her, but Helen stepped away. "Is getting the vote more important than us?"

Inga winced visibly. "Of course not." Her eyes shone in the lamplight. "I know it's hard to understand now, but the biggest reason I'm working for the cause is because I love you. I want to help win the vote soon, so you won't have to fight for it."

Leaving C.J and the girls had been harder than Inga expected. They'd had so much fun together at the masquerade ball and in the following six days. She spent much of the train ride steeling herself for resuming her work for the party.

When she arrived back in the District of Columbia, she marveled at the number of women who had come from all over the country to show their support for Alice and the other prisoners.

"Doris has received intelligence from one of the cleaning women at the jail," Inga told Emma when she arrived back at headquarters on Tuesday. "Alice and Rose have started a hunger strike."

How horrible for them! Yet it was another demonstration of their commitment to the cause.

Emma's eyes widened. "Has anyone gone to see them recently?"

"Yes, but most of the time visitors are turned away. And when they are admitted, they're only allowed a brief meeting." Inga returned to the desk where she had been writing thank-you notes for the numerous donations that had poured in. Emma followed, seating herself next to the telephone.

Emma watched a pair of strangers walk out the front door. "Isn't it amazing to see all these volunteers here?"

"Those two are from New York." Inga thought about Sarah, whom she hadn't heard from for more than a year. "New York is voting on woman suffrage tonight. Carrie Catt has invested a great deal of time and money in the state. It was part of her 'Winning Plan' to win suffrage on a state-by-state basis."

"Do you think it will pass?"

Inga lifted a shoulder. "I hope so, but I still think pursuing a national amendment is a better strategy."

The next day the New York contingent brought champagne and passed around newspapers with headlines proclaiming the referendum had passed.

"Congratulations, I'm happy for you." Inga smiled, but had to admit to herself that she felt more than a twinge of jealousy. She handed the paper on to Emma.

The following evening, Doris Stevens gathered those still at headquarters into the large front room.

"I've received a note smuggled out by Alice Paul," she announced. "She is in quite a weakened state."

"We got one last week from Rose Winslow," Emma whispered. "She said she and the others are mixed in with syphilitics, and that the jail is alive with roaches."

Inga shuddered. Conditions were worse than they'd expected.

"On this Saturday, November 10, we need to have a massive picket in support of our imprisoned leader. If you are interested in participating, please sign your name on this sheet, which I will leave on the reception desk." Doris held up a piece of paper.

Murmurs rippled through the group. Inga pinched her lips together as she considered whether she was willing to risk her freedom.

"Jail is a torture, so if you are the mother of young

children or if you have a physical infirmity, please do not sign up," Doris instructed. "We need to have enough people here to carry on the work of the party." She paused. "We will meet here tomorrow to make final plans."

The women parted to let her pass by. She made her way to the desk and set the page on the corner. Behind her, women lined up and added their names to the list.

Inga fell in behind Emma.

"You're not going, are you?" Emma asked, louder that Inga would have liked.

Doris strode to their side, lines of concern etched in her face. "Your family needs you. You should stay here, Inga."

If she stayed here to help at Cameron House, she could see C.J. and the girls whenever she wanted. But she couldn't stay. She had to do everything possible to secure the vote for her daughters.

"They'll be fine between my husband and my housekeeper," Inga argued with enough false bravado to cover the twinge of niggling guilt. "And I'm younger than many of the women here in the house right now. I would be much better able to withstand the rigors of prison than they are."

Frowning, Doris glanced at the women in the hallway. "Have you ever been in jail?"

"No." Inga waited until she caught Doris's gaze. "But there was a first time for you, too."

On Friday afternoon, the forty-one women who had signed up for the picket gathered in the parlor.

"Tomorrow, we will break into five groups," Lucy Burns announced. "We'll post the list at the reception desk."

"Mrs. Brannen, you will lead the first pickets." Doris nodded in her direction. "We fully expect arrests, so as soon as they begin, the second group will be dispatched and so on."

"I will bring up the rear of the fifth group," Lucy said. "Doris will stay behind to keep the party's work going.

"Arresting forty-one women will certainly be taxing on the police and the court," Doris said with a wry grin. "We expect you will be released and given a date to appear in court."

"Of course, the authorities could change up their procedures." Lucy sighed. "We'll just have to see what happens. In any case, we will demand to be treated as political prisoners."

"Does Miss Paul know we're going to do this?" a voice from across the room called.

Doris and Lucy looked at each other and shrugged.

"Someone should go to the jail tonight and tell her," another voice said.

"Maybe we should all go," Katherine Morey suggested.

Murmurs ran through the women. Inga shifted her weight from one foot to the other.

"What if we're all arrested?" The voice of another person rose above the din, voicing Inga's concern. "Who will march tomorrow?"

"They'll probably have to release us," Catherine Flanagan replied. "Or at least most of us, but if you want to stay behind, that is fine. Katherine and I can lead the group tonight."

Emma edged closer to Inga. "Are you going?"

Inga inhaled a steadying breath. "I think so."

"Then I will, too."

While the leaders worked out the details, the others retrieved their overcoats and together they traipsed through town to the prison hospital.

"Wait here." Katherine pointed to the brick structure. "Alice's room is behind that boarded-up window on the third floor. We'll go to Warden Zinkhan's house and ring the doorbell. When we give the signal, run to the space under Alice's window and let her know we're here before the guards arrive."

Inga was close enough to see the door open. One of the leaders asked to see the warden.

"He's ill and not receiving visitors," said the

woman who answered the door.

The leaders gave the signal.

Inga moved as quickly as she could toward the window, although the younger women were much faster. The suffragists shouted up their names.

Thuds of running feet on the earth sounded from both ends of the building.

Someone called out the amount of money that had recently come into the party's treasury.

The guards moved to surround the demonstrators, pushing and jostling them.

"Forty-one suffragists will stand on the picket line tomorrow to protest your arrest!" The woman's voice carried above the crowd as the officers shoved and herded the women out of the yard.

Inga stifled a yawn. She had slept little after the excitement of the previous night. Sipping her coffee, she watched as the first picket assembled.

Some of the members bore white banners with gold letters, demanding the vote and protesting the imprisonment of Alice Paul. Others carried purple, white, and gold flags.

Led by Mrs. John Winters Brannan, the first fourteen women walked slowly across the square to Pennsylvania Avenue and took up positions at the East and West gates of the White House. There they stood, stately and silent.

Inga wandered to the upstairs windows, hoping to be able to see the pickets well enough to determine if any were being arrested.

A shout echoed through the house. "Second Picket! Time to Go!"

Ten women, led by Agnes Morey, proceeded on their orderly march to Pennsylvania Avenue.

"Everyone else who is going out today should get ready, now." Lucy carried an armload of flags into the hallway. "Now that the arrests are beginning, they will probably go quickly. We need to make sure we have pickets there to take their place as each group is removed."

Inga donned her coat. She inhaled several deep breaths to calm her jittery nerves and roiling stomach.

Emma caught her gaze as she took her place.

"Good luck," Inga mouthed.

"You, too."

Moments later, Emma's contingent walked out the door.

The final group lined up behind Mary Nolan. Inga worried that the frail, seventy-year-old woman's overcoat might be inadequate. She was from Florida and not acclimated to the cold.

She limped valiantly across Lafayette Square, with Inga and the others following and Lucy bringing up the rear.

Applause, cheers and calls of encouragement heartened Inga. Energy infused her steps.

But as they approached Pennsylvania Avenue, shouts of "It is folly for women to aspire to the world of men," and "A woman's place is in the home," as well as despicable name-calling became more frequently interspersed with the expressions of support.

Holding her flag high, she kept her attention focused straight ahead, her expression bland. As she got closer to the White House gate, she could see that the police were quickly arresting the pickets and pushing them into the patrol wagons that lined the curb.

More and more people stopped on the sidewalk to stare.

Inga's muscles tensed as her fear rose. She concentrated on putting one foot in front of the other until her group reached positions along the fence outside the gate.

"Shame! Shame!" male voices shouted.

Hoots rose from men on the other side of the impromptu audience.

Inga shrunk away from them, her back touching the fence.

A fashionably-dressed woman strode along the line

sentinels. "Traitors!" she screamed. "How dare you be so unpatriotic?"

Almost immediately, the police moved in on the pickets.

A tall, stocky officer in a black uniform with shiny buttons halted directly in front of Inga.

She gulped in several quick breaths.

"Come with me," he said, a sinister note in his baritone voice.

Swallowing, she tried to regain her balance on shaking legs.

An officer grabbed tightly onto Inga's left arm. A man wearing a black wool coat and a bowler hat jerked her flagpole from her right hand and broke it over his knee.

Her heart raced.

The policeman dragged her through the crowd.

Faces blurred as she passed.

Pain shot through her arm at the pressure of his grip. Abruptly, the policeman stopped at the back of the black patrol wagon.

Inga peered into the dim space with only tiny windows for light. Her feet slipped out from under her as the policeman picked her up and hoisted her into the wagon. He dropped her unceremoniously on the floor and gave her a shove, knocking the breath out of her.

Another officer hauled Lucy toward the open back door. Inga glanced up to see the shadowed faces of the other picketers.

With much effort, she righted herself and sat up. She swallowed against the bile rising in her throat.

Lucy landed in the wagon, crashing into Inga. The officer who had tossed Lucy into the box smiled and dusted his hands together.

"Sorry, Inga." Lucy murmured. "Here we go again."

The door slammed shut. Musty, foul-smelling air closed around them.

Lucy pushed herself to a seated position. Inga followed suit.

She squinted, trying to help her eyes adjust to the

faint light. In her mind, she went over and over the details of the day in an effort to memorize them for a future article and to push out her dread of what was to come.

Finally, the patrol wagon stopped moving.

The women looked at each other. Inga saw her fear reflected in their faces.

After what seemed like an hour, but was probably a matter of minutes, the back door opened.

One by one, officers yanked the women out of the box.

Inga tightened her muscles to mitigate the pain from the manhandling.

When she was safely standing on the ground, she narrowed her eyes to reduce the glare of the late afternoon light.

The officers roughly herded Inga and her fellow suffragists into the District Jail. As she waited her turn to be processed, her stomach roiled.

After she gave her name, address, and other information, she stepped back. She clenched her hands together so tightly that her fingernails dug into her flesh.

When everyone had been dispensed with, the whole group was summarily released and told to return for a court hearing on November twelfth.

Relieved at not being locked in a cell, Inga's knees went soft and she had to focus to keep herself from collapsing.

C.J. held tight to the receiver, trying to make sense of what Inga was saying.

"The hearing is Monday." Inga's voice came strongly through the line. "I'll phone you and let you know how it goes."

He bit back his anger. How could she do this to him? To the girls? "What if they take you directly to jail?"

"Then someone from the party will contact you." Her voice carried a barely perceptible waver.

He wanted to see her. "I could come down for the hearing."

"That's not necessary."

He barely heard her.

"I could bring the girls down tomorrow."

The line was silent for a long time. He feared the connection might have been lost.

"Thank you, but no." A hiss of breath came through the receiver. "I'll need the day to get ready for whatever might happen at the hearing." Another pause. "I love you. Kiss the girls for me." Her voice quavered.

"Inga—"

A click.

His gut churned. He rose and paced the library.

On Monday, Inga sat in the courtroom with the other forty women who had been arrested with her on Friday. She blinked back tears as she observed her fellow picketers. Some had children. Some were frail and elderly. But all were willing to risk their liberty.

Judge Mullowny looked out over the courtroom. "You've been charged with obstructing traffic. How do you plead?"

"Not guilty."

Several witnesses, who had not been picketing, spoke on behalf of the suffragists.

"The responsibility for an agitation like ours against injustice rests with those who deny justice, not those who demand it," Mrs. Brannan stated. "Whatever may be the verdict of this court, we shall continue our agitation until the grievance of American women is redressed."

Would they? Would she? Inga swallowed back bile rising in her throat.

Mrs. Wiley spoke for some time, concluding with, "The Constitution says that Congress shall not in any way abridge the right of citizens peacefully to assembly and petition. That is exactly what we did. We peacefully assembled and then proceeded with our petition to the president for the redress of our grievance of disfranchisement. The Constitution does not specify the form of petition. Ours was in the form of a banner. To say that we 'broke traffic regulations' when we exercised our constitutional right of petition is therefore unconstitutional."

As the judge spoke, Inga straightened her spine. Her colleague was right. Their fight wasn't only for the vote, it was to protect their first amendment rights.

Judge Mullowny raised his voice. "I find that you are all guilty. I will take your case under advisement in the matter of sentencing. For now, you may pay your bail and go."

Relief coursed through Inga. She glanced at the large wall clock. It was a little after three. She would still have time to phone C.J. at his office.

Right now, she just wanted to hear his voice.

The next afternoon, Inga and thirty other protesters went back out on another picket in front of the White House. She was pleasantly surprised to find that the large group of onlookers was friendly.

Their protest line stretched from gate to gate. The women stood silently, holding their flags and banners.

From out of nowhere, a uniformed man seized Mrs. Lewis's banner and tore it.

Inga tightened her grip on her pole.

He grabbed another banner. And another.

"Stop him!" shouted someone in the crowd. Others joined in.

He ripped Emma's flag from her hands and smashed it on the sidewalk.

"Arrest him!" someone else shouted.

He grabbed Inga's flag, tearing off a section. He wrestled the pole away from her and threw it to the ground.

A policeman clutched his shoulder, but he wrenched himself free and destroyed another banner.

Finally, two officers subdued and arrested him.

Inga released a breath she hadn't realized she was

holding.

She and the others resumed their Silent Sentinel positions. They stood in their picket line, with six fewer banners.

Several hours passed before they were arrested and again ordered to pay bail.

"But our bail has yet to be refunded from yesterday's trial," said someone at the front of the group.

"That doesn't absolve you from paying today's bail," the officer replied.

"Well, we're not going to pay a second bail."

Inga swallowed. She had been prepared to open her pocket book and hand over the cash.

"Does that apply to all of you who were tried at yesterday's hearing?"

His question was greeted with nods and shouts of "Yes!"

With her throat so tight she couldn't croak out a word, Inga lowered her chin.

"Those of you who are unwilling to pay your bail, move over to that wall." The officer held out his left arm, making a flicking gesture. "The rest of you step forward."

A few women stepped forward, forked over their cash, and were allowed to leave.

Inga and the others who remained were escorted to the house of detention. There they found two relatively small rooms, each with only eight beds. Since there were more than sixteen women, the attendants brought straw mattresses for the others. At least there weren't barred cells.

"Older women in the beds, younger ones on the mats," Lucy called.

For once, Inga was thankful for being over forty years old. She sank down onto a lumpy mattress supported by a squeaky frame and settled back, wriggling until she found a tolerable position.

Staring up at the ceiling, she tried not to worry about what tomorrow would bring.

Chapter Twenty

Although she had slept little, Inga was wide awake and felt as though an electrical current ran through her body. The court convened and the judge spoke.

Inga shifted in her chair and clutched her hands tightly together. She forced her concentration on the judge's words. "I am fining each of you twenty-five dollars."

"But we have done nothing wrong," Lucy replied.

Judge Mullowny frowned and pronounced sentences. Mrs. Nolan was sentenced to six days

Inga briefly closed her eyes, sorry that the frail little woman would spend any time behind bars, but thankful her sentence wasn't longer.

Three women were sentenced to fifteen days.

Twenty-four would serve thirty days. Inga heard her name in this list. She bit her lip. A whole month away from C.J. and her daughters.

Mrs. Lewis and Mrs. Brannan received sixty day terms.

Lucy Burns was sentenced to six months.

All were to be confined in the District Jail for 'obstructing traffic.'

Inga fought back tears.

Every nerve in Inga's body was on edge as she waited in the hallway outside the courtroom. She tried to calm herself by watching the placid demeanors of the women who had previously been jailed. They seemed to be taking everything in stride.

Emma moved to her side. Concern etched her face. "Are you doing all right?"

Inga nodded. "I'm trying." She inhaled a steadying breath. "How about you?"

"The same." Emma dabbed a handkerchief to the corner of her eye.

Inga looked up. C.J. strode down the marble-floored hallway in her direction. Her empty stomach felt heavy.

"Miss Reed. Inga." He glanced toward the courtroom door. "I'm so sorry about what happened in there."

Emma moved a few steps away. Inga clutched his hand. "Thank you for coming. Where are the girls?"

"At home. In school, I assume."

"Good." Inga sighed. "I want their lives to be as normal as possible."

"As normal as possible without you." His voice carried a note of accusation. "I have to ask this once and then I'll drop it." He looked directly into her eyes. "Will you let me pay your fine and take you home?"

She bit her lip to keep it still and shook her head.

Disappointment clouded his face. "Is there anything I can do for you?"

Closing her eyes momentarily, she inhaled yet another steadying breath. Then she gazed up at her husband. "You can stop by Cameron House and pick up my things. I won't be needing them for a while." She paused. "And make sure to give the information about our situation to Caroline Katzenstein—she might be here today, but I didn't see her—and make sure she gets our story to her newspaper contacts."

"I will." His fearful expression nearly broke her heart. She hadn't considered that he might be as afraid for her as she was.

"Time to move, ladies," a male voice called.

Inga squeezed C.J.'s hand. "I love you. Kiss the girls for me."

"I'll visit you whenever I can." He leaned forward and gave her a peck on her cheek.

She released his fingers and turned to follow the others.

"Take care of yourself," he called after her.

"I'll try."

Pushing down her trepidation, she followed her suffrage sisters into the unknown.

Inga and the others who had just been sentenced were taken directly to the District Jail. Three prisoners were assigned to each cell, cells that were designed for two people at most.

The air smelled of body odor, rotten food and urine. Inga looked around and noted every window was closed.

She was assigned to stay with Mary Ingham and Emma. The room was small and dirty. Mary sat on one cot. Emma and Inga sat on the other.

Words failed Inga. She stared at the gray wall.

"Watch out for the rats!" called a female voice from somewhere on the left.

"They're especially bad at night," someone else called.

Inga shuddered. Emma trembled. Mary's face turned white.

"I'm the youngest," Emma said in a quavering voice. "I'll take the floor."

Inga placed her hand on Emma's arm. "I'm small. You can share my cot."

No one slept.

The next morning, after an inedible breakfast, some of the women were herded into a pen with numerous convicted criminals.

One-by-one uniformed men loaded them into small wagon boxes with tiny windows. Inga, Emma and two other suffragists sat crammed into the space. Two blurry-eyed men who reeked of stale alcohol swayed back and forth on the wooden seat. A busty woman to their left continually scratched at her arms. Another woman immediately laid her head back against the wall and snored. A wild-eyed, bearded man with dirty clothes, and a clean-shaven man in a rumpled suit perched on their seats. Several others rode at the other end of the box, but Inga couldn't make them out in the semi-darkness.

The door had been closed and locked. In the cramped, repulsive space, where the outside world was completely shut out, Inga lost all sense of time. After a few minutes—or maybe an hour—the wagon began to move. As her sight adjusted to the shadowy dusk, Inga made eye contact with the other suffragists. None of them spoke.

The vehicle lurched and rocked along the streets for an indeterminable period. Finally, the patrol wagon stopped. After another wait, the click of the lock sounded, the door opened, and the guards unloaded the passengers.

Inga blinked in the sunlight. She looked again. They were at the railroad station. Although she had known the Occoquan Workhouse was located in Virginia, she wasn't sure how far across the state line it was situated. The thought of taking a train had not occurred to her.

The guards formed the suffragists into lines, shepherded them into a group separate from the general prisoners, and marched them through the crowded station. Other passengers gawked.

"Shame!"

"You shouldn't be persecuted like this."

"Be strong."

"Give 'em hard time!"

"Traitors!"

"Good luck!"

"We'll pray for you."

One woman offered Inga an apple. Another gave her a chocolate. The other women received similar gifts.

Line by line, they were settled into railway cars and whisked into the countryside. The farther they went, the more rural the passing scenery became.

Somewhere in the middle of nowhere, they stopped at a tiny depot.

Inga's heart beat fast and hard. Her chest felt as though it might burst open as she descended the steps from the coach.

Black police wagons lined the platform.

An icy chill slithered up her spine. Where were the guards taking them?

Inga clutched tight to her handbag, trying to keep

her hands from shaking as guards channeled her and her cohorts into the front room of one of the small cottages near the entrance.

"Remain silent," their escort ordered.

Inga's empty stomach rumbled. She tensed her abdominal muscles in an attempt to quiet it. The only food she had eaten today was that given to her by strangers as they passed through the depot.

Directly behind the desk, a large placard proclaimed 'Rules and Regulations for Prisoners.' Inga scanned the list.

- *Prisoners shall bathe once a week and as much oftener as management shall require.*
- *Strict silence must be observed within the enclosure when under orders, in the dining room and in the sleeping quarters.*
- *Each prisoner must labor silently, faithfully and diligently at whatever work may be assigned.*

A tall, thin official stood and strode to the front of the desk. "I am Matron Herndon. I will call your names one at a time. When your name is called, step to the desk, and I will assign you a number. You will turn over all of your jewelry, money, and personal possessions. Everything except the clothes you are wearing."

Inga's stomach swooped. Her muscles stiffened.

"We will not." Mrs. Lewis's words were strong and clear. "We are political prisoners. We want to speak to the warden."

Mrs. Herndon frowned. "Mr. Whittaker is not available."

Mrs. Lewis straightened. "We will wait."

"You will sit here all night then." The matron returned to her chair.

Inga forced her attention back to the rules.

- *Prisoners must not at any time leave the line or their place of employment without permission of the officer in charge.*
- *Prisoners must always approach an officer in*

a respectful manner and give the military salute.

Really?

Hours passed. Inga shifted her weight from foot to foot. Finally, she found a place to lean against the wall. Some of the women sat on the floor.

- *Prisoners must be prompt to move in line at the proper signal, march in military order silently and yield obedience to the officer in command.*
- *Insolence from any prisoner will not be tolerated, nor will profane, vulgar or in any manner disrespectful language be permitted.*

The words began to blur. Inga blinked until her vision cleared.

- *If a prisoner has any complaint to make, he or she will be heard by the superintendent.*

The door opened. A man in plain clothes walked into the room. Then another. Then two more.

"Prisoners, we are going to try again to get you registered," Mrs. Herndon said.

One of the men took a step toward the suffragists. "You had better answer up, or it will be the worse for you."

"Alice Cosu." The matron called.

There was no response.

"Dorothy Day."

No response.

"I will handle you, so you'll be sorry you made me," another man said, his lip curling.

Mrs. Herndon's face tightened.

"Inga Wakefield."

She drew in a steadying breath, straightened to her full height, and clamped her jaw shut.

The door flew open. A man rushed in, his face red with rage. A gang of men followed.

"Warden Whittaker!" The matron stepped back.

Mrs. Lewis rose from her seat on the floor. "We demand to be treated as political pris—"

"You shut up!" Whittaker sneered. "Seize her!"

Two men descended upon Mrs. Lewis. Roughly,

they grabbed her arms and hauled her out of the room.

Inga's heart skipped a beat. Her fingers flew to her mouth.

A burly man, his suit coat flapping, jumped on Mrs. Nolan and jerked her off the floor. The little woman grimaced.

Inga swallowed back a sob.

Another man jerked Inga's arms behind her back. Her handbag slipped from her grip. Pain tore through her, as though her shoulders were being ripped from their sockets. Before she could catch a glimpse of her captors' faces, they wrenched her off her feet, holding her face about eighteen inches above the floor. She squirmed, in an attempt to relieve the agony.

She focused on the scuffed shoes and mud-splattered trousers of her tormenters as they wrestled her across the floor, down the steps, and into the black night where they trooped through the darkness. One of her abductors stumbled.

A fresh stab of pain shot through her shoulders. She shrieked.

Readjusting their grip, they wrangled her into a more upright position.

She inhaled a breath.

In front of them, stood a low building with a brightly-lit window. Mrs. Nolan was being rushed through the open door.

"Damned Suffrager! My mother ain't no Suffrager!" A deep, raspy voice erupted from the entry. "I will put you through hell!"

After Mrs. Nolan had passed inside, Inga saw that she was being taken to a large room. A uniformed guard stood at the threshold, brandishing a billy club.

"Damn you! Get in there!" he growled.

Inga wasn't sure if his words were aimed at her or at Mrs. Nolan.

Her porters rushed her through the space. She caught glimpses of iron benches. Two brutes lifted a slight young girl. They slammed her down on one of those benches. She screamed.

Before she could see more, Inga was whisked from the room and into a corridor. Ahead of them, Mrs. Nolan's guard pushed her into a cell.

At the next cell, the men flung Inga so hard that she crashed against the wall, knocking her breath from her. She crumpled to the floor.

A thud sounded next door.

"Mrs. Cosu! Are you all right?" Mrs. Nolan shrieked.

Inga lifted her head, but otherwise did not move. Her temples throbbed. The salty, metallic taste of blood dampened her lips.

A single bed and a mattress on the floor furnished the cell. There was a toilet in plain sight, with no shred of privacy. The murky light and dank smell of the small space closed in on her.

A missile hurtled into the room and banged against the cot. A groan rose from the human mass.

Inga struggled to a sitting position. "Emma?"

Outside the door, two men carried what looked like a flour sack in Mrs. Lewis's clothes.

A crash came from Mrs. Nolan's cell.

Someone else was shoved into a dusky cell across the hall.

Inga's left arm smarted as she crawled to Emma.

Emma had slid into a sitting position.

"Are you okay?" Inga asked.

"I think so." Emma's voice shook. "My ribs hurt."

"She's dead! They've killed her!" Mrs. Nolan's cry came from next door.

Inga held her breath.

"Who?" someone called from the other side of the corridor.

"Mrs. Lewis." The reply came between sobs. "No, look! She's breathing."

Inga released the breath she'd been holding.

"Are there three in there?" Emma whispered.

"Yes." Inga inhaled a deep breath. Her whole body ached, but she was still wearing her heavy overcoat. It had cushioned her impact.

"Doctor! She needs a doctor!"

"Shut up!" a male voice yelled.

A guard walked down the corridor, throwing blankets into the cells and slamming the barred doors shut.

The sound of retching echoed off the walls.

"Mrs. Cosu is sick! She's having a heart attack!" Mrs. Nolan called in a thin, wavering voice.

Moments later, Mr. Whittaker, lit from behind by the corridor lights like a devil in a picture book, passed by their cell door.

"If you don't shut up, I'll have you gagged." His hard voice was low, menacing.

This was hell.

Emma shivered.

"Let's get off this icy floor," Inga whispered.

"You're bleeding." Emma reached a hand toward Inga's face.

Inga shied away from the touch.

They climbed onto the cot and huddled together under the two foul-smelling blankets that had been tossed to them.

"I'm going to call roll." Lucy's strong, clear voice rang out through the hall. "Mrs. Nolan."

"Here."

"Miss Reed."

"Here."

"Shut up!" a guard growled.

"Mrs. Cosu."

"Here." Her tone was thready.

"Mrs. Wakefield."

Inga inhaled a stale breath. "Here."

"Mrs. Lewis."

Silence.

"Where is Mrs. Lewis?" Lucy sounded frantic.

"They've thrown her in here," Mrs. Cosu replied. "She's unconscious."

"Shut up or we'll put you in straight-jackets." The guard's threat slithered through Inga.

Lucy called a few more names.

"Stop it!" The official's words came from roughly the same place as Lucy's.

"Miss Day."

Scuffling sounds rolled down the corridor.

"Are they putting Lucy in a straight-jacket?" Emma asked in a terror-filled whisper.

"I don't know."

When the ruckus ceased, the guard shouted, "Speak again, and we'll put you in a buckle gag."

Goose flesh spread over Inga's skin. She had no idea what a buckle gag was, but it sounded like more torture. Beside her, Emma stiffened.

After a period of silence, Inga looked up to see the woman in the cell directly across from theirs standing at the barred door.

Inga rose with a groan and walked to the door of their cell. She studied the women in the cells opposite them. Most were also at their doors. A petite woman diagonally from Inga stood with her arms above her head, wrists together against the bars.

Emma joined Inga at the bars.

A few moments later, a whispered message reached them. "Lucy's been handcuffed to the bars in the position Julia is showing."

Inga shook her head. When would the cruelty end?

The ventilator had been closed. Inga and Emma passed the frigid night side by side under their coats and both blankets. Still they couldn't find comfortable warmth. Soft shuffles confirmed the presence of rats roaming beneath the bed. Inga prayed they would stay on the floor.

Between the lack of food, the rodents, and the cold, Inga slept fitfully.

"Are you awake?" Emma whispered.

Inga blinked to banish the visions of Susan, Elizabeth, and Helen flooding her mind. "Yes."

"It was nice of your husband to come to court today."

"He's a good man." A small smile curved Inga's lips sending pain across them.

"It's good that he supports your work for the party." Emma sighed. "My parents don't."

"Don't support the vote for women or don't support the party?"

"My mother wants to vote, but she thinks the efforts should be passive, like the NASWA." The cot creaked as Emma shifted slightly. "My father opposes woman suffrage. He wanted to cut off all financial support to me unless I start acting like a *proper* woman, but my mother convinced him to keep giving me a small allowance to live on."

"Yet you live with them when you're in Philadelphia," Inga whispered. "That must be awkward."

Emma sighed. "It is. But I try not to talk about the cause when I'm with them."

They lay in silence for a few minutes. Inga lifted her cold fingers to her hot, throbbing lips. The coolness of her touch gave her momentarily relief. The skin surrounding her mouth was tight and swollen. She ran her tongue over her top and bottom teeth to make sure none were missing.

"How do your daughters feel about your work?"

Stinging tears built behind Inga's eyes. "They support it, but they didn't want me to come back to Washington after my last visit home. They worry when I'm gone." She swallowed. "I've explained that I'm doing this for them, so they won't have to fight for the vote. But sometimes I wonder if I've made the right decision."

"You have."

Emma's emphatic words brought a momentary smile to Inga's lips.

"Sometimes, I think about Susan B. Anthony and the others who fought all their lives for suffrage but never won the vote and wonder if that could happen to me."

"Miss Anthony passed away when I was a young girl, but I think about them sometimes, too. I have to believe we'll prevail soon."

"If we don't, I'm ready to move back to Wyoming with my girls." Inga clenched and released her toes, trying to warm them. "C.J. wasn't happy about the possibility."

"I've been thinking about going to New York, now that their referendum passed."

"I wouldn't blame you." Inga shifted to her back and glanced around the murky cell. Particles floated in the air, reflecting the light from the hallway.

Her left arm still ached, but the throbbing had stopped. She roused herself off the cot, trying to stretch the knots out of her muscles. When she had gained her balance, she eased toward the corridor light coming through the bars.

She scanned the cells in her line of vision. To her shock, the little woman, Julia, was standing in the same position she had been in last night. Inga gave her a slight wave. Julia nodded silently.

That must mean Lucy was still handcuffed to the bars. She said a silent prayer for Lucy and more for the rest of them.

Footfalls sounded down the hallway. Loud clangs echoed one after another. The walls seemed to shake.

Inga stepped back.

A uniformed guard whacked his club against their door. Inga flinched.

Once he had moved on, Inga noticed that the door had popped open a few inches. She moved in for a closer look. The bolt appeared to be stuck in the unlocked position. Shaking her head, she chided herself for not even trying to open the door last night.

She backed away as footsteps approached. Mrs. Nolan was being escorted by a male and female, both wearing official uniforms.

"Where are they taking her?"

Inga startled.

She hadn't realized Emma was behind her.

"I don't know."

Moments later, Mrs. Lewis was escorted past their cell.

Later, the rest of the suffragists were directed to

the large room they had passed through last night. In the light, Inga noticed a large red welt blooming on Emma's chin. One by one they were taken into a small room to meet with Warden Whittaker.

When it was Inga's turn, she took a breath, straightened to her full height, and walked on shaky legs into his office. She tried to lick some moisture onto her swollen lips, but her mouth was dry.

He was seated at a small table.

"What is your name?" He asked, without looking up from the paper in front of him.

"Mrs. Charles James Wakefield."

He raised his head, looked up at her, and arched his brow. "Will you go to the workhouse, obey the regulations, and submit to the orders of the matrons?"

She held his gaze. "No."

He returned his attention to the paper on the table. "Will you wear the uniform of a prisoner?"

"I will not. I expect to be extended the rights of a political prisoner for the—"

"Silence." He turned toward the door. "Trusty! Take this criminal back to her cell."

Criminal! She was not— She clenched her teeth.

A tall, burly woman entered the room and reached for Inga's arm. She pulled away. "I will go with you voluntarily."

She followed her escort back to her cell.

A long while later, Emma returned also.

In mid-afternoon, a workhouse employee delivered a dirty metal tray with two glasses of milk and two slices of bread.

Inga was so thirsty, she picked up her glass of milk and brought it to her lips. Her nose wrinkled. It was warm and had a sour odor. She took a deep breath, held it and filled her mouth with the disgusting liquid. She swallowed it in one gulp before releasing her breath.

Emma watched her wide-eyed.

Heat filled Inga's cheeks. She put the glass back on the tray.

Inga licked welcome moisture onto her tightly puffed lips.

"I needed the liquid," she said apologetically.

Emma took a small sip and set her glass near Inga's.

Neither touched the bread.

They hadn't been given soap or water to clean up. Inga cast her gaze around the dirty brick walls of their cell.

For the rest of the afternoon, they took turns lying on the bed and the floor mattress, attempting to rest. Inga missed the comfort of C.J.'s warmth beside her. She pictured his face, grown more handsome through the years. During these past weeks, he had clearly struggled to keep his long-ago promise to support her suffrage work. How must he feel now that she was in jail?

She thought of her daughters. Would they one day understand her dedication to the cause? Or would they hold her absences from their lives against her? If they moved back to Wyoming, would the girls appreciate their right to vote or take it for granted?

Closing her eyes, she imagined being home in her own bed. As she started to doze, memories of her miscarriages swamped her. The doctor had told her it was not uncommon for women to lose their babies, especially early in the gestation period, but Inga had never known any.

Some time in the early evening, a worker removed the tray from earlier and left another, again with bread and milk. Again, Emma and Inga each took some liquid, but did not touch the bread.

Inga noticed that single prisoners were being removed from their cells, taken out of the area for a while, and then returned. When one of the three women in the cell across from them was returned, Inga waved to her.

"Where did they take you?" Inga whispered as loudly as she dared after the trusty was out of sight.

"To another interrogation like this morning," she replied quietly before moving away from her door.

The temperature in the cell seemed warmer than the previous night. Inga wasn't sure if the temperature outside was warmer, if the warden had decided to allow them some heat, or if she was becoming feverish. With nothing better to do, Inga pondered the options and ruled out illness.

When they were told to go to bed, Emma claimed the mattress on the floor. Inga lay on her back, staring up at the ceiling.

She had survived the third day. Only twenty-seven more to go.

The next morning Inga woke feeling lightheaded. She eased herself to an upright position, careful not to disturb Emma.

She glanced in the direction of last night's tray. Mealy bugs and roaches crawled over the bread. Her empty stomach flipped.

Breakfast and lunch were again bread and milk, since Inga and Emma both declined the chicken offered as a bribe to move out of their cell to the workhouse. Whispering campaigns and codes tapped on bars allowed the women to communicate. Other prisoners had also discovered their non-locking doors, and gradually a few brave individuals occasionally stole into the corridor.

In the middle of the fourth night, Inga was roused from sleep. Dizzy and weak, she sat on the edge of the bed. Two female guards jerked her to her feet, placed their hands beneath her arms, and walked her to the office where Mr. Whittaker had questioned her that first morning.

This time, Mrs. Herndon was seated at the table. While the guards supported Inga, the matron asked the same questions the warden had. Inga gave the same answers.

But the matron went on. "You refused the fried chicken we offered you today. If we gave you steak and potatoes, would you go to the workhouse and follow the rules?"

Thinking of the note Lucy had circulated that disparaged the chicken bribe, Inga almost smiled. That wouldn't do.

She pressed her lips together and shook her head. "No."

"If I let you go without paying your fine, will you promise not to picket any more and go back to Philadelphia?"

"I will not."

The matron's eyes narrowed. "Take her back to her cell."

During the ordeal, Inga had regained enough strength to walk without support, but the trusties half carried her back. As she passed the cells, she studied what she could see of the occupants. Lucy's cell appeared to be empty. Where was she?

Inga's escorts cast her toward her bed. She was able to avoid kicking the rancid broth and milk still sitting on the dinner tray. Thankfully. Emma lay on the mattress on the other side of the space so Inga had not stepped on her.

Each day, the guards placed an open pail of water in the corridor. The suffragists now freely left their cells to ladle water from the bucket into their tin cups. As days passed, prisoners more frequently dipped their cups directly into the pail. Although the practice irked Inga, she and Emma made sure to drink plenty of the disgusting liquid, as their stomachs were no longer able to tolerate the sour milk. They still refused to eat.

Without warning, Emma, Inga and six other prisoners were marched—or dragged—to the workhouse one morning. Even though Inga was weak, she was still able to walk.

It was the sixth day. Mrs. Nolan should be released today. Inga hadn't seen the elderly woman since she was led away on the first day, and she wondered what condition the brave lady was in.

Matron Herndon met them there in the bathroom. Shower heads protruded from the gray wall. Wooden benches stood in the middle of the room. "You all must have showers today. Remove your clothes."

Inga's head snapped up. She met the gazes of wide-eyed suffragists as she scanned the room. Emma's lower lip was quivering. Slowly, she fiddled with the buttons of her jacket. When she had finally undressed, she covered her breasts with one arm and held her hand in front of her other female part.

Inga offered what she hoped Emma would interpret as a sympathetic expression.

They were provided with only one bar of soap, so they passed it around. Without a scrap of privacy, the showers were completed in silence.

The matrons issued a suit of clothes to each prisoner. Inga accepted her pile and held them against her body in a belated attempt at modesty. The rough gray fabric scratched her skin. The concrete floor was cold on her bare feet.

She donned oversized undergarments of coarse, unbleached muslin. She pulled a heavy woolen stocking over each foot, rolling the tops over and over in an effort to keep them from puddling at her ankles.

The gray dress was a loose wrapper-style that could have encircled her twice. She positioned the matching apron and crossed the long ties in the back, bringing the ends to the front, where she knotted them.

Lastly, she studied the bulky shoes. The two were identical. They were not cut to fit one left and one right foot. Although the shoes looked large, Inga had to force her feet into them due to her bulky stockings. She wished she had her own dirty clothes back.

She stood up. The leather shoes pinched her toes.

"We will now proceed back to the cells," Matron Herndon ordered in her commanding voice.

Inga concentrated on each careful step back to her cell in her awkward shoes. She wasn't sure she could muster the strength to get back up if she fell.

Chapter Twenty-One

On Friday, November 23, Inga and her fellow prisoners filed into the small Alexandria, Virginia courtroom. The blur of conversations faded. A loud gasp rose from the people packed inside.

So weary she felt she might collapse, Inga concentrated on each step, willing her legs to sustain her. Passing Mr. Malone and Mr. O'Brien, the attorneys for the suffragists, she reached her chair and dropped onto it. Other prisoners who still had enough strength also took their seats. Some, too weak to sit, laid on benches.

Lucy Burns' flaming red hair caught her gaze. Beside her sat Mrs. Lewis, three chairs down from Inga.

"What happened to you?" someone closer to the pair asked.

"They tried to forcibly feed me, and then they took us to the District Jail," Lucy said.

"They didn't want us here today," Mrs. Lewis added.

"Then how—"

"Mr. Malone outwitted the authorities." Glancing in his direction, Lucy smiled.

Not far from them, Inga caught sight of Emma. She was slouched in her chair as though she had passed out. Inga regarded Emma's sunken bloodshot eyes and gaunt cheeks. The fist-sized bruise on her jaw had faded to ghostly shades of purple, brown, and yellow. She roused, caught Inga's gaze and nodded. Inga returned the silent greeting.

She swept her gaze to the other side of the room. Warden Whittaker, looking clean and professional, sat at the table wearing a smug expression. He was flanked by Matron Herndon and the warden from the Washington District Jail. Inga's eyes drifted closed but she could still hear conversations buzzing around her.

The bailiff announced Judge Edmund Waddill. The room quieted, and the proceedings began. The lawyers argued whether or not it was legal for the Commissioners of the District of Columbia to send prisoners to the workhouse. Inga was too tired to follow every word. She forced herself to concentrate on the judge's ruling, which came more quickly than she expected.

"I hereby find that the transfer of the petitioners from the District of Columbia Jail to the Occoquan Workhouse was undertaken without due process," Judge Waddill said. "I order that the petitioners be removed from the workhouse and remanded to the custody of the Washington, D.C. Jail to serve the remainder of their sentences."

Shouts of approval rose from behind her. Tears collected in Inga's eyes. She slumped back on her chair.

At a touch on her shoulder, she flinched.

The familiar scent of a spicy aftershave greeted her. A sob escaped her, and tears spilled down her cheeks.

"I've been trying to see you all week," C.J. whispered in her ear. "Now I know why they wouldn't let me in. They didn't want me to see what they've done to you."

With great effort, she lifted her hand and lay it on his.

"I'm going to do everything I can to get you out of the District Jail." His tightly controlled words belied his anger. "Without paying the fines."

"Don't forget the others," she whispered.

He gently squeezed her fingers. "I'll work with the party's attorneys."

A ray of hope flickered in Inga.

When they were taken to the District Jail, Inga and the other prisoners were determined to continue their hunger strike in sympathy with their leaders.

After a few days, the doors to the cells were

opened. Warden Zinkhan announced, "The administration has decided to commute your sentences. You may claim your possessions in the office as you leave."

Inga's initial rush of joy was quickly tempered by the realization that this might be another move in the game of cat-and-mouse that the government had been playing with the suffragists. She grasped the bars beside the door.

"Are there any conditions associated with the commutation?" came a voice from another cell.

"The commutation is unconditional." Only a small touch of resentment wove through his words.

Prisoners who were still able to leave their cells on their own power did so. As time passed, members of the National Woman's Party arrived to assist women who were not able to stand or walk on their own.

As Inga made her way slowly toward the office, she spotted C.J. approaching. Her chest warmed with a rush of love. He wrapped his arms around her, and she allowed herself to collapse against him.

She flashed Emma a weak smile as she passed by on the arms of two women with familiar faces.

"Thank you for getting us out," Inga whispered to C.J. once the others had passed.

"I didn't." He kissed the top of her head. "Oh, I talked to everyone who would meet with me since last Friday. I even joined the Men's League. But the jail couldn't afford—monetarily or politically—to force feed all of you, and they didn't want anyone to starve to death on their watch. Either way, the public wouldn't stand for it."

"So the president gave in."

C.J. nodded.

Inga smiled at the victory she and the other prisoners had won.

"You're weak, let me carry you." C.J. started to pick her up.

"No." The words came out with more strength than she expected. "Just give me some support. I want to walk out of here on my own two feet."

C.J. carried a tray with ice cream, cookies, and tea into the bedroom where Inga had been recovering. She was dozing, so he set the tray on the table and studied her injuries, as he did every day.

The cut on her lip had nearly healed. The bruise under her eye and the one above her temple were fading. Although the doctor had assured him that her arm hadn't been re-broken, he said the muscles were seriously battered. He had wrapped the injured limb and given her a sling.

She was still so thin that her ribs and shoulder bones were visible. Her wedding ring kept slipping off her finger, so C.J. had tucked it into her jewelry box for the time being. She had gained enough strength to walk short distances on her own, and she turned laps in the upstairs hallway to build her stamina. Since she could only tolerate a few bites at first, he, Ada, and the girls had offered her small amounts of food frequently throughout the days and evenings.

He sat in the chair beside the bed, poured himself a cup of tea, and munched on a cookie.

Soon Inga's eyes fluttered open. She smiled. "While I laid on my bunk in jail, I imagined your face. It's so nice to wake up and see you in person."

He grinned. "Are you saying that jail has made you appreciate me more?"

Her smile faded. "It made me appreciate everything in my life more."

Setting down his cup, he took her hand. "I learned I don't ever want to live without you." His worst fears had been realized, and he didn't want it to ever happen again. He glanced at the tray. "Would you like some melting ice cream?"

"Sure." She maneuvered into a sitting position.

He handed her the bowl. She took a bite of the soupy treat.

"These came for you today." He pulled two envelopes from his jacket pocket and set the letters beside her on the bed. "One is from Rachel, and the other is Miss Paul's statements since you were all released from jail."

She raised a brow. "You opened my mail?"

"No." He chuckled. "Miss Reed called today to ask how you are doing, and told me she'd sent it. She's at the emergency conference in Washington."

Inga pinched her lips together and narrowed her eyes. "I knew we couldn't trust Wilson to support suffrage in his message to Congress."

"She said the party is filing damage suits against the two wardens, the district commissioners, and another person or two I don't remember."

Her expression relaxed as he spoke.

"They want to know if you wish to be a party to the suit," he said.

She brightened. "If they think it will help, of course."

He took a sip of tea while she took a few more spoonfuls of the melted ice cream.

"Miss Reed also said that they're planning a mass meeting at the Belasco Theatre to honor everyone who has been arrested." He paused. "She wanted to know if you feel up to it."

He feared the stress and excitement might impede Inga's recovery, but after all she had endured, the decision had to be hers.

She lifted her chin. "I wouldn't miss it."

"Mama, can I see your jail pin?" Helen asked one cold mid-December evening, as the family sat together in the parlor.

"Of course, dear." Inga unhooked it from the jacket she had worn to work that day. Although she still tired easily, she had wanted to turn in her article on the suffragists' experience at Occoquan.

She handed the pin to Helen, who held it carefully in both hands.

C.J. finished lighting a fire to take the chill off the house. He crossed the room and sat in the armchair adjacent to Inga's.

"How many people got those 'Jailed for Freedom'

pins at that ceremony?" Elizabeth asked, looking up from the book she was reading.

"I think there were eighty-one. The women carried banners of purple, white, and gold down the aisles of the theatre." Inga smiled at Elizabeth. "Many of those brave women have been arrested more than once. Sóme many times. And there may have been others who have not yet recovered who will receive pins."

Susan slid to the end of the sofa closest to her parents. "Are you going to picket again?"

Visions of the 'Night of Terror' flashed in Inga's mind. Her stomach swooped.

C.J. raked his hand through his hair.

Inga forced a nonchalant shrug. "That will depend on what the president and Congress do."

Helen handed the pin back.

"If you do, can I go with you?" Susan asked.

The thought of her daughter being battered and bruised sent a chill through Inga, though some of the women who had resisted with her were not much older than Susan. Inga shot a glance in C.J.'s direction. He was staring at her, his jaw clenched.

She inhaled a steadying breath. "Your father and I will need to discuss it, but I think you should be at least eighteen before you picket."

C.J.'s relaxed expression.

Susan's shoulders slumped. "What if you win the vote by then?"

"That would be wonderful, and we would all rejoice." Inga fastened the pin back on her collar. "But remember, women have been fighting for suffrage since 1848. Many worked their whole lives for the cause and passed away without ever winning the right. So even though we've made some recent progress, the future is uncertain."

Susan squared her shoulders. "Well, I want you to know I'll do my part."

C.J. frowned.

Inga thought of all the gray-haired ladies she'd met years ago at the suffrage convention in Des

Moines. Would she be one of them some day? Would her daughters?

"I'm proud of your commitment." Her gaze brushed over her daughters. "But I pray every night that you won't have to continue the fight."

When C.J. had insisted they forgo their Christmas trip to Iowa and Wyoming so Inga could further recover her health, she had objected. But he took it upon himself to contact both families with the promise that he, Inga and the girls would spend a month with each family next summer.

She had been annoyed at the time, but now she was glad he had taken the initiative. In the past few weeks, she and her cohorts working for the cause had each contacted all of their friends and relatives to request they write letters in support of the Susan B. Anthony amendment.

The House of Representatives Committee on Woman Suffrage held its first meeting on January third. After a few days of testimony from Carrie Chapman Catt and other supporters of enfranchisement for women, they issued a report in favor of the amendment on January eighth.

Throughout the period, members of the National Woman's Party conducted daily polls of the House on the positions of its members.

Wyoming's representative, Frank Mondell, declared that at least two-thirds of House Republicans would vote for the amendment. This put pressure on the Democrats and the president for securing passage. Inga sent him a note of thanks.

The House vote was scheduled for January tenth.

At Inga's urging, C.J. and Nathan sent telegrams asking Wilson to put pressure on his party members to support the amendment.

The day before the fate of the House's amendment would be decided, Inga sat in her office, staring at her typewriter. She rubbed her aching temples. The hour was late and she was disheartened. The president had not declared his support for the amendment.

She scanned the newspaper. There was the new Employment Service that had just opened in the Department of Labor. Could she make an interesting article about that?

Footfalls pounded down the hall and C.J. burst into her office without knocking.

"I just got a call from our man in Washington," he announced breathlessly.

Every muscle in her body tensed.

A grin spread across his face. "President Wilson is going to come out in support of the suffrage amendment. Tonight."

Staring at C.J., she processed his unexpected words.

The amendment might have a chance!

She leapt from her chair and into his arms.

All afternoon, Inga paced the halls of *The Chronicle*, waiting for word on the vote. She should have gone to Washington to wait at the new NWP headquarters on Jackson Place so she could have heard right away.

"You know they'll be debating it for awhile," C.J. said, as he walked a lap with her.

"I know, but I can't sit still." She frowned. "This is too important."

"Have you thought about what you're going to write if it passes?"

"Not really. I'm afraid I might jinx the vote." She stopped and turned to face him. "There are two things I know, though. Today is exactly one year since Alice Paul and the other women picketed the White House because Wilson refused to consider the memorial resolutions for Inez." She sighed. "I wonder what she would think of where we are now."

C.J. wrapped an arm around her shoulders, and his warmth radiated into her. Her heartbeat slowed to nearly normal.

"Today is also exactly forty years since the suffrage amendment was first introduced into Congress." Her gaze drifted into a blur. "I can't help but think of how hopeful Susan B. Anthony and Elizabeth Cady Stanton must have been on that day. And how many times their hopes were dashed."

C.J. gently placed a hand on each cheek and turned her face toward his. "But they stayed with it, and look where we are now."

He kissed her forehead.

"Where we are now," she echoed. "I hope the two anniversaries are a good omen."

"Do you feel like getting a cup of coffee or a piece of pie?" he asked.

"No. I don't want to leave in case—"

"Then let's go back to my office." C.J. released her face, grasped her hand, and led her back down the hall.

As they approached his door, Nathan emerged from the elevator carrying four bottles of root beer. "Thought maybe you could use a break."

"C'mon." C. J. shepherded them through the door.

Nathan left one of the bottles on the secretary's desk.

C.J. followed her and their boss into the office. Nathan passed out the root beers.

"I guess you haven't heard anything yet," Nathan said, lifting the bottle to his lips.

"Not yet," C.J. replied.

Inga shook her head. She walked to the window and stared out at the city. How many people were waiting for—worrying about—the vote? She took a sip of the root beer.

"Must be a lot of controversy in the debate," Nathan speculated.

Inga cringed.

"I don't think we should read anything into—"

The telephone's ring interrupted C.J.

"I'll get it," he called through the open door.

Again, it rang.

C.J. lifted the receiver. "Wakefield."

The silence seemed to last for an eternity. Inga searched his face, trying to read his expression.

He grinned. "It passed."

Her chest felt light. A wide grin overtook her face. She set her bottle on the window sill and clapped her hands together.

He listened again.

"Two seventy-four to one thirty-six." C.J. scribbled notes as he spoke.

Inga danced to Nathan and gave him a hug.

C.J. hung up the receiver and crossed to Inga.

She threw her arms around his neck. "I can hardly believe it!"

He enfolded her in an embrace.

"We did it!" he declared, as he swung her around in a circle.

Her heart raced.

It was only a first step, but it was a big one.

By early March, many of the National Woman's Party leaders had left on speaking tours to promote Senate passage of the amendment, and Inga's life had fallen back into a comfortable routine.

One afternoon she sat at her desk, compiling notes from her interview with the United States Food Administrator, Herbert Hoover, about his call for 'meatless' and 'wheatless' days to help with the war effort. Despite the serious subject of their meeting, their conversation had been delightful—until he refused to consider the suffrage question until the war was over. After that, their dialogue had become tense. She was trying to figure out how to convey his demeanor without making the story sound frivolous or petty.

A knock sounded on her partially open door.

Inga looked up to see a familiar face poking inside. "Caroline!" Inga cried. "Come in. To what do I owe this pleasure?"

Miss Katzenstein stepped inside and claimed the chair across from Inga. "Well, I always enjoy seeing you." She smiled. "But I confess I'm here on business. I have a request and some good news. Where should I start?"

"With the request."

Caroline pulled a paper from her handbag. "The D.C. Headquarters has learned that you will be in the west this summer."

"Iowa and Wyoming," Inga clarified. "Emma must have called you." She missed Emma since her friend had returned to Washington.

Her guest nodded. "She asked if you could give a few speeches to ask for support of passage of the amendment in the Senate."

For several moments, Inga considered how to answer. "I will do a few, but I don't want them to interfere too much with our family visits. It might be best if Emma calls me directly to work out a schedule."

"That sounds like a good idea." Caroline's grin returned and her face brightened. "And now for some happy news. The D.C. Court of Appeals declared that all the suffragist arrests were unconstitutional and voided all the convictions."

Tears welled behind Inga's eyelids. She blinked them away. "I'll need to be sure to thank our attorneys. I'm so grateful to have my record cleared."

The aromas in her mother's kitchen brought Inga back to memories of her childhood, and the Danish coffee strip she was making was a treat from the past. Inga was happy to be in Iowa for their summer visit.

Moder stood at the stove, stirring the fruit mixture. Despite her gray hair and slightly stooped posture, she was as active as ever.

"I was really hoping all your brothers and sisters could come home at the same time, but at least you'll get to see them over the course of your stay," Moder said.

"It was nice having Uncle Peder, as well as Erik's and Greg's families at my speech last night. It felt very strange to be back at the Normal School." Inga ran the rolling pin over the sweet dough. "It's hard to believe it's been more than twenty years since I taught there."

Susan rolled her eyes. "It's called the Iowa State Teachers College now."

"Right." Inga chuckled. "I'll try to remember that, but I fear it will always be the Normal School to me."

Moder's gaze fixed on Susan. "Do you think you might consider going to college there next year?"

The hopefulness in her mother's voice touched Inga's heart. She would be happy to have her daughter in Cedar Falls with so much family to support and look after her.

"I don't know." Susan lifted a shoulder. "We stopped at Iowa University, Oberlin and Grinnell colleges on the way here, and I'll look at the University of Wyoming, too."

"You still have almost a year to decide." Inga hoped her independent daughter would pick a school closer to Philadelphia.

Moder set the pan on a trivet on the counter and moved closer to Inga. "Your talk last night was very interesting." Moder frowned. "I had no idea you were treated so badly in prison."

"I found it harder to talk about than I expected." Carefully keeping her flour-dusted hands from touching anything, Inga gave her mother a hug. "I am still shocked about the illegal arrests and the abuse the officials inflicted. I hope the audience will keep that in mind when they cast their votes."

"And that they'll tell their senators to vote for suffrage," Susan added.

Inga smiled at her daughter, pleased with her active interest in current political issues. "If only more women—and men—took their civic duty seriously, we could get the Susan B. Anthony amendment passed."

C.J. swept his gaze around the big table in the Hansen's dining room. Everyone was eating, talking, and laughing. The pocket doors to the sitting room were open, with smaller tables set up for the children, but Susan and Torsten's oldest daughter, Dorothy, were seated across from him. Of Inga's brothers, Torsten was the one C.J. knew least. He was pleased to have this opportunity to talk with him.

"Uncle Torsten." Susan set down her fork and turned to him. "I want to become a lawyer like you. Where did you go to college and law school?"

His blue eyes twinkled. "I went to Iowa University my whole way through. Have you decided on a college?"

Susan tilted her head. "I've been thinking about New York University for law school, like Inez Milholland, but I haven't decided where to enroll next year."

Torsten looked to C.J. "Next year?"

C.J. gave a single nod. "She skipped another grade."

Torsten grinned. "She's her mother's daughter."

"Come to Iowa University," Dorothy implored. "We could live together."

Susan raised a brow. "You've already decided?"

Dorothy nodded. "It's perfect for me. It's far enough away from Chicago and my parents, yet close enough to go home for a weekend if I want."

Torsten grimaced.

"You don't want her to go there?" C.J. asked.

"I'd be proud if she did." Torsten's face softened. "I just hate thinking about her leaving home."

"I know what you mean." C.J. watched his daughter chatting with Dorothy.

"It's funny, isn't it?" Torsten said. "We take it for granted that our girls will get a college education. So many men and women don't even consider the possibility for their daughters."

C.J. thought about how Ruth had pushed their parents to allow her to attend the university. "I think I owe that belief to my sister. And, of course, Inga."

"And my mother," Torsten added. "She always preached to us children about the importance of education."

C.J. glanced at his mother-in-law. "She's remarkable. It's no wonder Inga became the woman she is.”

CHAPTER TWENTY-TWO

July 24, 1918
Laramie, Wyoming

Dear Rachel,

It seems strange to be writing the return address from Laramie again. I hope all is well with you.

We spent last month with my parents, and it was wonderful to be home on the farm. It's been a delightful respite from the crucible of politics that often engulfs me at home. I enjoyed watching my children rediscovering the joys of nature, and engaging in activities like horseback riding and feeding baby animals. We had planned on getting the girls a kitten for Christmas, but with all of the hubbub surrounding my imprisonment and recovery, we didn't get around to it. Watching them with my parents' cats and those here on C.J.'s family's ranch, I think I may work on finding one when we get back home at the end of the August.

I gave talks at Iowa University and the Normal School about my experiences in Occoquan Workhouse, and the importance of passing the suffrage amendment in the Senate. They went well, but were much more difficult than I expected. The difference between lecturing students in class and giving public speeches has always surprised me. These events have given me a renewed respect for the work Mrs. Wells-Barnett does on the lecture circuit.

Next week, I will speak at the University of Wyoming. It is my last scheduled speech. When it's over, I'll be able to relax for the rest of my visit.

At Christmastime I dropped a note to Sarah, congratulating her on winning the vote in New York. I haven't received a response from her. I think she is angry that I have associated myself with the National Woman's Party, since she has always been loyal to the NASWA. In my opinion, neither group has treated

Negro women fairly, so I appreciate the fact that you haven't held my work for the NWP against me.

I was pleased to note that Theodore Roosevelt campaigned for passage of suffrage in New York again last year, as he did in 1915. I hope he'll work for the cause on the national level.

When I get back home, I hope we can get together for lunch, or better yet, that you and Herman can join our family for dinner.

Lovingly in Friendship,
Inga

Inga descended the steps that led off the stage of the auditorium. She readjusted the coarse fabric of her outfit, an imitation of the garb from the workhouse. Now that her program was over, she was eager to change into comfortable clothes.

Ruth, Jess, and their daughter and three sons joined her.

"It's so nice to see you," Inga greeted them.

Ruth gave her a hug, aggravating the chafing from the rough cloth. "I'm so glad we'll have some time together this week when you come out to our house."

"So am I." Inga grinned, despite the irritation of her skin. Even with the discomfort, she chose not to line her outfit so that her memories remained more vivid when she spoke.

Jess shook his head. "It's hard to believe what all you went through."

"You should have seen her when she was released from jail," C.J. said, walking to her side. He started to put his arm around her, but when his fingers brushed over the fabric he took her hand instead.

She shot him a smile.

"Her face and arms were covered with bruises." His tone was tight. "She was so thin her bones were sticking out, and she was so tired she slept most of two days."

Jess's gaze dropped to his shoes then rose to meet Inga's. "I never knew voting was that important to you," he said. "That you'd go through all that."

She squeezed C.J.'s fingers. "I didn't know I would have to."

A small smile curved Jess's lips. "Ruth showed me that women should be given the vote."

"If the suffrage amendment passes, it won't *give* us the vote." Inga lifted her chin. "We will have won it."

A few days later, Inga stood at the counter in the spacious kitchen of Ruth's large ranch house, cutting green beans. She smiled. "This is so much more convenient than canning was in your cabin, but we sure had a lot of fun back then."

"We sure did." Ruth lifted quart jars into the canner. "I'm looking forward to the time when Mildred is old enough to help."

Inga sighed and slid the cut beans into a bowl. "My girls don't get much opportunity to learn to can, since we don't have a garden. It's too bad."

"It's different in the city than on the ranch." Ruth filled another jar.

Her twins rushed into the kitchen.

Robert reached for the cookie jar. "Can we have some cookies for us and our cousins?"

Ruth shook a damp finger in his direction. "Don't touch that. When Aunt Inga and I get to a stopping point, we'll all have cookies and iced tea."

His face fell. He shot a glance at his brother, Lester, who only shook his head.

"Go back outside." Ruth kept filling jars while she spoke. "It won't be long."

The boys trudged outside, closing the door behind them.

Inga scanned the room. "While we're alone, there's something I want to mention to you." She moved closer to her sister-in-law. "I'm worried about your father."

Ruth's head popped up. "Why?"

"Sometimes, he seems to have a hard time breathing, especially when he's working hard." Inga kept her voice low. "And there were a couple of times his face seemed to turn pale, or even bluish."

"I've noticed the same thing," Ruth said. "But he keeps telling me it's because he's getting older and the work is harder for him. He promised to have his hired men do more."

Inga took a breath. "I know it's really none of my business, but it happened several times just in the week we were at their house."

"Of course it's your business. You're family." Ruth turned to face Inga. "I'm glad you told me. I'll talk with Mom when we take you back to their place."

"I'm sorry your father didn't feel well enough to see us off," Inga said to Ruth as they stood on the platform, waiting for the eastbound train. "But I'm glad he's agreed to see a doctor."

"Me, too." Ruth said.

"Let us know what you find out." Inga squinted, looking for a sign of the locomotive.

"I have your brother's telephone number. I'll call before I go back out to my place."

C.J. and his mother walked toward the concession end of the depot.

"There is talk of raising the draft age to forty-five," Inga confided to Ruth. "All four of my brothers will be eligible. I'm really worried, and I'm sure Moder is beside herself. I'm glad we'll be stopping at their house for a few days on our way home." Inga clutched her handbag tighter. "My only consolation is that C.J. would be too old."

Ruth frowned. "Jess would qualify, too. I don't know what Congress is thinking of."

"I'm still angry that young American men are dying for European democracies on foreign soil, when so many American women are denied the right to vote." Inga's temples began to throb. "And I'd feel even worse if one of my brothers was sent there to fight."

A shrill whistle sounded. Inga flinched.

As she watched the approaching train, she continued. "We'll just have to keep praying that the war ends soon."

Two days before they were to leave Iowa, Inga, her mother, and her daughters took a stroll around the farm. They had agreed to spend the whole walk speaking French. As they were leaving the stables, an automobile pulled into the dooryard. Inga recognized the vehicle as Erik's.

He parked, got out, and started toward the house.

"*Vous les filles pouvez continuer*," Moder said. "*Je vais voir ce qu'il veut.*"

"I'll go with you." Inga turned to her daughters. "You girls continue your walk."

"Can we go back to the stable and play with the cats?" Helen asked in halting French.

Inga smiled. "*Oui.*"

As she and her mother neared the house, she noticed Halvor and C.J. approaching from the old bunkhouse. They all exchanged greetings.

Erik's face was pinched. "Let's go in and sit down."

Inga's throat constricted.

Moder bit her lower lip as everyone followed him into the parlor. "What is it?"

"I got a call from Torsten this morning."

Erik raked a hand through his brown hair. "A draft registration has been announced for September twelfth for all men under forty-five. We'll all have to sign up." A small tremor wove through his words. "He also said he heard the war is winding down."

Inga cast her eyes upward and said a silent prayer that her brothers would not have to fight.

The day before they were scheduled to leave, C.J. was at the table with his wife and daughters, his in-laws, and their housekeeper. As always, they served a farm breakfast with eggs, ham, and an array of delicious Danish pastries. He made it a point to have a piece of each one, as he knew it would be a while before he would have them again.

"Do you think you'll be back at Christmas?" Inga's mother asked.

C.J. and his wife exchanged glances.

"I think we'll have to get back to Philadelphia and see what happens." Inga held her mother's gaze. "This summer we've been away longer than ever before. We'll have a lot of catching up to do."

Anna frowned. "Please let me know as soon as you make—"

A knock sounded at the back door. The housekeeper rose and headed into the kitchen.

"—a decision."

"We will," Inga promised.

C.J. silently thanked her for responding to the question by leaving them options.

The housekeeper returned with Erik in tow.

C.J. looked, then looked again.

Erik wore a grim expression. He cleared his throat. "Can I talk with C.J. and Inga in the parlor? Alone."

C.J.'s heart sped up. He shot an alarmed glance to his wife. She was rising from her chair.

His body felt heavy as he pushed himself to his feet. With leaden steps, he followed Inga and her brother into the other room.

Inga and C.J. sat side by side on the davenport. She took his hand.

"Your sister telephoned this morning." Erik focused directly on C.J. "Your father was admitted to the hospital yesterday."

C.J.'s chest felt as though a weight had been dropped on it.

"How is he doing today?" Inga asked.

"Ruth told me the doctor said that you should come soon." Erik leaned forward. "She told me how you can reach her at the hospital. If you want to come to town with me to telephone her, and maybe change your train tickets, I can bring you back here this afternoon."

C.J. looked to Inga.

"You need to go back to Wyoming," she said.

He could only nod.

"School starts next week. Do you want me to take

the girls back home?" She gently squeezed his hand. "Or do you want us to go back to Wyoming with you?"

He cleared his throat. "This might be the last time we see Dad. And the last time he sees us."

He gripped her fingers as though they were a lifeline. "I want you and the girls to come back with me."

On the third night of their stay in Laramie, C.J. and Inga lay in the hotel bed. His father had looked so pale and weak this afternoon. His mother was beside herself with worry. Was keeping his daughters here the right decision?

C.J. stared into the darkness, trying to collect his thoughts.

"What did the doctor say this afternoon?" Inga asked.

He swallowed. "That it could be days or it could be weeks, but he doesn't expect Dad to live to Thanksgiving."

She groped along his arm until she clasped his hand in hers. "I'm so sorry." She sniffled. "He's such a wonderful man."

"He wants to go home." The words irritated his scratchy throat. "Mom thinks we should take him to the ranch tomorrow or the next day."

"What does Ruth say?"

"She thinks it's a good idea since there's not much the hospital can do for his congestive heart failure that we couldn't do ourselves." C.J. paused. "I'm not sure she and Mom can handle his care, but she thinks having him at home would make it easier to keep an eye on the ranch and make plans for what happens after—" A sob choked off his speech.

Inga drew his hand to her lips and kissed his fingers then wrapped an arm around him.

They lay in silent blackness until C.J. was able to talk again.

"Ruth sent Jess and their kids home to take care of their place, so we'll have plenty of room at the ranch house." He drew in a breath. "She'll handle the folks' place until we figure out what to do with it in the future."

"How does your mother feel about that?"

"She's so upset that she can't think about it. She's glad Ruth is stepping up." He paused. "So am I."

Inga's arm tightened around him. "Of course we'll stay as long as we need to. Since we'll be here for a while, I'll go out tomorrow and try to buy some textbooks so I can help the girls keep up with their studies. That way, they won't be so far behind when they return to school."

An unexpected chuckle broke through his sadness. "If you're their teacher, they'll probably be ahead of their classmates."

She chuckled, too. The lilting sound was welcome after so many serious days.

"Are you saying I'm a cruel taskmaster?"

"The worst," he teased.

She lifted his arm and snuggled her head against his shoulder. Her presence comforted him.

"Did you telephone Nathan today?" she asked.

"Yes." C.J. pulled her closer. "He wants me to call in twice a week. He was glad you turned in your September and October stories before we left, but he wants you to work on an article for November."

C.J. buried his lips in her hair and kissed the crown of her head.

"I'll try to call Emma before we leave town." Inga sighed. "She can tell me what's happening with the amendment in the Senate. Last time I talked with her, she said the party had begun protests in Lafayette Park."

"You're going to write an article on that?"

"Yes." She shifted her position. "And I want to find out if I'll have to go down there and picket when we get home."

C.J. clenched his teeth. With his father's failing heart, he didn't want to even think about her picketing again.

By early September, C.J.'s father had been settled

in his bed at home, and the household had fallen into a routine of sorts, although his condition deteriorated. Ruth, her mother, and Inga took turns caring for him.

Weekdays, Inga conducted lessons for her girls and assigned homework, which freed her to work on her article.

On September twelfth, Jess registered for the draft, putting Ruth and the rest of the family on edge.

Twice a week, C.J. and Inga drove into town to make their telephone calls. Although only a couple of her former colleagues at *The Boomerang* were still employed there, Inga insisted upon stopping in the office to purchase a newspaper on each trip.

On one such foray, Inga called Erik to catch up on the family news.

"Torsten received his draft notice a few days ago." Erik's voice was calm and even. "He has to report to Camp Grant in Rockford in two weeks for training."

"Oh, no." Inga pressed her lips together to suppress a sob.

"Moder is very upset. She and Halvor have gone to visit him and offer to have his wife and family stay with them until he is discharged."

Inga sucked in a breath. "I'm glad we got to see him this summer."

"Torsten said it's possible that the war will end before he finishes training." Erik's voice sounded hopeful.

"We can only hope he's right." Inga tamped down her anger enough to keep her voice as calm and even as his. "But I think it's wrong for the president to send our men to fight for liberty abroad when we women are denied our rights here at home."

"There's not much we can do about that now." Erik sounded resigned.

"Write to your representative and the president." Inga would do the same.

When they returned to the ranch, their daughters greeted them at the door.

"Did you talk to Miss Reed today?" Susan leaned forward, her eyes bright with interest. "Is there any word about the suffrage amendment?"

Inga sighed. "Nothing for certain, but she said the party has been assured that it will be introduced in the Senate soon."

Ruth and C.J. joined them.

"That doesn't sound very certain," Ruth said.

"Emma said that Washington newspapers started reporting influenza cases the last week of August, and more since. They seem to think it's more of a problem at the naval stations and army camps than in the city, but she's worried it might interfere with the Senate's work." Inga shrugged. "I suppose it would give them an excuse for not dealing with the suffrage amendment."

"We also heard there has been a case or two in Laramie," C.J. added.

Ruth grimaced. "We'll have to be careful when we're there."

Inga agreed. She wished they wouldn't have to go into town at all.

One morning in early October, C.J. sat with his father while he waited for Inga to finish dressing for their trip to town. He watched as the man who had always been so strong, so vigorous, lay in his bed, sleeping, gasping for breath.

C.J. rubbed his jaw, trying to ease his fatigue.

Inga appeared at the door.

"I'm ready when you are," she said quietly.

He rose and walked to her, thankful she was here to support him through this difficult time.

When they arrived in town, he parked in front of the grocery store.

"I'll drop off the list here, and then stop in the *Boomerang* office to get my newspaper and make my calls." She patted her handbag. "I need to turn in the article I promised as payment for the use of their telephone."

"The Night of Terror column?" C.J. asked.

She grinned. "If we're here much longer, the editor

will probably want me to write another one."

"I'll meet you here when we're both done." He headed up the street toward his friend's livery, where he would visit and make his calls.

He placed his call to Nathan. While waiting to be connected, he pulled his notes out of his jacket pocket.

"C.J." Nathan's voice came over the line. "How is your father?"

C.J. inhaled a deep breath. "He is failing fast. I don't think he can last much longer."

"I'm sorry." Nathan's tone became serious. "I think you should stay in Wyoming for a while."

"Why?"

"The influenza is rampant here in the city. A lot of people have already died. It would be safer for you and your family to stay where they are."

"Are you and your family okay?"

"For now." He didn't sound certain. "But we've taken our children out of school."

The line was silent for a few moments. C.J. glanced at his friend, who was polishing the buckle on a harness. "Did you get Inga's story on solar eclipses?"

"Yes, and we were lucky enough to obtain a couple of photographs of the one in June to go with it."

C.J. smiled weakly. "She's still working on an article about the amendment, but so far it's mostly a civics lesson. When she finds out what the Senate's going to do, she'll finish it."

"It's been introduced in the Senate," Nathan said.

"She'll be happy to hear it." C.J. couldn't wait to tell her. It would be welcome good news in the midst of the sadness surrounding his father's condition. She hadn't once complained about being so far away from her work for the cause, even though he knew it was hard on her. "I don't think she talked to Miss Reed last week."

They finished talking about the layout for the November issue and C.J. hung up.

"I didn't mean to be eavesdropping." His friend wore a sheepish grin. "But were you talking about the influenza?"

C.J. nodded. "I was."

"I read that the university closed, and the health officials are shutting down schools and telling people to stay away from public places." His friend searched through a stack of newspapers and handed him one.

"Here in Laramie?"

"Yes."

C.J. handed the paper back. "I need to go tell Inga."

He hurried to the drug store and purchased medicines the druggist recommend to help his father breathe easier. Then he returned to his father's automobile. Inga wasn't there.

He waited. After looking up and down the street and not seeing her, he went into the grocery store and picked up her order. He stowed the items in the back seat.

And waited some more.

Inga trudged toward the street where C.J. had parked. With so much bad news to process, she felt as though she was carrying the weight of an elephant on her shoulders.

As she approached the automobile, she picked up her pace.

C.J. rushed toward her. "Where have you been?"

"It's a long story." She glanced at the store. "I'll get the groceries."

"I already did. Do you want to get some lunch?"

Her stomach roiled. "No, thank you. I just want to go home."

His face brightened. "The Senate introduced the suffrage amendment."

He hurried to the passenger side and held the door for her.

"I know. I called Emma." It was about the only good news she had received.

When she was settled in the seat, he closed her door and took his place behind the steering wheel. He turned toward Inga.

"She also said a lot of people in Philadelphia are sick with the influenza, and many have already died," she continued.

"Nathan said the same thing." C.J. slipped the key into the ignition. "He said we should stay out here until the worst passes."

"But there's flu here, too." She hesitated. "And the health authorities have closed all public places, including the churches. I think we should talk with your mother and Ruth about that."

The line of his mouth thinned.

"I also telephoned Ada and told her she can stay at our house. I let her know she's welcome to bring her parents and sisters, too, if she wants." She fiddled with the handles of the handbag in her lap. "I know I should have asked you first, but I thought I needed to make a decision while I was talking with her."

"That's fine."

Inga swallowed back a threatening sob. "I also talked with Moder." She inhaled several breaths. "She said Torsten has fallen ill with the influenza at Camp Grant. The military medical personnel are caring for him and the other affected soldiers, as well as the civilians in Rockford." She gripped the handles of her handbag with tight fists. "I feel like I was surrounded by influenza today. I just want to go back to the ranch and hide away until the sickness goes away."

Their daughters greeted them as soon as they walked through the door.

"Did you talk to Grandma Hansen today?" Elizabeth asked.

Inga's throat thickened. She set her handbag on the table. "Yes."

"Is Uncle Torsten at the training camp, yet?" Susan asked.

"He is." Inga sensed a joyful note in her daughters' voices. "Why do you ask?"

"We wrote letters to him today." Elizabeth smiled.

Helen pursed her lips. "Susan said we could."

Now was not the time to tell them of their uncle's illness. Inga managed to smile at her oldest daughter.

"Well, I think that was a fine idea." She gave each girl a hug. "May I read them before you send them?"

"Sure," Helen said, speaking for them all. The others nodded.

Inga hoped their letters would help cheer him in his fight to overcome the influenza.

Chapter Twenty-Three

October 30, 1918
Laramie, Wyoming

Dear Moder,

I hope this finds Torsten on the road to recovery.

We are very sad here. C.J.'s father passed away three days ago. At his end, he was constantly gasping for breath. I felt so sorry that we could do nothing to help him. Laramie is fighting the influenza, and all public gathering places have been closed by the health officials. Consequently, the pastor came to the ranch for a small funeral for family and only the closest friends. C.J.'s mother wanted her husband to be buried under a beautiful oak tree at the back of her dooryard, so C.J. and the hired hands dug the grave and laid him to rest.

Ruth has asked C.J. to stay until they can take care of the will and figure out how to handle the ranch since their mother wants to stay but doesn't want to supervise the hired hands. C.J. thinks one of the men could be made manager and take care of the day-to-day work, but his mother is trying to pressure him to stay here. He definitely doesn't want to do that, so he and Ruth are trying to figure out a solution.

We're not in a hurry to leave because when C.J. telephoned the owner of The Chronicle *day-before-yesterday, he learned that the influenza is still widespread in Philadelphia. The owner has closed the magazine and they won't be printing a December issue. This is the first time that has happened in all the years I've been writing for them.*

I was so pleased to learn that the Senate introduced the suffrage amendment in late September, but not surprised that it failed the vote on October 1. Members of the National Woman's Party are now picketing the Capitol and Senate Office Building. Hopefully they will change some senator's minds.

For now, we are all well here. We hope the same is true for all of our Cedar Falls family.

Love,
Inga

Inga sealed the letter and set it aside. Tomorrow she would put it in the mailbox for the rural letter carrier to pick up.

"Do you want to check my algebra problems?" Elizabeth asked, sliding her paper across the dining room table.

Inga smiled. "Yes, thank you."

"May I go outside and help Daddy with the chores?"

Inga smiled. "Of course."

"I've finished my book report on *Oliver Twist*," Susan said.

"Good. Then you may be excused."

Helen was still working on her report about the Preamble to the Constitution.

Inga pulled out her draft of the article on the suffrage amendment and skimmed it. Outside, the dogs began barking. The sound of tires crunching on gravel carried into the house. She glanced out the window. She didn't recognize the car, so she returned to her editing.

A few minutes later, C.J. came through the front door, followed by Elizabeth and a man Inga had never seen before.

"Here she is," C.J. said.

Inga shot him a questioning gaze.

"Mrs. Wakefield, I have a telegram for you," the stranger said. "It's from ah—" He checked the page. "Anna Hansen." He held out the paper.

She shrunk away from it. Telegrams were rarely good news, especially from family. Her limbs felt like lead.

"Do you want me to read it to you?" C.J. asked in a soft voice.

She wasn't sure if it would be worse to see the words or hear them out loud. Reluctantly, she accepted the telegram and unfolded it.

Torsten passed away yesterday.

Most of Iowa quarantined.

Burials banned.

Memorial service later.

Moder

Tears pooled in Inga's eyes. She pressed her lips together to keep them from quivering.

Handing the paper to C.J., she fled to the bedroom.

C.J. returned to the ranch and parked the car in the dooryard. He felt lighter than he had in months. If he was able to whistle, he would have done so as he entered the house.

Inga and his mother were in the kitchen,

"The war is over!" The words burst from him.

Both women stared at him.

"Thank goodness," Inga said finally. "Now Erik, Paul, and Greg will be safe from fighting in Europe. And Jess." She smiled. Something he'd rarely seen since she'd received word of Torsten's death.

"And the boys who are there can come home," his mother added.

"I brought a bottle of champagne to celebrate." C.J. placed it in the icebox. "Ruth and I got the paperwork filed on Dad's will before she left for her place."

"Jess and her kids will be glad to see her," Mom said.

C.J. wondered how his mother could acknowledge that while still insisting that Ruth come every week to meet with the hired man they'd appointed to manage the ranch. With the distance between the two places, his sister would have to be away from home at least two days out of every seven. Hopefully they could reduce the frequency when winter set in.

"I also secured train tickets for the Saturday before Thanksgiving." C.J smiled at Inga, "And I telephoned Erik to let him know when we'll arrive. He said your mother is excited that we'll be there for the holiday."

"Especially since we won't be back for Christmas. She wasn't very happy when I gave her that news on Monday." She held his gaze. "What did Nathan say about the influenza? Is the number of people dying still declining?"

"Yes. And he said most public places have reopened now that the quarantine was lifted." He snatched a cookie from the batch cooling on the counter.

"C.J.!" his mother scolded.

He grinned at her. "Thank you."

"When is Nathan planning to get *The Chronicle* going again?" Inga pulled a sheet of cookies from the oven.

"The Monday after Thanksgiving. That should give us plenty of time to get the January issue out on time." He eyed the rest of the cookies.

"But that won't give us much time to settle in at home." Inga began removing warm cookies from the baking sheet.

"You can take the week off, since you've already finished your January story."

"I might do that." She set the baking sheet next to the sink. "It will give me a chance to help get the girls into their school routines, and start finding some returning soldiers to interview for my February article."

He winced. "Are you sure you want to write about that? Don't you think it will be too hard since your brother—"

"I want to do it in honor of Torsten." Her eyes shone. "Because they served their country, like he was preparing to do."

"I won't stand in your way."

She cleared her throat and swept her gaze around the kitchen and toward the doorway to the dining room. "And I'll try to find a kitten to give the girls for Christmas."

"Maybe we should get a cat for each one," C.J. whispered. "Then they won't be fighting over one."

Her eyes widened. "When did you become such a Santa Claus?" She grinned. "Granting everyone's wishes."

Moving behind her and encircling her waist with his arms, he whispered, "You and the girls have been such good sports about spending nearly half of the year here, I'd like to make it up to you."

"If Congress doesn't pass a suffrage amendment in the next year or two, I'm ready to move here permanently."

He frowned. The last thing he wanted to do was move back to Laramie and get roped into taking over his mother's ranch. When he got home to Philadelphia, he would help the Men's League lobby the Senate for passage of the amendment.

"It seems like forever since I've seen you," Inga greeted Rachel outside the café where they always met for lunch, one of the few in the nation's capitol that wasn't segregated. "But that's mostly my fault since I was out west for five months."

"At least you missed the worst of the influenza." Rachel grimaced.

"We were out on the ranch through most of it," Inga said. "Was it terrible?"

Rachel frowned. "All of the relief stations were set up for whites only until they finally opened one in our community near the end of October, barely a few days before the quarantine was lifted." Her gaze met Inga's. "But that was no surprise since Wilson instituted segregation in all federal agencies."

"Between that and his attitude toward suffrage, he's been a real disappointment as a president." Inga clenched her teeth.

"At least he urged passage of the suffrage amendment in his annual speech to Congress two weeks ago." Rachel sighed.

A couple approached, so Inga and Rachel stepped aside to avoid blocking the door.

"Only because it was to his political advantage." Inga wrinkled her nose. "He's such a scoundrel."

"He's definitely not popular in my community," Rachel told her.

Inga glanced in the direction of the Capitol. "At least the proposed suffrage amendments haven't discriminated based on color."

"No. But they haven't passed yet either."

"Tomorrow, when the conference is over, we're going to protest in Lafayette Park." Inga smiled. "We're going to burn Wilson's speeches."

Rachel lifted a brow. "Aren't you afraid of being arrested again?"

"We'll have several hundred women there." Inga let her smile bloom. "I doubt they'll want to arrest all of us." She shivered. "Let's go inside where it's warm."

C.J. sat at the desk in his library, forcing himself to read through articles that had been submitted during his absence.

He glanced at the silent telephone. Why hadn't Inga called yet? He checked the mantel clock. Half past seven. Had the protesters been arrested?

Directing his attention back to the papers, he forced himself to skim the piece about the terms of the Armistice. The piece was dry, and most of the material had already been covered in the newspapers. Maybe if the writer had explained the implications of the provisions—

A knock sounded at the half-open door.

He looked up to see Helen peeking around the panel.

"May I come in, Daddy?"

"Sure, baby." He put down the page he was holding.

"I haven't heard the telephone ring," she said. "Mama hasn't called, yet, has she?" Her face was tense with worry.

He hated seeing his daughter so anxious. "Not yet." He forced a smile. "It's still early."

"Can I stay here and read a book while we wait? I'll be quiet so you can work."

"Is your school work done?"

She nodded. "Yes."

"Then you may." He smiled again, trying to reassure her and himself.

She selected a volume from one of the shelves and curled up in a corner of the sofa.

Over the next quarter hour, his older daughters joined them.

"What if Mama is in jail again?" Susan asked.

She had hit on C.J.'s biggest fear. A chill ran through him.

"Let's not worry yet." He kept his voice even although his heart pounded.

Helen's lower lip quivered. "Christmas is only nine days away. Would she have to stay in jail for Christmas?"

C.J. pushed the idea out of his mind. He inhaled a long breath. "Whatever happens, we'll be fine." He forced another smile. "Let's all go to the kitchen and make some cocoa."

He stood and followed the girls into the hall.

The telephone rang.

He stopped mid-step. His throat constricted.

"That's her!" Helen cried, running back into the library.

"It has to be." Susan's voice was barely audible.

C.J.'s heart beat so hard, he felt it in his breastbone.

Another ring.

He hurried past the girls and picked up the receiver. "Hello?"

"Hello, dear." Inga's voice came through the line. "Just calling to let you know I'll be home on tomorrow morning's train."

His muscles relaxed, and he sat on the corner of the desk. "I'll pick you up at the station."

He looked at his daughters. They were all grinning.

On Christmas morning, Inga watched as her daughters unwrapped the last of their gifts. They had helped her decorate the parlor with evergreens and festive red ribbons. The multitude of candles the girls had insisted on placing on the tables and mantel cast a warm glow across the room.

Susan had already curled up in the corner of the sofa reading the new book, *Summer* by Edith Wharton, that Ruth and her family had sent.

Elizabeth and Helen were dutifully picking up the wrapping paper, when C.J. leaned forward, reached in front of the lamp table, and touched Inga's arm. "Shall we do it now?"

Inga nodded. "I can go."

She started to rise, but C.J. stood before she could. "I will."

As soon as he left the room, Helen whirled to face her. "Do what? Go where?"

"You'll see." Inga smiled as she heard the distant squeak of the basement door. "When Daddy comes back, you must remain still and quiet."

A few minutes later, C.J. returned with the half-grown calico kitten in his arms.

The girls' eyes widened. Their mouths dropped open then they broke into grins.

"Is it ours?" Helen whispered.

"Yes." Inga said quietly. "Remember how we introduced ourselves to the cats on the farm and do the same here."

Susan walked to the door and closed it slowly.

C.J. bent down and set the kitten on the rug.

The girls sat at intervals on the rug, each holding out their hands for the feline to sniff.

"You three are going to be responsible for taking care of her," Inga said.

C.J. walked to the desk and picked up a sheet of paper and held it up. "We've made a schedule of who is responsible for feeding and cleaning out the sandboxes each day."

Inga nodded. "We'll put this on the door to the back stairs, and you need to check it every day."

"And you must keep her in the house at all times,"

C.J. cautioned.

"Why?" Helen frowned.

"It's too dangerous for a cat to be outside in the city." Inga looked from girl to girl. "She could get run over by an automobile or truck. Or a bigger animal could hurt her."

Helen's lip quivered, then stiffened. "We'll need to tell Ada when she comes back tomorrow."

"She already knows," Inga said. "We talked about it when I asked if she would be okay with having a cat in the house."

"Does the kitty have a name?" Elizabeth asked. The cat sniffed her fingers then rubbed its cheek against them. She stroked its furry back.

C.J. grinned. "Not yet. What do you girls think we should call her?"

They each threw out names, then argued for or against the options. Inga thought back to cats that she and her brothers had named in their childhood. She hoped having an animal to care for would help teach her girls responsibility, patience, and kindness.

Finally, Helen suggested, "She's a girl. Let's call her *Fille.*"

"Fille," Susan and Elizabeth said in unison, each studying the cat.

"That's a good idea," Susan smiled at her sister.

Elizabeth scratched behind the cat's ear. "Do you like that, *Fille*?"

In a small meeting room at the Philadelphia suffrage headquarters, Inga sat across the table from Emma. Her friend's skin was pale and drawn thin across her cheekbones. Both hung their coats over their shoulders to stave off the February chill.

"I thought the memorial article that you wrote about former President Roosevelt was a nice tribute," Emma said.

"Ever since I interviewed him, I've had a soft spot in my heart for him." A sad smile played at Inga's lips. "He always seemed so vital, so vibrant that I was shocked to learn that he had passed."

Emma nodded. "I know what you mean. I didn't realize he was sixty."

They sat for a moment in silence.

"Have you been down to Washington for any of the watch fire demonstrations?" Inga asked.

Emma frowned. "I've been to party headquarters to answer telephones and do paperwork, but my doctor says I can't go out in the cold for long periods until I'm more fully recovered from the influenza."

"I'm so sorry you had to go through it." Inga tried to keep her tone even. "My brother was drafted, and then he died when the epidemic swept through his training camp." In the past few months, her grief had morphed into anger at Wilson and Congress over raising the draft age so close to the end of the war.

"I'm sorry." Emma blinked several times then lifted her tear-filled gaze to meet Inga's. "Did you hear that Martha Scott and two of her children also passed during the outbreak?"

"Yes." Inga inhaled a steadying breath. "It breaks my heart to think about them."

They sat in silence.

"We got word just before you arrived that the watch fire protesters who were arrested for the protests on the ninth were released today." A small smile played at Emma's lips. "I hear they had started a hunger strike."

Inga remembered their horrible days at the workhouse. "I'm glad they weren't jailed for long."

"Maybe the judge felt the Senate had dealt enough punishment after the suffrage amendment failed by one vote," Emma suggested.

"I'm not sure the D.C. judges have that much compassion." Inga pursed her lips. "Does the party have a plan going forward?"

"The 'Prison Special' speaking tour starts day after tomorrow." Emma rubbed her hands together.

"I was invited to participate, but didn't feel I could after being away for nearly six months last year."

"I couldn't go either, but they had plenty of

volunteers." Emma paused. "Their train is called the 'Democracy Limited.'"

Inga chuckled. "Clever. I like the double meaning, but I wonder how many people will comprehend it."

"I'm sure the speakers will explain how U.S. democracy is limited as long as women can't vote." Emma pulled gloves from her coat pocket and donned them.

"I still can't believe that we were shy only one Senator." Inga shook her head. "I'm sure it would have succeeded if Wilson had worked harder for passage."

"I think a group plans to address that with him when he returns from Europe."

"It feels like Congress is playing the same cat-and-mouse game with suffrage that the Iowa Legislature was playing when I lived there twenty-plus years ago. And still are as far as I know." Inga sighed. "I only hope this is not the federal lawmakers' plan."

Inga sat in one of the large wing-backed chairs in the library. Rachel sat in the other. Both waited for the phone to ring. A refreshing May breeze wafted through the open windows.

"I'm so glad it worked out that you're in town and free to get together today." Inga clasped her hands together in her lap. "I don't think I could have dealt with the waiting as well at the office."

Rachel sighed. "It's nice to be out of D.C. for a while. I wish Herman could have come with me, but he couldn't get off work. The tension between the races there is growing."

"Because Wilson segregated the government?" Inga studied her friend's face, drawn with worry. "There was no reason for him to do that."

"No, except he bows to pressure from the southerners. And truth be told, I think he and his cronies prefer it." Rachel frowned. "I've lived in Washington most of my life, but I don't remember ever being this nervous."

"If you ever need to get away for a while, you and

Herman are welcome to use our guest room." Inga's glance strayed to the telephone.

"My aunt has already offered me Minnie's old room." A gentle smile softened Rachel's features. "But I appreciate your invitation."

Ada brought in a tray with coffee and cups and set it on the table between them. "I'll be back with sandwiches."

As soon as she left the room, Inga leaned toward Rachel. "Do you mind if I ask her to join us?"

"Of course not." Humor glinted in Rachel's dark eyes. "Only you would invite the help to lunch."

"Not only me." Inga grinned. "My mother does, and I'm sure most of my siblings do the same." She picked up the pot and poured two cups of coffee, handing one to Rachel. "I was thankful to see that the amendment the House is voting on would enfranchise all women, not just white women."

"I was a bit surprised, but it hasn't passed yet." Rachel brought her cup to her lips.

"Emma Reed—you met her years ago at the parade where my arm was broken—is in Washington at the NWP headquarters." Inga picked up her cup and saucer. "When I telephoned her yesterday, she said their canvass showed it should pass, but I'm trying not to get my hopes up."

"Even if it passes, I won't be able to vote in the presidential election, since I live in the District of Columbia."

Inga frowned. "That is so unfair."

"But at least that law applies equally to men and women, Negroes and whites." Rachel sighed. "In the states, I'm sure the same procedures being used to suppress the vote of Negro men will be applied to Negro women."

Inga closed her eyes. "That will have to be the next fight."

Ada returned with a plate of sandwiches and a relish tray.

"Please bring yourself a plate and cup and join us,"

Inga said to her.

"Sure will. Thanks." A wide smile spread across her face. "I own to being curious of how it will come out."

"What is your brother going to do, now that Prohibition has been ratified?" Rachel asked.

"He said last year that he feared it would become law." Inga picked an open-faced egg salad sandwich from the plate. "He was planning to convert to distilling vinegar and looking into bottling root beer and other soda pop. So I hope he'll be okay."

"It's been hard on some of the tavern owners in our neighborhood." Rachel placed a few carrot sticks on her plate.

Ada returned. She filled her plate and placed it on the corner of the desk, then poured herself a cup of coffee.

Rachel watched. "Are you planning to go on to college like Minnie and Sadie did?"

Setting her cup on the desk, Ada nodded. "Someday. I hope—"

The phone rang.

Ada's wide-eyed gaze fixed on Inga.

On the second ring, Inga set her plate on the tray, stood, and walked to the desk.

She lifted the receiver and spoke into it. "Wakefield residence."

"It passed." C.J.'s voice came through the line.

"That's wonderful." Inga grinned and nodded to Rachel and Ada.

"Three-o-four to eighty-nine." The incredulity in his tone was unmistakable. "Can you believe it?"

Inga did some quick mental math. "That's forty-two more than we needed." She could hardly fathom it. "I hope that bodes well for the vote in the Senate."

Rachel and Ada were both smiling.

"Word is they're going to take it up soon," C.J. said.

"I hope so." Inga closed her eyes and inhaled. "Thanks for calling."

"See you tonight."

Inga hung up and caught Rachel's gaze. "How are

we going to celebrate?"

"Ice cream!" they said in unison.

"Now that the Senate passed the suffrage amendment and the president signed it, when do you get to vote?" Helen asked, as everyone sat down to dinner.

Inga smiled at her. "We don't know yet."

"The states still need to ratify it." Susan plopped a spoonful of mashed potatoes on her plate.

Helen's eyes widened. "All of them?"

"No." C.J. snagged a roll, then passed the plate to Ada. "Thirty-six of them."

"That could take a long time," Elizabeth lamented.

"That's why Daddy and I are going to Harrisburg next week to talk to lawmakers." Inga looked forward to the opportunity to make her case in person.

"May we go with you?" Elizabeth asked.

Inga caught C.J.'s gaze and gave a slight nod.

"Do you all want to join us?" he asked.

"Yes," Susan and Elizabeth replied in unison. Helen nodded.

C.J. grinned. "Okay."

"Before we go, we all need to write letters to our representatives, politely asking them to vote for the amendment." Inga looked from girl to girl. "We'll leave the letters as a reminder of what we want them to do." She turned to Ada. "Would you like to send a letter, too?"

"I would." She nodded. "I'll write it tomorrow."

"Do you want to go with us, Ada?" Helen asked.

The housekeeper's eyes widened. "Oh Lord, no." She smiled at Helen. "I'd rather stay here and take care of *Fille*."

Susan frowned. "But Pennsylvania is only one state."

"Maybe you girls could write to Grandma Hansen and Grandma Wakefield and ask them to contact their legislators about supporting the amendment," C.J. suggested. "That would add Iowa and Wyoming."

Elizabeth's brows knitted together. "Women can already vote in Wyoming. Do they have to approve the amendment?"

"Yes." Inga lay a hand on her shoulder. "Even the states where women have the vote will need to ratify it."

"Are you going to write our grandmas, too?" Helen asked.

"Yes," Inga said. "But I think it will mean more to your grandmothers if they hear from each of you."

Chapter Twenty-Four

July 18, 1920
Philadelphia, Pennsylvania

Dear Moder,

Now that Northern Schleswig has once again officially became a part of Denmark as South Jutland, I'm sorry Fader did not live to see it. I wonder what he would have thought about the southern part of Schleswig staying with Germany. I doubt he would have approved, although I can't remember which part his family home was in.

Although the Senate has rejected the Treaty of Versailles again because they don't want to ratify the League of Nations, I am working on an article about the League. I think it's a good idea in theory. I'm hoping to travel to The Hague to learn about the International Court of Justice, but so far Nathan hasn't approved it. The election this fall will be interesting, since Cox supports the United States becoming part of the League and Harding doesn't. If Nathan doesn't let me go to Europe, I'll have to center my article around the candidates' competing positions.

I am worried about whether the Susan B. Anthony Amendment will be law in time for this year's election, since only thirty-five states have ratified it. I'm pleased that Pennsylvania, Iowa, and Wyoming are in that group. C.J. says I shouldn't be so nervous since we only need one more state, but I can't help it. No states have ratified since Washington on March 22. That was almost four months ago, and the election is less than four months away.

The Democratic Party is supporting ratification, and they have a strong suffrage plank on their platform. The Republicans have a weaker one. Why do they always have to be so backwards, especially since they were the party of Theodore Roosevelt? I wish he had lived to run again. I think he could have won.

We look forward to coming west for Christmas. Hope to see lots of family while we're there.

Love,

Inga

The early August afternoon was hot and muggy. Inga's office was stifling, even with her window open and two oscillating fans blowing.

"Although I don't favor the NASWA's approach, I have to give Mrs. Catt credit for telling those men in Tennessee—" Emma looked down at the newspaper clipping she held. "'Tennessee will be made ridiculous in the eyes of all citizens of this country who know the U.S. Constitution if she refuses to ratify on the grounds of unconstitutionality.'" She looked up. "Unconstitutionality! What a stupid argument."

"I find it troubling how many American citizens do not know and understand what the Constitution says." Inga frowned. "And fewer yet have read the Federalist Papers to understand what the founding fathers were thinking."

A blush of color rose in Emma's cheeks. "I must confess. I haven't read all of the Federalist Papers myself."

"Oh, Emma." Heat rushed up Inga's neck and into her face. "I didn't mean to offend you. I'm so sorry."

"It's okay." A small smile curved Emma's lips. "I agree that all citizens, not only the judges and politicians, should know the Constitution inside and out."

Inga grinned. "And that's one of the reasons we're good friends."

Emma sobered. "I do feel badly that Mrs. Catt had a heart episode. She has worked hard to get states to ratify."

"I do, too. Word is that she's recovering. It is unfortunate that she prematurely declared victory in Tennessee. Doesn't she understand that when a woman predicts what men will do, it only serves to prompt them to do the opposite?"

Emma dropped her gaze, then raised it to meet Inga's. "I'm not very familiar with the ways of men, but Mrs. Catt has been married twice, so she should be." Her eyes twinkled. "Is Mr. Wakefield that contrary?"

Inga laughed. "Not always, but often. It took us being jailed and assaulted for him to join the Men's League for Woman Suffrage, even though I had expected him to do so long before that."

Emma sobered. "However the men react, the anti-suffragists are fighting hard against the amendment. They're playing up the NASWA's historical associations with the Temperance Union and with the abolitionists, neither of which is popular in Tennessee."

"The influence of the Quaker origins of equality in the association fell away decades ago." Inga recalled Rachel's prophetic comments from way back at the Iowa convention. Her chest tightened. "And the influence of the segregationists has only increased. But I can't say the NWP is much better on that score."

Emma's eyes widened. "Were you raised a Quaker?"

"A Lutheran." Inga gave her head a small shake. "But I was raised to believe that all men and women were created equal, and I still value that principle, although it hasn't prevented my support of the NWP." She inhaled a breath. "My friend, Rachel, said that the Nashville Federation of Colored Women's Clubs is standing with the new Tennessee League of Women Voters, despite the demeaning treatment they often received at the hands of white women."

"I'm glad." Emma paused. "Are you going to Tennessee for the vote?"

"Nathan said I could since he won't let me go to The Hague, but I don't think so." Inga shook her head. "I know this sounds crazy, but I don't want to jinx the outcome. And, if the ratification doesn't pass, I want to be around friends and family who can distract me from the disappointment."

They sat in silence for a few moments.

"I was glad you shared with Alice what you learned about the Republicans' failure to support ratification in Tennessee, and about the Democrats' waffling."

Inga's spirits rose. "They didn't see how suffrage related to their positions on the League of Nations. I told them it was tangential, so I was surprised they answered my questions."

"Alice said she had received several similar reports." Emma lowered her voice. Her tone became conspiratorial. "Alice sent Abby Baker to Marion, Ohio to confront Senator Harding about his position and remind him that many women in this country can already vote. She will tell him if the amendment fails in Tennessee due to his party's position, the Woman's Party will be forced to unleash the women's vote against the offending party in this fall's election." She grinned.

Inga couldn't force a smile in return. "I just hope we won't have to."

"The Woman's Party needs money," Inga said as she entered C.J.'s office a few days later. "It looks like the Tennessee governor and Senate are in support of the amendment, but there is a huge fight in their House." She hesitated. "I'm going to send them a hundred dollars, but can you get Nathan to donate the money he would have spent if I had gone to Nashville?"

"I have no objection to him doing that, but you'll have to ask him."

Inga lifted her chin. "I will."

She marched out of her husband's office and down the hall. In Nathan's outer office, she inhaled a breath. "Is Mr. Bender in?"

"Inga!" Nathan's voice boomed through his open door. "Is that you?"

She walked into the room and smiled. "Good morning, Nathan."

He rose, rounded his desk, and pulled an easy chair closer, gesturing for her to sit.

She stood behind it until he returned to his chair, then sat.

"Have you changed your mind about going to Tennessee next week?"

"No, I haven't." She decided to engage in the conversation on the Tennessee trip, before making her request. "We don't know when the final vote will be held, and I can wait here better than there. Besides, there's no guarantee it will pass."

"That Harding has really bungled his comments on ratification, hasn't he?" Nathan shook his head.

Inga only nodded in response.

"Chairman Hays says the Republican candidates and the party are being clobbered with complaints," he continued.

As they should be, Inga thought. Harding had damaged the chances of ratification.

"And Franklin Roosevelt is calling Harding out at every stop." Nathan scratched his chin. "I think he might turn out to be a better presidential prospect than Cox. Too bad he's only the vice-presidential candidate."

"I agree, but there's not much we can do about it."

Nathan frowned. "I suppose not."

"But there is one thing we can do something about," Inga ventured.

Nathan raised a brow, but didn't speak.

"We can donate the money you were going to spend on my Tennessee trip to the National Woman's Party to help with their efforts toward ratification."

Nathan broke eye contact. "But then we won't have an article if the amendment is ratified."

"There will be lots of articles if the amendment is ratified, or if it isn't. The press is all over Nashville." She lay her hands in her lap. "If you want an article, I can interview people who are down there now." She rushed on. "But I thought maybe it would be better to have a story after the election, about women voting for the first time or women who are still prevented from voting."

A sly smile crossed Nathan's face. "Or we could have both."

"We could." Inga pursed her lips. "If you donate the money."

Nathan chuckled. "I'll bring you a check this afternoon."

"Thank you." Inga was gratified that he and C.J. had kept the promise they'd made after her release from prison to support the cause.

Inga took her donation and Nathan's to the Philadelphia headquarters on her way home, since Emma was planning to go to D.C. the next day.

"Promise you'll telephone me if anything comes up," Inga said.

"I will." Emma sighed. "I'm sure the party will appreciate your help. I'll write a thank-you note to Mr. Bender before I go."

Throughout the week, Inga waited impatiently for a call from Emma. None came.

On Sunday afternoon, Inga accompanied C.J. and the girls on an automobile ride in the country. Upon their return home, Ada came running from the house to meet them.

"Miss Reed is on the telephone," she said breathlessly. "It's the second time she's called. I saw you drive up and told her to wait."

Inga flung open her door and rushed into the library. "Emma." She tried to catch her breath. "What's happening?"

"The Anti-Suffragists are bringing up Mrs. Catt's support of Elizabeth Cady Stanton's *Woman's Bible*." Panic tinged Emma's voice. "They're saying the cause is anti-Christian. We fear it will offend the legislators since most of them are Christian."

Inga closed her eyes and sank into the chair. "*The Woman's Bible* was decades ago."

"And Mrs. Catt stated that she spoke and voted for a repudiation of it." Emma sniffed. "But the Antis won't let it go. They're running ads and the papers supporting them keep publishing articles to keep the topic before the lawmakers."

Inga rested her elbow on the desk and her head in her hand. "Thanks for calling, Emma. Keep me posted."

When Inga replaced the receiver on its cradle and looked up, C.J. and the girls were standing in the doorway.

"Bad news?" C.J. asked gently.

Inga nodded. "The vote hasn't happened, and it doesn't look good."

On Tuesday afternoon, Nathan called Inga into his office.

"I got a call from my friend over at the *Inquirer*," he began as she walked in. His expression was grim. "His man in Nashville is reporting that the corporate supporters of the Anti-Suffragists are bribing and threatening lawmakers supporting the amendment."

Biting her lip, Inga dropped onto the chair across from his desk.

"And when that doesn't work, they're sending false telegrams telling them their family members are ill to keep them from voting." Nathan's frown deepened. "Luckily, the legislators have mostly figured out what is happening and have been telephoning home to check."

"Good." Inga croaked out the word.

Nathan shook his head. "They're even plying some of the lawmakers with alcohol, trying to get them too drunk to vote."

Inga clenched her teeth. "But, prohibition."

"It's Tennessee. They have a Jack Daniels Suite at the hotel."

Inga closed her eyes and rubbed her temples, wondering what would happen next. "I'm glad I'm not there."

Susan poked her head around the door jam. "Any word yet?"

"Not yet." Inga forced a half smile. "But you can wait here with me if you like."

Susan shook her head. "I'm too nervous. I think I'll go see if I can help Ada make lunch."

She disappeared from view.

Inga shuffled her notes once more. She checked the wall clock. Was Nashville in the Eastern or Central time zone? She couldn't remember.

Turning her attention back to the page, she added a sentence to the article.

Her thoughts drifted back to Tennessee. Emma had called last night to say the last poll of legislators had come up one vote short, but that the suffragists were still working to change some of the less settled minds.

But the antis had probably done the same.

At mid-day, Ada and the girls brought a lunch of chicken salad and grapes into the library. The meal proceeded with little conversation. Inga forced a few bites and nibbled on a handful of grapes, but her nervous stomach wouldn't allow her to consume more. The housekeeper removed the remnants of the meal, but the girls remained.

"Let's play rummy," Inga suggested. "It'll take our minds off the silent telephone."

Susan retrieved a deck of cards. Inga and Elizabeth lifted the card table away from the wall. Helen and Susan gathered chairs. They seated themselves, and Elizabeth shuffled the cards and dealt their hands.

The telephone rang.

Inga froze, then rose so quickly she nearly knocked over her chair. She hurried to grab the receiver. "Hello?"

"You should have gone to Nashville." Nathan's jovial voice came through the line. "The amendment passed by one vote."

Inga was proud to have been invited to Philadelphia's celebration of the ratification of the Nineteenth Amendment. It seemed a fitting way to mark the fulfilment of her life's dream.

"Why is the Independence Square decorated in red,

white, and blue instead of the purple, yellow, and white for woman suffrage?" Helen asked as Inga and her family walked into the square.

Inga bit back her bitterness and tried to answer blandly. "Because our mayor opposed enfranchising women."

"That's probably why so many men are here compared with the number of women," Elizabeth said.

Inga looked around. While there were many familiar faces, many loyal Pennsylvania suffragists whom she had expected to be invited, were not present.

"The mayor probably did that, too." Susan's tone betrayed her scorn. She turned to her father. "I hope you won't be voting for him when he stands for re-election."

"I don't plan to," C.J. muttered under his breath.

Inga waved to Emma, who made her way toward them.

"Would you like to join us?" Inga asked, when Emma had picked her way through the crowd.

"For a while." Emma smiled. "I'm so glad Connecticut ratified. Now, no matter what happens with the challenge to the Tennessee vote, we'll be able to vote in November's election."

Inga returned her smile as the police band struck up the opening notes of their concert. For the next half hour, the musicians played and the attendees sang familiar songs.

At three o'clock, Mayor Moore took the podium.

"The Nation expects better things. Better things because of the advent of women into the realm of American citizenship...Welcome, women of the land...welcome here in the presence of the sanctity of this sacred building...."

Inga shifted her feet and bit her lip. This from the man who wouldn't allow use of the suffrage colors in decorating for this event.

She waited for him to finish.

He was followed by Mrs. George Piersol, who

represented the League of Women Voters. Inga had only met her a few times, but Emma spoke well of her. After mentioning this event occurring 'at this hallowed shrine of Liberty to celebrate the completion of democracy and the dawn of an era of justice.' She went on to say that she spoke for women who had dreamed of this day. "For all—whatever be their creed or color."

That wasn't technically true. Inga thought of the Native women who were not enfranchised. And those, like Rachel, who could not vote for president because they lived in the District of Columbia. And how many more women would be excluded from voting by poll tests or taxes?

There was still much work to be done.

Inga shook off her fretfulness. At least the Nineteenth Amendment was a start. It was a time to celebrate. She inhaled a cleansing breath, worked up a smile, and focused her attention on Governor Sproul. He spoke of four important milestones in the history of the country. These included the Declaration of Independence, the Constitution, the Civil War, and the granting of equal franchise.

Granting. Inga's jaw clenched. It was not the appropriate word to encompass the seventy-two years of effort, tears and struggle that had gone into winning the vote.

She turned her attention back to the governor, who was concluding his address by asking women "not to lose one bit of the sweetness, tenderness, and devotion which have characterized you in the past, but to carry that sweetness, tenderness, and devotion into your public works."

Hypocrite! Inga almost gagged. She looked at Emma, who was rolling her eyes. Quickly, Inga diverted her gaze so she wouldn't burst into laughter.

Several more women spoke on behalf of women voters and women who had worked for the cause. Two of Susan B. Anthony's nieces were recognized.

Finally, Katharine Wentworth Ruschenberger, who had commissioned the forging of the Justice Bell, spoke of its history and symbolism. While she gave her remarks, a contingent of girls and women dressed in white with green and gold badges marched toward the Justice Bell.

"Forty-eight," whispered Helen. "One for each state."

"That's right," Inga whispered, blinking back joyful tears. "Because now women in all states can vote."

Helen huffed. "I figured that out myself."

Inga placed a hand on her daughter's shoulder, now the same height as her own. "Good for you."

When Mrs. Ruschenberger finished speaking, a woman in a striking green robe trimmed with white, with sandals on her feet and a crown of oak leaves, marched out of Independence Hall.

"That's Lady Justice," C.J. whispered.

"We know, Daddy," Elizabeth replied without looking at him.

Two young girls, one carrying a sword and the other carrying a scale, accompanied Justice to the bell. She silently unchained the clapper.

Mrs. Ruschenberger introduced her niece, Miss Catherine Wentworth, and stated that she would ring the Justice Bell at exactly four o'clock, when bells in communities across the country would ring out in recognition of women's suffrage. The ringing of the bell would symbolize hard-won justice for women, for her daughters and girls like them throughout the country.

Inga checked her watch. Four more minutes.

She cast a loving gaze over her daughters' faces, all filled with anticipation.

Again Inga checked the time. One more minute. Her pulse raced.

Finally, Miss Wentworth rang the bell.

It tolled forty-eight times.

Inga straightened to her full height, clasping her hands to her chest.

"I'll always remember this day," Emma said.

Inga turned to discover tears streaking her friend's

cheeks. Inga patted her arm. "I will, too."

Emma bade them farewell and wandered toward the bell.

"And now you can vote in November." Elizabeth smiled at her mother, her wide eyes sparkling.

"Yes, but first I need to prepare." Inga slid her gaze over her daughters. "And you girls can help me."

Susan's expression turned skeptical. "What do we have to do?"

"We need to learn all we can about the candidates for each office and study the party platforms," Inga replied.

"Is Daddy going to help us?" Helen asked.

Inga glanced at C.J. "If he wants to."

He grinned. "I will."

"What if you learn all about the men running for some office and you don't like any of them?" Elizabeth's solemn expression touched Inga's heart.

C.J.'s grin faded. "Then I can write in the name of someone I think would do a good job in that office."

"That's one option." Inga kept her gaze on Elizabeth. "But I think it unlikely that the person I might write in would get enough votes to actually win the election." She paused. "I think I would review the duties of the office and the qualifications of the candidates. As if I was hiring someone for a job. Then I would vote for the one who I think is best qualified for the office."

"Hmmm." C.J. grinned. "You have a very smart mother."

Inga grinned back at him. He had supported her through even the worst of times. Her heart swelled. "And a daddy who is best qualified for his job."

On November second, Inga took the ballot the election worker handed her and stepped into the voting booth. It didn't seem real. She stood there for a few moments while the enormity of this day washed over her.

As she marked her choices, she was engulfed by the same awe for the responsibility that had overcome her the first time she voted, years ago in Wyoming.

She grieved for Susan B. Anthony, Elizabeth Cady Stanton, and all the other women who had given their lives to the cause, but never reaped the rewards.

She thought of her mother and half-sisters who would be voting for the first time and of C.J.'s mother and sister who had cast many ballots.

She pictured her daughters, voting in all the elections in their future, glad they would not have to do battle for this right.

She took a deep breath and submitted her ballot.

This had been a cause worth fighting for.

ACKNOWLEDGEMENTS

Many, many people helped in the development of *The Cause*. I will try to mention those whose input was critical to the writing.

As always, I depended upon feedback from my critique group – Mary DeSive, Mariah Ambersen, Debra Hines and Jenn Thor as I was writing the manuscript. After completion, the reviews by Kristin Wells and the suggestions from Kim Louise and Joann Heckroth helped me polish the story. My deepest appreciation to all of you for your support and encouragement.

The research for this book was more complex than any of my previous works. The Reference Librarians at the Library of Congress have been invaluable in helping me to track down references and resources. Additionally, the following individuals and entities have been instrumental in helping me to conduct the research for this story:

In Cedar Falls, Iowa, I would like to thank the staffs of The Cedar Falls Historical Society, The Cedar Falls Public Library, and the University of Northern Iowa Library, Archives Department. In Des Moines, Iowa, the staff of the State Historical Society of Iowa were particularly helpful.

In Laramie, Wyoming, my thanks go to the staff of the American Heritage Center at the University of Wyoming, the staff of the Albany County Historical Society, Joel Funk at *The Laramie Boomerang*, and Nathan Bender at the Albany County Library for helping me to track down resources and obscure details I needed for the Wyoming portions of the story. Thanks also to Nathan Bender for allowing me to name a character after him.

In Philadelphia, Pennsylvania, my appreciation goes to the staff at the Free Library of Philadelphia, the staff of the Historical Society of Pennsylvania, and Sara Falch at the Independence National Historical

Park.

I'd also like to thank Dr. Cynthia L. Robinson, Chair of the Department of Black Studies at the University of Nebraska-Omaha, and Louisa Hoffman at Oberlin College Archives for helping me to track down references.

Finally, thank you to Cheryl St.John and *lizzie starr for their help and guidance.

Thanks to all of you for helping me to bring *The Cause* to fruition.

A list of References is available on the "News" page of my web site, www.annmarkim.com

Ann Markim has enjoyed a three-act career, with each act allowing her to pursue a personal passion. After graduate school, she pursued her love of people, working in and directing programs providing care and services to improve the lives of elderly people and individuals with disabilities.

In her second act, she owned and operated a retail nature store. This afforded her opportunity to share her love and knowledge of birds and nature with customers, children, and other interested people through conversations in her shop and presentations to school groups and various nature and gardening organizations.

Now, in her third act, she is devoting full time to her passion for writing. Her interest in writing historical novels began some time ago with her curiosity about her ancestors and evolved into a fascination with researching historical events and imagining what life must have been like in those earlier eras. Although the stories she writes are fictional, they are set in actual historical settings and she includes authentic details about real occurrences.

Ann lives in Omaha, Nebraska, with her two cats,

Ripley and Riley. In addition to writing, she enjoys gardening, quilting, and traveling.

Sign up for her newsletter at
www.annmarkim.com
Follow her on Facebook at
www.facebook.com/AnnMarkim

Books in the Stryker Legacy Series
The Legacy – available now
The Cause – available now
The Claim – coming Summer, 2020